SANCTUARY

PATRICIA DIXON

BLOODHOUND
— B O O K S —

For Manchester

PROLOGUE

Isle of Wight Festival, Hell Field
1970

I don't want to do it. Leave her behind. But I know I'll have to. Say goodbye to all this. Freedom. To love and think and feel. To be me. The real me. Not the one they want me to be.

Here, with her, in this magical capsule in time, colours burst inside my mind and every single one of my senses take me, like she took me, to another dimension where I came alive. I didn't know it could be like this.

It's been perfect and she's perfect and so is this place full of people like me. Well, the person I could be if I wasn't such a thoroughbred coward. If I hadn't been conditioned. Trained to stay inside the box, to succeed, to make proud.

I just want this day to last forever and for the night to melt away and take us with it, to the other side of the moon, another galaxy so that before dawn breaks, we become nothing more than atoms. Joined together for all eternity, floating, as one, forever. A mist of swirling carbon, melded as one like we were the first time, my first time, with her or anyone.

Thinking about it causes my breath to catch in my chest and strange, beautiful things happen to every part of my body. Urges I never experienced pulsing through me. She brings me alive. She gives me life and hope and possibilities that I never knew existed and all I have to do is find the courage to do what she asks.

She made it sound so simple, blissful and when I close my eyes I can see the future, us. We are in the van, driving away from here, to Dover and then across Europe to freedom.

It's exactly the same as the painting. The one she created from words that is now daubed across my heart and soul. Smeared onto my eyes in a vivid technicolour palate so that I see it all. We are picking grapes in Bordeaux, riding horses bareback in Spain, sleeping on rooftops in Greece, and travelling along dusty highways through Turkey on our way to Egypt and beyond.

She wants to escape. The man whose ring she wears and the life she leads. I told her we would go together. Disappear in the morning, at first light. And she believed it. And for a beautiful moment so did I when I said the words. It was as though I could touch it. Touch destiny.

I need to think. There's time before we meet. I don't want to ruin our last night together because I already know that's what it is, even though she doesn't.

Then I remember. That here I am on Desolation Hill, and I wonder if it's a sign. Because I couldn't make up a name more apt if I tried. One that sums up where I am in my life. The irony tempts me to weep but years of conditioning serves me well. Weepers aren't allowed. Not in my family.

Instead, I focus on the sounds of the campsite waking. Long-haired bearded men and tousled women with painted faces, smudged by sleep and sex, crawling from tents into the breaking day. And those who haven't slept, still high on life and chemical love. Laughter too. Beautiful joyful laughter. And below, the strains of the artists as they soundcheck the stage while closer by, singing and the strum of a guitar.

Scents glide overhead on a balmy breeze that brushes my skin, my bare chest bronzed from the sun and scorched by the touch of her fingers. Woodsmoke, patchouli, cooking and spices.

I am attuned to it all. Soaking it in. Committing it to memory.

As I lie here, arms folded behind my head, the soft grass beneath the bare skin of my back, the first rays of sunlight caressing my chest, I remember the touch of her lips as they skimmed my body. As she ran her fingers through my hair, winding coils of sun-kissed strands that turned a lighter shade of chestnut and have grown longer over summer. Her words, telling me I was her John, and she is my Yoko. That I am beautiful, perfect.

And so is she. This girl, barely a woman, who married too young to a guy who owns a van selling burgers. He is her jailor and I'm not her saviour. Tomorrow she will have to go back. To the Black Country and her job in a mill. And I will go back to York and a charmed middle-class life as the son of a respectable barrister and his even more respectable wife.

I laugh, a silent bitter reaction to the thought of taking her home to Mother. I can see a face twisted with distaste as she looks upon the willowy goddess with the long blonde hair. Irritated by the bangles that adorn her wrists and clink and rattle when she waves her arms during an animated tale. By her home-made floaty skirts and dusty sandaled feet. Mother wouldn't see the kind heart beneath the pale creamy skin. Or look behind the bluest eyes that spark with excitement and innocent wonder, with hope and acceptance, devoid of malice. We would have no chance.

They think I'm staying with a friend from Oxford for the summer. A nice family, I told them. Good stock and with a house by the sea. Dorset to be more precise. Instead I've been travelling alone. Wherever the mood and the wind took me, and it brought me here. To Hell Field and her.

I saw her, watching me as I painted and I knew that she'd seek me out, later, at some point. I just had to wait. And while I did, I allowed my soul the freedom it yearns for, that I yearn for. To paint. That's what I want more than anything in this world – apart from her.

What am I going to do?

Practically, and with regards to the next few hours this question is easy to answer. I'm going to stand in a crowd of dancing, swaying, beautiful people like me and listen to Hendrix, and Joplin, Baez and The Who. I'll be like them, believe every word, believe I can be part of their generation, for a while.

I'm going to get high. So high that nothing can touch me or trap me or tie me down, stick a label on me and rob me of my desires and dreams. And in the gloaming moonlight, I will wait for her to come to me, like we arranged. When she can sneak away and make love to me in our secret place. We will lie in each other's arms and sleep beneath the stars, wrapped in her belief in me, our eyes closed to my lie. My imminent betrayal.

Tomorrow I'll have to come down. Face reality. Say goodbye to my first love, to the woman who stole my heart. Can I do it, can I leave her behind?

And then, I hear a voice. Brought to me on the strains of a guitar, blown on the breeze through a marijuana haze of a most magical trip. It whispers the answer. A way to keep her close to me always. And then I know how.

I can take her with me. My beautiful Krystle.

1

Blacksheep Farm, Hathersage, Derbyshire
Present day

Cathy lived for days like these. Where she could walk the wild, wet and windy moors under moody charcoal grey clouds set against an ice-white sky, illuminated by the sun that was determined to thwart their malevolence. The rays that escaped the cumulonimbus in shards, lit the craggy moss-covered peaks like a searchlight, while all below was cast in shadows making the valley appear deep and cavernous.

It was late March, the promise of Easter was heralded by longer days and the bloom of spring, along with the new life that accompanied it. She could smell it in the air, see it, hear it. A dewy scent, buds of plant life dotted on the fells and tree branches, the cries of newborn lambs.

Yet the weight of such joyous things and the light that shone bright on the world sat heavy in Cathy's heart and as they moved through April towards May, it would become a lead weight. An anniversary to circumnavigate, or get over, blot out and then she'd be on the other side and the burden would ease eventually. It had been the same every year. Six of them to be precise.

And that was why the cloak of winter appealed to Cathy more. Coal fires, the blanket of ebony darkness that made her part of the world seem even more isolated and safe. Cut off from temptation, interference, horribleness and anything she couldn't close her eyes to. Cathy wished someone would invent a remote control that she could point at all the bad things out there and switch them off with a push of a button. In the meantime she could just stay where she was, protected by the hills and cocooned in the sanctuary of her mind.

Stopping at the stile to catch her breath, Cathy took it all in. This was her place and she'd known it from the moment she'd stepped outside, at daybreak one frozen January morning, six years ago.

In those pivotal moments, after finding the door unlocked, as she'd lifted the latch and yanked open the creaky hunk of wood, Cathy had been desperate for fresh air. To breathe freely and relieve that restrictive band of anxiety tightening her chest.

Trying to cope alone, not giving in, not telling anyone how she truly felt, not admitting even to herself that she was struggling, determined that terror wouldn't win. Instead she'd craved silence, because it was her friend in a world that was full of noise and horror and hate and blood-soaked tears.

It was impossible though, to find sanctuary because at work they just didn't shut up. All day, their voices tunnelled down her ears, boring inside her brain; and laughter, some stupid ringtone, a door slamming had her on the verge of screaming like that poor person in the Munch painting.

Outside it was worse. The sound of passing traffic seemed magnified and the wheels of a bus would crunch and grind through her head. A blaring car horn had her grasping her coat, pulling it around her for protection while underneath her heart pounded a wild, frantic beat. There in the bustling city centre that she once loved so much, everyone came too close. Jostling, rushing, impatient. It, they, everything, made her want to run just like she did that night.

Flee the memory of what she'd endured in there, the sights, the stench, the screams, the fear. No wonder the urge to run again, barefoot, as fast as her wobbly weak legs would carry her and never stop, consumed her like a deep, gnawing hunger.

Eight months. That was how long she'd kept the trauma at bay, fighting off a rabid beast as best she could. But December had done for her. The festivities, the neon lights, the expectation and even more noise and crowds swarming all around. The thought of putting on a smile, let alone a party dress, had been too much and after crying off the works do, then enduring Christmas Day with her family, it had been the fireworks on New Year's Eve that brought it all crashing down.

Cathy had turned her phone to silent. Closed the curtains and with her hands clasped over her ears, lay in the darkness praying for the night to end. When her phone bleeped at two minutes to midnight, through tear-misted eyes she read the message on the screen. From someone she hadn't expected to hear from ever again, because since she had ignored texts and deleted her social media, he, and most people really, had taken the hint.

They'd met on a night out. She was with friends, cruising the bars of the gay village, and he was with his brother and his on–off boyfriend. The two groups had merged, and Cathy had been enamoured by the two burly farmers, the younger one especially.

They started seeing each other, as people who dance the modern dance say of a relationship where neither party feels bold enough to commit. It came naturally, revolving around her hectic work schedule that took her up and down the UK and across to Europe, and his commitments on the family farm, intriguingly named Blacksheep.

Cathy knew she was falling for him, and he said he felt the same. So even though it was a trek for him after a long day at work and a red-eye from wherever for her, when they managed to get together it was always worth the wait.

And then *it* happened. And she knew she'd hurt him by cutting him off and he didn't deserve it because he was one of the nice guys and after searching for one for ages, she had to let him go. It was the only way to cope, and he'd taken her message explaining that she needed a break and why with grace.

This out of the blue text was typical of him, because that's who he was. Kind and decent with a heart of gold. The one she almost let get away.

> Hello stranger. Was thinking of you. They're playing our song on the radio. Just wanted to say hi and wish you all the best for the new year. Hope you're okay. You dropped off the face of the earth but don't forget, the offer still stands. If you ever want someone to drive you home, all you have to do is pick up the phone.

And Cathy did.

After he'd driven south, along winding roads battered by rain and then through streets thronged with revellers, he'd picked her up and taken her to safety like he promised.

Cathy had laid her head against the window and watched the road in a trance, while the rhythm of the battered Land Rover Defender soothed, as did his silence and a strong hand holding hers.

They arrived in the early hours of the blackest night and then cocooned in a duvet under a mountain of blankets, Cathy slept the sleep of the dead, in a strange house owned by a family she'd never met but heard plenty about. But he was by her side and knowing that, for the first time in eight months, Cathy felt the most beautiful of things. Safe.

Two days later, when she stepped outside onto the cobbled yard, into minus degrees with a howling wind that nipped and pinched her pale, spotty face, she stalled and looked across the valley. It wasn't the cold that caused her shallow breath to hitch in her chest. It was the view.

Dark peaks and rolling hills towered on either side. A monochrome scene from a gothic classic. While below, in the valley, a platinum sliver of meandering water wove its way towards the horizon. Then, like a portent, the watery sun slowly lifted through the misty haze.

Cathy didn't want to run anymore. All she wanted to do was stare.

She still remembered every second of what happened next. The footsteps approaching slowly from behind, a blanket placed gently on her shoulders and the words, spoken softly, 'It's beautiful, isn't it?'

'Yes, I've never seen anything like it.' And it was true. She hadn't.

The city girl with city ways and a city life. Her vocal cords, worn and exhausted from hours of crying in her bedroom, struggled to croak the words foremost in her mind. 'It's as though the hills are protecting this place, but they're showing us the way out, too. Lighting up the road ahead, like a new dawn. It's magical.'

He took a step closer and gently placed his hand on her shoulder, reassuring, not restricting. 'You can go back home if you want to. All you have to do is say. But for now, why not come back inside where it's warm. I'll make us some breakfast before the others get up.'

It had been hard to drag her eyes away, but her feet were

numb, and her body trembled, from hunger or the cold – both probably – so she turned, and he was there like he'd been every day since. Her saviour. Alfie.

That was six years ago. Cathy had stayed and never wanted to go back to the city, her old life or the real world. This was home.

As she leant against the stile, not for the first time Cathy reminded herself of that day, unafraid to face the past anymore, but still terrified of returning. And while she ran like the wind from the things in the world that scared her, she wasn't one for shying away from her own truth. That Alfie with the good heart, and the most glorious view, the one her eyes currently rested upon, had saved her life.

After taking one last look before she headed upwards towards home, Cathy climbed over the wooden ledge and with a following wind aiding her ascent, made her way along the rugged footpath, her hiking boots just visible beneath a generous coating of mud, her jeans warming her legs and her body huddled in a thick Barbour.

Every now and then, as she picked her way along, she'd fall foul of muscle memory and have to stop herself from turning to see where Skip was, and it was in those seconds her heart dipped. She missed the company of Alfie's loyal sheepdog and was denying any thought of what was to come.

Skip was too old for walks along craggy paths and his days of racing over the hillside bringing in a flock were long gone. He spent his time by the fire or guarding the yard, and recently just the kitchen door. For now, Skip would be waiting by the hearth when she returned from her early-morning walk and the sight of him, along with the thump-thump of his tail, was welcome enough. And what awaited as she rounded the jutting lump of sandstone rock that skimmed the edge of the path, never failed to lift her spirits. And there it was.

Nestled at the foot of one of the taller peaks, set on a gentle slope of pastureland, looking out across Cathy's precious valley was Blacksheep Farm. Her very own Wuthering Heights.

It didn't matter that this was the Peak District. The essence of Brontë country was in the air, due north along the hikers' trail into West Yorkshire. Cathy could simply close her eyes and imagine she was there, walking in the footsteps of her namesake, searching for Heathcliff.

As she left the path and made her way towards the sturdy farm, built from local sandstone, she ran her eyes along the long low walls where a golden glow from the miner's lamp guided her home on that dull, misty morning. The narrow windows dotted along the length top and bottom, allowed in just enough light to take the edge off sombre evenings and keep the wind that buffeted the façade in winter at bay.

The downstairs rooms were cosy, especially when the fires were lit; and cool in summer when the sun toasted the south facing walls. The large square kitchen in the centre was – well it used to be – the hub of the home. To the left was the farm office and to the right what they quaintly referred to as the parlour.

Upstairs there were five bedrooms and a box room with a family bathroom plonked in the centre. En-suite living hadn't reached Blacksheep but even when the farm had been full, they'd managed. The yard to the front was empty save for Alfie's Defender and her beat-up, mud-splattered Fiesta that was on its very last legs. Like the farm had been for far too long.

Even though the flock was long gone, their bleating a mere memory, the essence of them couldn't be erased. Cathy would still find tufts of wool attached to the fences which she'd pluck away, relishing the feel of it between her fingers. And in the barns, their animal scent lingered, a subtle blend of lanolin, sweet grass and droppings that had been absorbed in the ground and the sandstone walls. She'd used up the last of the wool, crocheting blankets for the parlour and giving them away as gifts. She regretted not saving some skeins if only as a keepsake.

Brushing aside thoughts of what used to be, Cathy clicked the latch and opened the door into the kitchen and breathed the smoky scent of the wood burner as she listened for signs of life. Thump, thump, thump. Her heart lifted; after kicking off her boots she made her way over to where their old faithful Skip waited in his basket for a ruffle of his ears and a kiss on the head.

As she straightened, she heard the stomping of size-eleven feet on the wooden stairs followed promptly by the appearance in the kitchen of her very own Heathcliff in the form of her six-foot-four hulk of a man, Alfie.

'Morning, love...' He paused and stopped to give Cathy a hug and a quick smacker on the lips before heading over to the fridge. 'Can't stop. Mam's been on the bloody phone, ringing and ringing like it was end of the flaming world...'

Alfie pulled a carton of milk from the shelf and made his way to the wellie rack by the door. She didn't comment that she'd asked his mother only yesterday if she wanted anything from the shop in Hathersage village, to be told, 'Got plenty to last me till end of the week. Now leave me in peace.'

As Alfie shrugged on his lumberjacket and gave Cathy a quick wave as he bolted out of the door, she looked at Skip who lowered his head and sympathised through rheumy eyes. Cathy sighed and before she went to flick the kettle on, said, 'I know, mate, I know.'

Peering through the narrow window Cathy watched as her curly-haired man pulled on his beanie and marched across the yard, up the farm track towards Shepherd's Cottage and the home of Bertha Walker. The most thoroughly disliked member of the family, the farming community, Hathersage village and – it wouldn't surprise Cathy – the whole universe to infinity and beyond. And a bit further than that, too.

2

ALFIE

Alfie stopped for a moment and inhaled a fortifying breath. He did it every time he reached the door of his mother's cottage in the hope it would see him through the following minutes. Never hours. Nobody could put up with her for that long.

After slipping off his work boots and leaving them on the step to avoid a bollocking for tramping muck into her hallway, he pushed down on the latch and let himself inside. 'Mam, it's me. Brought the milk.'

Closing the door behind him, Alfie followed the aroma of stale cigarette smoke and whatever his mother had crucified under the grill for tea the night before. Dipping his head slightly so that it wouldn't scrape along the low ceiling, he trudged towards the back of the cottage to the kitchen.

The farm worker's dwelling wasn't built for six-foot-four giants such as he and his fifteen stone bulk barely squeezed between the narrow walls of the corridor. Reaching the kitchen always made Alfie feel like a ferret emerging from a rabbit warren and even though the kitchen wasn't vast, it was certainly less claustrophobic.

'Took tha' bloody time. I'm gaspin' for a brew.' The familiar twang of Yorkshire vowels came from the lounge to the left and deep inside the wings of the armchair set by the fire.

'And a very good morning to you, too, Mam. Shall I stick the kettle on then? Don't want you keeling over now.' No matter how much he tried to contain the thought *and do us all a favour*, it still slipped into his head and as always, made him feel ashamed.

'Aye, go on then... and stick some bread in the toaster while yer up. Me legs have been bad during the night, and I'm jiggered.' At this point Bertha shuffled forward and watched through the doorway as her younger son did her bidding.

It beggared belief that the short dumpy figure with the frizzy mop of shoulder-length hair, who watched beady-eyed as Alfie pulled out two slices of Warburton's from the bag, could strike fear into the hearts of grown men and most people in a twenty-mile radius.

That's why every sentence Alfie uttered was processed before it left his lips, so as not to get his head bitten off in a sarcastic retort. As he emptied the old teabags from the pot before placing it on the table with a clean cup and saucer, he felt he was taking part in a well-rehearsed dance routine. It was just easier to do it how she liked.

There was no point in asking if she wanted jam and butter, because she'd want marmalade, and if he took a tray in she'd want to eat at the table, or vice-versa. He didn't bother complaining that there were tea-stained lumps in the sugar bowl that held a crusted silver spoon or that there was something grim stuck to the butter in the crystal dish.

Bertha liked things done her own contrary way and had trained her pups, all three of them, well. The only thing was, two of them had buggered off and left the middle one to bear the load. And a heavy load it sometimes was.

'Where's that lass of yours? Sat on her arse making tat, I

s'pose.' Bertha had raised herself from the armchair and was on her way to the table, making a great show of what Alfie presumed was pain from her aching, stiff legs.

Ignoring the familiar jibe, Alfie prayed for the knackered old toaster to ping and busied himself with fetching the butter dish from the side. At least the kettle had boiled, so as he poured the water onto fresh teabags, he attempted to jolly the torture along.

'Sit yourself down, Mam, and I'll bring the pot. Cathy's got an order to finish today that's why she's not come up. She's sold some of her jewellery this past week so needs to get it posted out, but she asked if you wanted her to plate you something up for your tea. It's no trouble.'

The harumph answered that question before Bertha even replied. 'No I do not want any of that fancy muck what Cathy makes. Turns me stomach it does. There's never any meat in it on account of her being a wotsit... veganarianist.'

Alfie sucked in his temper. 'A vegetarian. But you know very well she makes things for me with meat or chicken in it so you could have some of that.'

'No chance. Tastes like crap with or without. I've got a tin of stewed steak in the larder and some mash from last night. I'll 'ave that. Proper food. And anyways, how can a farmer's wife be a vegetanarian? Bloody ridiculous is that.'

Alfie heard the whistle of exasperation as it escaped his pursed lips. 'Mam, I'd hardly call lasagne "muck" or "fancy" and Cathy's just trying to look after you.' What he didn't say was that he and Cathy weren't married but that would elicit a whole new pain-in-the-arse conversation. And he didn't say that it wasn't a farm anymore, not since she sold the livestock from under their noses.

And again that voice in his head, *You don't deserve Cathy's attention. I don't even know why she bothers with you, you nasty old—*

His thoughts were interrupted by Bertha who responded to the mild chiding with a counter blow. 'I don't fancy jam today. I want marmalade or maybe an egg. Yes, that'd be nice. Can you do me a couple of boiled eggs, son? You don't have to stay. I know you'll be too busy to spend a few minutes with your old mam... just pop 'em in and I'll do the rest.'

The grating sound of the wooden chair leg being dragged from under the table was almost as bad as her voice and the same old mind games she'd been playing for years. Ever since Alfie could remember really.

Sucking in his annoyance, as he turned, Alfie prayed hard that the old larder set into the kitchen wall would be empty. *Please let her be out of eggs, please don't make me have to stay for three extra minutes while the water boils.* Yanking open the rickety door, Alfie peered in and for a few seconds at least, believed in God.

'Sorry, Mam, looks like you're out of eggs. I'll bring you some up later when Cathy's checked the coop. But at least you've got marmalade so it's not too bad.' The click of the toaster brought further relief and even the loud tut from Bertha didn't ruin the moment. Freedom was within his grasp.

'I'd set me heart on eggs an' all. Bloody typical is that. Oh, and I've got a list you can take with you, for when your lass gets me shopping in. I need some ciggies and a bottle of gin. That's if it's not too much trouble for her. You know, seein' as she's livin' rent free and floggin' tat from my kitchen table. I still reckon I should get commission.' Bertha was pouring tea from the pot and didn't see the look that Alfie cast her way.

She never missed a chance to remind him that the farmhouse still legally belonged to her, as did everything. Shepherd's Cottage, the barns and outbuildings, and thousands of acres of prime arable and grazing land that surrounded them. Blacksheep Farm was firmly in her grasp and all of them – he, his elder brother and his sister – knew that it would remain so until Bertha Walker buggered off to wherever their dad was.

Being an atheist Alfie believed there was no heaven and he hoped he was right because his poor old dad did not deserve to spend eternity in the afterlife with the wife he'd left behind. Or escaped, depending on which way you looked at it. Then again, his dad had loved the bones of the grumpy old bag. Something none of them could ever fathom.

The kitchen table comment had pissed Alfie off. Cathy had turned a relaxing hobby into a way of bringing money in, by making and selling holistic bracelets online. She said her jewellery was her way of sending love into the world. Not that he'd tell his mother that because he couldn't bear Cathy being ridiculed.

He snatched the toast from the machine, slapped it on the plate and unceremoniously plonked it on the table in front of Bertha. 'Right, I'll be off. Got a delivery coming today and Dave the Rave is giving me a lift so I need to crack on. Either me or Cathy will bob back later. If you want owt, just ring, okay.'

Bertha didn't reply immediately, leaving Alfie to hover by the table like an attentive waiter and instead, slowly dipped her knife into the crumb-laden butter. 'Suit yerself. And there's nowt I need, 'cept a bit of company now and then. You know I'm bad on me legs and can't get down th'ill like I used to if I get lonely, but you just go. I'll be fine here on me own. You can show yerself out.'

Alfie wanted to say, *Thank fuck for that because the last thing we want is you coming down the hill to stick your neb in every five minutes.* The scrape, scrape, scrape of knife against dry toast may as well have been spreading acid across his brain but he held his nerve and didn't rise to the bait.

Instead, he went for fact to counterbalance her fiction. 'Mam, I've told you before that if you want to come down to the house I can easily bring the Defender up. And Cathy says Mrs Ives from the wool shop is getting rid of her husband's wheelchair. There's a card on the noticeboard in the Post Office and she only wants fifty quid, so say the word and I'll go get it.'

The slap of her palm as it connected with the tabletop brought back memories that were seared on his brain, just like leather belts and the old coal hole in the garden of the farm.

'I'd rather crawl down that hill on me hands and knees or stay right here for the rest of me life than be pushed in a bloody wheelchair, so you can tell your lass to keep her nose out. Now, if you don't mind, I'd like to eat me breakfast in peace so like I said, see yerself out.' Bertha's eyes had been boring holes into Alfie's but had refocused on slathering an inch of butter onto her toast.

He'd been dismissed and was glad of it and after a terse, 'Right, I'll be off then,' he turned and made his escape on socked feet that couldn't get him down the dismal hall quick enough. And just when he thought he'd made it out alive, as his fingers lifted the door catch, the chill of Bertha's voice, like a cold ghostly hand touching the back of his neck, stopped him in his tracks.

'And don't forget me ciggies.'

3

Alfie trudged back down the hill towards the farmhouse that was just around a gentle right-hand bend in the track and, thankfully, hidden from view by a huge oak tree that was already budding into life. Its branches shielded him and Cathy from the monster on the hill, leaving only the gable end and the front yard of Blacksheep Farmhouse exposed to watchful, mistrusting eyes.

Even now, as he made his way to the barn to open up for when Dave the Rave arrived later, the thought of his mother monitoring the comings and goings, taking note and complaining about who was visiting 'her farm', was driving him insane and away. Just like it had with Albie, his elder brother, and Annie, his sister. The only reason Alfie stayed was for Cathy, because despite the crone on the hill, she loved it there.

Alfie was the one who'd persevered in the misguided hope that someday his mother would see sense and turn the farm over to him and Albie, who would then come home. He missed his brother more than he let on because, with a five-year age gap between them, Albie had always been his hero, after their dad of course.

Following a huge row and showdown with Bertha that had been on the cards for years, Albie said he'd had enough. But rather than taking some time out, maybe holing up in the city with one of his friends or even jetting off on holiday, he'd gone the whole bloody hog and buggered off to New Zealand and had no intention of coming back.

At least Annie hadn't deserted him completely. She lived down in the village with her partner Joe and three wild but lovable kids.

Not that he blamed either of them for cutting ties with the farm and their mother. Ties that were threadbare while their dear dad was still alive, but once he was gone they'd been trampled into the mud by Bertha. Just like she'd trampled on her children and their feelings all of their lives.

Mother. That wasn't really an apt word for Bertha Walker but it's what it said on their birth certificates so as much as they'd all wished otherwise, it had to be true.

Alfie didn't ever think of her as *Mam,* although that's what they had to call her out loud. What he called her under his breath and in his head was another story. To him, the word *Mam* should have been a term of endearment but there was nothing endearing about the woman who'd brought them into the world.

Bertha was a hard-hearted narcissist and why she'd had two more children after Albie, Alfie couldn't fathom because it was clear she despised all of them. It could only have been to please her husband who came from a big family and wanted one of his own.

The second conundrum was that whilst she couldn't show even a hint of warmth to her children, Bertha miraculously loved and worshipped her husband. Jacob Walker was the one person Bertha Walker truly cared about and, as Annie had said as she marched down the path on the day she left home, her kids were just in the way.

Their mother had masked her cruelty well, using the façade of rearing children in the old way, as she and her husband had been raised, with tough love and respect. According to Bertha, farming wasn't for soft lads and simpering girls, so she was doing them all a favour.

In actual fact, the best favour she could have done for her children would have been to drop down dead, well before their dad. That way, Albie would still be there and all the plans they'd had for the farm would be under way. It would have been perfect, but *she'd* ruined it all.

Alfie didn't even feel bad about wanting his mother dead, and neither did Albie and Annie. They'd all wished for it enough times especially after they'd gone to bed hungry without their tea or supper. Or cried themselves to sleep after she'd lashed out verbally or physically.

Yes, on the face of it they'd lived in a spick and span home, been well fed with three home-cooked meals a day. They'd worn clean, decent enough clothes that wouldn't give the mothers at the school gates cause to comment. And they slept each night in warm beds with laundered sheets. Those were the precise things Bertha had used as tools, weapons with which to control them all.

Poor Annie had sobbed herself to sleep many a night and for a while, at around six years old, had been haunted by nightmares after Bertha told her gruesome stories about what animals in the wild did to offspring they didn't want. Annie knew her mother meant her.

Alfie had his own demon in the form of the belt which had hung on the hook of the coat rack for years. It was a silent threat. Another of Bertha's mind games that worked a treat. Their dad would never have allowed their mam to hit them with the strap but in the back of Alfie's mind there was always a 'what if?'

Dad knew that Mam often gave them what she called 'a clout', but when she was in a rage, it was more than that. Alfie lived in fear of the day she would really lose it and reach for the strap. And then, out of the blue, one glorious day, Albie summoned some inner strength, or maybe it was just that he'd had enough, and banished the demon so that fear left the building for good.

Annie had been for tea at her friends and was late home, which meant she'd not done her chores. Albie and Alfie had promised to do them for her, but it wasn't acceptable, not to their mother.

When Annie bounded through the door and into the kitchen, worry etched on her thin face, Bertha had pounced on the opportunity to punish her eight-year-old scrap of a daughter. Alfie knew that Annie was due for a slap. They'd been at the receiving end of their mother's rage and gone to bed with sore, slapped bottoms but with Annie, Bertha's favourite target was her daughter's face. It was as though she literally wanted to wipe a smile, or Annie's beauty away.

It would have happened had Bertha's six-foot, nineteen-year-old son not stepped between them.

Their mother's mood swings had been getting worse and one minute she'd be too hot and flinging open doors and windows then the next, berating them for letting all the heat out. And God help them if she ran out of ciggies. And her favourite tipple of gin and orange could send her one way or another: maudlin or mean. So they never knew if they were coming or going. On that occasion, the gin had made her mean. When Bertha made towards the coat rack where hung the leather belt, Albie stood in her way. 'No, Mam.'

Bertha hissed, 'Move, soft lad, now! She's late and she knows the rules.'

Albie towered above his mother, who in those days had more meat on her bones, but nothing compared to the rugby team's star player. He had benefited from years of manual work and was certainly not a 'soft lad'.

He held his ground. 'We said we'd do her chores, and we have. So there's no reason to punish her and you know what, Mam, from now on there'll be no more slaps and no more belt.'

'Oh really, and how've you come to that conclusion? This is my house and I make the rules.' Bertha was a smirker and from the look on her face, she was amused by her eldest's protest.

'If you touch us again, I'm gonna ring the police.'

Alfie and Annie gasped in unison.

'You wouldn't dare.' Bertha had gone a funny colour and Alfie could've sworn she was shaking, though whether it was from anger or fear, he wasn't sure.

'Try me. Go on. Hit me. I dare you.' Albie's fists were balled by his sides. 'I'm sick of it. We all are. If Dad saw what you did, he wouldn't be happy, because it's not just a quick crack round the ear like you tell him, is it? Dad's never had to hit us, ever, so why do you?'

'Cos he's too soft and it's my job to keep you in line while he works himself to the bone to put food on the table for you three ungrateful buggers.' The rage in her voice reverberated around the kitchen, like waves of hate rippling in the air.

'Our dad's not soft. He's a good man and we love him. Everyone round here does. But I swear, Mam, if you hit our Annie again, or any of us, I'm going to ring the coppers on you, and we'll make Dad believe what you do to us.' Albie turned to Alfie and Annie and said, 'Won't we?'

As Alfie and Annie nodded, never had Alfie loved his big brother as much as he did right then. And when Bertha screeched and grabbed a full mug of tea and hurled it at the wall, leaving a brown splatter mark and shattered pot all over the quarry tiles, they all stood firm.

It was only a sound in the yard, dogs barking and the familiar voice of their dad that broke the spell and by the time the latch on the door flicked, Bertha had stormed off down the corridor leaving a triumphant Albie and his stunned siblings alone in the kitchen.

The next morning when they came down for breakfast Alfie's eyes slid to the coat rack and his heart flipped when he saw the peg where the belt used to hang was empty. Round-eyed, he looked to Albie who just smiled and gave Alfie a wink.

The memories of that night in the kitchen seemed as clear as if they happened yesterday. And there was something else. A lump of sadness stuck in Alfie's chest that weighed heavy because, his mother aside, he'd loved living at Blacksheep, and he'd loved his old dad even more. Alfie wished he was still there, and it had all turned out differently.

It was just him and Cathy now though, and Alfie bore no grudges towards the others and understood why they had to go. He wished them well, especially Annie who, being the youngest child and God forbid a girl, had taken the brunt of their mother's warped behaviour.

The apple of her dad's eye, Annie often stole the limelight because, as the photos in the family album proved, she was a heartbreaker from the day she was born. She was adored and protected by Albie and revered by Alfie and as the years rolled by, Annie had repaid their love in bucketfuls.

She was the link that held the Walker children together. She was queen of the Zoom calls, which she religiously organised once a month. No matter how near or far they lived from one another, their bond held firm.

If only they could Zoom their dad. He'd been their idol and

while Alfie and Albie wanted to make Jacob Walker proud by learning the business so they could one day take over, little Annie was content to follow her dad and brothers around. Like a lost lamb looking for its mother because after all, her human one shunned her – but only when her dad wasn't there to see; Bertha was clever like that.

Albie was the brains of the family with a degree in agriculture. In a perfect world, he'd have married someone from the village or thereabouts and settled down to run the farm with Alfie. But they didn't live in an ideal world and Albie had been living a lie.

Happy to play the local heartbreaker during his teenage years, as soon as he was able Albie found the kind of love he really wanted in the gay quarter in Manchester. That was where he could be the person he hid from not only his parents but the community around his home. Those he trusted implicitly knew the truth. His brother and sister and Cathy.

It made Alfie so sad that his brother had been too scared of the ridicule his mother would heap on him if she knew; and as for their dad, Albie hadn't wanted to put him to the test. Alfie got that. He also suspected that even though it was their mother selling the flock that made Albie flip, being sick of living a lie also had a lot to do with it.

It was a crying shame because it could have all been so perfect. For years it had been their dream, his and Albie's. As they'd walked the fells, herding the sheep or down at the pub huddled round a table, they'd shared ideas and dreamed big, of the day they'd turn a failing sheep farm around.

But there was one huge insurmountable obstacle that their loyal, down-to-earth dad had never factored into the equation. His wife, their mother. Bertha.

It had become clear from the moment the curtains closed around Jacob Walker's coffin, that there would only be one boss at Blacksheep Farm and that was Bertha. The farm was hers. The fate of Albie, Annie and Alfie was written in black and white and no matter how much they tried to talk her round, get her to see sense, no way was she going to honour her husband's unwritten but well-known wishes.

Which was why Albie packed his bags, hugged his sister, shook his brother's hand and left without saying goodbye to his mother. With a work visa and a bubble-wrapped mug that said 'best big brother in the world' in his hand luggage, Albie headed for New Zealand and hadn't looked back.

Annie had already escaped and was living with Joe which left Alfie and Cathy home alone with the monster. But that didn't last long, thank God.

At the farmhouse door, Alfie sighed and not for the first time thought, *What a waste*. He also resisted the urge to turn around because he could still feel that ghost-like hand of doom on the skin of his neck. Bertha's glare could penetrate hills and trees, sandstone walls and definitely hearts – but so far the one thing that she couldn't tarnish or turn to dust was the love he had for the woman waiting on the other side of the door.

His love. His life. Cathy.

4

CATHY

Cathy always had a happy vibe when she visited Annie's house and as she made the journey down the hill to Hathersage, she looked forward to their regular Monday morning together.

Annie's was one of those homes where you could drop in any time and be sure of a welcome. The small estate where she and Joe lived was made up of pebble-dashed family dwellings, a remnant of seventies social housing and a testament to either a lack of imagination on the architects' part, or a limited council budget.

No doubt at the time, the simple but built-to-last boxy homes had seemed incongruous in their rural setting, plonked on the edge of picturesque Hathersage but conveniently close to the Snake Pass, and then a hop and skip to Sheffield and the surrounding mill towns.

It was there, in Rotherham to be precise, that Joe worked for a construction firm and seemed happy enough driving his digger on building sites while Annie stayed home and took care of their tribe. The eldest was five-year-old Eliza. Bright as a button and the family chatterbox. Then there was three-year-old Ezra, boisterous with a capital B who wanted to be a digger-driving rabbit farmer. And then the most cuddly, bonny bouncing baby Cathy had ever seen, with his rolls of puppy fat, dribbly chin, and a smile that would light up the whole of the Hope Valley, ten-month-old Eli.

As she made her way along the side of the house with her carrier bag of treats for the kids and a giant one containing the clothes she'd bought from the sale rail at Asda, Cathy could already hear the radio coming from the open kitchen window, accompanied by an awful clanking sound.

Pushing the back door open, she immediately spotted the source of the noise: Eli in his highchair beating the lid of a saucepan with a big metal spoon. Seeing Cathy he stopped immediately and gave her a gummy smile followed by a shriek of delight.

'Hello, gorgeous,' she said to the dribble monster, dropping her carrier bags to the floor and responding to his outstretched arms as she called out to Annie, 'It's only me. I'll stick the kettle on.'

Seconds after hauling the dribbler from his highchair and covering his face and neck with kisses and raspberries, Cathy was joined by Annie carrying an overflowing washing basket.

'Hello, love, sorry. I whizzed upstairs to grab this lot while the terror was occupied. Anyone'd think he didn't have any toys because that bloody spoon and lid is his new favourite thing. I reckon the noise has made a permanent dint on my brain so thank God he's stopped. Right, brew, biscuits and a nice sit down. You occupy him and I'll do the honours.'

Not needing to be asked twice, Cathy did as she was told and took Eli through to the lounge where they settled on the floor. While Annie brewed up and loaded the washer, Cathy took in the room and read all the signs that said 'This is a home'. As always it smelt fresh and clean, a faint hint of Dettol from the mopped wooden floor, and the scent of Lenor rising from the row of pyjamas airing on the maiden under the window.

Yes, it was littered with toys, and the furniture was battered round the edges; there were scuff marks on the skirting boards, and a three-piece suite that had seen better days, its war wounds disguised with throws and squashy cushions.

But Eliza's books were, just as she liked them, arranged neatly on the shelves next to a row of family photos: birthdays; Christmases; beach days at Blackpool, the tower resplendent in the background; and the ubiquitous school snaps.

And wellies and shoes were lined up in the hall and coats hung on the rack above.

What Cathy would give for that.

'Right, here you go.' Annie bustled in carrying two mugs and the biscuit tin. 'Leave me laddo on the floor while we have this. I'll give him a rusk before he asks for that bloody pan and spoon again.' She placed the mugs on the coffee table and yanked off the lid of the tin before passing Eli his treat. 'There, that should keep him occupied for five minutes. If he thinks it's out of here, he'll eat it. To be honest, Cathy, sometimes I feel like giving him a four-finger Kit-Kat! Anything to keep him quiet.'

'No you won't. You're too good and I know how strict you are with the kids about sugary stuff. Has he had you up again in the night? You do look a bit peaky.' Cathy had always admired Annie's parenting which was a gentle mix of following the rules as laid down by those in the know, and her own brand of mothering, which was firm, fair but smothered with love. And from what Cathy had been told, it was the antithesis of how they were brought up at Blacksheep.

Annie took a sip of her tea and sighed. 'Yeah, he's teething, poor bairn, and woke up with rosy cheeks and a runny bum. The other two were the same but it'll pass.'

Cathy watched as Eli sucked his rusk and rubbed it on his irritable gums. She absolutely adored him, Eliza and Ezra, and her love for them only made the yearning for a baby of her own harder to bear. Pushing that thought away, she remembered the bag of clothes she'd bought for the kids. 'Now don't go pulling your face but there were some fab bargains on the sale rail at Asda, stock they were getting rid of, so I nabbed some for the kids.' Cathy knew that Annie and Joe were proud and did well to manage their finances and keep a roof over their heads. But making ends meet was getting harder for everyone so she liked to help out where she could.

To bring them a bag of groceries that just happened to be on the 'reduced to clear' shelf, or a new top for Annie and a foodie treat for Joe was her way of looking after them and also, to say a silent thank-you for welcoming her into their family when she needed it the most.

Annie paused mid-sip and raised an eyebrow, as though not quite believing Cathy's story but going with it anyway. The haul of clothing hadn't really been in the sale, but the kids never stopped growing and Ezra wrecked most of his things when he was playing out. And Eliza would love her new dresses and sparkly rainbow leggings, so it was worth a tiny fib.

'Thanks, love. It's appreciated. So, are we still on for your birthday meal on Sunday? I wish you'd let me cook for you. It doesn't seem right that you'll be slaving over a stove on your special day.'

Cathy waved away the idea. 'It's fine. You know I like buggering about in the kitchen and anyway, you're making me one of your gorgeous cakes so that's enough. It'll be nice having everyone round the table and Albie's going to Zoom us. He can watch us eat while he misses out on my magnificent giant Yorkshire puds. I'm hoping to entice him home via food envy.'

Annie snorted. 'I wish it were that easy. I suppose you've invited *her*.'

'Yep, but I don't think she'll come. She's making out that her legs are bad again, but I saw her wandering about the yard early hours this morning, just as the sun came up.'

A loud tut preceded a question from Annie. 'The bloody weirdo. Did she know you'd seen her? And what's she doing wandering round at that time of the morning? The nosy old bag.'

Of all the Walker children, Annie was the most vocal and bitter with regards to their mother and for good reason. But while she was honest about the goings-on up at the farm, Cathy tried to play devil's advocate and keep the peace where she could. 'No, I just watched from the crack in the curtains. I only knew she was there because I'd been for a wee and I love looking out over the valley as the sun comes up. She gave me goosebumps when I saw her wandering about like that. It made me wonder how often she does it. But perhaps it was a one-off. And as for Sunday, I told her you're all coming and that I *will* be cooking meat so she can't refuse because I'm serving what she calls "vegetarian rubbish".'

At that Annie rolled her eyes. 'Well I won't miss her if she doesn't come. In fact, I'll be glad. I can't be arsed looking at her sour face or listening to her crap, and she scares the kids and puts them off their food, constantly criticising everything they do.'

Hearing it put like that made Cathy wish she'd not invited Bertha. It was supposed to be a nice occasion, not one filled with tension and uncomfortable silences. But what could she do? If Bertha wasn't invited and spotted everyone arriving, Alfie would get it in the neck for weeks and he couldn't deal with the guilt trip she'd lay on him.

'Well, let's just hope she gets another one of her imaginary illnesses or her legs really do stop working for at least a day and then Alfie can take her a plate up later. That way everyone's happy.'

Annie huffed. 'Well I'm not going up there to see her if she's pretending to be ill. Sod that! I've got a night off from the pub and I've been looking forward to having some fun, so not a chance am I pandering to her. I don't know how you or our Alfie have the patience but thank fu–' She looked over to Eli whose big eyes were watching so she changed tack. '...furry animals that you do. At least she doesn't live at the farmhouse anymore. Imagine how hideous that would be. Anyway, stuff her. I'll get my boots on, and we'll take this little man for a walk and get some fresh air. Shake away the cobwebs before we pick Ezra up.'

Cathy nodded and watched as Annie took her mug and the biscuit tin into the kitchen, pondering her caustic words, knowing they were true. The idea of Bertha under the same roof didn't bear thinking of. The only reason she actually moved out of the main farmhouse when Albie left was to thwart Alfie's plans for Shepherd's Cottage.

They'd almost finished the refurbishment just before Jacob died and the tiny farmworker's dwelling had been transformed. With new plumbing, heating and electrics, freshly plastered and painted and fitted with a small but functional new kitchen and bathroom, it was ready to go as a holiday let for hikers and cyclists who visited the Peak District in all weathers.

And then out of the blue, Bertha announced that she wanted her independence and peace and quiet so installed herself in the cottage. She justified it by saying, 'Seeing as I paid for that building work from my bank account, I've got every right to move in.' Then she sweetened the medicine by saying she felt in the way and there was only room for one woman in the kitchen. But she and Cathy had rubbed along for years so they all knew it was rubbish.

Soon after, she'd vetoed Annie's dream of rearing goats and setting up a business making artisan produce from their milk.

The goats had always been Annie's ambition, and one Jacob had given the thumbs-up, over-ruling Bertha and promising to support his daughter's new enterprise. With money from a small start-up loan that Annie had secured with a meticulous business plan, one of the old barns would be converted into a mini-factory unit where she would make cheese and ice cream and sell it along with milk at local farm shops and markets.

Once the barn refurbishment was complete and a small herd of goats established, she and Joe had hoped to secure a mortgage and convert one of the barns to make a home at Blacksheep. Annie's little dream would have been a reality if only Jacob hadn't suffered a heart attack and died on the fells he loved as much as his family.

Annie told Cathy that she'd known, the minute the paramedic confirmed that her dad was gone, that so were her plans. That her and Joe's hopes for a better future were doomed and that the baby growing inside her wasn't going to have an entrepreneur for a mummy. What was worse, baby Eliza would never meet her grandad and that still broke Annie's heart.

She had a lot to answer for, did Bertha Walker. Cathy understood why Albie, Annie and Alfie couldn't stand the sight of their mother.

But the reason why Bertha behaved the way she did, why she shunned everyone and seemed hellbent on making those around her miserable remained a mystery. A mystery that Cathy's overactive imagination was determined to solve.

5

They'd taken their usual Monday morning route through the village, detouring via St Michael's churchyard where they stopped by the grave of Little John so that Cathy could read the inscription on the stone:

> HERE LIES BURIED LITTLE JOHN THE FRIEND & LIEUTENANT OF ROBIN HOOD. HE DIED IN A COTTAGE (NOW DESTROYED) TO THE EAST OF THE CHURCHYARD. THE GRAVE IS MARKED BY THE OLD HEADSTONE AND FOOTSTONE AND IS UNDERNEATH THE OLD YEW TREE.

No matter how many times she saw it, Cathy had to say the words out loud and channel the connection to those gone before. It was the same connection she had felt when she visited North Lees Hall, as Charlotte Brontë had when she was gathering inspiration for Jane Eyre. The whole area, from Hope Valley to the Dark Peak moorlands spoke to Cathy in a way she'd never experienced before.

The ghosts of the past soothed and settled her soul, welcoming her home and promising to keep her safe. That's what she felt, and what she told herself when the demons from the past threatened to invade her world.

Dragging her mind back to the present Cathy focused on the sleeping boy swaddled in his pram, cheeks rosy from fresh air and, hopefully, not from sore, irritated gums. She and Annie occupied a bench in the grounds of St Michael's, both lost in quiet contemplation.

Annie's surprise statement broke the silence. 'Remember how she wanted to put Dad here in the memorial garden, but he'd stipulated in his will that he was to be scattered on the fells? Pissed her right off, that did. I was so proud of our Albie when he took the urn off the dresser in the kitchen and refused to give it back. I can see him now, disobeying Mam.'

Cathy smiled, remembering the hoo-ha in the kitchen and Albie's stand-off and how the whole thing had upset Alfie. Not just the row but the fact his dad was inside an ugly black vase with a lid.

'Poor Alfie, it really freaked him out.'

Annie nodded. 'You know what our Alfie's like. Keeps too much inside and doesn't like to speak ill of folk or cause a fuss. Thank fuck,' she glanced at Eli who was still fast asleep, 'that it was Albie who collected the ashes from the undertaker, otherwise I reckon she'd have brought them down here, dug a hole herself and hid them underground, just to piss us off. I swear she's mentally unstable. It's like she takes pleasure in causing us pain and going against everything. I mean, if she'd been sad and said that she wanted to keep him close or couldn't bear the thought of Dad being chucked on the muddy fells, I might have got it. But to go against his wishes for no reason whatsoever... that's what told me she was doing it for devilment and exerting her power because it gave her a kick.'

'I think it's all about keeping control, like she's scared of not being in charge of her life now your dad's gone. But she goes about it all the wrong way. She's definitely very bitter about something. I just wish we knew what. Then maybe we could help put it right.'

Annie hummed, then replied, 'Yep, it's all about control, which is why she kept all Dad's personal belongings, you know, stuff that's been in his family for generations. Like my great-grandfather's war medals and his pocket watch. That should have gone to the lads but oh no, big bad Bertha hoards it all, up her arse on the third shelf, no doubt.'

And even though Annie's barbed comment made her chuckle, Cathy knew she was right in her evaluation of Bertha and again the question pecked at her brain: *Why is she like this?* Cathy tucked a strand of hair behind her ear and wished she'd tied it up. Her shoulder-length curls were going wild in the wind, and she'd look bedraggled and witchlike by the time she got home.

Annie rocked the pram to and fro as she spoke, a frown creasing her face. 'I was so proud of Albie when he said we were all going to scatter Dad there and then and if she wanted to come and say a few words then that was fine, but he wasn't giving the urn back. Do you remember, she issued the usual threats that came to be part of life after Dad died? The power went right to her head, and she loved to tell us we'd be cut out of the will if we went against her, or she'd sell the farm from under us and give the life-insurance money away, rather than let us have it. If it hadn't been for Dad tying that will up good and proper I reckon she'd have done it.'

Cathy nodded. 'Alfie says she can't change the will because it's joint and they made it together. So surely part of that's a load of rubbish.'

'Yes, that's true. She can't disinherit us or change the will in any way but unfortunately she could sell the farm and spend all the money – not that she will because she'd have nothing left to dangle like a carrot and torment us with. Like I said, she's mad as a box of frogs.' Annie leant over and tucked the blanket under Eli's chin and looked deep in thought.

Cathy gave Annie a nudge. 'I do get it, you know. Why you're all so bitter towards her and I don't mean because of how she was when you were kids. It's like she's constantly punishing you for something, even though you've not done anything wrong. And by preventing all of you from being together on the farm and making it profitable again she gets the last laugh.

'It's so weird. And she could have such a good life, too. With all her family around her and I just wish there was a way to make her see that. Life is precious, and I can't stand the thought of anyone wasting it when it could all be taken away in the blink–' Cathy stopped mid-sentence because she'd heard the crack in her voice and recognised the familiar wave of panic and despair welling up inside.

Without saying a word, Annie reached over and took Cathy's hand and gave it a gentle squeeze and together they waited for the storm to pass. Minutes ticked by to the sound of traffic beyond the churchyard walls and maybe, if they listened hard enough, that of Eli sucking his dummy. Faint, comforting and blissfully innocent.

Annie broke the spell of silence. 'You shouldn't upset yourself on her account, Cathy. She's not worth it and neither is the time you'll waste trying to fathom what makes her tick. All in the hope you'll somehow make it all better. You can't, because she won't let you.' She gave Cathy's hand another squeeze as if to affirm her belief.

'I love you for wanting to try, though, and I know what you mean about life being precious. After what you went through, what you saw and everything, the way us lot carry on must seem petty, but I assure you, *she's* a lost cause so if you can, just let it go. Look after yourself and my daft brother. You two are more important, believe me.'

Cathy sighed and leant sideways, resting her head on Annie's shoulder, glad of the comfort of another human being even though the tweedy fabric of Annie's jacket scratched her cheek. 'I don't think you're petty at all. I swear. I overthink everything and get lost in my own world sometimes, dreaming up scenarios and hoping they'll come true if I focus hard enough. And for someone who's about to turn thirty that's sad, I know it is.'

'It's not sad at all. In fact it's very sweet, that you fill your head with positive thoughts and get lost in a world of your own.'

Cathy gave a wry laugh. 'What? Like wandering the fells and moors pretending I'm Cathy and Alfie is Heathcliff. Yes, that's very sensible and bound to make all the bad things in the world disappear and at the same time, make my dreams come true.'

On hearing this, Annie dislodged Cathy's head so she could put her arm around her shoulder, pulling her closer. 'Oh mate. I wish I could tell you they will come true one day, but I can't. And I won't, because to say those words is stupid and tight. I can't make promises or wave a magic wand even though I wish I could.

'And that's another reason why I bloody despise Mam, because she has the power to put it all right, heal our family, let me and the lads have our dreams and give you the chance to have a baby. I will never ever understand why Dad didn't see through her and stand up to her more because if he had, things would be so different.' Annie began to tap her hand on the arm of the bench and her jaw was set firm, annoyance radiating from her.

Cathy sighed. 'It's because love is blind. It's as simple as that. I didn't know Jacob for long, but I could tell he loved the bones of Bertha as much as he loved the bones of his kids, so he was stuck in the middle. I think he was a lonely single farmer and wanted someone to love and work beside him, give him a family. Yes, I know Bertha was quite young when they met and there was a big age gap, but they were definitely in love. And she never talked about her own family. That makes me suspect that they were horrible, which is why she and your dad eloped. I reckon when they met, they both needed each other for different reasons.'

'Yeah, you're right. Talk of her family was banned and we never met any of them. And if she's anything to go by, I bet they were all vile or, perhaps she was lying and they kicked *her* out and were glad to be shot of her. Probably would've packed her suitcase if they'd known she was going to do a flit. You know, the one Dad said she arrived with, oh, and a carrier bag, like a little orphan he said. I actually believe my version more.'

Cathy couldn't stifle a chuckle at that because Annie did have a way of putting things. 'Well, whatever the reason, while Jacob was alive, he was the glue that kept the family together. A quietly reassuring presence, that's how I always thought of him and even though he didn't say a lot, I'm sure he saw her faults. My mum and dad have plenty, but they tolerate and forgive and move on. Perhaps your dad just wanted a peaceful life. Sometimes it's as clear cut as that.'

'Hmm, maybe. I think she just knew how to play him and us. She chose her battles well, like when I wanted the goats. I reckon it came down to money because we weren't making any on the flock, so maybe she thought that my idea might actually be a winner. She's crafty like that, because when Dad gave me the go-ahead, after she'd put her ten-pence-worth in, she backed down. Still, she won in the end, didn't she.' Annie sounded more defeated than angry at this point.

'Well, if you can call pissing your eldest son off so badly that he packed his bags and buggered off to New Zealand, and having your daughter despise you for taking away her dream, then selling the flock and leaving your younger son jobless a win, she really is warped!' Now Cathy was annoyed.

Annie laughed. 'I rest my case, your honour.' Releasing Cathy from her grasp Annie made a decision. 'Right, no more talk about Bonkers Bertha for today. Let's go and get one of them fancy coffees and a cake to take back to mine for after our dinner. I'll make us some butties. This one'll zap awake soon so thank goodness his aunty Cathy is here to play with him and barmy Ezra while I crack on with the ironing. You don't need to rush back, do you?'

They both stood and set off down the path, Cathy taking a turn to push the pram. 'Nope, so I can stay a while and anyway, Alfie is expecting a delivery so he'll be busy, and Dave the Rave said he'd help so he can keep him company.'

'Agh, yes, I remember our Alfie mentioned something...' Annie trailed off lost in thought.

Cathy glanced across and gave her a nudge. 'And you need your roots doing. If you order the stuff online, I'll do them for you.'

'Phew, thanks, mate. I'm starting to look like Winnie Witch, but I didn't want to ask because...'

'It's fine. I don't mind, honest.' Cathy pushed the button on the pelican crossing, and as they waited for the lights to change, despite their mirth and the supposed shaking off of the spectre of Bertha, there was a faint shadow following them on their way.

Was it the memory of the life Cathy had left behind? From the dream career working with the cream of the industry that took her all over the country, to luxury hotels and high-octane trade events and photo-shoots... to making bracelets to sell online.

Or was it the fact that Annie was right. Because the

hundreds of thousands of pounds that sat idling in Bertha's bank account, the pay-out from Jacob's life-insurance policy, could be the one thing that would change everyone's lives.

Instead it was doing absolutely nothing. While Albie remained on the other side of the world, Annie worked three nights in the bar at the George Hotel and Alfie bought and sold cars to put food on the table. In the meantime, from her spanking new home on the hill, Bertha lorded it over them all, dangling the carrot that was Blacksheep Farm.

And Cathy? Well, she was happy in her own way. Hidden from the horrors of the world. Tucked away in the hills with a man she loved more than anything and anybody ever. Content to stay exactly where she was, wanting one thing that maybe money could buy if only Bertha would help them out. A baby.

6

ALFIE

Alfie stood behind Cathy in the big barn, his hands over her eyes, his heart beating. He was nervous and not sure how she'd react, even though Dave had insisted she was going to love her thirtieth birthday present.

'Right, I'm going to count to five. Keep your eyes closed, okay...'

'Alf, just let me see, you bloody nutter.'

He heard a giggle of excitement in Cathy's voice which boded well so instead of counting down, he removed his hands and quickly stood beside her so he could gauge her reaction. 'Okay, open your eyes.'

He watched as Cathy blinked then focused on the heap of blue rusty metal before her.

'What do you think? I bought it for you. It's a Bedford CA, a proper classic. Worth a fortune once it's done up... which I'm going to do, obviously, but I thought you could do the interior because you're good at making stuff. I'll sort out the engine and the exterior, and I think we should keep the colour original... unless you want something special...'

Alfie realised he was panic-rambling because she still hadn't said anything. She probably couldn't get a word in, so he had to ask, 'Do you like it? You hate it, don't you?'

'Is it really for me?' Cathy rested her hand on her chest then stepped forward, walking towards the neglected van that was covered in mildew and bird muck.

'Yep. I thought we could get out and about in it, you know, when it's been tarted up. We've not had a holiday for years and we could just shoot off anywhere we wanted whenever the fancy takes us. Do the east coast hippy trail.'

Cathy turned for a second to ask, 'Is there even such a thing?'

Moving swiftly on because he was getting worried, 'Or we could head for Scotland and look for Nessie, or wherever you want...' He was rambling on again so forced himself to shut up, be patient and allow his body and tongue to relax.

When she turned towards him, her pale face flushed pink at the cheeks and a wide smile on her lips, he silently hoped for the thumbs-up.

'Alf, I love it, I absolutely bloody love it, you big superstar.' Cathy launched herself at him and wrapped her long arms and legs around his sturdy frame, covering his face with kisses. 'This is the best present I've ever had. And yes, I'll do the inside so let's have a look. Come on.' Releasing him from what felt like a wrestling move, Cathy planted her feet on the earth floor of the barn then shot off, opening the passenger door and peering in before racing to the back and yanking wide the rear ones.

'Oh look, look, Alf, it's got a little kitchen and everything. I love it so much.'

By the time Alfie got there she was in the back, bouncing on the bench seat, running her hands over the tatty curtains and talking ten to the dozen. 'I'll make new covers for the seats in retro fabric... Do they turn into a bed? They must do. And matching curtains, and new lino for the floor.' Then she leapt outside and ran her hand along the paintwork. 'I think you're right. We should deffo keep it original when you paint it. The same blue and white. And it needs a name, too.'

'It's a camper van not a person!' Alfie was laughing as he watched her jump into the driver's seat, turning the wheel like a child pretending to drive.

'Don't be such a philistine. Of course it needs a name, but I have to decide if it's a girl or a boy first. I'll wait till I get to know it better before I choose. Does it start? Where's the key?' Cathy was looking around the cab, opening the glove compartment and pulling down the visors.

Alfie took the key out of his pocket and passed it to Cathy. 'And the logbook's in the dash. It's only had one owner from new. Bought in 1968. Like I said, a classic.'

Cathy turned the key. Nothing happened and after a couple of goes she gave up, a forlorn expression replacing her previous excitement.

'Don't be disappointed, love. Me and Dave got it going this morning, but it sounded a bit rough so I'll take a look at the engine and give it a service. Nothing to worry about. These little beauties are easy to work on; not like new cars that are bloody computers on wheels.'

She wasn't listening though. So Alfie signalled he was going to make them a brew and went back to the house to put the kettle on, leaving her lost in one of her worlds.

He knew Cathy's mind would be racing, taking her on journeys to happy places. Exactly what he'd hoped for when he spotted the van on the auction website, because while Cathy was content to hide from reality on the farm, he wasn't.

She preferred the company of family and their close group of friends, safe in their hilltop haven away from whatever threats she perceived lurked down there in the big city. And he got it, he really did, and for the most part he had no need or desire to venture out either. He'd had everything he'd ever wanted right there, at Blacksheep Farm until, bit by bit, it was all taken away.

And sometimes he felt like luck wasn't on their side, especially after trying for a baby for ages and with every month, he saw Cathy's mood dip and disappointment written across her face no matter how much she tried to hide it. So he'd decided it was time they made some luck of their own rather than waiting around for something to happen. Okay, so an old camper that needed a lot of work doing to it wasn't going to change the baby situation, but it might give them both something to focus on and divert their attention. They could even go and lie on that Cerne Abbas Giant that was supposed to symbolise fertility. It was worth a try. Anything to make Cathy happy and get away for a while from Blacksheep and his mother.

7

Back inside the kitchen, after giving Skip's ear a scratch, Alfie put teabags into mugs and waited for the water to boil. Unlike Cathy who was lost in the world of her camper, Alfie became lost in the past. It was a place he longed for and at the same time, felt an increasing desire to shake off.

Annie had been the first to free herself from their mother. She moved in with Joe, happier in a studio flat than on the farm, simply because she couldn't bear being under the same roof as Bertha for one more minute.

Annie was feisty, but she'd fallen in love with Joe, saw her chance to escape and took it, moving far enough from the likelihood of throttling their mother, but not so far away that she'd be parted from her beloved dad and brothers.

Despite losing one of his crutches and dedicated bodyguards, Alfie was in some part glad that particular war, between mother and daughter had ended.

He expected to see Annie every day once she started her new dairy venture, so it wasn't like he'd miss her. And, he'd thought, there was always a chance that being apart might miraculously bring her and his mother closer together. He'd actually laughed out loud when that thought popped into his head. Ever the optimist, often the fool.

His dad dying was the next blow – but once the shock and grief somewhat abated, Alfie and Albie did what Jacob Walker had always expected of them, talked about and trained them for. They focused on the flock and reviving the dwindling family business they were determined to save. And then *she* ruined it all.

The first strike was when Bertha vetoed Annie's dairy. Permanently. The brothers were incredulous. Not only had their dad deemed a holiday let and the dairy viable projects that would bolster the farm's future, his hefty life-insurance pay-out would have easily financed all of their dreams.

So when the price of livestock fell again and she called a meeting to tell them that they were selling the flock, Albie gave up, packed up, and left.

At first Alfie was bitter, hurt and very confused because as much as he wanted Albie to stay, he understood why he had to leave. Albie was the headstrong one. The fighter of the family and the least malleable of the Walker children and there was only so much a man could take before pride called time. Albie was also getting tired of living a lie on so many levels.

It had been a huge relief to Alfie when his mother moved into Shepherd's Cottage and left him and Cathy alone in the farmhouse. A tactical step on her part because, as Annie wisely pointed out, with their dad gone, mother dearest had nobody to impress, to cook and clean for, and she no longer had a need to prove she was the perfect wife.

It had pained Bertha to care for her kids when they were young, because what she did do, was all for show and so that nobody could criticise. Not a chance was she going to keep house for adults. People she hated. Her own children.

And as much as Annie's words, or one word in particular,

had stung Alfie, he knew she was right. Bertha *hated* her kids and probably always would.

And that left him and Cathy to look after the farm, not that there was much to do. No job. No focus. A roof over his head at least, but with the constant threat of his mother's return.

Bertha wasn't stupid, though. She'd moved her pieces on the board and lay in wait. Watching from the cottage up the lane. She held the purse strings. Lorded it over them in the knowledge she had the power to sell the farm and had she been so inclined, spend the lot on wine, men and song.

It was Annie who'd explained the rules of the game to Alfie. 'Don't think for a minute she'd put the farm up for sale, Alfie. For a start, who in their right mind would want to be a farmer these days? And who would pay what that greedy bitch expects? To do what? Live up there in the middle of nowhere.' Annie had reached over and tried to cover her brother's strong hands with hers, rubbing his calloused skin with her thumb. She was trying to give comfort, but her words bruised his heart.

'She'd get a pittance for it and then, where would she go? She's got no friends to go on holiday or stay with. She disowned her Yorkshire family when she married Dad, so they won't be interested. That's why, by staying at Blacksheep and preventing anyone from stepping foot into Shepherd's Cottage she can play queen of the castle. Dangle the carrot now and then with her idle threats. Have you and Cathy at her beck and call and at the same time, make sure you're beholden for having a roof over your head. She's sick and twisted and I hate her fucking guts.'

On hearing that, Alfie had felt more down than ever. 'So what do you suggest I do? Bugger off like Albie has or ask Joe to get me a job on the diggers? And where would we go? Oh yeah, doss down on your sofa because no way will Cathy move back to her apartment in Manchester.'

Annie sighed. 'Yes, you could, that's a given and I'm sorry if

I've made everything worse. But look, what I'm trying to say is she needs you as much as you – at the moment – need her. Hopefully she'll pop her clogs soon and then we can all move on.'

Alfie had gasped. 'Annie, you don't mean that!'

But when his sister raised her eyebrows and shrugged, he knew she did.

The flick of the kettle switch brought Alfie back to the task in hand and as he finished making the tea, his thoughts meandered once again to Cathy. It had been a gamble using some of his savings to buy her the van, but he was desperate to escape the farm, even if it was for a couple of wet weekends in Scarborough. She was becoming increasingly insular, like she was living inside her head more and more, distant and daydreamy, and purposely reducing the outer limits of the circle she'd drawn around them.

They had a great group of friends who often asked them to go for days out and on holidays, but she always found an excuse. Instead they hiked or cycled, which Cathy insisted was good for them.

If they walked over the fells, Alfie knew there was a high peak from where, on a clear day, you could see Manchester on the horizon. They never took that route because if they did, Cathy wouldn't want to look towards the city where she'd abandoned her life, leaving her fancy apartment in the hands of a letting agent. The rent covered her mortgage and left some spare, which she saved. For what, Alfie had no idea.

And then as if to make things worse, their failed attempts at starting a family had made her close in on herself even more, locking in her disappointment, like she was avoiding anything that might send her spiralling again.

Their name was down for IVF with the NHS, but the waiting list was huge, and they could be in limbo for years. His mother could have lent them, or even given them, some money to have tests and go private to speed things up. But that would never happen, and neither would he lower himself to ask.

And it was that, and the thought of being stuck at Blacksheep, marking time and praying for a miracle or three, that was slowly suffocating Alfie.

Since the flock had gone, he'd had to re-invent himself. Find something to give structure to his days and, a way to put food on the table. It was his pride, more than anything, because Cathy was happy to use the rent money from the apartment, and what she earned from selling her jewellery, which wasn't a lot, tided them over.

He bought, restored and sold classic cars and laboured at neighbouring farms that were just about clinging on, like Blacksheep had done. For now, he and Cathy were managing because they didn't crave a fancy lifestyle, which was most likely their saving grace.

Lately though, Alf had noticed a shift in himself, too. He'd been used to labouring all his life and despite working manually during the day, on the cars or maintaining fences and keeping the farm tidy, no matter how tired his bones were, his restless mind kept him awake at night.

His thought process then took him to New Zealand and his brother who he missed like a limb. Or on backpacking trips to Asia. Or to a farm that he'd always imagined would one day be his, for the family he was yet to have, for the future.

During those long hours, as he waited for the bedside alarm to ring and alert him to the start of a day that would stretch on forever, he tried to come up with a way of luring Cathy out of her comfort zone.

There was no way he'd force her to go away with him or tell her how he felt, because her happiness and peace of mind came above all else. She'd been through enough and even though the physical scars had faded, the ones in her mind hadn't.

He could only hope that the little van in the big barn would be the catalyst they needed. A safe haven on wheels that might take them far, far away from the black cloud that seemed to follow him everywhere.

8

CATHY

The kitchen table was littered with fabric swatches, magazines, coloured pencils and a brand-new scrapbook that Cathy was going to turn into a diary showing the before, during and after of Maggie's restoration.

She'd ignored the sniggers from Alfie and Dave the Rave when she'd first told them what she was calling her van and also when they pointed out, as they slurped tea and ate their bacon sarnies, that it would be a lot less buggering about if she made a virtual scrapbook.

'Why don't you just take stage-by-stage photos on your phone then bang 'em in a folder on that there laptop?' Dave waved his free hand at Cathy. 'Nobody uses real photos anymore. Can you even get 'em printed off these days? I've not done that for yonks.'

Cathy rolled her eyes. 'Course you can. You can order them online and anyway, get you being all tech savvy. But I want a physical memento that I can touch and feel and ooh-and-ah over. Something I can add to as Maggie's journeys begin.'

A bit like a baby album. There, she'd admitted it but thankfully only in her head and nobody else had heard. Because it had occurred to her that she might be acting out some weird replacement therapy, swapping photos of prams and cots for paint charts and handy foldable washing-up bowls.

'I told my Sheena that you'd called the van Maggie and she's as barmy as you. Said it suits it.' Dave took a bite of his sarnie, oblivious to the brown sauce that was trickling onto his ginger beard.

He was an original, was Dave. Lean, and tall with muscled biceps and a neck covered in colourful tattoos. A mop of long hair to match his mountain-man whiskers, too many piercings to count and a fondness for shorts no matter what the weather. He was a conundrum too. His tendency to be a bit gormless belied the fact he was the most intelligent of their group, a senior paramedic, a saver of lives with a heart of pure gold.

'It does suit her, and reminds me of that song, "Maggie May" and I bet any money that whoever drove the van back in the day would have listened to that song on the radio.' Cathy didn't care if they thought she was daft: she loved the name she'd chosen, and the fact Sheena agreed with her.

Alfie was next with his ten-pence-worth.

'Well, while you're sticking and gluing and colouring in, we're going to strip the van out. Those interior panels will need replacing I reckon so that's something you can be sourcing online. There's plenty of companies that do them but don't go ordering owt till you've shown me, okay? It's easy to pick the wrong thing and you have to be sure it's the right make and year.' Alfie had stood and kissed the top of her head before turning to drop his mug and plate in the sink.

Cathy smiled. 'I promise I won't go mad on eBay. Anyway, maybe some of the panels are salvageable and I can re-cover them, so don't *you* go throwing anything out. Deal?'

'Deal.' Alfie jerked his head at his right-hand man. 'Oi, lazy arse, let's get a move on.'

He waited while Dave deposited his breakfast things in the sink. Then they both headed off – but not before Dave, lingering in the doorway, dropped one of his big unsubtle hints. 'We'll be back at one for us dinner, lass. And I wouldn't mind one o'them nice cheesy pies you make, and some chips if you fancy gettin' the fryer on.'

Cathy turned, and smiled at Dave's cheeky wink that was just about visible from under the rim of his tatty bobble hat. He'd worn it for as long as she could remember and it never left his head during the colder months, replaced in summer with an even tattier bucket hat.

'Go on then, seeing as it's you! Ya cheeky bugger. Just make sure you look after Maggie for me, or else!'

Alfie, bellowing from somewhere in the yard interrupted their banter, 'Dave. Will you stop gabbing like a fishwife and get your bloody finger out, you lazy sod.'

With a grimace and quick salute, Dave was gone, and Cathy put aside her swatches and grabbed her pad and pen and ran through the shopping and guest list for her birthday meal and drinks that weekend. She still wasn't one for crowds in the pub – hence the small gathering at the farm.

Since moving in with Alfie, she'd swerved what she knew was the approach of full-on agoraphobia. She could now manage the supermarket by being there first thing when they opened the doors. Outdoor events, like the summer fair at the village school were doable; but not Alfie's rugby matches because the roar of the crowd was too much and certainly not bonfire night because Cathy knew exactly how pets felt when they heard the booms...

Don't go there. Refocus. Breathe.

Cathy scanned the list of names who'd been invited up to the farm in the evening, once the family birthday lunch was done and dusted. She was looking forward to seeing her mum and dad but her brother lived in Canada and she didn't expect him to fly back for a Sunday roast, vegetarian or meat option!

Cathy remembered the days when Bertha would serve roast lamb at the weekend, taking the meat from a freezer stocked to the brim with it. Even though she didn't miss seeing what she regarded as a frozen coffin full of dead animals, it still made Cathy sad, knowing that a huge part of what made Blacksheep tick, was gone.

Returning to her list and swiping away any maudlin thoughts, she checked everyone off, smiling at how almost all of Alfie's friends had a name plus a description, just to make sure everyone knew who was who.

He said they'd always had nicknames, because some of them shared names.

Dave the Rave, Cathy's secret favourite of all Alfie's mates, was so named on account of the one and only time he organised a party at his parents' house while they were in Rhyl for the weekend.

What had meant to be a bit of a piss-up with a few mates somehow morphed into a full-on rave with people turning up from miles around. Word had spread by mouth and text and the house was totally wrecked.

It all kicked off (according to legend) when some bright spark channelling The Who did a Keith Moon and threw Dave's dad's new twelve-inch flat screen telly out the window.

There was what the locals described as a teenage orgy in all of the bedrooms, which Dave swore on his granny's life was a lie. And then the uninvited started ripping down curtains and smashing ornaments, drawing on his mum's favourite painting of the Spanish lady with the long black hair, and filling up the sink with wee.

When Alfie, helped by Dave's real, invited friends tried to stop them, it turned into a huge punch-up. By the time the police arrived, the scumbags had scarpered and most of the furniture was on the lawn with Dave sat in his mam's armchair crying into his can of beer.

After the massive bollocking off his dad, he handed over the contents of his Post Office account. Then the whole terrible event made it onto Monday night's *Look Northwest* and into the *Daily Mirror*; and Dave the Rave became a legend in the village.

His mam, once over the shock of seeing the contents of her knicker drawer dangling from the cherry blossom tree in the front garden and the fact someone had stuck a row of frozen sausages in her herbaceous borders, had the double-page spread mounted in a frame in the lobby where it remained to that day.

It was stories like that, and Alfie's bond with his friends from the village, lads and lasses he went to school and grew up with, that added to the sense of calm and security that living at Blacksheep gave Cathy.

She'd memorised the names of all of them. Irish Dave (for obvious reasons), Ponytail Tony who shouldn't be mixed up with Chippy Van Tony (who just for the record was bald). Then Fat Pat who went to Turkey for a gastric band and now looked like a supermodel who needed a chip butty but would forever be Fat Pat. There was Tommy Dog (kept whippets), and there was Colin the Scrapman and Eddie the Skip. Old John was not to be confused with his son, Young John who owned the pub in the village.

There were many more, and if you were married or going out with one of them, then you'd be, for example, Dave the Rave's Sheena. Because clearly other halves were only memorable when attached to their menfolk.

Cathy was quite proud, though, of being Blacksheep-Alfie's-Cathy. He was the best person of the male variety that she'd ever met and being absorbed into his life and his name in some ways soaked up what remained of her past.

She could pretend her old life hadn't existed because even thinking about it – her job, her apartment, her city friends – would lead her mind back to that night. So she'd blocked it all out and carved her life into three sections.

The before, which entailed growing up in Droylsden, a suburb ten minutes outside of Manchester, with her parents and brother. School, holidays, fun bits, happy times, her grandma and grandad, ended at the middle section. When she got her first job, in a top city-centre salon as a Saturday girl.

She was fifteen and it was her first taste of what would become her career. One in which she progressed, thrived and reached the top. And had now wiped from her memory with the skill of a surgeon. It was a no-go zone and if a mere flicker, an unbidden snapshot of that time breached the barrier, Cathy squashed it like a fly.

Section three was all that mattered now. Where she was at. Where she belonged with Alfie. By his side and safe.

Cathy was setting the table, lost in her task while cooking aromas of home made pie filled the room. No doubt Dave would be devastated to hear that the deep fat frier wasn't switched on and he'd have to make do with oven chips. To make up for it, there was apple crumble for afters and as she heard male voices on approach, she opened the oven door to check everything was ready.

When they burst through the doorway, stamping feet and removing work boots, calling 'dinner smells good', Cathy noticed Alfie was carrying something.

'What's that?' She pointed to the long tube, the type you keep posters in.

Alfie made his way over to the table and after he gave her the regulation kiss and bear-hug, his three-day stubble leaving Cathy's cheek tingling, he waggled the tube. 'We found it in the van when we stripped the interior out, wedged behind one of the side panels. There's something rolled up inside but we didn't want to look in case we got whatever it is dirty. We were thinking it might be a painting and Dave's already got us on *Antiques Roadshow*. He's talked himself into it being a masterpiece, but I reckon it'll be some old tat. I bet it's a poster of the bloody Spice Girls or S Club Seven.'

'Hey, don't diss the Spice Girls, and c'mon, pass it over. Let's have a look.' Cathy was intrigued and wiped her hands on the tea towel before joining Alfie at the table where he was sliding plates and cutlery to one side.

'Look.' Alfie popped the plastic lid off the end of the tube and turned it upside down allowing sheets of rolled paper protected by polythene, to slide out.

After discarding the tube, Alfie let Cathy with the clean hands take over. Unfurling the papers, she smoothed them out on the table. They were each covered by a sheet of tissue held in place at the corners by masking tape which she carefully peeled away. Then, rather than Scary Spice, they were met with something entirely different.

'Oh my goodness. She's beautiful... it's beautiful. What a gorgeous painting.' Cathy was mesmerised by the image before her and reached out to gently touch the paper, tracing the watercolour brushstrokes that brought the woman to life.

Whoever she was, the artist had caught a look, a moment in time that was just between them, her wide blue eyes staring straight into those of the beholder. She wasn't smiling but there was a hint of amusement at the corners of her full lips, as though she knew a secret and it was something that made her happy. And while her face was the focal point, her expression and presence drawing you in, she was framed by her long blonde hair, tumbling and cascading over her shoulders like a waterfall of yellow that faded as it met the edges of the parchment.

Also attached to the painting was an old photograph, quite

faded and nowhere near the quality of those taken in the present. In the background Cathy could see lots of tents – a campsite perhaps – and the sky was clear and blue so maybe summer. But where could it have been taken? This question was swiftly swept aside when she noticed something else.

In the bottom right-hand corner was a name, presumably the artist. It looked like it said *Guy Alexander,* and then on the left there was a name and a date. Leaning in to get a closer look and as she read the words out loud, the hairs on her arms stood on end and her skin was peppered with goosebumps. It said 'Krystle, 1970'.

9

The scene around the kitchen table was one of contentment, due entirely to the feast Cathy had served, plus a copious amount of real ale and the good company of friends and family. Easter had come early and although it was the last day of March that year, there was still a buoyant springlike sense that always lifted her.

It made up for the disappointment of her parents not being there owing to her mum having a migraine. They'd plagued her for as long as Cathy could remember and often wiped her out for days. Her parents promised to call up during the week and celebrate on her birthday proper, the 7th of April, and bring her presents and Easter eggs for the kids.

Talking of which, two were currently fast asleep on the battered old sofa in the corner, with Skip squashed in between them keeping guard. Eliza was still going strong, dressed up in her best *Frozen* costume and holding court at the head of the table in the chair they'd left empty, just in case Bertha had made an appearance. She hadn't and Cathy knew she wasn't the only one in the room who was secretly relieved.

Alfie was well on his way to being merry, as were Dave and

Joe. And true to her word, Annie was letting her hair down and, with two willing childminders in Cathy and Sheena, had the rosy-cheeked glow induced by afternoon drinking.

On the side was a plate of Sunday dinner, covered with tinfoil that someone, most likely poor Alfie, would have to deliver to Bertha and truthfully, Cathy wished he'd take it straight away so as not to tempt fate. They'd had a lovely afternoon, and she didn't want anything to spoil it, or their pudding.

'Right, let's clear this table then I have a *huge* chocolate fudge cake if anyone is interested, and yes, Alf, before you ask, cream and ice cream!'

Cathy smiled as she saw Alfie close his mouth on the question she knew he was about to ask and instead, he rubbed and patted his tummy. 'Ooh, go on then, lass. I reckon I've got some room left for pudding, just about. What do you think, our Eliza? Shall I chance it?' He pushed his already ample belly outwards so she could reach across and give it a pat.

Eliza grimaced and in a voice laced with wisdom said, 'Yes, you definitely have a *bit* of room in there, Uncle Alfie, but only for a tiny slice cos I think a big piece might make you sick. Aunty Cathy says you eat three potatoes more than a pig and that's a lot!'

Deciding it was time to gather the plates Cathy averted her eyes from Alfie, laughing with the others who were agreeing with Eliza and ignoring Alfie's protests that he was still a growing lad, and his blubber was an essential bit of kit that kept him warm all through winter.

As always, from her position at the sink Cathy couldn't help taking in the view before her and it was from there, looking out across the peaks, she had spent many a happy washing-up session. The magnificent scenery made light work of a chore.

She was soon joined by Sheena bringing plates and cutlery,

and after feeling the bump of hip-against-hip, took the hint and moved aside. 'You shouldn't be washing up on your birthday, so go and sit. I'll do these.'

'It's fine, love. I like to be busy and between us we'll have this done in no time. So, tell me how the wedding plans are going.' Cathy squirted Fairy Liquid into the sink as Sheena scraped leftovers into a bag.

'It's all good and thankfully not till August so we can keep saving. I wouldn't mind but we're only having a small do, but it all adds up and my mam keeps dropping hints about white doves and a horse and carriage. Bloody doves! What a waste of money that is. I'd rather have another tier on the wedding cake.' Sheena passed Cathy the plate and continued scraping.

'Well, I think it's going to be perfect and I'm looking forward to it. We'll all have a lovely day.'

At this Sheena paused and her expression, as she asked Cathy a question, was one of concern. 'Are you really, though? You know that if it gets too much, I'll understand if you need to leave. I don't want you being upset in any way.'

Her hand covered in soap suds, Cathy reached over and wrapped her fingers around Sheena's. 'I promise, I'll be fine and if I get a bit panicky I'll sneak off and wait outside the church and the same at the restaurant. It goes both ways, Sheena, and I don't want to be the one who ruins your big day. So you just focus on looking gorgeous and making that man over there legal, and I'll go puff into a paper bag or something while you say I do. Deal?'

'Deal. Right, I'll fetch the rest of the plates. Won't be a mo.'

Cathy turned back to the sink and carried on washing dishes as she thought of Dave and Sheena's trimmed down wedding. After moving in with Dave's parents, they'd finally managed to save enough for a deposit on a house, one that was being built on a brand-new estate on the far side of the village.

Seeing as Sheena had been waiting for years for a home of her own and for Dave to propose, the only way to achieve both was to keep the nuptials sensible. It was close friends and family only, followed by a meal in the carvery in a fancy pub on the tops.

Sheena, who worked as a home help for the local authority, and Dave, had been scrimping for years and Cathy admired them both more than she could say. No way was she going to be the one who cast a shadow on their big day.

And there was Alfie to consider, too, because he was best man and would want her by his side. Even though they were a couple, he did a lot of things without her, like going to watch the local rugby team and social nights down at the pub, simply because she preferred to stay right there, at Blacksheep.

That's why Cathy was determined to go to the wedding if it was the last thing she did. And now Dave had taken the plunge, she was expecting that Alfie would soon follow his lead and pluck up the courage to ask her. They'd discussed marriage plenty of times and it was something they both wanted, but deep down, Cathy had a very good idea why Alfie hadn't proposed.

All of the reasons made her incredibly sad because regardless, if he asked she'd say yes, immediately. No hesitation. And while Cathy was of the mindset that it didn't have to be a leap year to ask him – she was, after all, a modern woman living in the twenty-first century – Alfie needed to be the one to say the words for his own self-esteem and pride.

It's who and how he was, old-fashioned, principled, loyal and salt of the earth and she loved him for it. And for the fact he wanted to provide for his wife, to be independent, detached from his mother and the hold she had over him emotionally and financially. And from his own lips, that saddest indictment of all, that she'd just ruin the day and cast a cloud on everything.

'When I get married I want it to be perfect and part of our lives. But I know her presence or her refusal to attend will tarnish something special.'

And for those reasons, Cathy would wait because he was right. She wouldn't allow Bertha to spoil their wedding like she'd ruined Eliza's baby-naming ceremony with her tutting during the service and acerbic comments about airy-fairy ideas and offending God, like she was the most devout woman in the village!

Or all those Christmas Days, where she'd left it till the last minute to say she was too poorly to show up. Her pretend, spontaneous illness cast a shadow on the day as everyone wondered if maybe she really was ill, and whether it was wrong to be pulling crackers and reading out jokes while she lay in bed, alone. Everyone bar Annie who refused to let Bertha into her headspace.

And, as if by magic, the woman herself appeared by Cathy's side – Annie, not Bertha.

'Looks like Sheena has been commandeered by Eliza into colouring in so I'm on drying-up duty, seeing as them three's arses are glued to their chairs.' Annie jerked her head at the table, then grabbed the tea towel.

'I see mother misery couldn't be bothered to show her face again. What was the excuse this time? She's lost her broom?' Annie was vigorously making circular motions with the towel and in danger of rubbing the pattern off the plate.

'Bad legs.'

Annie rolled her eyes. 'Ah, that old chestnut.'

Cathy had also heard the leg excuse before and many more ailments besides but knowing Annie was easily riled where Bertha was concerned, attempted to douse the flames.

'And by the way I like the little flowers and gold paint on my plate so chill, just ignore your mam, because in the end we've swerved a bullet and had a nice time. I only invited her to keep the peace. You know how it is.'

'Hmm, exactly. And that's what does my nut in. That she uses every nice event in our lives to mess with our heads. And you know what pisses me off the most?' Annie grabbed another plate, this time treating it with a bit more care.

'What?'

'That it bothers our Alfie, and it's getting to him more than it ever did. I was watching him earlier and he couldn't help looking over to the window, as though he was waiting for her to appear, and I don't know whether it's because he feels sorry for her or wants her to stay away.'

Cathy nodded. 'It's probably a bit of both. It's the same when he goes up there to see if she's okay. He dreads going but feels duty-bound and I hate it, which is why I do my bit too. Otherwise she'd drive him mad.'

The tut from Annie sounded like a stone on glass it was so sharp. 'Bloody woman. She's got a lot to answer for. I can still remember when the cattle wagon came for the flock and if rounding them up wasn't bad enough, watching the sheep being loaded... poor Alfie, it was just awful. I always say to Joe that you coming into his life saved him, 'specially after our Albert buggered off.'

Something in Annie's words raised the hairs on the back of Cathy's neck, and her heart contracted, remembering the melancholy that had swamped Alfie during the worst time of his life.

She had to ask. 'Annie, you don't think it's coming back, do you? Because he *has* been subdued lately, but I put it down to winter blues then spring being on its way. It was his favourite time of the year, the lambing season and when everything came to life. You have to be honest with me, then we can do something about it, before it gets a grip. Blokes are known for keeping stuff like this to themselves, aren't they? Men's mental health awareness is always on the news, and we can't ignore the signs.'

A swell of panic was making its way upwards from the pit of Cathy's stomach. She couldn't let her Alfie fall apart because he was her rock to lean on and make her feel safe. Scrutinising Annie's face for even a hint of a lie, Cathy waited for an answer.

'No, love, I don't.' Annie looked Cathy in the eye. 'So don't start panicking and doing the brown-bag-puffing thing on your birthday. That's an order!' Annie raised her perfectly arched eyebrow, a crinkled hint of humour at the corner of her eyes lightening the mood. 'But I do think that he needs to feel there's some purpose in his day like there used to be. Or maybe have something to look forward to because buying and selling them bloody heaps of rust isn't what he imagined for his life, not since he was old enough to carry a lamb round the yard.'

'Has he told you this? That he feels unfulfilled here?' Cathy bridled and felt judged for not noticing and maybe being part of the problem. Had she put herself first and allowed him to coast, in order to keep her world, her sanctuary intact? Living here at Blacksheep with Alfie by her side or a few metres away in the big barn.

Annie rested her hand on Cathy's arm as she replied, a reassuring gesture that had zero effect. 'No, I swear he hasn't said anything of the sort. It's more of an observation, like there's something going on behind his eyes and that blustering Alfie vitality we know and love seems as though it's waning, as if he's weary.'

They glanced over to see Alfie throwing his head back and laughing at something Joe had said and the tension ebbed slightly.

Annie turned and smiled reassuringly at Cathy. 'See, he's fine. And, as you say, it could just be the back end of the winter blues and let's face it, January and February up here can be bloody bleak. Or he's missing the lambing season and I'm just an annoying big sister who can't let go. I wish I'd kept my gob shut now because I can see from your face I've worried you... Are you okay? Please tell me I've not just rained all over your birthday.'

Cathy, seeing the crestfallen look on Annie's face, forced herself to rally. 'No, of course not but I think we need to keep an eye on him.' And then before Annie could reply, she added, 'And as for raining on my birthday, I think there's a storm on its way.'

For a second Annie scrunched her eyes in confusion, then spotted the dark shadow of a stooped, limping figure moving slowly past the window.

They braced themselves for trouble.

Bertha had arrived.

10

ALFIE

While they waited for her to enter, it was as though someone had sucked all of the joy from the room, like when the tide goes out before a tsunami.

The happy birthday vibe had been replaced with a balloon full of tension, the rubber stretching to the max and whoever spoke first would pop it, should they say the wrong thing. Then they'd all explode, and their body parts would splatter over Cathy's newly painted kitchen wall, and he'd never get to eat the chocolate fudge cake with a double helping of cream and ice cream.

And even as he thought it, and absorbed how ludicrous it was to be gutted about not getting his pudding, Alfie realised he didn't care that his mother had arrived. And even better, this time, he was *not* going to be the one to jump from his seat and jolly things along, or smooth the jagged edges of conversation.

The latch shook and clicked and along with a gust of cool air, Bertha stepped into the room like a portent of doom, and slammed the door shut behind her.

Hearing Skip's low growl, Alfie reached down to stroke his faithful dog who now lay on the floor by his side. Dogs knew, and Skip had never taken to Bertha, and Alfie didn't blame him. Not after hearing her harsh, cautionary tales about how they did things in the old days on her dad's farm. How they treated runts, calves of the wrong sex and anything deemed not useful. As a child it had always made Alfie shudder and hold back tears and even as an adult he didn't like to dwell on the images she'd conjured for their young minds.

This led to a memory he'd buried deep, when his mother had gone mad when Albie brought home a tiny rabbit for Annie. One of his friends was giving them away and he and Alfie scoured the yard for bits of wood and chicken wire to make a hutch as a surprise for their sister.

Obviously Annie had been overjoyed, even their dad tickled Daisy's ears – that's what Annie named it – but the balloon went up when *she* came into the barn and saw what they were up to. 'Rabbits,' she'd said, 'were good for nowt but the pot or a pie and a waste of money.'

It was only when their dad stepped in and said that as long as they bought its food from their pocket money, Daisy could stay.

Whether or not the glint in her eye, just before Bertha stomped off in a huff was real or imagined, to that day, nobody ever really knew what happened to poor Daisy and why she only lasted a few months. It had broken Annie's heart when she found her little rabbit cold and stiff in her cage.

This was why Skip's instinct and wariness around his mother told Alfie all he needed to know.

Back in the present, everyone in the kitchen remained silent and stared at the figure who, after making her point by not bothering to knock or say hello, just stood there.

To Alfie, she looked like the absolute spit of the woman in *Home Alone Two*, the scary bag-lady in Central Park. Apart from lacking a hundred pigeons and a coat of white bird shit,

Bertha was her double. And for some reason, the thought made him laugh, out loud, and once he started he couldn't stop and as his shoulders shook, everyone swivelled their heads and stared at him.

Tramp-lady by the door was momentarily forgotten as Alfie wiped away tears.

'Uncle Alfie, what are you laughing at?' That sensible and obvious question came from wide-eyed Eliza who'd previously been frozen to the spot by the appearance of her nan.

Sod it. Once Alfie managed to compose himself he decided to answer honestly because in truth, he was buggered if he could think of a feasible fib.

'Sorry, Eliza. It was just for a moment there, your nan reminded me of that lady in your favourite Christmas film, you know, *Home Alone Two.* Remember the scruffy one who stands in the park and has birds sitting on her head.' At least he'd managed not to say *shitting* because Annie would have told him off for that.

At this, Eliza's eyes were like golf balls, as were everyone's around the table.

Bertha gave a loud tut and visibly sucked in a deep breath, which meant she was annoyed. They all knew the signs. 'Well I'm glad I've provided amusement, Alfred, but I'm not actually here for your entertainment.' Bertha made a cursory sweep of the kitchen letting her cold grey eyes rest on each member of her silent family. Then, 'I thought someone was going to bring me dinner up, but seein' as you can't be bothered, I came to get it meself.'

Cathy was hovering by the sink, and after giving her the side eye, Bertha fired her next barb, 'An' I hope it's not any of that vegenarian rubbish because I'd rather have toast.'

To this Cathy replied, 'No, it's roast pork and stuffing and I put some crackling on the side for you—'

She was rudely interrupted by Bertha whose gaze had rested on the two sleeping boys who were blissfully unaware that the old hag from up the lane had turned up to give them nightmares.

'What you letting them bairns sleep for in the day? You'll not get 'em off at bedtime. Asking for trouble is that. Too soft on them kids, you are.' Another tut was followed by a steely glare at Annie.

But it was Joe who replied. 'Never you mind, Bertha, they'll be fine. Now, do you fancy a drink? Wine, tea?'

Arsenic. Petrol. A deadly nightshade sandwich while you wait? Alfie wondered if any of the others had had the same thought yet still he sat, refusing to interact or pander to Bertha. Instead he took a swig from his bottle of beer and waited for Annie to steam in because he knew she would. Any second.

Bertha huffed. 'I'll pass. Like I said I didn't come to chat. I came for me dinner.'

And to that, just as Alfie predicted, Annie waded in. 'S'all right, Mam. We'd expect nothing less and Cathy's already done you a plate. I'll fetch it for you then you can get off. Can you manage to hobble back with it on them bad legs, or shall I get our Joe to carry it? Don't want you falling over and breaking a bone, or your neck or anything, do we?'

Alfie didn't try to stifle a laugh, and even though he knew Annie shouldn't really say stuff like that in front of Eliza, he was glad for his hot-headed sister because today, he really couldn't be bothered with their mother.

It might have been the alcohol making him belligerent, or the fact he was bone weary from fitting fences all week, and really pissed off that Cathy's birthday meal had been cast into shadow. But right there and then he just wanted his mother to sod off home.

Sheena poured herself another glass of wine and glugged it

down in one shot while Dave excused himself to go to the loo as the others watched on. Annie, giving Bertha a hard stare as she passed by, then holding up her palm to Cathy who appeared to have been struck mute, marched over to the range from where she grabbed the plate covered in tinfoil. Turning she thrust forward Bertha's dinner.

Bertha raised an eyebrow and stared at the plate. 'No pudding, then?'

Annie's eyes widened and before she could reply Cathy found her voice and stepped in as Alfie and the others watched the show. 'Yes, I've made chocolate cake or apple crumble and custard. Which do you prefer? Or you can have some of both, it's no bother.' Cathy was already rushing around finding a bowl and a knife, and something about it riled Alfie, seeing how Bertha had rattled her.

'I shan't bother. Not fond of either so I'll just take me dinner.' Bertha snatched the plate from Annie and turned to leave, resting on her stick with one hand, food in the other then, 'Can one of you get off yer backsides and open this door, or do I have to stand here all day?'

The swell of anger inside Alfie rose as his cheeks flamed and weirdly, his ears went red hot. It was like they were huge and burning and inside he was going to pop or steam really would spurt from his head like it did on cartoons. There was no way he could hold in his temper. He had to do something so simply said, 'Thank you.' He heard his words, loud and clear, and then again, sharper in tone. 'MAM. Say "thank you". To Cathy, for your dinner. And while you're at it, a "happy birthday" would be nice.'

All eyes were on him for a second and then they turned to Bertha. It was like a tennis match, and everyone was waiting to see if bird-woman would bat the ball back to Alfie.

Silence. Just for a second. Then from Bertha a tut. And

next, Annie piped up. 'Why do you do this? You knew it was Cathy's birthday and she invited you, so why couldn't you be normal for once and come and sit with your family and be pleasant. Say hello to your grandkids and pretend that you're a decent human being but oh no... you have to cause a scene and make it all about you, don't you. You know exactly what you're doing, turning up late, ruining the atmosphere. For what? Go on. Tell us why. Amaze us.'

Although Annie's words were strong and true and spoken to her mother's back, everyone in the room could hear the tremor of frustration in her voice. Whether through anger or desperation, and in spite of her being Bertha's staunchest critic, Alfie suspected that his sister still craved a breakthrough, some softening or hope that their mother might change or show them she had a heart. Because he did believe, even though deep down it was a fool's errand to hope she'd change.

Bertha turned slowly and showing not a trace of emotion looked Annie straight in the eye and then said, '*Me*, make a scene! Well, madam, I think the only person around here whose done that today, is *you*. You should be ashamed of yerself, bawling in front of your bairns and what kind of example are you setting, eh? Talking to an old woman in that way. People like you shouldn't be allowed to have kids.'

There was a gasp from Sheena as Bertha turned her focus on Alfie, her face hard and uncaring as she delivered the killer blow. 'And neither should you be allowed to spawn young'uns, not going by how you've just behaved, sitting there chucking beer down your throat and speaking to me like that. But then again, ain't likely to 'appen, is it? Not now you've picked the barren mare.' She jerked her head at Cathy. 'So praise be to the lord because the world is spared having to put up with another waste o'space like you.'

The gasp from Annie, and the choke of a sob from Cathy

ricocheted around the room and before Alfie could tell her to get out, Bertha had slammed the plate down on the draining board and was yanking open the kitchen door. 'And you can stick your dinner. I'd rather 'ave toast.'

Then she was gone. Leaving the kitchen in turmoil as Joe blocked the doorway to prevent banshee-Annie from chasing Bertha, and while Alfie tried to console a sobbing Cathy, the boys awoke to pandemonium and, picking up the vibes, both burst into tears.

In the absence of Dave who was hiding in the loo, Sheena flew over to the sofa to comfort them.

Eliza, unperturbed by the ruckus simply rolled her eyes and carried on with the drawing in her sketchpad. Of an old woman in a tatty overcoat and wellingtons. With frizzy grey hair and huge devil horns, a giant, pooing bird flying over her head, and just above, carefully written in bold red pen, were the words, *My Very Nasty Nan.*

11

From the kitchen window, Alfie watched Cathy who was in her usual spot at the table, the five paintings he'd found hidden in the van spread out as she took photos for her scrapbook. She was keeping busy, as was he. Re-focusing and getting on with it.

In the forty-eight hours since their family get-together crashed and burned, nothing had been said about Bertha, or her cruel words. They weren't exactly being false. It was more a case of being jolly and avoiding the issue because, after all, there was bugger all they could do about it.

Alfie was determined not to go up to Shepherd's to check if his mother was okay. He was still too angry to contemplate speaking to her; and it would feel like a betrayal of Cathy, even though she was the first to tell him to go and make the peace. Not this time. Not for a while.

He was seething about it all. After his mam left, he'd offered to ring their friends and cancel the birthday drinks scheduled for the evening. But Cathy had insisted they came: she didn't want to let people down or waste the party snacks she'd prepared.

Her heart hadn't been in it, though, and his went out to her.

Knowing how hard she found being around large groups of people, made it even harder to forget the hurt his mother's words had caused. He'd been glad of one thing though: that Julie and Mark, Cathy's parents, hadn't been there to witness the scene, because on top of everything else he'd have been shamed to death of his mother.

And then there was Annie. Who after consoling Ezra and Eli, had smothered her own anger and refocused her attention on Cathy, making sure her birthday ended on a happy note. The utter opposite of their mother, his big sister embodied being a mother and a wife and de-facto head of the family, throwing herself into the role like her own life depended on it.

It had been a knife to the heart because despite what Annie said, not caring about or needing Bertha, he'd heard something in her voice that afternoon. It was more than sadness, disappointment and anger. It was a very simple question.

Mam, why are you like this?

Recognising a maudlin mood creeping up on him, something that was happening with more frequency lately, Alfie shook it off and let himself into the kitchen determined to leave the black dog at the doorstep.

Cathy, looking up, paused her snapping and gave him a smile worth coming home to. 'There you are. We were wondering where you'd got to, weren't we, Skip?' The collie raised an eye, wagged his tail then curled up and went back to sleep.

'Sorry, love. Got engrossed in a job and wanted to get it finished today. Have you thought about what you're going to do with those?' Alfie nodded towards the paintings that, thanks to whoever had carefully preserved them in tissue paper and polythene to protect them from damp, were in remarkably good condition.

Cathy stepped back and folded her arms as she stared at the

paintings and considered his question. 'I'm not sure. It seems a shame that they're stuck in that tube. Maybe I could get them framed and hang them in the hall. What do you think?'

Alfie's heart sank. Even with his limited knowledge of art, gleaned mostly from the telly, his own eyes told him that the artist was talented. But there was something disconcerting about those watercolours. When he looked closely at the faces of the women, their eyes stared right at you, and bored into you, and they gave Alfie the creeps.

Then he had an inspired idea borne of panic and the thought of five creepy women watching him from the wall as he went past. 'What if you tried to track down the owner? I bet he's gutted his paintings got towed away when his van went for auction.'

At this Cathy's eyes widened. 'Do you think I could? Alfie, you big clever clogs. I love that idea! But how would I go about it? And maybe the last owner of the van didn't know they were there, and they belonged to the previous one.'

Alfie shook his head. 'No, that's not possible. Remember, there's only ever been one owner of that van from new, which is what makes it more valuable. I remember seeing the details on the logbook but didn't think much about it. I was too concerned with getting it bought, paid for and back here to surprise you. Where did you put that envelope that I left in the dash? With the receipt and all the paperwork.'

Cathy scooted over to the Welsh dresser and pulled open the top drawer from where she extracted the manila envelope. 'Here it is. Let's look. Ooh this is exciting.' Cathy pulled out a chair and tipped the contents of the envelope onto the table.

Alfie, not only feeling buoyed by his skilful swerving of the creepy paintings on the wall dilemma, was also glad of the diversion from the cloud that Bertha had left hovering over the farmhouse.

He quickly located the section of the logbook given to him at the auction house. 'Right, let's have a gander. From what I know, the van was taken by bailiffs and sent to the auction so, if I'm not mistaken, and unless the owner moved house and didn't change the details of where it was stored, the address is on here.' Alfie scanned the logbook. 'Ah, there it is. This is more than likely where you'll find the original and only owner of Maggie.'

Cathy leaned in; her eyes scrunched in concentration as she read. 'Orchard House, Cross End Road, Wetherby, Yorkshire. And the owner's name is Guy Alexander. Oh my goodness look, Alfie. Here, it's the same as on the paintings.' Cathy pulled one of the pictures over to where they sat and pointed to the signature in the right-hand corner.

She looked up at Alfie, her face a picture of delight. 'So that means that the owner of the van is very likely the person who painted these, and he lives or lived, not a million miles from here.' Then her shoulders sagged as did her expression. 'But there's no contact phone number on the logbook so apart from writing him a letter, how can I find him?'

Alfie was firing on all cylinders and full of bright ideas. 'The internet. Start with searching the address and artists by that name and then if that doesn't throw anything up, try social media. I have every faith that you'll track him down, love, and then hopefully you can return his paintings. Job done. Now, what's for tea? I'm bloody starving.'

Alfie pushed back the chair and made for the range so he could put the kettle on and check if there was anything in the oven. He found it cold and empty, though, which prompted Cathy's next suggestion.

'I fancy a chippy for tea. It'll be a nice treat and you can get your mum a fish. Take it up as a peace offering.'

Alfie bridled, and he couldn't decide whether he was more annoyed with Cathy for being a pushover and wanting to make the peace already, or with his mother for... well, just being a nasty, poisonous woman.

It was unlike him to snap at Cathy and the second the words began spilling from his mouth he wished he could recall them. 'Why would I want to make peace? After what she said to you the other night, I don't think I ever want to speak to her again so stop trying to force me and if you want to play best friends, you go to the chippy and you buy her a bloody fish because I'm not!'

Cathy took a breath, and then got up from the table and came to where he stood, wrapping her arms around his waist and pulling him close. There was no escaping her willowy embrace. Regardless of her slight frame, she had him trapped in a vice-like hold, squishing his pie-belly. 'Because, my gorgeous but very grumpy man who I love most dearly, you know my outlook on life. And that is?' Cathy stood on her tiptoes, gave him a soft kiss on the lips and waited for his answer.

'That we never know when it's our last day on earth which is why we won't ever go to bed on a row, *and,* say I love you every day and before we go to sleep.'

Cathy raised one eyebrow as she waited for the rest.

He continued, '...And that my mother might be the most weird person any of us have ever met in our entire lives but life's too short for regrets and...' – he sucked in a deep breath – 'I need to be the bigger person because one day she will be gone.'

Cathy rewarded him for remembering her mantra with a gentle tug of his beard and a smile. 'Well done, my love. So, I'll have fish, chips and a carton of curry sauce to build up my strength for yoga later. And get whatever you're having, plus a fish for your mam. I'll put the plates on to warm and set the table.' And after another more lingering kiss, she released Alfie and got on with bustling about the kitchen.

Later, from the wooden bench underneath the window, Alfie watched as Cathy sped out of the yard in the Defender and off down the hill to her yoga class. He felt a swell of pride because she was being brave, pushing her boundaries. But still, in amongst all that, the sign-writing on the cab still stung him.

Encircling a logo, the side-on silhouette of a sheep, were the words *Blacksheep Farm*. A name that had been synonymous with the family business for almost 200 years.

That lone sheep reminded Alfie of the ones he'd lambed, or bottle-fed as orphans in front of the kitchen fire, watched over into maturity as they roamed the fells, and had saved from lonely deaths in cruel winters. And it reminded him of the sheep his mother had sold, trotting nervously up the ramp onto the cattle truck, leaving their home, and him, behind.

It made Alfie feel so sad. Like a weight pressing down on his shoulders that crushed every bone in his body, diminishing him, squishing his heart and lungs, making him feel small, breathless and tired, and much older than his thirty-five years.

What the hell was wrong with him?

Alfie had never felt like this his entire life, not even when Father Christmas hadn't brought him Marine Action Man despite it being right at the top of his list, written in capitals and underlined in highlighter pen. He'd given it to his mother to post and for years he chose to believe his letter got lost. It was easier than giving credence to that voice in his head. The one that said she'd thrown his letter away. He knew better now and understood why he'd not got Marine Action Man. Mind games.

To quell the panic that was taking hold of his body, Alfie tried to talk it through with himself.

Did he feel this bad when his dad died?

I miss you, Dad.

Or when Albert buggered off?

I miss you too and I don't blame you for going, not anymore.

Alfie didn't think so.

And there was something pecking his brain, reminding him of the things he'd seen on telly and online about men's mental health and he wondered if perhaps... no, it couldn't be that.

He was a Walker. All six foot four and seventeen stone of him. He told Cathy he was fifteen and a half stone, so she wouldn't put him on a diet.

He drank real ale, could eat two pies more than Fat Pat before she got thin. He had four Weetabix for breakfast and toast! He had biceps and a manly beard. He had scarred, calloused hands that'd delivered lambs, chopped wood, fixed oily engines, dug ditches and hammered fence posts into the earth and he'd even had a punch-up with the captain of the rugby team and won. Men like him didn't get depression, for God's sake.

Walker men were strong and weathered storms and drought, and whatever Mother Nature threw at them. He knew all about death and the circle of life and accepted it was the way things were, no matter how cruel and unfair and sometimes sodding futile. So why did he want to put his head in his hands and weep? Right there and then on the wooden bench outside the back door.

And there it was. That elastic band that made his chest go tight like the strings on a banjo. He was struggling to breathe, and he was hot despite the chill of the evening air. Then something nudged his leg and when he looked down, Skip was there, laying his snout on Alfie's knee. Big black eyes bored into his and said, *It's okay, I'm still here. I get it.*

Sliding off the bench and onto the cobbles, Alfie reached for his faithful dog and pulled him close, pushing his face into the soft fur that felt so familiar, smelt of woodsmoke and oil and dog. And love and trust.

It was as Alfie breathed in the scent of Skip and held tight to his warmth, knowing he and his beloved friend didn't require words, that his panic eased, and the strings of the banjo loosened in his chest.

With the arrival of calm came clarity and Alfie realised one very simple thing. That he needed help.

12
GUY

Orchard Cottage, York

I still can't believe what that stupid woman did. That she actually gave them the keys to my beloved van, my Luna, and now all I'm left with is the crate I'm sitting on, and an empty garage. They even took my record player and vinyls, and the radio and my bloody tools. Not that I'll need them now Luna is gone. Vultures.

Apparently my loss is nothing compared to hers and I'm entirely to blame for the situation we're in. Well yes, I suppose that's very true, but I don't care. About her, or anything she says, or the cottage that's been my prison for more years than I can bear to contemplate and, more than likely, will be the next thing to go.

Just like I don't care that they took all her bloody stupid china cats and her mother's jewellery. In fact, I'm glad.

It's all phoney. Our marriage. The homey cottage that she abhors since we had to downsize from the big house. Smoke and mirrors. That's what it is. To give the neighbours and her friends the impression all is well on her film set of life, as if she's popped out of a page from one of her country magazines that says, *Home is where the heart is. Yes, we decided to downsize. It was the sensible option, being just the two of us. We're very happy there, a contented couple in our twilight years living the best life with roses round the door.*

We are *not*. Apart from the roses that is.

It was a means to an end. Marriage for a start. Surely she's realised that by now. And downsizing didn't bother me half as much as it did her. It's just somewhere to rest my head in the spare room. A place to return to from my travels. But now, thanks to her, my travelling days are over.

My precious Luna. My home on wheels. My sanctuary and the one place that allowed me to grip on to sanity, has gone. But worse, so much worse than that, is the loss of my paintings because they were the link to something precious – my youth and my beautiful ladies who I loved. Profoundly. And that love will endure to my dying day.

Those paintings, those faces, those smiles, were only for me. And what I cannot bear is the thought that someone else will look upon them. It will taint their memory, sully what we had.

The men that came here have stolen what for me, was pure and perfect. They're akin to thugs who invade churchyards, kicking over headstones and dancing on the graves of the dead. Desecrating something holy. That is what *she* allowed to happen, and I will never forgive her.

According to her, the letter from the court, telling me time was up, was on the pile in the hall, waiting for me to open. It wasn't *her* fault I'd been lying in hospital for weeks. She's never opened my mail in all the years we've trudged along together. *So why start now?*

Apparently, she tried to call me the day the thugs arrived. *Really?* And she had no option but to let the warrant-wielding bailiffs in. I'm not stupid, though, because she must have pointed them in the direction of the garage. You can't see it from the cottage, hidden behind a bank of trees on the edge of our wood.

She did it out of spite. Her china cats for my van. I can just imagine her self-satisfied smile as they took my beloved Luna away and I can imagine her parting shot of, *Serves you right, you philandering, gambling, alcoholic, waste of space.*

Yes, I am all of those things but how dare she try to shift the blame onto me! I was under anaesthetic, for pity's sake! Sleeping the sleep of the almost dead as the surgeon fiddled with my heart that, he'd jollily assured me pre-op, would soon be in tip-top condition, extending my life by many years.

Well, I wish he'd ended it right there and then on that gurney. That would have served *her* right! I bet she was hoping I'd peg it. Probably said a few Hail Marys to be on the safe side. Waiting by the phone, fingers tapping, gagging for bad news so she could claim the insurance money. Well dearest one, have I got news for you!

Oh the irony. What joy my imaginings bring me, picturing the scene... 'I'm dreadfully sorry, Mrs Alexander. We did everything we could but he's a goner. Oh and by the way, some more bad news. Before he went under we had a bit of banter. You know, patient–surgeon humour, and he told me not to bloody well mess up because he'd cancelled his life insurance in 2009. Wink, wink. Sorry about that, old girl.'

That little nugget will no doubt come out in the wash when the time is right but at least I'll be spared the wrath of my dear wife, and instead, face the wrath of the big man upstairs. Actually, I doubt very much I'll be heading *tout de suite* to the pearly gates, so the thought of me burning in the fires of hell will soften the blow for my dearest wife.

The worst thing is, apart from not pegging it and being

almost bankrupt and enduring an arranged marriage to a harridan, is that in the dust of the garage floor, I can see the tyre tracks left behind when they drove Luna away. As though my beloved trailed her hand along the earthen floor as she departed, nails digging into the ground, beseeching eyes locked on the fading image of home, delicate fingers tracing a path of despair as she was extricated from her sacred resting place.

I can't bear to step on the tracks. They're all that's left of my monument to love. The best part of me and my life. It was my haven and the guardian of my ladies and now, it has been sullied.

You know, I used to sit here for hours whiling away the time and avoiding *her* indoors. It was my man-shed on wheels. Most days I'd bring my packed lunch and just sit in splendid isolation. Reading or listening to music while the kettle whistled away. In the summer months I often started Luna up and moved her outside so we could camp out, just beyond the doors under a canopy of trees and stars.

I kept her in tip-top condition, too. Bought a Haynes manual and taught myself how to make repairs, which came in handy when I was on my travels. She often broke down, but I learned how to care for her, keep her alive. I've not actually been out and about in her for many years, though. Not to festivals like I used to because... well, because they make me feel things I don't want to anymore. I'm too old for all that now.

Listen to me, talking like my little Luna is real, was real. But to me, she was. We were amigos, we were pals. Just the two of us out on the open road ever since I was twenty-one. That's when I bought her, with a little nest egg left to me by my grandmother for when I came of age.

Whenever I could escape it'd be the two of us and my paints and easel. That was all I'd needed. Until that first time, when I met Krystle, and it all began. With her and that first portrait.

I dare myself to wonder where Luna is. Where all my paintings are. What if someone finds them and discards them or burns them not knowing their worth. Not in monetary value, I mean, what they symbolise. The happiest times of my life, being the true me, taking control, the adrenalin rush, the greatest thrill, knowing pure love and harnessing it forever.

Perhaps I should be optimistic. Perhaps whoever has Luna won't care about the faded interior and leave her as she is and then, my ladies will stay hidden forever.

And so will my secrets.

13

CATHY

Skip's ears pricked up a few seconds before Cathy herself heard Alfie shouting down the stairs to announce the arrival of visitors.

Their sleepy sheepdog, whilst enjoying his retirement still took his role of guard dog seriously and even though his eyesight was poor, his sense of hearing was still as sharp as ever. He'd decide whether to bark or not when he knew if the caller was friend or foe and again, some deep-rooted instinct, probably scent, would kick in soon enough.

Alfie bellowed from the bathroom, 'Cathy, did you hear me? Your mam and dad are here. They're just coming up the lane.'

'Yes, thanks, love, I reckon the whole valley heard you.' Cathy smiled as his footsteps clumped across their bedroom floor, and then made their descent of the stairs.

Cathy was already waiting by the door as her parents' car crunched across the yard, pulling to a stop by the Defender.

Her dad was making hand signals that told her he was taking a call and would be two minutes so after giving him the thumbs-up, she turned her attention to the other half of the double act. Cathy chuckled as she watched her mum tell her dad off, then climb out of the car before straightening the crinkles in her smart work skirt. She was the epitome of what Cathy imagined a bank manager to look like. As far back as she could remember, even when her mum was still a cashier, she was perfectly presented as she went through the door and out to work.

In contrast, Cathy stood before her mother wearing an old pair of ripped jeans, a full-length crocheted cardy made by her own fair hands, a pair of Alfie's holey socks under her lime green Crocs, and a smile. She should've changed because her attire would send alarms bells ringing and result in twenty questions, but she'd been caught on the hop.

Bugger.

'Hiya... you're early. I thought you'd get stuck in traffic at this time of night.' Cathy had reached the car and was immediately swallowed whole by a bear-hug.

'Hello, chicken. So did I but it was plain sailing straight from town. Probably because it's the Easter holidays and everyone's off somewhere. Now, let me look at you. That's a nice cardy... different but nice and colourful. Have you lost more weight? You feel a bit bony.'

After giving Cathy, who was stuck for words, the once over, Julie bustled around to the boot and pulled it open. 'Your dad's talking to your brother... something to do with how to fix a leaky tap. He's had to take the day off work to sort it and he can't fathom the YouTube tutorials... Knowing our Stevie it could take a while. He's not the handiest of lads, is he? I told him to ring the plumber save everyone the grief of a flooded kitchen.'

'Well at least he's having a go but you're right: him and DIY don't come naturally, do they.' Cathy's brother was useless in a practical sense, end of.

'Exactly! But oh no. Stevie is adamant he can change a tap so I said don't come crying to us when you have to claim on your insurance and the premium goes up. But what do I know? Anyway, come and give me a hand with these bags and then we can get inside and have a cuppa. And where's that lovely lad of yours? Don't tell me he's out.' Julie looked crestfallen.

'No, Mum, he's inside getting changed.'

Skip's barking and wagging tail heralded the arrival of Julie's clear favourite. 'Oh, talk of the devil, here he is.'

Cathy was exhausted already by her mum who never stopped talking, walking, working, gardening or otherwise, so indicated towards the door, knowing that as soon as her mum spotted Alfie, she'd be surplus to requirements.

With arms outstretched and a big sigh followed by, 'There he is,' Julie made her way towards Alfie who she tried to bear-hug, and instead was lifted off her feet and spun around a few times until he was told to, 'Stop, you daft bugger, you're making me dizzy.'

Alfie gently placed the diminutive Julie back on terra firma, 'Hello, love. Nice to see you and look, our Skip's all of a do-da now he's heard your voice. See, he's waiting by the door. You get yourself inside and I'll bring your bags. Go on, I'll hang on for Mark.'

Cathy took her mum's arm and led her over to Skip who really was all of a do-da and more waggy than she'd seen him in a while, but it was as she followed Julie inside, the sensation of being watched made her look up the lane, towards Shepherd's Cottage.

She may have been imagining it, yet she was sure she wasn't, but in that split second, the sight of a figure darting behind the oak tree brought Cathy out in goosebumps. It also made her feel rather sad.

The kitchen table held a mountain of wrapping paper, a caterpillar birthday cake, a pot of tea and two bottles of pink Prosecco. The countertops were laden with what Cathy presumed was half the supermarket, thanks to her mum's insatiable appetite for shopping and stocking up other people's cupboards with enough groceries to feed the village.

'Thanks for this, Mum. You didn't have to, you know. We're managing just fine but I do appreciate the gesture, and my lovely cake. I knew you wouldn't forget.'

There was no point in being proud and it was easier to let her mum do what made her happy. And if that meant Alfie got his favourite biscuits and treats and Cathy got her regulation Colin the Caterpillar cake, all was well in the world.

'Oh, it's nothing, love, and I know how much things have gone up and the cost of living is having an effect on everyone. Anyway, this lad here needs his carbs, don't you, Alfie?' Julie patted Alfie's arm not giving him a chance to answer as she continued, 'And we're sorry we couldn't make it to your birthday meal, but you know what I'm like when I get one of my migraines... no good to anyone, am I, Mark? Mark, are you listening?'

Mark opened his mouth to answer but was too slow.

'Let's give her our pressie. Go on.' Julie nodded to her husband who swivelled round to delve in the inside pocket of his jacket that was hung on the back of the chair. He passed an envelope over to Cathy.

'What's this?' Cathy flipped the sealed envelope, noting that it wasn't a card.

Getting in before Julie took over, Mark replied, 'It's a surprise from me and your mum. Our Stevie got exactly the same on his thirtieth, but we made him promise not to say anything so it wouldn't spoil the surprise for you. Go on, open it. Been waiting for a long time to give you this, haven't we, love?'

Julie was nodding vigorously and looked like she was fit to burst. After a quick glance at Alfie, who gave her a wink, Cathy sliced open the seal.

Inside was a cheque and typed on the front was her name and in the small box to the right, the sum made her gasp and cover her mouth with her hand. It took a moment or two to sink in, and then Cathy looked up and from one parent to another. 'Mum, Dad... where on earth did you get all this... I don't understand... it's too much.'

Spotting Alfie's bemused look she passed it over the table and watched his eyes widen, just as Julie answered the question. 'We took out some bonds with the bank when you and Stevie were born. They matured on your thirtieth birthdays, which is why he's already had his. Me and Dad wanted you to have something special, didn't we, love?'

Her dad nodded and Cathy thought he was going to say something but then he stopped as if he'd thought better of it. She took the opportunity to lean over and give him a hug. 'Thank you, Dad, and Mum. This means the world to me, and I promise I'll use it wisely. I'm just a bit overwhelmed to be honest... I really didn't expect that at all.'

Julie, quiet for far too long, piped up, 'Well I should think not, because otherwise I'd have known our Stevie blabbed and spoilt the surprise, and then he'd have been in big trouble, but he's a good lad and I knew he wouldn't. Right, now let's cut this cake and have some fizz. I bought the posh stuff, and we need to toast the birthday girl. Mark, do the honours, love.'

Her beleaguered dad sighed and did as he was told, while her mum chattered on about recycling wrapping paper, folding it into squares and tidying the table as Alfie fetched the glasses. And amidst the hubbub, from his bed by the hearth Skip gave a low growl as his rheumy eyes focused on the window.

Instinctively, Cathy snapped her head in the same direction

and although it was gone in a flash, the unmistakable face of Bertha, staring through the window caused her skin to ripple with goosebumps.

Leaping from her chair, Cathy shot to the door and was in the yard in seconds, calling out to the receding image, 'Bertha, why don't you come in and say hello to Mum and Dad? We can have a drink together...'

There was no reply, just the sound of wellington boots crushing gravel and the sight of her stooped back. Before Cathy could make another attempt Alfie was by her side, taking her hand. 'Come inside, love, you're wasting your time. She's just messing with your head, and I don't want her here today, not after she spoilt your last party. Leave her be.'

'I just felt bad, that she was on the outside looking in and I wanted her to know she doesn't have to be.'

She heard Alfie's sigh, felt it almost because it came from deep inside. 'It's where she likes it, love. She does it on purpose and won't ever change. We all know that. Come on. Your mum wants you to cut the cake, and so does Skip.'

And Cathy knew that Alfie was right, so nodded and smiled and did as he asked. But no matter how hard she tried to wipe out the memory of Bertha's face at the window it was impossible to ignore, just like the question nagging inside her head. *Why is she like this?*

14

Alfie had taken Cathy's dad for a stroll around the farm which left her alone in the kitchen with her mum and Skip. If ever Julie was building up to one of her heart-to-hearts, the moment was nigh, and Cathy prepared herself for the inevitable. She even had a good idea what the topic of conversation would be.

They were settled in opposite armchairs by the kitchen fireplace, logs and the last of the winter coal crackling in the grate, which added much-needed warmth to a cooling spring evening.

Skip rested his snout on the bridge of her mum's stockinged feet while Cathy sipped her tea and considered heading her off at the pass but really, there was no point. Spotting the shift of position, the plump of the cushion and a pre-emptive sip of Prosecco, Cathy braced for impact.

And we're off.

'So, love, how's things here, with barmy Bertha for a start? Alfie looked furious when you went outside to speak to her earlier. What's going on there? He always seems so patient where his mum's concerned.'

Cathy cringed and decided to water down the truth for

Alfie's sake more than anything. 'Oh, that. She turned up on Sunday at my birthday meal and was her usual caustic self. Alfie took the huff and he's struggling to make peace with her this time. He's just keeping it civil and doing the bare minimum at the moment.'

'What did she say?' Julie loved a bit gossip.

'Oh, nothing much. It was more her and Annie sniping at each other. Thing is, I doubt those two will ever get on, but I don't want Alfie having regrets and I *really* believe he should make the most of the time he has with Bertha, no matter how bloody annoying she is. Which is why I try my hardest to forgive her and show him the way if I can, that's all.'

'Hmm.' Julie fell into deep thought for about ten seconds which was something of a record, before she asked, 'Is he okay, Alfie? He looks tired, a bit sunken round the eyes which is surprising seeing as he's well-padded everywhere else.'

'Mum!' Cathy laughed. 'I hope you're not insinuating my Alfie is chubby.'

'No of course not.' Julie smiled and wafted away Cathy's question with a flap of her hand. 'He's big boned with plenty of meat covering them, that's all. And muscly too, might I add, but he just has a faraway look in his eyes now and then. What can you expect though? Having a barmy mother isn't helping on top of everything else, you know, with looking after you.'

Now we're getting to it. 'Mum, may I remind you that I'm not an invalid and I don't need looking after, thank you very much! Bertha does need care now and then because she struggles walking and is semi-housebound.' Cathy was going to add, *when she wants to be,* but thought better of it as it would only add fuel to her mum's fire. 'She's just becoming more and more belligerent and tries his patience and yes, he does have things on his mind about the future and the farm. But we're working through it, together, so try not to worry.'

Julie didn't miss a beat. 'Oh but I do worry, love, especially with bloody interest rates and inflation... don't forget that I see the figures and forecasts at the bank and it's not pleasant reading which is why I'm glad you kept the apartment. It's a solid investment for the future and you really must hang on to it. Then you'll have a nice little pot for your retirement, seeing as your pension has been frozen.'

Cathy sighed, not missing the huge hint her mother had dropped. They'd had this chat many times before. Always very tentative and designed not to stress her out or apply pressure but her mum's motive was clear.

'Mum, just for the record and so we can move on to another of your favourite topics, I promise I won't be tempted to sell the flat and spend the profit on a boob job, or whatever it is you think I might do with it, okay? I bow to your greater wisdom in these matters and, as for the cheque, that's going into my savings account for emergencies only. I promise.'

It was Julie's turn to do the dramatic sigh, but instead of another gentle lecture, she surprised Cathy with her next words. 'But that's not what it's for, love. Me and Dad, we want you do something with that money now. Anything you fancy that will make you happy, anything at all and not that you need fake boobs, but if it puts a smile on your face, and maybe Alfie's too–'

'MUM!'

Julie raised her hands and grinned. 'Okay, too far. But I'm echoing your words from earlier. You know, the advice you're so fond of giving Alfie about not having regrets, making the most of the time you have, to plan, dream, live in the now if you want. You have my blessing, and Dad's, to do something to make your wishes come true.'

Those last few words were laced with things unsaid, too painful to say out loud so they hung in the air like pollen waiting to make your eyes sting and tears flow, and they lapsed into their own thoughts. It was unusual for her mum to remain quiet for so long, which meant Cathy felt the urge to fill the gap and mop up the silence that was as unbearable as the truth of the matter.

'I didn't expect you to say that, you know. About the cheque. I thought you'd want me to squirrel the money away or use it to re-invent myself, so I'd be the me I used to be because I know you want her back. The other Cathy. Not the basket-case who's scared of her own shadow and the outside world. You miss the go-getter with a bright sparkly career and a plan and...' She could feel the tears pricking the corner of her eyes and her throat was getting tighter, preventing her from saying the words that would hurt her as much as they'd hurt her mum.

'Cathy, love, don't upset yourself. I didn't mean for you to... I'm sorry, it came out wrong.'

'No, it's okay. I get it.' The words escaped as a croak and things needed to be said, to clear the air otherwise her mum would fret and not rest until they'd sorted it out.

'I know you want me and Alfie to be okay and yes, we do struggle with lots of stuff right now, financially and emotionally. Especially the baby thing, because each month brings another disappointment and having to face the fact that there's something not working with one of us, maybe both of us. When I add it all up, I feel like such a failure. Giving up my job and the life I'd worked so hard for. And it makes me angry because I don't want to be like this, because it impacts on you and Dad and our Stevie, too.'

Cathy rubbed at a dried blob of Colin the Caterpillar that had landed on her T-shirt, while she grappled for words that would comfort her mum. 'But I need you to know that I'm still that little girl who wants to make her mum and dad proud. Get a prize in school assembly, ace her GCSEs, be top of the studio bonus board, employee of the year and all that malarkey.' She flicked away a lone tear then tried to reassure her mum and maybe deep down, herself.

'And I promise, I am working at it. Getting my head right and waiting patiently for the hospital to say it's our turn, so they can try to fix the faulty bits in my body so we might have a baby. Honestly, just the one will do.'

Cathy swallowed down a sob and as she looked up, saw her mum doing the same. 'So that money is a breath of fresh air and a ray of hope, and I promise you once I've mulled it over I *will* use it in the spirit it was given, okay?'

Julie nodded, and as if he sensed something was up, Skip stood slowly and put his head on her knee, gentle eyes staring through the mist into hers.

'It's okay, boy, don't worry. Just me and my girl getting a bit weepy on her birthday.' Julie bent and kissed him on the head which did the trick, and after a cautionary glance at Cathy, he lay down at Julie's feet and went back to sleep.

And then they sat a while, watching the orange flames flicker amongst the logs and Cathy was glad that the air had been somewhat cleared but there was one more topic, another mountain to get over so before her mum mentioned it, Cathy did. 'I'll be okay, you know, on the anniversary.' She said it with as much conviction as she could muster but the look on her mum's face told Cathy she wasn't convinced.

'Are you sure? It'll be seven years since... well, you know, and please don't take this all wrong because I understand you have to do what's best, but I just worry that hiding away up here isn't the answer, love. So perhaps you could use some of that money to see someone, a therapist or a counsellor, whatever they call them.' Julie took a nervous sip of her drink and waited.

It was impossible not to bridle at her mum's words because she didn't understand at all. Cathy had tried therapy and hated it, every single second. Her mum was wrong. Being there, at

Blacksheep was the answer and had been, ever since Alfie went to rescue her on that New Year's Eve in 2017.

While fireworks, that to Cathy sounded like bombs going off around her head, had exploded into the night sky, they'd left the city and its revellers behind. As they got closer to Blacksheep, with every mile they travelled, the silence of the peak-top farm, its isolation and solitude soothed her.

As the days, weeks and then months went on, the attraction they'd felt for each other when they'd first met, being on the verge of saying the L-word had quickly blossomed into exactly that. An accident waiting to happen but this time, it wasn't a seismic catastrophe or an act of terrorism. It was simply two people ready to fall in love at the right time in the right place, when they needed someone the most.

Cathy had no desire to go back to her old life and Alfie had no desire to let her go, either. It was as though out of a terrible thing, something good had found a way to thrive. A new start borne from the seeds of hate that an evil mind had scattered around the arena.

Finally Cathy addressed her mother, her voice calm but firm. 'You say you understand but you can't, because it's so many things all rolled into one and they add up to why I want to be here. Hiding away as you put it. But if that's what it takes to get through each day, what's the problem?' She waited for her mum to answer but unusually Julie was silent which, as always, made Cathy angry, determined to fill the awkward void and ram her truth home.

'You see, to me, it's all about variables. Fate, bad luck, timing. Wrong place wrong time, right place right time. Picking the lucky ticket out of a hat or getting the booby prize.' She sucked in her temper, and enough air to continue.

'That night, while Mel nipped to the loo, the rest of us lingered, letting those in a hurry make for the exit and taxis and lifts. Because I lived in the city, and it was a short walk home, everyone was crashing at mine, so it was *me* that suggested we let the people around us go first. Variables. That one decision saved our lives. If we'd gone out minutes earlier, then I probably wouldn't be here telling you this.'

Her mum leant forward and placed the glass on the slate floor, then, hands clasped, said, 'Love, I know all this, you've told me before–'

'Yes I have but you're clearly not getting it because hate, evil, a sick and twisted bad person did that. Following the orders of other evil people who helped him to kill and maim all those poor innocents. Like Mel. Nobody knew it was going to happen, did they? So how do you know it won't happen again anywhere in the world, in any street or town or building and I can't bear the thought of it, Mum.'

A swell of what she could only describe as anger fuelled her on, not for her mum, but a man with a rucksack filled with nails and enough explosives to kill and maim.

'So you see, being here, I've made my own variables and reduced the odds. Hate and evil won't come looking for me at Blacksheep, or in the library or at the church hall while I do yoga. Well, that's what I tell myself when I manage to get into the car and drive down the lane and do something many people wouldn't think twice about. I'm trying, Mum. I really am. Step by step. And with my patient, kind Alfie by my side, making me feel extra safe, I believe I can get better. I really do.'

Her mum sighed and put her head in her hands and paused before she looked up, Cathy instinctively knew that whatever she was going to say was not going to play into her carefully remembered narrative, the mantra that had become her life since surviving a terror attack and moving to her haven on the hills.

'And, my dear wonderful daughter, that all sounds so

perfectly doable. It's a great plan that has got you this far and you *have* made brilliant strides. And be assured, I'm really proud of you for that. But there's something – or someone –that you've forgotten in all of this.'

'Who? My old friends and colleagues... well I'm sorry we lost touch but it's easier to distance myself. Mel healed from her terrible injuries on the outside, thank God, but who knows what goes on in her head. I know what goes on in mine, remembering the state she was in... all of us covered in blood splatters, our own and other people's, the ambulance, the hospital...' Cathy was trembling at the memory, and she wished so much that she could get through to her mum; but more than anything, she wished she could forget. 'And actually, I do hear from some of them from time to time but–'

'No, love. Not them. I'm glad you still keep in touch, and I swear I do understand why it's difficult even if I will never truly grasp what you all went through. But it's someone closer to home I'm worried about.' Julie paused for a second. 'Someone who has lost his father, his brother, his livelihood, and his dreams for the future and from the look of him, he's as lost as you were a few years back.'

Cathy's head jerked upwards, eyes wide. 'Alfie?' She could hear the disbelief in her own voice yet at the same time, a dollop of home-cooked truth came and slapped her hard around the face. How could she be taken by surprise when she knew all of this? Because she was selfish, self-absorbed?

Julie confirmed it. 'Yes, Alfie. You see, I've watched him over this past year, and I've listened, too. And that spark he used to have, the ability to laugh things off, the belief that somehow he'd turn the farm around or carve out a new life for himself, it's diminished, and we all know who is responsible for snuffing out his dreams.'

'Bertha.' Cathy was so moody that she was glad to have the old woman to blame and take the heat off her.

'Yes, that old harridan. But that's by the by. We can't change what she's done but the future is still up for grabs.'

Cathy retaliated and wasn't quite sure why she felt so... attacked. 'Yes, Mum. We both know that and when the time is right we will get our heads together and... and... come up with a new plan.'

At hearing this Julie sat back in her chair and held Cathy in her sights, her voice taking on a firmer tone. 'Good, so all that's left now is the big question. When? Oh, and how long do you expect Alfie to wait? For you to get better. Spending his days marking time fixing up old bangers to make ends meet, missing his brother, being tied to this godforsaken place that will only stand a chance when Bertha is bloody dead and buried.'

'MUM!' Cathy's high-pitched response resulted in a low grumble from Skip and a dismissive wave from Julie.

'I'm only speaking the truth and you know it. So, am I right? Is that the taboo, unspoken plan? To hang around in limbo waiting for her to pop her clogs because I hate to be the one to break it to you but people like her, they usually cling on while the good ones go young. It's called sod's law. A bit like your variables, I suppose.'

Cathy slumped back in her chair. Her mum's words had knocked the wind out of her. And as much as they had stung when they'd hit home with a blast force, one delivered by her own mother, Cathy couldn't deny that the impact had an effect.

It gave her no other option than to look in on herself and their lives at Blacksheep and ask two simple questions. Was Alfie struggling? And was she so wrapped up in her own head that she hadn't noticed, not properly?

Hearing voices in the yard, Julie stood quickly and came over to where Cathy sat and enveloped her in a hug.

'Remember, sweetheart, I'm telling you because I love you and I love Alfie too. It's as pure and simple as that, so please don't be angry with me.'

And even though she was thoroughly pissed off, somewhere deep down, Cathy also understood that very often the truth did actually hurt, and saying such words to someone you love came at a cost, with a risk. Her mum had been brave and as Cathy returned the embrace, the swell of anger subsided and with its departure came a moment of pure clarity.

She *was* safe there at Blacksheep, with Alfie and Skip. She *was* going to get better and then work out a plan, a way forward. She'd pay more attention to Alfie just in case her mum was right. And no matter what, she *wouldn't* let bad people like Bertha ruin their lives and dictate their future. Or, let evil win.

15

It was going to be one of those weeks. Cathy just had a feeling. May Day Bank Holiday had been and gone, with a barbecue down at Annie and Joe's. Then on the 11th, she and Alfie and Skip had stayed up late to watch the northern lights. Thanks to it being dark on the Peaks, the borealis gave them a wonderful show.

Week three had begun with a phone call and Alfie being asked to cover for one of the farm hands over in Holmfirth. It seemed he'd come a cropper and broken his leg wrangling a boisterous heifer from the top of a stone wall.

Yes, on the one hand the money would come in handy for the next few months but on the other, it meant that work on the camper would come to a halt. Not that Cathy minded too much but Alfie did, she could tell. He'd set his heart on getting away in it.

September was the date he had in mind, when the midges were at their least ferocious. He'd spent ages plotting a road trip around the coast of Scotland and even saved a folder on the laptop that contained photos of lochs, castles and campsites and, bizarrely, the motorway services at Scotch Corner. Apparently he remembered stopping there on a school coach trip to Edinburgh. When he'd seen the sign, he had imagined that they'd actually turn a corner and drive into Scotland. Which was why he wanted to go back to that exact service station, and to Edinburgh to buy a box of toffee in a tartan box and also, to see the Forth Bridge which had been the grand finale of that school trip.

It had occurred to Cathy as he told the story with a glint in his eye, that the teachers at his school could rest easy knowing that at least one of the kids on that coach had the best day out, ever.

Tuesday saw Alfie leave the house at 6am and at 9.30 came the phone call from Annie, freaking out because they'd had a letter from the landlord. When the lease on their home renewed at the end of the year, he was putting the rent up to an astronomical amount that they couldn't afford.

This had re-opened the inheritance can of worms, and Bertha was back to being public enemy number one because Annie blamed her for ruining everyone's life. They'd ended the call with them arranging a family pow-wow that weekend to try to come up with a plan. In the meantime Annie was going to get her calculator out, do her sums again, and hope for a miracle.

Wednesday was the day Cathy faced up to the fact that she was never going to make any money selling her jewellery on Etsy because there were just too many competitors out there, and well-known designers were suing people for copying their designs and really, she wasn't exactly entrepreneur material and could do without the stress of it all. She decided she would make some wedding favour bracelets for Sheena and then after that, whenever Eliza came to the farm, she'd let her go crazy with the beads and charms that were left. She loved doing crafts, so it would be something relaxing to do together.

Thursday was spent running back and forward to see

Bertha. She'd come down with a bad cold, which had gone to her chest but she was refusing to call the doctor. Knowing they'd never get an apology for her horrid outburst, Cathy and Alfie had just ploughed on and did their best not to throttle her. She was a cantankerous old goat in good health, but God help *anyone* who came into contact with her when she was poorly. It was like she had the devil in her.

All Cathy could do was pray for patience, fetch over-the-counter medicine from the chemist and make a pan of chicken broth because according to the ratbag up the hill, it was the only thing that'd get her better.

By the end of the week, after collecting eggs and weeding her vegetable patch, Cathy was hoping that she'd get the Friday Feeling. But by midday, it still hadn't arrived. Which was why the sight of Annie's car pulling into the yard lifted her spirits. It wasn't until Annie reached the little gate that kept the chickens out, that Cathy spotted her drawn face and red-rimmed eyes. Something was up.

Half an hour later, after Annie had got it out of her system and explained her current situation, that unless they were blessed with a miracle, or a money tree started growing in the back garden, by the end of the year they'd have to move out of their house.

'So no matter how many times I do the sums, even if we cut back on everything and I take on more evening shifts at the pub – which basically means every bloody night – and Joe picks up overtime at work, no way can we afford that rent. It's too risky. All it takes is an emergency that we have to fork out for and we'll be finished. I've heard about it happening to people and then they start using credit cards and robbing Peter to pay Paul.'

Cathy nodded because it was something her mum had seen a lot recently in her job at the bank.

'And you know what's worse? It's dead money, isn't it,

renting. If we had a deposit we could at least get a mortgage and then we'd actually be buying our own home but that,' Annie tapped the new rent figure on her notepad, 'is just ridiculous. I spoke to your mum yesterday and she got one of her colleagues in the mortgage department to do some provisional calculations. She said that going off our income, we'd definitely get one.'

'So it's the deposit you need, the lump sum?' Cathy was sure she knew what was coming next.

'Exactly. And it boils my wee that her up the lane is sitting on a huge nest egg from Dad's life insurance, not to mention his pension and the private health policy that paid-out, and what does she do with it? Nothing! She's loaded and the most she spends it on is her bloody lottery tickets, gin and cigarettes. And that's the really hilarious part. I bet if she did win the jackpot she'd keep the lot, every penny, because she's warped. Got serious issues in my opinion.' Annie tapped the side of her head with her finger.

Cathy had heard this before, from all three siblings. She was incredulous that a mother would behave the way Bertha did – but maybe this landlord news might be the thing that would encourage her to help out.

Another alternative pinged into Cathy's head. 'Okay, let's take your mum out of the equation because it just winds you up. We should focus on the big issue, which is saving up for a deposit.' Then came inspiration and with it, a giddy beat of her heart.

'What if you tell the landlord to shove it and you move in here. There are three spare bedrooms upstairs, plus the box room, and you could use the rent money to save for a deposit. Let's work it out, how long it'd take... go on, get the calculator up on your phone.'

Annie wasn't convinced. 'We can't move in here, Cathy. Three kids would drive you bonkers and *she* wouldn't be pleased either.' Annie jerked her thumb in the direction of Shepherd's Cottage. 'She can't stand the sight of me and was over the moon when I left home so she won't welcome me back. Remember, she still sees this as her house. It's only her benevolence that allows you and Alfie to stay, that and needing you around to take care of her.'

Cathy made a huffing sound, because Bertha was a stumbling block and Annie rammed that point home.

'I've told you before, Cathy. She played a blinder when she sold the flock and pushed Albie too far. I'd already gone so she was left with the most malleable child at her beck and call. You were a bonus because you've got a kind heart, and she also knew you loved living here where you felt safe and Alfie would do anything for you, simple as that.'

And there it was again. The reminder that it was Cathy's PTSD that tied them to the farm and Bertha had capitalised on that. Even though Annie didn't mean anything by it and her words weren't intended to hurt, they did because they were true. Glancing over to the calendar on the wall where the two May bank holidays were circled, as was Ezra's birthday, there was a date near the middle of the month that she refused to acknowledge.

The 22nd. The day of the Arena bomb.

Dragging her eyes away, Cathy watched as Annie tapped the screen and reluctantly did the sums. Yes, it would be strange having a house full again – but fun, too. Cathy remembered the days when Jacob and Bertha lived there, along with Albie, her and Alfie. Even though Bertha hadn't welcomed Cathy with open arms, she'd accepted her as Alfie's new girlfriend.

Perhaps she'd been playing the long game even then, probably, because she was sly. And after Jacob died, she'd moved herself into Shepherd's Cottage, saying she needed her own space to grieve. They all knew it was rubbish and a ploy to scupper their plans to rent out the renovated cottage and also, with Jacob gone there was no need to play at being a mother.

Cathy could see her now, walking up the lane, carrying nothing more than her handbag and a tatty brown suitcase that looked like it had once belonged to a child. Behind her, Alfie pushed the wheelbarrow full of bin bags containing her clothes, the old record player from the parlour, and whatever knick-knacks she'd decided to take.

It had come as no surprise to any of them, Annie especially, that the framed photos of them growing up were left on the sideboard in the parlour. Unwanted, much like her three children.

Breaking the memory spell, Annie caught Cathy's attention with the results of her maths test.

'Three years. That's how long it'd take to save up a decent deposit. Bloody hell, Cathy. That seems like forever, doesn't it. And the only way we can do it is, as you suggest, move in here.' Annie put her head in her hands and stared at the scribblings and figures on the notepad.

'Well there you go. I swear me and Alfie would love to have you and really, this is your house too, or will be one day, even if it's a part share. And I reckon three years will pass quicker than you think. Or there's another alternative.'

Annie's head snapped upwards. 'What?'

This flash of inspiration had even surprised herself. 'You could ask Bertha for a loan and do what you wanted to do when your dad was alive. Do a barn conversion and while you're at it, turn the old pigsties into a milking shed for goats and start your business. In fact we could do it together, that's if you fancy it. I'm jacking in the jewellery thing – too much competition. I'd love a new challenge. I was thinking... I was thinking I could get some bees and make honey.' Cathy's heart skipped a giddy beat, then she saw Annie's eyebrows rise, already sceptical.

'As if Mam'd do that.'

Cathy didn't expect Annie to believe it was possible, but she was on a roll. 'Hear me out, okay. I know she put the mockers on this after your dad died, but that's because he was going to fund the goat cheese business and she didn't want anything coming out of their pockets. But, if you ask her for a loan – not a handout – to convert the barn and the pigsties, in her own weird head she will see it as a business transaction and even better, love thinking she's the big *I am* who has some kind of hold over you... you know what I mean, like you'd be grateful. You should play her at her own game and use some reverse psychology on her.'

'No way! I would bloody hate it. Knowing I'd had to grovel and be at her mercy because that's what it is, no matter which way you look at it.' Annie slumped into the chair, a petulant expression and the tightly folded arms across her chest signalling she wasn't buying the idea at all.

Cathy wasn't going to give up that easily. 'Yes, I get that but it's how you approach it. For a start, we could tell her that you don't expect it to be a nought per cent loan and you'll pay her interest and regular monthly instalments. She's a proper Shylock and loves money, so that'll appeal to her straight away. As for the goats, tell her you'll pay rent, too. Anything to get her to agree. The other advantage is that this way, you'll be able to hold your head up and not feel beholden to her like me and Alfie sometimes do. Because every now and then she reminds us we live here rent free and it really does piss me off which sounds ungrateful, but she does.'

Cathy kept to herself the fact it also hurt like hell that Bertha had the means to help them have some fertility tests carried out, but she and Alfie couldn't pay her back, so they were waiting for their turn on the NHS list. And no way would Alfie go cap in hand to his mum. Deep down, she'd hate it, too.

If they didn't hear soon, though, she was thinking of using the money her parents gave her. But for now, her monthly disappointments caused Cathy too much pain, so she concentrated on Annie's predicament.

Sitting straight in her chair again, Annie picked up her pen and tapped it on the table, as though keeping time with the cogs that were clicking in her head. 'So it will be a straightforward business transaction. She loans us the money and we pay her back with interest, using what we'd save on renting a house. And we could live here while the barn conversion is done. Is that still okay? Do you think Alfie would mind?'

Cathy nodded. 'Of course it is, and I think Alfie would love having you all here. He always says how much he enjoys it when the kids come up and help around the farm and it'll put some life back into the place. And I reckon a barn conversion will take less time than saving up for three years for a deposit and, if you want to start a business, you'll be on site to project manage both builds while Joe is at work.'

A smile spread across Annie's face. 'Oh my God, do you really think this is possible, Cathy? I don't want to get my hopes up because it was awful the last time when she shut it all down. And we haven't got the best relationship, have we? And she'll take great pleasure in turning me down, I know she will.'

Cathy took Annie's hand. 'But like I said, this is different because Jacob's not funding it out of their bank balance. That's what irked her originally, and you know what, maybe it was grief that made her act that way, and now time has passed she'll see things differently. For a start she'll be making a few quid. Lord knows what for. More lottery tickets and a bigger bottle of gin, probably.'

That made them both laugh and the tension in the kitchen receded. Annie had another question, though. 'So what do we do next?'

'Well first, I'm going to make us some dinner and then we can have a mooch online and get a rough idea of what barn conversions cost. Then I think we should ring my mum and see if she has any financial advice, and you'll need to speak to Joe. No point in steaming ahead if he's not on board, and I'll talk to Alfie tonight. Once we've done that you'll have to put your big-girl pants on and approach Bertha with all the facts and figures.'

At this Annie grimaced, and then, putting her hands together in prayer asked one more question. 'Cathy, please will you come with me, when I go and see Mam? I don't think I can face her on my own and Joe's shit-scared of her as it is. I'll feel more confident with you and you're the only one she seems to tolerate.'

The thought of having any kind of financial conversation with Bertha filled Cathy with dread but Annie was right. If anyone could get through to the old dragon, it was her, so the answer was simple. 'Course I will.'

16
BERTHA

It was all very inconvenient because their impromptu visit was making her miss the *Jeremy Vine* show and it was all about whether they should send them boat people to some country beginning with R. She'd intended ringing up to have her say and now they'd ruined it.

Bertha liked ringing radio shows when it was discussion time and once got through to BBC Manchester and told them what she thought of her licence money being spent on the Eurovision Song Contest, but she got cut off for being abusive about Ken Bruce and gay folk and them that didn't know if they were lads or lasses or neither. Bertha didn't know what the world was coming to and there was the soft lass opposite, wanting to bring a bairn into it!

Looking from one to the other, Bertha absorbed what Annie and Cathy had just said. She also noted they both looked nervous as hell and Annie was getting right on her nerves by twiddling her bloody pen while Cathy made what appeared to be a business pitch.

It was soft lass Cathy that spoke up next, asking if Bertha

wanted a warm drink. The silence was clearly making her uncomfortable.

'No, I want you to bugger off so I can watch the telly but seein' as you're 'ere, I'll have a milky coffee. Make one for yerselves if you're stopping, which it looks like you are.'

Annie shot off, obviously eager to avoid conversation unlike Cathy who never bloody shut up, and went on, 'I know it's a lot to take in straight away, so we'll leave you the paperwork to look over, but I honestly think it's a viable business transaction that'll help Annie and Joe build a lovely home for their kids. And you'd be profiting from it, too.'

'Hmm. You reckon, do you.' Bertha only managed a few words before she succumbed to a bout of coughing. She wasn't feeling great, and her chest hurt when she breathed, not that she was going to let on, otherwise they'd have the doctor up. Or worse, cart her off to hospital and everyone knew at her age, once you went in you rarely came out again.

So she certainly wasn't in the mood for chatting or doling out money for them that didn't deserve it, especially Annie. Talk of the devil, she was back, still avoiding contact like the sly little minx she was.

Bertha had never trusted her daughter. She was sure she used to pinch money out of her purse, *and* she was bone idle. Always trying to shirk her chores and stir trouble between man and wife, currying favour with Jacob and pushing Bertha out. And as for the lads, they doted on her for some reason. Thorn in her side, that's what Annie had been ever since the day she was conceived. On the day she left home to shack up with that Joe, Bertha had almost cheered.

'Right, kettle's on. So, what do you think, Mam? Initially, of the idea. Would you mind us doing the barn and the pigsty up if we paid for it ourselves?'

It speaks, thought Bertha, *and eye contact too. Very bold.*

'Would I mind forking out my hard-earned money for the privilege of being disturbed by wagons going in and out of the yard for months on end, and the noise of cement mixers and builders banging about, day in day out? Oh yes, I'm totally thrilled about that prospect, I can tell you.' Bertha huffed and then set off coughing.

Annie bit her lip. *Holding her temper in like always, the huffy mare,* thought Bertha.

Cathy decided to chip in. 'I doubt you'd hear the builders from here, Bertha. It's nowhere near the cottage. You know which barn we mean, don't you? The one right at the back of the farm, by the copse of trees. It's where Jacob used to keep the–'

'Yes, I know exactly which one you mean and exactly what my husband kept there – the winter feed, thank you very much.' Bertha added a tut to her sentence just so they knew she was cross. Cheek of it. Telling her about her own bloody farm.

Annie was next. 'I promise we'd do our best to limit any inconvenience to you and keep the noise down. But about the loan... Do you think it's possible?'

Bertha tilted her head to one side and looked at the ceiling, feigning deep thought. The white plaster was actually more interesting than her daughter whose face got on her nerves. Still, she could have a bit of fun with them both before she gave them her answer, which she already knew. She'd made up her mind more or less straight away. 'I'll need to think on it a while. Can't be making decisions like that at the drop of a hat.'

A look was passed between Cathy and her desperate daughter, which Bertha read as hope. As if.

'Okay, well thanks for thinking about it, Mam. It'll really help us out. What the landlord is asking for the new rent is beyond our means and it's going to be bad enough telling the kids they're leaving their home, never mind finding somewhere else with three bedrooms for a decent price. There's hardly anything in the village to rent so we'd probably have to relocate to Sheffield and none of us want to move to the city.'

Bertha couldn't think of anything that'd please her more, seeing the back of Annie but she kept that to herself. 'Hmm. And what does Alfred think about the prospect of his home being invaded by three kids, never mind you and that lump of a husband of yours?' Bertha tried not to smile as she watched Annie's knuckles go white from gripping her pen.

And right on cue, the chatty one stuck her oar in, trying to keep the peace. 'Alfie's fine about the whole thing. In fact, he's looking forward to it, having his family around him and he'll help Joe work on the barn at weekends. If they do as much as they can themselves it'll save Annie and Joe loads, and Alfie's really handy at DIY, isn't he?'

Annie appeared to have swallowed down her annoyance and with a smile as false as that tarty Sheena's eyelashes, said, 'And maybe you can spend more time with the kids if they're here every day. You could get to know them a bit better.'

'And why would I want to do that?'

The two sharp intakes of breath were music to Bertha's ears.

Annie couldn't resist taking the bait. 'I beg your pardon?'

A quizzical look preceded Bertha's reply. 'What don't you understand? You know I'm not fond of kiddies so why would I want your three up here driving me round the bend? 'Specially that baba, never bloody stops crying. You're obviously spoiling it, and as for the other two–'

'I do not spoil my children and Eli is a good baby and by the way, do not call him it. OKAY!' Annie was now sporting two red cheeks while Cathy had gone so pale that her face almost matched the ceiling.

This is more like it, thought Bertha, and would have embellished on the matter but a coughing fit took hold and forced her to drink some of her water. She also noted neither of them asked if she was all right, so they were most likely hoping she was going to choke to death. Shame she had to disappoint them. When she recovered, she decided to twist the knife.

'And while I think on, as for this house business... You've made your bed so maybe you should lie in it and learn your lesson. In't my fault you can't keep your legs crossed and in my book, folk shouldn't be 'avin kiddies if they can't afford to keep 'em and you obviously can't. Otherwise you wouldn't be up here askin' for a handout.'

At this Annie rose to her feet and pointed a finger at Bertha. 'How dare you! I can look after my kids and have been doing so quite nicely since they were born but this new rent has ruined that and just remember, I am *not* asking you for a handout. I'm asking for a loan which will be paid back in full, with interest, and it's not like you can't afford it, you tight-fisted old cow!'

At last, Annie had shown her true colours and lost her temper. 'Well that's charming, I must say. Here's me, a poorly old woman, considering dipping into her life savings only to be verbally abused by her nasty daughter. Never known anything like it and that's a fact.'

For a second Annie was stumped but she rallied quickly, much to Bertha's delight. 'Verbally abused! Are you serious? After the things you've done and said to this family, calling you a tight-fisted old cow is nothing, and that's a bloody fact.'

'Why, what have I done? Apart from bring three whining kids up, putting a roof over their heads and food on the table, clothes on their backs. You've always been an ungrateful so-and-so, Ann Walker, and nowt's going to change that. I did me best for you all so stop feelin' sorry for yerself and grow up.' Bertha shook her head in disgust, but knew that out of everything she'd said, calling Annie *Ann*, would've annoyed her the most. She'd always hated her plain name, but Bertha always thought she was a plain baby so if the cap fit...

Annie was now holding the sides of her head as though it was going to explode and her whole face was blood red. Cathy, now also standing, looked like she was going to pass out as Annie let rip. '*You did your best?* Don't make me laugh, Mother. You did the bare minimum and put on a front just to please Dad who genuinely loved all of us, while you... you acted like you despised me and the lads. And you did, didn't you? Go on. Admit it. I dare you.'

Bertha pondered on her answer, not because she didn't know it, more because she was weighing up just how honest she should be. She knew it was wrong, to say the things she thought in her head but that knot of bitterness she stored deep inside, a pulsing ball of hurt and shame, of being unworthy, swelled up every now and then, like a big pan of soup boiling over. And once it began to flow, spewing her frustration over everything and everyone in its path, she found it hard to turn the gas off and let the anger simmer down. Which was why her lips were about to run away with her. When Bertha answered, she went for brutal.

'I never pretended to be the motherly type and Jacob knew I found it hard to show you all affection because I weren't brought up with any, but that's by the by. So it's not my fault I never took to motherin'. I gave him the sons he wanted and thought I'd done my bit so no; I wasn't best pleased to find out I was carrying you. That's probably not what you wanted to hear but you dared me to tell the truth and now you have it.'

Annie's eyes welled, her voice shaking as she spoke. 'Yes I do, and it comes as no shock at all. I always knew you didn't want me and I'm also sure you've enjoyed kicking me in the teeth while I'm down and at my wits end, so well done, Mother. Job done. At least you spared me the bit where you tried to get rid of me because I wouldn't put that past you either.'

Bertha chose not to answer, then again, the fact she didn't deny it sent out its own, very obvious silent message.

'Oh Jesus. I'm right, aren't I? So enlighten me, go on. What did you try? Was it a bottle of gin and a hot bath or did you just chuck yourself down the stairs?'

At that, Cathy gasped, her hand covering her mouth, her face a picture of shock which didn't surprise Bertha one bit because the lass was mardy as they come.

Deciding not to confirm or deny Annie's suspicions as it wasn't anyone's business but her own how she'd tried to end her third and very unwanted pregnancy, Bertha ignored Annie and focused on Cathy. It was about time she heard some home truths, too. Do her good it would.

'I don't know why you're lookin' so horrified. It's real life, not the one you see through them rose-tinted glasses you're so fond of. An' if you want my opinion, you should be glad you can't have bairns because, believe me, they're more trouble than they're worth. Lasses 'specially. No use for nowt.' Bertha folded her arms and sat back in her chair and waited for the explosion she knew was about to come.

Annie blew first. 'Oh my God, you evil cow! How could you say that to Cathy who out of all of us gives you the most time and even sticks up for you? She doesn't deserve being spoken to like that. So apologise right now. I MEAN IT!'

Bertha wasn't having that, being shouted at, not in her own home. 'Do not take that tone with me, Ann Walker. And I will not apologise because it's true: see for yerself.'

Addressing Cathy, Bertha jerked her thumb towards Annie. 'The proof is right there in front of me. My plain, gormless daughter who got herself up the tub just so some bloke would put a roof over her head and then, as if it weren't bad enough, turned into a baby-making machine cos let's face it, she's good for nowt else. Apart from working in a pub. If she'd been an animal the kindest thing would've been a sack, a brick and the river. Job done.'

The room fell silent, like the ears of the walls were listening in stunned horror, mimicking the expressions worn by Cathy and Annie who appeared to have been struck mute. Bertha took this as an opportunity to embellish on the theme.

'So you mark my words, Cathy, keep yer legs crossed like this one should've done. An' thank your lucky stars that our Alfred's probably firing blanks or there's summat wrong wi' your bits and bobs. Now, if you don't mind I want to watch the telly, seein' as I've missed Jeremy, and you're stood in the way. Show yourselves out.'

Bertha picked up the remote control and pointed it at the telly, giving them both a stern look as she waited for them to move. She was expecting Annie to implode, but instead, Cathy grabbed her arm and spoke in a voice calmer than Bertha would've thought her capable of under the circumstances. 'Come on, let's go. Enough's been said this morning. Annie, come on, leave it.'

With one last stare, Annie held Bertha in her sights and even though there were no tears just yet, they were on the cards, she could tell. With a nod to Cathy, Annie turned to go and as they both made their way to the door, Bertha called out, 'And take your poncy business plan with you. Don't be leavin' your rubbish here.'

Without a backward glance Annie shouted, 'Why don't you shove it right up your arse, Mother, you know, in the same place you keep Dad's blood money! You twisted old hag.'

Along with that parting shot, Annie gave the door a good old slam as she left the room, reminding Bertha of many a teenage tantrum and mother-versus-daughter slanging matches of the past.

On hearing the front door thump closed, Bertha pointed the

remote and was relieved to see she'd not missed too much of *This Morning* and as she settled into her chair, managed a wry smile as she remembered Annie's words. It was a great parting shot and one that Bertha herself would've been proud of.

Touché, Ann. Maybe you're more like me than you thought. Fancy that!

17

CATHY

Shaken to the core by what she'd just witnessed, so much so she couldn't even cry, Cathy focused on Annie who was scrunched into a ball on the parlour sofa, breaking her heart, totally inconsolable. All Cathy could do was make more tea, which was a waste of time as neither of them had drank the first one yet. Instead she opted for holding Annie's hand while she cried it out.

She had no idea what had come over Bertha. The vitriol in her words was unlike anything Cathy had witnessed before. Yes, she knew Bertha could be cutting and blunt and she got away with most of her barbed comments by playing the honesty card, as if that made her hurtful ways somehow acceptable. The scene at the cottage though, that was next level.

To tell your daughter she wasn't wanted and more or less admit to trying to get rid of her in the womb was abhorrent, never mind the bit about the sack and the river. And the things she'd said about her own grandchildren were uncalled for because they were all great kids.

Most of it was a blur of hurled insults but snippets were drifting back slowly as though her brain was trying to process them bit by bit, but the part that hurt Cathy most was when Bertha mocked her and Alfie and their longing for a baby. No way was she going to repeat to Alfie the things she'd said about him firing blanks, because she wouldn't want him feeling the way she did.

Maybe it was because Bertha wasn't feeling well she'd behaved that way. Cathy had read that sometimes, salt imbalances or water infections in the elderly made them act in really strange ways, hallucinating and saying odd things. Deep down, Cathy knew that probably wasn't the case. What they'd witnessed was the real Bertha with her 'nasty dial' turned up to devil level.

Still, it had been a poor decision to go up there while she wasn't feeling well. Cathy regretted allowing Annie's infectious enthusiasm to convince her to visit Bertha as soon as possible because it had got them nowhere.

For a moment, though, Cathy had dared hope that Bertha was going to give it some proper thought but now, she wondered if the whole thing was a fool's errand. Worse, it had all been her idea and that made Cathy feel terrible for getting Annie's hopes up.

It took a few seconds to realise that the sobbing had stopped. Turning to Annie, Cathy gave her a smile as she squeezed her hand gently. 'Your tea's gone cold. Want me to make you another?'

Annie pushed herself upright on the sofa and shook her head. 'No, it's okay. I'll drink this one. I'm used to it. Nearly all the brews I make end up going cold. Comes with the being-a-totally-shit-mum territory.' When once again, Annie's lips began to tremble, the conversation at Bertha's flooding back.

Cathy grabbed both of Annie's hands and gave them a shake. 'Listen to me right now! Everything your mum said about you before is a load of bollocks, do you hear me? And we are not going to allow her vile words inside our heads or to bring us down any more than she already has, okay?'

Annie didn't nod or say she agreed and instead pointed out a fact. 'It's too late for that, Cathy. Her work here is done because I'll never forget what she said today. At least I can stop kidding myself because now I know for sure that she never loved me or wanted me and even though she's sick in the head, she's still my mam and it hurts that she's the way she is. I get that it sounds weird, wanting someone so horrible to love or even like you, but I did. All the time I was growing up.'

Cathy sighed. 'It's not weird at all because you were a little girl who just wanted her mum to be nice and love her, which for any child isn't too much to ask. It's what they deserve and I'm so sorry that you never had that, and Alfie and Albie too. But from what I can tell, she was far worse to you than them.'

Annie huffed. 'You can say that again. None of us had an ounce of affection from her and I swear, I can't remember being cuddled. By my dad, yes. Her, no way. And it shocked me, before, when she said Dad accepted that she found it hard to mother us. It sounded like he condoned her behaviour but I'm sure he didn't. I don't want to feel badly towards him, because he can't speak for himself, but it's really rattled my cage and not for the first time, I'm wondering why he wasn't tougher with her. You know, putting his foot down when she tried to make stupid rules and spoil our fun.'

Cathy knew the answer to that straight away. 'Because she's a gaslighting narcissist and they're always very skilled at what they do. Sly and manipulative and good at masking their true nature, using excuses or emotional blackmail to stay under the radar. In fact, I think that's exactly what she did earlier, laid the seeds of doubt about your dad by making out he was okay with how she was.'

'Bloody hell, I bet that's exactly what she was playing at.

And did you hear her call me *Ann*. I reckon she chose the plainest name possible for me, or one that started with the first letter of the alphabet because she couldn't be arsed thinking of another. And she chose the most old-fashioned names for the lads, too, which was why they shortened them. I added the ie to mine, so we all matched. I honestly haven't got anything against the name *Ann*. It's just this weird hunch I've always had that she used it as a weapon, which sounds totally bloody paranoid.'

Cathy shook her head. 'After what I heard today, I really don't think you are. It makes me shudder wondering what goes on in her mind.'

'You mean like the sack, brick and river thing? Seriously, how sick was that? But I told you about Daisy my rabbit, didn't I. That she was so bent out of shape that Albie brought her home and Dad said I could keep her. I reckon she waited for the opportunity to take Daisy from me and in the worst way possible. I swear she killed her somehow because there was absolutely nothing wrong with her when I went to school and when I came home... well, she was gone. Dad was baffled, too. Obviously I bawled my eyes out, but *she* told me it was just nature's way and to toughen up. I lived on a farm, and it was no place for cry-babies. I was six.'

'Christ, what a cow. And how could anyone do that to a little rabbit? It's too gross to imagine.' The way Cathy was feeling she didn't want to speak to Bertha ever again.

'She's warped through and through. About a year later I fell off my bike and broke my arm. It was in plaster for six weeks and back then we didn't have a shower, so we had to wash our hair over the sink or when we had a bath. I struggled to do it myself with one arm, but she kept making excuses not to help me, saying she didn't have the time. In the end I asked Albie to do it.

'It was as though she wanted me to look a mess, and went

out of her way to criticise, telling me I was getting tubby and spotty so not to eat chocolate and biscuits, or my hair was boring and mousey, and when I hit puberty, she made comments about my flat chest. If anyone complimented me she said they didn't mean it and were just being kind. I had to ask my friend's mam about periods and sanitary towels because I had no clue, and no way could I mention it to Dad or the lads.

'I swear on my life she's never said *well done* or given me any praise. Once, I got the star of the month award at school and when I brought it home her reaction was, "They must have been giving them away" or when I was in the Christmas play, "Oh you're just in the back row of the chorus. Is that because you can't sing?"'

Cathy was tempted to tell Annie to stop torturing herself with Bertha stories but realised that maybe she needed to exorcise the ghost of her horrid mother.

Annie continued, 'I was constantly told that I didn't deserve things, and if I complained about anything she'd say I should be grateful because without her I wouldn't be alive, which I now realise was true – but only because she failed to get rid of me.'

Annie paused and looked around the parlour, deep sorrow reflected in her eyes as she took in the room that Cathy had redecorated once Bertha left, taking her favourite bits and bobs with her.

'You've made it so cosy in here, Cathy, and I'm glad you kept the rogues gallery.' She nodded towards the contemporary IKEA sideboard where a row of framed photos stood, showing the three siblings on their journey through life, plus some shots with their dad. Bertha was nowhere to be seen because she hated having her picture taken, unless of course it was with Jacob.

'There's not one photo of us up at the cottage and I've stopped giving her any of my three because she just shoves them in a drawer like she used to do with cards we made her. I bet she threw them on the fire at the first chance she got.' As if exhausted by the unhappy memories, Annie sighed and dragged her hands down her tear-streaked face.

'What a bloody mess, eh. And now, after I lost my shit with her I've ruined any chance we had to make a new start here at the farm. I'd allowed myself to imagine it, you know. Us all being together here, me and you mucking in with the housework while the barn and pigsties were done up and now, it's never going to happen. I blew it and I'll have to explain why to Joe.'

Cathy disagreed with part of Annie's analysis. 'It wasn't your fault, Annie, because the more I think about it, and after what you've just told me, it wouldn't surprise me one bit if she was messing with your head and never had any intention of loaning you the money. I think she got a kick out of baiting you. Had you not had a row, she would've kept you dangling on a string for however long it amused her. In fact, I feel like I'm to blame for suggesting the loan in the first place, so I'm sorry if I made things worse. I truly am.'

'Hey, there's only one person at fault here and we both know who that is.' Annie swung her legs off the sofa and stretched them in front of her. 'Right, well there's no point sitting here moping. I'd best go and get Eli and Ezra from Joe's mam, and then plan my speech for when he gets in from work.'

'He'll understand, I'm sure he will. And let's not give up on the dream just yet because who knows what might turn up. We can get our heads together and think of an alternative. And I'll have a word with my mum in case she has any bright ideas. And don't forget, you can still move in here and save up like we said. No way can she stop you doing that and if she tries, we can all tell her to piss off. Or she can take us to court and have the lot of us evicted because if you go, then so will me and Alf.' As Cathy said the words she knew without a doubt

129

they were true. They would stand by Annie and Joe come what may.

'Well putting it bluntly, the only way any of us are going to get a shot at our dreams any time soon is when she kicks the bucket and God forgive me, I won't be shedding any tears when that happens, not after today.' With that, Annie stood but Cathy had one more thing she needed to say.

'Annie, when you explain to Joe, will you do me a favour and miss out the part where she was mean about Alfie because I really don't want him to know. It's taken ages for him to forgive her for what she said on my birthday, and he's been a bit down lately.'

'Has he? He always seems okay when I see him. What's up?'

'I think it's because Skip's health is deteriorating, and he wanted to get that camper done so we could go on holiday but now he's working over at Holmfirth, it might not be ready. Lots of little things, really, that all add up. I've noticed he's been quiet and not as cheery as he usually is.'

It occurred to Cathy as she explained that if Annie thought Alfie was fine, did that mean he was masking his true feelings, not just to his sister but to her, too?

'Aw, poor Alf. He bloody loves that dog, doesn't he. We all do. And yes, my lips are sealed, and Joe won't hear anything from me, that's a promise.'

They made their way down the hall and into the kitchen and after giving Skip's ears a tickle, Annie picked up her bag, dished out a huge hug, and made a promise to text later.

With a sigh, Cathy waved from the door as Annie drove out of the yard much faster than normal, stones flicking up in her wake as plumes of dust fogged the air. Glancing to her left, Cathy was in two minds whether to march up to Bertha's and give her what for.

But she thought better of it. There'd be no getting through to her and Cathy wasn't giving her the opportunity to go for round two. And just to make a stand, Bertha could cook her own tea, and her breakfast! That'd teach her. With that, Cathy went inside and closed the door, turning her back on a shitty day and an equally shitty person.

18

From the surprisingly comfy armchair in the corner of the silent room, Cathy watched the rise and fall of Bertha's chest as the antibiotics coursed around her purple veins, seeking out infection and hopefully, wiping it out. It was late and visiting time was over, but Cathy had been allowed to bring Bertha some home comforts and sit with her for a while.

On the whiteboard above bed 5 it said, *Bertha Walker* and her consultant's name. Not much more to indicate that below, lay a woman who had the day before wreaked havoc and now looked somewhat angelic. The sun had set behind the peaks in the distance and the light in the room was dimmed. It was peaceful and so was Bertha.

Alfie had been in such a flap when he'd rang from the cottage, telling Cathy he'd found Bertha unconscious on the floor of the kitchen. While she was racing up there, panicking and feeling guilty for not popping in after the row, he had called an ambulance.

Alfie went with Bertha to the hospital and he'd still had the... what was it? Goodness of heart and presence of mind to insist Cathy remained at home to wait for news.

The wail of the siren as the ambulance made its way up the track would have been enough to set her nerves jangling. She knew that he knew that hustle and bustle and panic of a busy A&E was no place for her.

Since then the hours had stretched – fifteen to be precise – while Bertha had been triaged and assessed and finally – when they found a bed – moved onto a ward and, as luck had it, into a side room.

Dave had picked Alfie up after his shift and brought him home. There had been no need for Cathy to make the trek to the hospital that night, but she'd been compelled to by nagging guilt and worry that the harsh words spoken between mother and daughter had in some way contributed to Bertha's sudden decline.

Alfie explained that Bertha had been lucky with only a cracked rib and severe bruising to her torso, right arm and face. She'd be in a lot of pain, but they'd given her something strong to relieve it and help her sleep. It was the pneumonia they were most worried about, and the next forty-eight hours would be key.

'Do you think... that we might lose her? Did they say?' Cathy sat opposite Alfie while he ate the warmed-up meal. Hers was still in the oven. She had lost her appetite.

Alfie had taken a gulp of tea, then shook his head. 'No, not in so many words but that's what they were getting at. The doctor said it was serious and her lungs were in a bad way, but they're doing everything they can and all that, and they'd keep us informed. I'll go back tomorrow and take her some clothes and stuff, but they said they'll manage for now.'

It was then that Cathy decided to go because she'd never forgive herself if Bertha died and she didn't see her one last time and say she was sorry for not taking her tea up and checking in at breakfast. And it didn't matter if she didn't receive an apology for the awful things Bertha said. There was actually more chance of pigs flying because Bertha didn't do sorry. But Cathy did.

Alfie had protested, saying it was a wasted journey, but Cathy had stood firm. 'Alfie, just let me do it. I'll be fine. You said she's in a separate unit to the main hospital and by the time I get there everyone will be asleep and hopefully, they'll let me see her for a minute. I really want to go. And I think we'll both sleep better knowing she has some home comforts and... and if anything happens, I'd like to see her. It's as much for me as it is her, okay.'

Then Alfie's face dropped. 'Do you think I should've stayed? You know, in case she goes... I'll come with you.' He began to eat quickly. 'Just let me finish this and I'll drive you back.'

Cathy raised her palm. 'No, Alf, you're staying here. I mean it. You're knackered, I can tell, and you've got work tomorrow. Please, Alf, I need to do this by myself. Remember, little steps.'

Of course he'd given in because he was emotionally and physically drained but not so much that he couldn't see sense. She'd left him with strict instructions to rest, ring Annie and Albie and keep Skip company. The dog had picked up on the atmosphere and been unsettled all afternoon. There was only one person who could calm him and that was his best friend, Alfie.

The creak of the door followed by the smiling face of the sister suggested to Cathy that her time was up, so she was surprised by the kind offer that followed. 'Would you like a warm drink? We're all having one.'

Cathy was actually parched and starving. 'That would be lovely but only if it's not too much trouble. I'm not outstaying my welcome, am I? I don't want to be in the way.'

The sister waved her hand. 'No, you're fine, love. We'll be in and out doing observations, but you can stay as long as you want.'

With that, foreboding washed over Cathy, and she was compelled to ask, 'Do you think the rest of her family should be here... I mean, Alfie wasn't sure if–'

Sister placed a reassuring hand on Cathy's shoulder. 'No, she's doing fine for now and it's nice that if she wakes up someone is here that she recognises. I'm told she was in and out of consciousness for most of the day and the painkillers are the good stuff, so she might be slightly woozy and disorientated when she comes round. Once she realises where she is and what's happened she'll be fine. So, what can I get you? Tea, coffee?'

After fearing they might lose Bertha, Cathy could feel the stress draining from her. 'Tea, please. Milk no sugar.'

And with a wink, the sister was gone, leaving Cathy and Bertha alone. It hadn't been as hard as Cathy imagined, doing something that for her was a brave step. Yes, she'd had butterflies on the way down from the Peaks and had scoped out the entrance to the unit, sitting in the almost empty car park for ten minutes having a one-way chat about big-girl pants.

But now she could add something new to her list of mountains climbed. Doctors' surgery; supermarket; yoga, which had been so relaxing and peaceful, like the library (which to be fair was a cinch, thanks to the rules of silence). And now a hospital – albeit visiting at stupid o'clock.

In between watching the zig-zag line on the monitor and the occasional flutter of Bertha's eyelids, Cathy drank her tea and wolfed down the packets of biscuits that Rebecca, as she now knew the nurse was called, had brought with the drink.

It was approaching midnight and Alfie and Annie had texted to say she should go home and that they'd go back in the morning. Cathy was quite surprised that Annie said she'd go, and then a wicked thought flickered, which she banished immediately.

She was beginning to flag and Bertha appeared to be deep in sleep, not even stirring while someone did her observations. So it came as quite a shock when, as she bent to pick up her bag, a familiar voice cut through the silence of the room, weak and barely audible. 'Din't expect to see you 'ere. Got no 'ome t'go to?'

Cathy's breath caught as her head shot up and her eyes met the perpetually steely ones belonging to Bertha. 'Oh good, you're awake. Let me get the nurse... two ticks...' For some reason, after waiting ages for the bloody woman to come round so she could say sorry, Cathy suddenly lost her bottle and sprinted from the room in search of help.

Thirty minutes later, once Bertha was settled and her medication topped up, she and Cathy were again left alone. An uncomfortable silence descended on the room.

Rebecca said the painkillers would kick in quickly and they'd relax Bertha and hopefully help her sleep. Cathy found herself praying that would be the case – but first, she had to make her peace, otherwise the journey and wait would have been for nothing.

Speaking to closed eyes, she had no idea if Bertha could hear, but got on with it anyway. At least she could tell herself she'd tried.

'Bertha, I'm going to get going soon. But I just want to say that I'm sorry for not coming to see you yesterday. I was hurt and angry about the things you said but that doesn't give me the right to judge you because I have no idea... Well, I don't know what's gone on in the past to make you... What I'm trying to say is that I hope we can move on from this and somehow find a way to be friends, for Alfie's sake at least.'

Nothing. Bertha remained still. Apart from the rise and fall of her chest not a flicker of movement indicated she was conscious. So having said her piece, Cathy decided to call it a night and was about to stand when the Sleeping Beast removed the mask from her face, swallowed and said, 'Where's Alfred? And Mam? They were here earlier. Was nice to see me mam. She looked well.' Bertha's eyes remained closed.

Finding it hard to hear, Cathy stood and dragged the plastic chair right beside the bed and rested her hands on the sheets next to Bertha's canula-free arm. Avoiding the subject of Bertha's long dead mam, Cathy focused on Alfie.

'Alfie's gone home for something to eat but he'll be back tomorrow. I brought you some bits from yours, but if there's anything else you need just say and I'll sort it.' Cathy noticed the flicker of eyelids, but they remained closed even as Bertha replied with a statement which caught Cathy totally off guard.

'I miss me mam, you know. Do you think she'll come back later on?'

Cathy swallowed down a lump that had caught in her throat and suspecting the drugs were making Bertha confused, decided to play along rather than cause her distress. 'I didn't see her, but I hope so. And I'm sure she knows you miss her, but she'll want you to have a good sleep and get better.' Cathy thought that sounded okay because it wasn't actually lying so her conscience was clear.

'It would have been different, all of it, if she'd been there. Me dad didn't know what to do when she went, and I was the only lass, so it fell to me to look after 'em all. Me brothers, five of 'em. I were only just thirteen. I did me best, but he were a hard man to please at best o'times so when Mam passed, it turned 'im to steel it did.'

Cathy had never heard Bertha speaking about her family like this and welcomed the opportunity to find out what made her tick. 'That must've been difficult for you, losing your mam and having to look after a family so young. I bet it made you grow up quickly but I'm sure they were glad that you were there for them.'

'Were they buggery. Selfish lot, all of 'em. Treated me like an unpaid skivvy, they did. Without a word o'thanks or kindness for owt. Wearing Mam's old clothes or second-hand stuff because he were too tight to buy me owt new. Still, made me feel close to her. Mam would've given 'em all a good hiding had she been there an' that's a fact. I'll bloody well tell her when she comes back, what they're like an' then she'll sort em out. Serves 'em right an' all.'

Even though Cathy hadn't been there she couldn't help agreeing. 'And so she should. I'd give them a piece of my mind too, if I could.'

It was then, that Bertha opened her eyes and seemed to be scrutinising Cathy before she spoke. 'Aye, I bet you would an' all, lass.'

And then, to Cathy's utter surprise Bertha did two things she'd never ever done before, in all the six years she'd known her. She smiled at Cathy and took her hand.

19

More than thirty minutes had passed since Bertha had gently held on to Cathy's hand, then gone back to sleep. Cathy had replaced the oxygen mask over Bertha's face and relaxed into the chair, her mind on overdrive.

To say she was stunned by the act of contact, let alone the snippet from the past, was an understatement and although she accepted that a stiff dose of morphine was likely responsible for the loosening of Bertha's tongue, Cathy welcomed it. So rather than heading home, with her free hand she'd extracted her phone and texted Alfie to say she'd stay a while longer.

Both her hands now enveloped Bertha's right, which was mottled with liver spots, the skin tissue thin enough to see the raised purple-blue veins beneath. Her fingernails were short and uneven, thick and yellowed. More than likely they had never seen a lick of nail polish, thought Cathy. She imagined the hours of work those hands had toiled as Bertha ran about after her dad and brothers while grieving her mother.

Had Bertha gone to school or did her dad make her stay home? Cathy tried to do the sums and worked out that Bertha's mum must have died in 1970 or '71, so maybe back then they weren't so strict about things like that.

And from what Annie had told her, Cathy knew that Bertha had met Jacob Walker at a farm and cattle auction and there were no prizes for guessing how Annie interpreted that scenario.

Yeah, Dad went to buy a tractor and came home with a prize cow!

Annie's sense of humour aside, the story went that Jacob was there looking for farm machinery and instead bagged himself an admirer and, not as Annie said, a prize cow. And despite the ten-year age gap – Bertha had just turned seventeen – it was love at first sight.

Cathy thought Bertha and Jacob's meeting was quite romantic, and their love story meant a young girl escaped a life of drudgery and an ungrateful family. Then a question pinged into her head. Why, knowing what it was like to be brought up in an unloving environment did Bertha perpetuate a similar one in her own home?

In contrast to Bertha's reaction to her own upbringing, Annie was hellbent on being the total opposite of her mother. It really didn't make sense. Unless Bertha was, as Annie said, *Just a wicked woman through and through.*

Bertha grimaced slightly as she shifted position and Cathy wasn't surprised when she opened her eyes. Her gaze roamed the ceiling as if to take bearings and then rested on Cathy. 'You're still 'ere then. 'As me mam been back?' Bertha's voice was raspy and laboured.

'No not yet but I'm keeping an eye out. Would you like a sip of water, or do you need the nurse?'

Bertha gave a tiny shake of the head. 'About what I said t'other day... about having babies... I need to explain while I think on... me bloody brain's like mush these days and I keep forgettin' stuff.'

Cathy was overcome by the urge to shut down any uncomfortable discussions and focus on good things so tried to avoid the subject of babies. 'You don't have to, it's fine. Let's just forget all about it and move on. There's no point dragging it up. It's in the past.'

The vice-like grip of Bertha's hand surprised Cathy as did the strength that had returned to her voice as she insisted. 'No, I must, because that's where it started, in the past. Made me like I am, and I've never told anyone the truth about it, not even my Jacob. Especially my Jacob.'

There are moments in life when you want to speak out in fear, smothering the possibility of hearing something you'll later wish you hadn't. Then an inner voice, instinct maybe, tells you to stay quiet. Which was why Cathy waited, almost dreading what she was about to hear.

Staring straight ahead, Bertha began. 'I loved my Jacob more than life itself. From the very first moment I saw him leaning over the fence at the auction, lost in his own world he was, gazing lovingly at a big rusty second-hand tractor. An' I thought, *I wish someone would look at me like that. Second-hand Bertha. And that they'd love me as much as I loved them.* Because that's what was missing from my life. Love.'

Cathy's breath hitched in her chest and the heart beneath her ribs broke a little bit more for young, motherless Bertha who seemed intent on getting it all out...

'I came to thinking I wasn't worthy of kindness, never mind love. An' I'd tried hard to make 'em be nice to me. I thought by cookin' an' cleanin' for 'em they'd appreciate me, and I'd be makin' Mam proud from up in heaven, but it wasn't enough. I knew, on me thirteenth birthday that they didn't care about me.

I weren't one of them. I was a lass and, in their opinion, the lowest on the ladder. Worth nowt an' that were that.'

When she closed her eyes again, Cathy thought Bertha was about to nod off so regardless of what she might hear asked, 'Why, what happened on your birthday?'

Bertha opened her eyes and took a moment before answering, as though she was turning the pages of her mind slowly, trying to find the place where she'd left off. And then she found it. 'We had a record player in the parlour and when the farm was quiet I'd go in there and play Mam's old albums but that year, I'd asked for one of my own.'

'What was it?' And even as she asked, Cathy already knew that whatever it was, Bertha hadn't got it for her birthday.

A sad smile played on Bertha's lips as she answered, '*The Donny Osmond Album*. I'd seen it in Woolworths and advertised on telly and it was all I wanted. I told Dad and Bill, my eldest brother, all of them knew. Instead I got a pound note left under the teapot on the kitchen table and a note that said *Happy Birthday*.'

While Cathy desperately scrabbled for something to say, Bertha's grip loosened and her jaw slackened in sleep. As once again silence descended, she was glad that Bertha slept and didn't embellish on what Cathy imagined to be a heart-breaking birthday morning scene in an empty kitchen, many years ago.

Instead they just held hands while time ticked by. Cathy's eyes were beginning to burn and her back and arms ached from sitting in an awkward position and she longed to stretch her legs. So when Rebecca appeared at the door with her faithful observation machine, which she trundled on squeaky wheels around to the other side of the bed, Cathy took the opportunity to stand.

'How's she been?' Rebecca asked.

Cathy rubbed tired eyes and replied, 'Surprisingly chatty. I think it must be the drugs because in all the years I've known her, I don't think she's ever spoken more than a sentence to me, and not much of that was exactly pleasant. But who knows, this might be the start of a new Bertha.'

Rebecca smiled as though she'd heard and seen it all before. 'Well if I were you, the next time she wakes up, tell her you have to go home because you look exhausted, or I can tell her if you prefer. She might sleep for hours now her meds have kicked in and you can always come back tomorrow if you want. Her obs are looking good and you can ring later on to check, if it makes you feel better.'

Cathy hesitated, then went for the truth. 'The thing is, I probably won't come back during the day. I've got a bit of a problem with busy places and noise, sirens especially, and the sight of the blue flashing lights. I only managed to visit tonight because it's quiet. This was quite a leap, and it's taken it out of me. I'm glad I came, though, because I got to speak to her, and it was important that I cleared the air.'

Rebecca tipped her head to one side and gave Cathy a knowing look. 'I suspect you've been through a trauma to feel like that and I understand, I really do.'

Relief flooded Cathy, just hearing that someone understood or was prepared to accept how she felt prompted a rare moment of honesty. 'I was there, at the arena when the bomb went off and after, I had a breakdown of sorts but I'm getting loads better than I was. It's about knowing my limits, I suppose.'

Rebecca had finished her task and was wheeling the machine towards the door and stopped to lay a hand on Cathy's arm as she passed. 'Anyone who was involved in that dreadful night will always bear the scars, love, and you're right. It's about knowing our limits.'

There was no need to ask questions because an unspoken message had passed between them before Rebecca continued.

'So, if you want to come back again, I'll be on duty for the next two nights and after that, I'll give my colleagues the nod, so they know the score. You're not in the way at all.'

'Okay, and thanks, Rebecca, for everything, you know, tonight... and getting it.'

This was answered with a wink and a gentle arm squeeze, then Rebecca and her squeaky observation machine were gone. Cathy checked her phone and presumed that Alfie had fallen asleep which was good but just in case, she sent a message explaining the situation.

She did intend taking Rebecca's advice though, and the next time Bertha woke, unless she was about to confess to some great crime, or spill a Walker family secret, she'd be heading home.

In the meantime, not wanting Bertha to wake up and wonder where Cathy was, she took up position by the bed and in a bold move, she gently folded her hand around Bertha's and waited quietly for signs that she was rousing.

Only minutes had passed before the patient opened her eyes and this time, seemed even groggier than earlier. It was clear to Cathy that Bertha really needed a proper uninterrupted sleep and her being there might be hindering that.

'Hello again, sleepyhead. I wanted to stay until you woke up so I could tell you I'm heading home soon, but I'll be back tomorrow night, if you want me to visit, that is.' Cathy tensed and waited to be rebuffed.

Pulling the oxygen mask from her face, Bertha implored, 'Will you bring me mam and Jacob with you, and make sure you feed the chickens. Don't let that fox get 'em. Bloody thing. If you see it shoot it.' Bertha shook Cathy's hand as if to make sure she got the message about the chickens that she always seemed to prefer to her family.

'I'll tell Alfie when I get back now, you go to sleep and get better soon. Okay?'

Bertha sighed and looked like she was going to nod off, then, her voice becoming laboured, 'It wasn't the kids' fault, you know... that I couldn't love 'em properly... but they ruined it all. No matter how hard I tried... 'twas impossible to forgive 'em. Still can't.'

Cathy tensed. 'Forgive them for what? I don't understand. I know you said you didn't want Annie and wished she wasn't...' it was even harder to say than it had been to hear, '...born. But I thought that was just you, well, being you. Trying to upset me and Annie, and you didn't mean it really.'

Bertha looked straight into Cathy's eyes as she spoke but unlike the previous day when they were cold and cruel, this time they looked not sad exactly, more resigned to an unavoidable truth. One she wasn't prepared to lie about, not for anyone. 'Oh I did mean it. Every word and I can't help it, either. Simple as that. None of you will ever understand and there's no point tryin' to explain. There's badness inside me, there must be. Sometimes it just all spills out like poison 'an I can't stop sayin' things to hurt them because it makes me feel better. P'raps I'm mad, too.'

'No, no. You're not bad or mad at all. You just had a tough start in life, Bertha, and it affected yo–'

Bertha halted Cathy's soothing with a sharp response, 'NO, you're not listening... I am bad. Like me da and me brothers. Black-hearted bastards all of us an' that's why I tried to stop it 'appenin... again.'

Cathy's brain couldn't compute so asked for help. 'What, happened? I don't understand.'

Bertha's breathing was becoming increasingly laboured, and there was a sheen to her forehead and Cathy was really scared that after feeling so guilty and going there to apologise, she might end up being the reason Bertha pegged it after all.

Yet despite her fatigue, and after shrugging off Cathy's hand as it stroked her arm, Bertha rallied. 'In the end I did it for Jacob because I loved him and 'avin bairns is a wife's duty they reckon, and I didn't want to disappoint 'im. Then, when they came along I hated sharing him with them... and I hated them because he loved 'em more than me. I gave 'im two strong sons an' that were enough, so there were no need for a useless lass like Ann. She were a mistake, like I said, and I couldn't stand her bein' the apple of her da's eyes. Simple as that.'

Cathy sucked in a breath, shocked by Bertha's brutal words. 'Oh Bertha, I'm sure Jacob loved all of his family the same and I think the way you were treated by your dad and brothers affected how you felt about having a daughter. Or maybe you had some kind of post-natal depression or trauma from the past because it sounds like something happened to...'

It was clear from the tut and shake of the head that the patient was becoming cranky. 'Don't start with all that namby-pamby stuff an' anyroad, it doesn't matter now because I can't change the past, or who I am... or their memories. Our Ann can't stand the sight of me, and vice-versa but I don't blame her. Our Albert feels the same... there's only Alfred left, and it won't be long before he throws in the towel, too.'

Cathy's lips wouldn't move, and for a second her brain pressed the pause button. All she could think was that the super-strength painkillers being pumped into Bertha's arm were the NHS version of a truth drug!

And in the meantime, Bertha was winding up the show. 'Anyway, you'd best go. No more talking. I'm tired and Mam'll be here soon. She said she'd read me a story and bring me slippers. Oh, an' don't forget about that fox. Blow its bloody brains out if it goes near me chickens.' And with that, before Cathy could say her slippers were by the side of the bed, Bertha closed her eyes and went to sleep.

After waiting a few moments, Cathy slowly retracted her

hand and stood in stunned silence, looking down on the peaceful woman snoring gently underneath the green hospital blanket.

She couldn't work out if Bertha was just under the influence of hallucinogenic drugs, or very, very weird. Or the most complex woman she'd ever met and badly damaged in some way. Or just plain nasty?

Then seeing it was almost 1am and she was almost too knackered to drive home, Cathy decided that right at that moment her priority was to get back safely. So she picked up her bag, and after a peck on the forehead, she said a whispered night-night to the lunatic in bed 5, and quietly crept from the room.

20

BERTHA

She kept her eyes closed until she heard the door click shut and once she was sure Cathy was gone, Bertha opened them and scanned the room. Realising it was empty, disappointment swallowed her when neither her mam nor Jacob was waiting by the bed.

Had they been there or was it a dream? It seemed so real earlier, and when her mam leant over to kiss her goodbye she'd caught the scent she always wore, lily of the valley. The soft wool of her cardigan had brushed Bertha's cheek as Mam had stroked her face when she told her to rest, promising to come back later. Mam wouldn't let her down, she just wouldn't.

She'd be patient and wait and then Jacob would be here too because Cathy was going to tell him to come, but there was something she wasn't remembering, about Jacob. No, it was gone. No, it was back, and she realised he'd be at the farm. That's why he wasn't there. Yes, that's what it was.

Still, she was glad Cathy had gone because while she'd been talking to the lass, Bertha was having trouble keeping her thoughts in order and kept getting muddled between past and present and knowing when to hold her tongue. And then, just as she'd had that thought, she heard it running away with itself. Saying things she'd never said before and to that bloody Cathy, of all people.

That was why she'd told her to go before the secret came out and then they'd find it and all hell would break loose. But at least Jacob never found out before he died, so that was good. Bertha's breath caught in her chest as the words in her head bounced around her skull.

Jacob had died.

He was gone and she was in charge. Her farm, her rules. Yes, she remembered now. Why was her head so fuzzy? Bertha turned it to the side and saw the clear bag hanging on the stand and the tube running all the way to the awful stingy thing in her hand. Drugs, now she understood. What had she done? How had she ended up here?

It was all too much to take in, being in hospital. Away from the farm, and she couldn't afford to be there too long because then they'd take control and start doing things their way and she was not having that!

But the pain in her ribs and arms and legs was bad and her face felt as though it'd been in three rounds with her punch-happy father. At least she knew one thing for damn sure. He was dead and buried and good riddance to him. And she was still free of her mean brothers, who'd taken the lot. She'd got nothing. Cut out of the will like an infection.

It was hard to breathe. At least now Cathy had gone she didn't have to keep taking the oxygen mask off to talk and spill her guts like one of her Christmas geese. Or maybe she should deprive herself of the oxygen that her lungs clearly required. Would that bring matters to a swift end? Probably not and anyway she needed to make her bloody mind up because she couldn't have it both ways. Stay alive or pop her clogs.

She was confused. Torn between the desire to leave and

leave them all to it. Then the obstinate side of her that wanted to stay until the bitter end because some poisonous part of her personality wouldn't let go. It was hard work being a bastard, and that was a fact. But then again, she did enjoy it and did it well. See. She was bad.

She also enjoyed the woozy feeling she got when whatever it was they were pumping into her got topped up and took hold, but that made her gabble on. No matter how much she'd wanted to tell Cathy to piss off home, she just couldn't stop bloody talking. *Just shut your gob, Bertha, and enjoy the ride,* she'd told herself, but it didn't work.

Worse, every time she opened her eyes, Sister Cathy Bride of Christ or whatever you called the scary nuns on that programme from the telly about midwives, was there. All agog, hovering and waiting to hear her confession. She hated that programme and switched it off as soon as it came on.

And then, through the fog of her drug-addled brain, Bertha wished she could get hold of that syringe the nurse brought in earlier and keep on pressing and pressing until she was released into a world where Mam and Jacob waited. That would be lovely.

Then she could cross over the fairy bridge into another realm, or was it a rainbow bridge, just past the pearly gates? If only she knew the way and now, she was sinking deeper and faster and all of what lay buried, the things she'd kept just for her, were swirling around in her brain.

She wanted to go back. But only so far, to when she met Jacob because that was the best bit, just the two of them, the happiest most wonderful time of her life.

21

BERTHA AND JACOB

1975

God, her dad would be so mad when he found out. Puce with rage at losing his skivvy and punch bag. But Bertha didn't care because she was in love. She was seventeen and she was leaving home. And there was nothing, absolutely sod all, that her dad or her brutish cocksure brothers could do about it. Nothing that was legal, anyway.

She'd worried for days that they might lock her in the loft or maybe the hay barn, but she knew Jacob would come eventually and kick three bales out of them or ring the coppers if they tried to stop her from going.

She didn't want any trouble though. Her eldest brother was a proper nobhead and thought he owned the village never mind the farm. As much as she'd like to see him get his head kicked in, being wily was the best bet.

That was why she was doing a flit, to save all the bother and at the same time, depriving the gossips down in Wetherby of something to yak about while they polished their steps and hung their knickers on the line.

Did you hear about that poor lass from up at Bradshaw's Farm? Buggered off and left her da and them brothers of hers to fend for 'emselves. Good on 'er I say.

Or maybe, *Makes you wonder what's gone on up there... I mean, all we 'ave is their word for it. Poor lass might be six foot under for all we know. Won't be first one who's gone missin' up on them moors an' she din't seem the type to do summat like that. Always shy she was, scared of her own shadow.*

Bertha didn't care what they thought of her or her family. All she cared about was getting away. Which was why breakfast had been the final trial to endure, and it had dragged on forever, eased only by the thought of Jacob. His face, lodged in her mind caused a bubble of happiness to tickle her tummy, turning to bile when the fear of being caught took hold.

Still, she'd pottered about like always, not attracting attention, fading into the background as she brought another pot of tea, made more toast, listened to their mindless chatter and ignored the breaking of wind and belching until they'd shoved down their eggs and bacon and left to start work on the farm. And as this entailed fixing walls on the far edge of their land after a most wonderfully powerful storm that had whipped across the moors, the coast was clear.

After keeping up appearances by taking away their plates and mugs, instead of washing the pots she'd left everything in the Belfast sink, swimming in cold water and grease. It was a tiny victory that preceded winning the whole battle and she'd enjoyed it immensely, her first taste of rebellion.

It had all been planned to perfection. It was perfection, the thought of her and Jacob and the life she would have with him.

'I promise to make things better, lass. We'll be a team, me and thee, and have a happy life away from here. Can't promise you diamonds and pearls, but I can promise I won't let anyone hurt you ever again. I swear it on my life.'

And Bertha had believed him.

It was market day which afforded her a perfect opportunity to head into town. Nobody would bat an eyelid as she wheeled the tartan shopper out of the yard and down the hill. It was part of her weekly role as unpaid housekeeper and probably the highlight of her week, going into town to stock up.

The only other time she'd been outside the farm boundary was when she'd been to the auction, a rare and unexpected errand because her dad had left his wallet on the table, and he'd rang and told her to fetch it. And what a marvellous day that had been because that's where she'd spotted Jacob.

As much as Bertha would have loved to spend all day swooning over their courtship, six months and four days of pure bliss, their increasingly urgent and passionate clandestine meetings seeming like torture when they said goodbye. As she counted down the minutes until she made her escape, Bertha decided it would be more productive to focus on the plan.

They couldn't risk Jacob picking her up from the farm, just in case one of her brothers had stayed behind. And even though Jacob would have preferred to do the gentlemanly thing and introduce himself to her father, shake his hand and ask for his permission to wed, Bertha knew only too well that her dad would make it difficult. He was a bitter, cruel man with a black heart and her brothers were cut from the same cloth.

It wasn't beyond the realms of fantasy that he'd take the shotgun down. It had been used for despatching many a living thing over the years and her dad was fond of blasting ramblers and their dogs who'd strayed onto their land. The man was a nutter, everyone said so. Jacob would be fair game and if her dad wasn't spoiling for a fight, one of her four brothers usually was. That's why her way was best.

Bertha would walk through the market, past the stalls and keep going until she reached the cricket club car park that was used by the stallholders once they'd unloaded their goods. Nobody would notice another farm truck amongst those that had transported a multitude of wares to Wetherby. Most of the village would be at the market so, fingers crossed, she could climb into Jacob's Land Rover unseen.

The thought of driving away conjured a glorious jumble of emotions that swung from happy hysteria to panic when a long-smothered memory resurfaced, reminding Bertha of another day when she set off to meet someone–

'NO! Jacob's not like that! He will be there. He said he'd wait all day if necessary. He *will* keep his promise and he *will* make me happy.'

There was only one more thing to do, and that was fetch from her room her belongings, which she was going to hide in her shopping trolley. As Bertha made her way upstairs for the last time, she ran the palm of her hand along the bumpy stone walls, knowing every ridge of plaster, remembering how many times she'd trudged upwards, bone weary or hurting from the bruises inflicted by her short-tempered dad.

It had to be better than this, a life with Jacob on his farm sixty miles away in Derbyshire. Far enough to avoid being recognised or found. Close enough to be rescued if it all went wrong – but that was a ridiculous notion because Bertha didn't see her family as her saviours. If it turned out she'd jumped from the frying pan into the fire, then she was doomed. No matter what, she was never coming back to Wetherby and even though the unknown filled her heart with fear, she would take her chances elsewhere if need be. Nothing could be worse than this.

Once in her room, from under her pillow, the bed already neatly made, Bertha slid out the note she'd written for her father saying she was eloping. No clues as to where or who with. No apologies for leaving them in the lurch with a week's worth of laundry and empty cupboards, no tea in the oven, the range unlit, just an empty chair at the corner of the kitchen table.

Next, Bertha opened the wardrobe door that held her meagre belongings in a Co-op carrier bag. She'd taken nothing of her mam's apart from the clothes her dad had said she could wear, even though she would have loved the gold wedding band that lay on the table by Mam's side of the bed. She didn't dare. Her dad would accuse her of thieving and tell anyone who'd listen. All Bertha was taking were her clothes and toiletries, and the framed photo of her mam.

And one more thing.

After placing the bag on the floor, Bertha knelt in front of the wardrobe and gathered her strength then, with trembling hands, carefully moved the blankets stacked there. She then prised the wooden base upwards to reveal a small brown battered leather suitcase. It was the type a child would use and as her mam used to tell her, had been a makeshift cot when Bertha was born.

Not expecting any more bairns, they'd given away the crib so when her mam had gone into labour with the 'time of life' baby that she didn't even know she was carrying, the suitcase did the job for a while. It was either that or a drawer.

Bertha hadn't seen it for over two years, ever since she'd hidden it there and tried to put it out of her mind. But it was impossible because every time she opened the door she knew. When she lay in bed at night it was feet away and its presence gave her nightmares. Had she known where else to hide it, without being seen, she'd have done so in an instant.

Instead she'd prayed hard that nobody would find it, which was why, she now had to make the decision. Leave it behind in the hope that one day the memory of its existence and what was inside would fade. Or take it with her. That way her secret would be safe always.

Bertha knew the answer. Leaving it wouldn't guarantee the end of the nightmares and she'd still be plagued by fear, wondering if her dad or anyone had decided to chuck the wardrobe out. She was sure one of her brothers would move straight into her room once they realised she was gone.

That left her with no other option because just like on the day she'd hidden it, the terror of what she'd done, and gone through and what might happen to her was too much to bear. As was the shame.

Lifting the zipped suitcase from its hiding place, the two straps still firmly held by brass buckles, Bertha placed it next to the bag and then set about returning the inside of the wardrobe to how it was. Picking up the three items, Bertha took one last look around the bedroom and leaving the door wide open, made her way downstairs. After propping the note against the cold teapot on the crumb-streaked table, she stuffed the case and the bag inside the shopping trolley, took her coat off the peg then slammed the kitchen door shut.

Without a backwards glance, saying a silent goodbye to her old life, Bertha went to meet Jacob.

22

CATHY

So much for flaming June. Rain. That's all they'd had for the past week. Proper deluges that were topping up the reservoirs nicely but leaving huge puddles in front of Blacksheep Farm. Filling the craters that dotted the farmyard was another job that never got done due to lack of funds and motivation.

Cathy couldn't sleep, so while Alfie had a lie-in, from the kitchen window she'd watched the sunrise emerging from a murky horizon, the sky exploring a colour palette of sludge greys through to grimy white. Skip hadn't been impressed by her early-morning appearance nor by having to go for a wee in the rain. But after Cathy had towelled him dry and made him a bowl of warm tea – one of their secret treats – he'd nodded off in his bed.

It was too early to go up and check on Bertha who, after a ten-day stay in hospital to fight off a nasty bout of pneumonia, had been allowed home and was once again installed at Shepherd's. To Cathy's disappointment, when she'd made her nightly treks to visit Bertha, there hadn't been a repeat appearance of the chatty version. And as the days went by and her health improved, she gradually returned to the grouch they knew so well.

Annie didn't venture to the hospital, once she knew Bertha was going to recover. The bitterness over their row was still raw. Instead Cathy and Alfie took it in turns to visit and both were relieved when Bertha was discharged, simply because the to-ing and fro-ing took its toll, as did trying to make conversation with a borderline psychopath. The nurses probably cheered when Bertha left the building.

It had been a performance though, because they wouldn't release her without making sure she had adequate care and accommodation when she got home. Once that was sorted, there'd been plenty of visits from the district nurse and other health carers, giving her physio for her bad legs and bringing equipment to aid her independent living, like a wheeled frame which she hated, and point-blank refused to use. Cathy, however, was glad of their help because while Bertha was complaining to the carers or about them, it took the heat off her.

One thing that had caused ructions was the doctor's serious warning about the state of Bertha's health, predominantly the clogged arteries in her heart and neck, and her tar-lined lungs. The doctor had pointedly told them that for a sixty-six-year-old, Bertha was in bad shape and if she didn't take matters in hand now, she was a stroke or heart attack waiting to happen. They'd given her a prescription for a new regime of preventative medication and nicotine patches and told her to quit smoking immediately. But Cathy and Alfie were convinced that would never happen.

And they were right, so while Bertha did as she pleased and harangued whichever unfortunate person stepped through the door at Shepherd's, they rumbled on as best they could.

Gripping her steaming mug, as the rain battered the glass Cathy traced the rivulets of rainwater that trickled along the crevices between the cobblestones at the front of the house, laid by Walker hands in the nineteenth century, 1826 to be precise, almost 200 years ago. The tiny streams found their way onto the mismatched section of yard that was earth and concrete, and the odd splodge of tarmac added in the twenty-first century. A veritable patchwork of make-do-and mending after tractors and farm vehicles had trundled back and forth day after day.

Cathy could feel a shroud of melancholy wrapping itself around her shoulders, remembering fondly her first couple of years at Blacksheep, when the farm was a hive of activity. Back then, as they battled to keep afloat after Brexit, the Walkers had made alternative plans to bring in extra income.

There was the holiday letting planned for the renovated Shepherd's Cottage. And there were plans for Annie's goat herd, a dairy and a farm shop. Cathy was to have been her assistant, so there was an entrepreneurial buzz about the farm as the younger Walkers brainstormed ideas, determined to make the future bright.

Cathy had joined in, too, voicing her ideas about beekeeping and producing honey which they could sell in Annie's farm shop. The moor heather provided a perfect feeding ground as did the crops grown on the surrounding farms such as oilseed rape and winter beans, plus an abundance of sycamore and hawthorn blossom, clover, lime trees and wild flora in the hedgerows.

There was something magical about the power of bees, Cathy was sure of it. Practicalities aside, like the fact that a third of the world's food production relies on them, it was their spiritual significance that made Cathy's senses prickle. In some ancient cultures, they were spirit messengers, the link from this world to the afterworld. And it's said their honey has the power to heal and bestow wisdom and fertility.

But even more special, the bee was the symbol adopted by

the city of Manchester in the 1800s, around the same time Blacksheep was being built. While the Walkers grafted on the land and their home, below them, in factories, on the smoky streets, canals and railroads, the industrial revolution was powering ahead. The bee motif reflected the notion of hard work and enterprise, resilience and the city being a hive of activity.

And then, the thing that resonated with every cell in Cathy's body, was that after the arena attack, the bee became a unifying emblem of solidarity and resilience in the face of tragedy, representing the city's spirit and determination to stand together in the aftermath of a dark day in its history.

For Cathy, the sense of connection was tangible and undeniable, perhaps spiritual, and it made her all the more determined that one day, she'd bring worker bees to live at Blacksheep, high on the hills above the city she once called home.

To top it all, Jacob had promised that if the holiday cottage and dairy started to make a profit, Annie and Joe could convert the far barn into a home, and then all of the Walkers could work and live on the farm, just like he'd always wanted.

Bertha, however, simply watched and listened and waited.

Cathy contributed to the household from the profit she made on her rented-out apartment, but still, in return for her safe haven, and desperate to show Jacob and Bertha she was grateful and willing, Cathy was up with the lark every morning, ready to muck in wherever she was needed.

Jacob was glad of the extra hands especially during the winter when they had to bring the flock down. She'd done her shift scouring the fields for lost sheep, helped when they scanned the ewes and marked their fleeces to show how many lambs they were carrying. Then through lambing, which for Cathy was the most wondrous part of all, she did her time in the sheds, ensuring the ewes gave birth safely. She loved seeing new life enter the world. A world that was so different to the one she had known and come to loathe.

It was a whole new lifestyle, a recurring cycle of long days and hard, outdoor work. Of caring for the land so that the flock had the best grazing conditions. And providing shelter and food in the colder months, and helping hands when their lambs arrived.

The months between January and March tested everyone because they were dark and grey, and bitter temperatures brought sleeting rain and heavy snow. Yet even though she collapsed into bed most nights, longing for spring and summer, she thrived on it all.

Working by Alfie's side, their love for one another grew stronger by the day, her respect for him knew no bounds as did her gratitude for the way he had saved her from the dark recesses of her mind.

In those days, Bertha recognised Jacob as the head of the family. And she behaved as if his final word was just that – but in her own subtle and conniving way, she was the one who controlled everything that went on at the farm.

Looking out towards the peaks obscured by heavy grey clouds that promised thunder, Cathy sighed, recalling the tiny breakthroughs she'd made back then with Bertha. Ones she'd hoped would develop into a friendship of sorts. Cathy had stupidly taken them as a prize, like being allowed to cook some family evening meals, no mean feat in another woman's kitchen. But she had soon realised that Bertha just fancied a few nights off.

Being the new arrival, a female one at that, Cathy made sure not to tread on Bertha's toes, watching and learning. All families have their faults and ups and downs and for the most part in between Albert and Bertha going head-to-head now and then, they'd muddled along, the five of them. In the evenings Jacob would go for a couple of pints down in the village with his farmer pals, or he and Bertha would sit in the parlour and listen to records, she with her gin and orange, him with a bottle of ale.

Cathy and the lads would remain in the kitchen chatting or watching television, unless Albie and Alfie snuck off to the farm office to 'bugger about on that PlayStation thing,' as Jacob would say. And on those nights Cathy would sit in front of the open fire in the kitchen and read, with Skip sprawled at her feet warming his belly. How she longed for those days once more.

It was that number, five, that brought with it a wave of sadness because now there were only three. Her, Alfie and just up the lane, Bertha. Cathy missed Albie like mad. He'd quickly become a friend and she'd understood instantly why everyone loved to be around him.

The funny brother, the joker of the family who talked constantly at the table while they ate, annoying Bertha who thought mealtimes should pass in quiet appreciation of the food she'd slaved over.

It might have worked when they were little but the days when Albie did as Bertha said were long gone.

Worldly wise, he wasn't shy of speaking his mind on whatever was on it, including politics – his left-wing beliefs in particular – Brexit, rugby and his favourite subject, 'them poncy pen-pushing bastards down in London at the Ministry of Agriculture.'

The brothers were similar in appearance, both six footers, with dark curls, broad shoulders and the strength of oxen, but in contrast to the bearded Alfie, Albie was clean-shaven and trim thanks to the gym he'd set up in the tractor shed. Hence why down at the Labour Club, he was a magnet for the ladies of the village who vied for the attention of the senior, eligible Walker son.

Not that it got them anywhere and he had a well-earned reputation for playing hard to get. Only Cathy, Alfie, Annie and Joe knew why. Even Dave and Sheena were in the dark because Dave had loose lips when he'd had a few, so it wasn't worth the risk.

Her Alfie was, as her mum would say, the cuddly one. Shy but not reclusive, just more private, introspective and focused on the farm, and luckily for Cathy, not so popular with said ladies of the village. So he hadn't been snapped up by someone who fancied being a farmer's wife. He'd been totally in thrall of his elder brother and still was, albeit from a distance.

Despondent at the loss of happy days gone by, as a bolt of ice-white lightning split the sky Cathy turned away from the incoming thunderstorm and made her way to the kettle. After flicking it on she went to take milk from the fridge, smiling at the photo of the three of them that was fixed under a magnet.

She knew exactly when it was taken. Thursday October 10th, 2019. Albie's birthday. Eleven days before Jacob died. Five months before the first lockdown. Two years before Bertha pulled the plug and Albie left them.

The photo showed Cathy in the middle of the brothers, holding the cake she'd made for the birthday boy. They were sitting on the bench in the yard and Jacob had taken the photo. It had been a lovely day. Annie, pregnant with Eliza at the time, had been there with Joe after another truce had been silently declared between mother and daughter. None of them knew it would be the last time they'd be together as a family, or what was on the horizon.

Changes. For them, the farm and the whole world.

23

Touching the photograph, her finger lingering on the faces of Alfie and Albie, Cathy made a silent wish that one day they'd be reunited there at the farm. And that all those plans they'd made as they sat around the fire pit outside the big barn, drinking beer long into the night, watching the star-show above, would one day be fulfilled.

Taking her drink over to the table, Cathy jumped as a crack of lightning lit the sky, and as her heartbeat returned to normal and thunder rumbled over the peaks, she tried to quell the anger that swelled inside. It was always the same, whenever she thought of those dreadful years after Jacob passed, and the havoc Bertha wreaked.

Throughout Covid, the brothers did what they'd been trained to do, and promised their dad. They kept the farm going and looked after their mam no matter how undeserving she was. Cathy also threw herself into farm work and took forced isolation in her stride. After all, that's what Blacksheep gave her – a haven where she could hide from the ills of the world and Covid was just another of them.

Seizing her opportunity, Bertha had already decamped to

Shepherd's Cottage, and in truth, nobody missed having her at the farmhouse and her absence meant that Annie, Joe and Eliza could join their bubble. A lighter atmosphere descended and for the first time in many years, the Walker siblings felt truly at home, free from Bertha's oppression.

Really though, they were kidding themselves because away from the curry nights around the kitchen table, they all knew that Bertha was standing in the way of much-needed revenue.

Which was why once the worst of Covid was over, and they could breathe again, like the rest of the world and every industry in it, the Walkers were playing catch-up. On the back of Brexit and EU regulations, exorbitant tariffs, dwindling wool and livestock prices, eye-watering costs of feed, never mind day-to-day living, Blacksheep and many other farms struggled, incurring loss after loss.

And then on a day very similar to this, as a thunderstorm raged outside, Bertha called a family meeting that sent shockwaves through them all. It was the most dreadful day. Memories of the moment Bertha told them what she'd done, the stomach-rolling, heart-lurching impact of it still travelled through time to reverberate around the kitchen, slamming into Cathy's body.

The words Bertha had used, to maim and hurt, to squash hopes and dreams, trample underfoot thousands of hours of hard work, tearing loyalty to shreds as once and for all she established herself as the head of the family. The holder of purse strings and master puppeteer. That scene could never be erased from any of their minds.

In a deal she'd brokered without anyone's knowledge, swearing the other party to utmost secrecy until the transaction was complete, Bertha had sold the flock at a knock-down price to a farming competitor and in one fell swoop, broke her children's hearts. Cathy's stomach had turned and so must have

Jacob in his grave. Annie sobbed, Alfie held his head in his hands and Albie, well, he just went mad.

Recognising the signs of an encroaching panic attack, Cathy had put her coping mechanism into practice and focused on what she could see and not her breathing that she swore was about to pack in.

The news was delivered by a standing Bertha, from her old place at one end of the long kitchen table that within seconds of hearing the words, seemed to have shrunk. Just like the walls of the room were closing in. Cathy had frantically scanned the faces of those told to sit. And they had, like obedient children, and this made her want to weep at the bitter, pathetic and cruel irony of it. Four adults bending to the will of a woman who they'd stupidly trusted, and dared hope that the meeting she'd called would be for a good reason. Fools.

I can see a wall clock. I can see the fridge. I can see the windows that need a good clean. I see Alfie. Oh God, poor Alfie.

Instinctively Cathy reached to her side and gripped his arm, the need to be strong for him outweighed and diverted her trauma. But when Albie, seated directly opposite, stood so abruptly that his chair flipped backwards onto the kitchen tiles, the noise of it and his two fists hammering into the pine table setting Skip off in a barking frenzy, she knew the worst was yet to come. And it did.

'NO! No you haven't. You're lying. Mam, tell me you haven't. Why the hell would you do that? No way. I don't believe you.' Albie was leaning on the table and Cathy was sure it was holding him up because his face was ashen, and he looked like he was going to pass out.

Calmly, in response to his question Bertha had pulled an envelope from her cardigan pocket and on the front she saw the gold recorded delivery sticker. Cathy gasped, remembering the post van shooting in and out of the yard earlier that day bringing what she now recognised as a death knell.

'There you go. The bill of sale. Money's already in the bank an' if you don't believe me, you can ring the solicitor and the accountant. Either ways, the flock's gone an' that's that.'

Alfie remained silent and Cathy kept her hand exactly where it was, because beneath her palm she could feel his body trembling, as was hers. While Albie grabbed the envelope and tore out the bill of sale, Annie, between sobs, spoke next.

'But Mam, why? Do you realise what you've done? The flock *was* Blacksheep Farm, its livelihood, hundreds of years of family history, our future and now you've taken it away. What the hell is wrong with you?' Annie's voice cracked, preventing her from saying more.

Bertha merely rolled her eyes then harumphed before she answered, *her* voice not betraying an ounce of compassion or regret. 'Because it's a lost cause, and someone round here needs to step up and make a decision, that's why. I'm not shelling out for feed and vet's bills and wages when there's nowt coming in. We've been scraping through for years and enough's enough. I told yer dad many a time he should have called it a day, retired and put his feet up, but did he listen? Well now it's my turn to make some decisions and after I saw the books...'

Albie leapt in. 'What, you've been to the accountants and checked? Since when have you ever been there in your life? That's my job and he has no right going behind my back. I keep the books and they're all balanced and in order. All he's there for is sorting the VAT and the tax out at the end of the year.'

Cathy winced at that comment, pre-empting the retort that Albie had just fed his mother.

'Oh yes, you're right there an' all. Been your job to manage the finances and the minute your dad's in the ground you've let it all go to pot and just so we are clear, I have *every* right and don't you forget it. This farm belongs to me an' you three will have to wait till I join your father before you get your hands on it. Then you can do what you want. Until then, I'm in charge.'

A hush descended and the only sound was that of the envelope and bill of sale landing on the table, then Albie began to pace. Back and forth with his hands on his head, like he was going insane or trying to stop his brain from exploding.

It was then that Alfie chose to speak. Lifting his head, he bravely met Bertha's contemptuous gaze. 'So what are we supposed to do now, to earn a living? We can't rent out the cottage because you're in it. We have no flock, and the only other thing we were banking on was Annie's dairy, which I already know you're going to put the mockers on, am I right?'

Cathy's attention was drawn away from Alfie into whom she willed calm and strength. After a quick glance at a pale-faced Annie, Cathy focused on Bertha, who preceding her response, allowed herself the hint of a smile.

'Looks like you and your brother are going to have to stand on your own two feet and get another job. Maybe one of the other farms will take you on but, seein' as you're family and out of the goodness of my heart, I won't charge you rent for living here. So long as you pay the bills and keep the house and land maintained. I think that's a fair swap.'

'Jesus Christ, have you heard yourself?' That came from Albie, who was still pacing as Annie blew her nose and wiped her eyes before asking a question of her own.

In a voice that sounded stronger than she looked she pinned her mother with a stare and a question. 'You haven't answered Alfie's question about the dairy, not that I really need to hear it. But go on, do your worst, Mother. Are you putting the mockers on that, too?'

'Pfh. Well that's always been a bloody daft idea. Oh and what was it after that... oh yes, llamas so you can sell the wool, or was it alpacas? Bloody ridiculous an' I told your dad as much. But my Jacob always felt he had to be fair, not show favouritism to the lads which was the only reason he agreed. And that's why I'm sticking to my guns and sayin' it's a no-go. I'm not pouring farm money into a pie-in-the-sky venture, so well done, you are both correct.'

'GET OUT!' Albie's command bounced off every wall in the kitchen, setting Skip off again, and even Bertha looked shocked, but she rallied, sticking out her chest, shoulders back, ready for a fight.

Albie was visibly shaking, his eyes wild as he repeated his command but this time his voice was a low growl. 'Get out now before I throw you out, you bitter, twisted freak, do you hear me, GO!' In temper he swept his arm across the table, swiping the bill of sale and the wooden salt and pepper pot at the same time, sending them crashing to the floor.

Cathy had the most bizarre thought, that it was a good job they weren't made of glass, otherwise they'd all have to throw salt over their shoulder to ward off evil, which meant dousing Bertha in the stuff, too.

And as Albie took three steps forwards, noses almost touching in a surreal mother and son stand-off, Cathy couldn't bear it any longer and leapt to her feet, grabbed Bertha by the arm and pulled her away from Albie. One more word would have ignited the pilot light and in the mood Albie was in, both of them were in, she really feared blood would be spilt.

'Bertha, you need to go so everyone can calm down,' Cathy held tightly to her arm and guided Bertha to the door, opening it with her free hand and as if on cue, a bolt of lightning lit up the sky while cold February rain poured through the gap. It was a scene from a gothic novel where the Machiavellian landlord turned up at the door to do his worst but on this occasion, theirs was being given the boot.

Maybe, realising she'd taken things as far as she could and having said her piece, Bertha tutted and shook her arm free. As Annie sobbed and Alfie wrapped her in a hug, Albie folded his arms and turned his back on Bertha who silently obeyed and stepped outside.

To Cathy's relief, and without a final sarcastic retort Bertha began walking towards the cottage but after a few paces stopped and turned. Expecting to get her marching orders, because that would have stuck the knife in Alfie one more time, Cathy waited.

'Oh, an' I've been thinking. Can't see you goin' anywhere fast, so I'll let you keep the chickens your so fond of. Give you summat to do, I s'pose. So long as you bring me a box of six up once a week. If you don't want 'em give me the nod and I'll come down and wring their necks. Your choice.' And with that she turned and disappeared up the lane.

In that moment, Cathy wished so hard that the oak tree would get struck by lightning and squash Bertha and every wicked bone in her nasty poisonous body. That day, Cathy finally accepted that no matter how much you want them to, wishes don't come true.

24

Hearing footsteps overhead Cathy rallied and flicked the kettle on again, determined that whatever caused the awful mood that had consumed her morning wouldn't infect Alfie. And the best way to make her man smile was with a cooked breakfast. As she pulled bacon and sausages from the fridge, she couldn't help but remember the teasing she'd got from Albie about being a vegetarian living on a sheep farm.

It had been a lot to take in, she admitted that; but the benefits of living and working with Alfie outweighed the negatives when her conscience whispered in her ear now and then.

Bertha was especially vocal on the subject but her sniping only toughened Cathy up. That was why she'd made a point of not shying away from preparing or cooking meat. Telling herself there must be loads of vegetarian chefs working in restaurants all over the world, helped immensely. She did make herself scarce though, whenever the truck came to take the lambs to the abattoir.

As she lifted the frying pan from the hook, Cathy couldn't erase from her mind the list of Bertha's barbed comments that she'd accumulated over the years and thanks to a Zoom call with Albie the previous evening, a memory of a particular comment was pecking her head more than others. It was the reason she couldn't sleep that morning. It came just after Albie had left and had hurt Cathy all the more, because it was true.

Unable to reconcile himself to working on with a neighbour's livestock when he'd had his own stolen from under him, Albie had wanted a fresh start somewhere he didn't feel everyone was sniggering behind his back. Nor could he stand the sight of his mother and had vowed never to speak to her again. Which was why he'd made the bold move to seek work overseas.

'And you could come with me,' he'd said to Alfie and Cathy.

Cathy's head swam at the mere thought of leaving the sanctuary of the farm and her head snapped in the direction of Alfie, her breath hitched and held, waiting for him to answer. But she shouldn't have worried.

There were only two things stopping Alfie from saying yes to his brother's proposal. The first was Bertha, because she'd played the sympathy card, saying she needed him to stay and maintain Blacksheep. She also had another ace up her sleeve, saying that after careful consideration she'd pay him a minimal wage to do so.

The second reason was Cathy, who was so crippled by anxiety and fear of the outside world that Alfie knew he couldn't ask her to go. And no way would he leave her behind to wait for him at the farm or, see her go back to the city and her apartment. The guilt was immense and Bertha, as an expert head-worker, had capitalised on it.

Cathy had been feeding the chickens when Bertha appeared from bloody nowhere. Her words sounded in Cathy's memory as if it were yesterday. 'I hear Albert's off on his travels any day.'

Cathy had ignored her and continued in her task.

'Alfred says he asked you two to go, as well. Is that right?'

'Yes, that's right but I heard that you persuaded him not to, seeing as you're basically an invalid these days and can barely put one foot in front of another. What was it you said? *Almost knocking on death's door,* is that right?' Cathy couldn't help the sarcasm that dripped out because it masked the feelings of guilt she harboured at her own incapacity.

'Hmm, well I 'eard *you're* the reason Alfred 'as to stay here. Like I said to Alfred, it's not my fault you've got mental problems and can't even manage going to the supermarket. So seein' as he 'as to babysit you, he might as well be useful round here. At least you 'aven't tried to trap him with a bairn like most lasses do. I reckon you being doo-lally is the least of his worries. Right, I'll be off then. Oh, and don't forget me eggs in the morning.'

Cathy hadn't even looked at Bertha or acknowledged her farewell because she knew the old woman was smirking. But whether the conversation with Alfie had really taken place or whether it was a figment of Bertha's imagination, the words had stung, which was why she'd never asked Alfie about the truth of it. Instead, she'd vowed to prove Bertha wrong and, for Alfie's sake, find the courage to defeat her demons and set herself and him free from Blacksheep Farm.

The thunderous sound of Alfie coming downstairs almost eclipsed that of the storm raging outside and as he appeared in the kitchen, stopping to stroke sleepy Skip, the first rasher of bacon was sizzling in the pan.

'Morning, love.' Alfie kissed Cathy on the cheek as he did every day. 'Don't do me a big breakfast. I'm not that hungry, so I'll just have a sarnie and a brew.'

Not thinking much of it, Cathy added more bacon to the pan and put the sausages back in the fridge.

'You were up early again. Couldn't you sleep? I thought you'd be tired after our late-night chat with Albert. He looks well, doesn't he.' Alfie pottered about making drinks and generally getting in Cathy's way. 'Still no mention of him meeting a nice bloke or coming back, though, and I didn't want to bring it up, you know, put any pressure on him...'

When his voice faded into thought as he stirred sugar into his coffee, Cathy sought to fill the hole created by missing his brother *and* being trapped on a farm scraping a living with a semi-agoraphobic girlfriend.

'Well, the weather forecast says this storm is in for the day, so why don't we spend an hour or so sourcing some parts for the camper, and you can show me your holiday scrapbook and tell me where you're whisking me off to. And a bacon butty, of course.' Cathy bumped Alfie's hip and was relieved when he smiled back. But it was only a glimmer and while she flipped the bacon, he went back to wherever he'd been seconds earlier.

The breakfast things were cleared away and there was still no sign of Alfie showing her his scrapbook or looking for parts. He said he'd already looked on eBay and everything was out of their price range for now. And before she'd even suggested it, he'd put his foot down and said they weren't using any of what had now become the 'rainy day emergency pot' her parents had given her.

Looking outside at the continuing deluge, Cathy pointed out, if only to herself, that it was in fact pissing down and Alfie's increasingly miserable mood swings made her feel quite desperate. In her book, that counted as an emergency.

He'd never been like this before: prone to quiet moments where she felt like he was out of reach, or hyper moments when he was making lists of things to do around the farm as though there was no tomorrow. And all those nights where he tossed and turned, then in the morning slept until noon.

From her observation post by the sink she watched him flick through his Facebook feed, a frown on his face and only the occasional weak smile. Giving it one more go, Cathy tried to engage him in conversation. 'So, I was thinking I'd have another go at tracking down the man who painted the portraits. What do you think? I keep meaning to do it, so seeing as I'll be stuck in all day, I may as well get my Miss Marple on.'

At first Alfie didn't respond, as though her words were floating in slow motion across the room. But eventually he looked up and said, 'Yeah, that's fine, love, whatever you want. I'm going to go and check on misery guts, then I'll watch telly for a bit. I'll go up the barn later and do some work on that Mini, see how it goes. Once that's finished we can flog it and buy the parts we need for the camper.'

Cathy just nodded and busied herself wiping down the worktops, watching through the corner of her eye as he performed his morning ritual. Seated before the unlit fire, he scratched Skip's ears in between fastening up his work boots and then shrugged on his waterproof. Then with a 'See you in a bit' and without a kiss or a wave, Alfie went into the storm.

It was speaking to Albie that had done it, she was sure. Hearing about the farm where he was working and the shared house in the town where he and three other labourers lived, the nights out and the weekends by the beach, the laughter and lightness in Albie's voice was in stark contrast to everything Alfie knew and was. Admitting that was like a punch in the gut for herself, so she had no idea how it felt for Alfie.

Determined to shake off the mood that was sticking to her like treacle, Cathy went to the dresser, yanked open the door so forcefully that it pinged against its hinges and startled Skip who gave a grumbly growl. She extracted the paintings in their tube and took care to close the door quietly afterwards. After spreading them on the table, she went back to the dresser drawer for the laptop and her notebook and sat down to search for Guy Alexander.

Looking closely at the portraits again, she made a list of each, in date order, noting their names – always written on the bottom left, in pencil, with the date underneath. The photographs were attached with a small piece of yellowed masking tape to the top right corner and Cathy thought this was sweet and old-fashioned, not using a staple or a paper clip, just the tools of the artist's trade. Flipping the photos over, she double-checked there wasn't any other information scribbled on the back – but each one was blank.

The only other clue was the signature on the bottom right-hand side, which she was confident read, *Guy Alexander* mainly because it matched the name on the camper van logbook so at least she was on the right track.

The list of names began with the blonde beauty Krystle in 1970. Then Deborah in 1979, with her straight dark hair flowing over her left shoulder. Next was another blonde, Miriam in 1983. After her, Guy had chosen a strawberry blonde – her name was Linda – dated 1988. And finally, Allison in 1992, a bobbed brunette.

They all had two things in common, though. The first was the way they looked straight into the lens of the camera at a man Cathy was sure they loved. Their eyes gazed into his soul whilst baring theirs, giving themselves totally to the artist who had immortalised them in watercolour.

Cathy mused that art in any form was supposed to speak to the voyeur and that's what these did, every time she looked at them.

The second thing the portraits had in common was that the women were all very beautiful, which made Cathy wonder if the artist was, too. What did Guy look like then, in 1970 as Krystle posed for the camera, and now? And then it occurred to Cathy that he may even be dead. Had a wife or a descendant sold the camper to pay debts? After doing her sums, presuming he would have been at least eighteen when he bought the van new, she estimated that Guy would be around seventy-four.

These thoughts spurred Cathy into action because time was of the essence, and the last thing she wanted was to track him down and find out she was too late to return his paintings.

Her previous scan of social media had produced zero results so Cathy decided to start with the address on the logbook. And if all else failed, she'd write a letter and do things the old-fashioned way. Flipping open the laptop, with the storm outside as an auditory backdrop and sleepy Skip for company, Cathy commenced her search.

Three-quarters of an hour later, after refusing to pay Yell.com for access to their stash of phone numbers and other assorted personal information, she'd resorted to Google Street maps and frustratingly, after going up and down what looked like a B-road that narrowed off to a single track, finishing at a gated wooded area, Cathy had drawn a blank.

The only property along that road that resembled the address on the logbook was a boutique hotel by the name of Orchard House so with nothing else to go off, she phoned their front desk. When someone picked up, Cathy's heart flipped.

Tapping her pen nervously, she explained why she was calling. The receptionist, Gail, sounded professional and polite and thankfully, was the chatty type. In her broad accent, she soon cleared up the mystery of the hotel's name.

'Agh, what it is, you see, this used to be the main house and was owned by the Alexander family back in the day. In fact, it's been here for a few hundred years, however,' – at this juncture Gail's voice lowered considerably – 'the last in the line got himself into... shall we say, a spot of bother financially and had to sell Orchard House to get himself out of a fix. Was the talk of the village a few years back.'

At this Cathy nodded, because it tied in with the camper van being sold at auction. 'Yes, that makes sense because that's how we came by the property I'd like to return to Mr Alexander. So if he's moved away, I don't suppose you have a forwarding address, do you? I was confused as the logbook does say he lives at Orchard House.'

Again, Gail was happy to fill in the blanks. 'Oh yes, that's the right address but maybe Mr Alexander never got round to changing it on the logbook? Lucky for you I know exactly where he lives.'

'Really? That's great. Where?' Cathy was smiling like a fool and already congratulating herself on her magnificent detective skills.

'Him and his wife, Cressida, live just down the road in what used to be the gamekeeper's lodge. Between you and me, that's a bit of a fancy name for it, because it's actually a small cottage. When they sold the main house to the people who own this hotel, the Alexanders kept the lodge and the patch of woodland next to it and moved down there.'

'That's great news! Do you have a phone number by any chance, so I can give them a call? Or if you don't want to pass that on, you could have mine and ask them to ring me.'

'It's fine, I'm sure they'll be pleased to get their stuff back and yes, I have a landline number somewhere, for emergencies. Not that we see much of them mind. They keep themselves to themselves really and between you and me, she's a bit stuck up. Always fancied herself as lady of the manor and now she isn't, she doesn't like living in an old staff cottage. Now, let me find that number...'

The sound of rummaging filtered down the line as Gail

searched and as she did, Cathy couldn't resist asking, 'And what's he like, Mr Alexander?'

'Oh, he's a sweetie. Always passes the time of day. Bit of a charmer with a twinkle in his eye but nice with it. Eccentric I'd say, what's the word? Flamboyant, yes that's how I'd describe him. Like he's stepped out of an album cover from the seventies, you know, ageing hippy meets bonkers lord of the manor. Long grey hair tied in a ponytail and a whacky hat and floaty coat, that kind of thing. The village kids make fun of him, the little horrors. Ah, here it is. Do you have a pen?'

Cathy could picture Guy in her mind's eye. As the man Gail had described in the present and then, taking a trip in a time machine, rewinding back to 1970, meeting him as a beautiful young thing in the throes of true love, painting a blonde-haired beauty named Krystle.

Sitting up straight Cathy flicked the tip of her pen. 'Yep, got one, go ahead.'

Minutes later, after Gail had promised to pass on Cathy's number to the Alexanders in case she couldn't get through, they said their farewells and the second the call disconnected, Cathy re-dialled.

Energised and excited at the prospect of doing a good deed and reaping plenty of karmic energy as a reward, she pictured Guy's face morphing from flaxen-haired seventies rock-god to distinguished yet well-aged artist. Listening to the ringtone, hoping the snooty Mrs Alexander was out, Cathy waited impatiently for Guy to answer.

25

Stretching her hand over to Alfie's side of the bed, Cathy tapped the mattress trying to locate a warm body. But after a few seconds, she realised he wasn't there. Then her heart lurched, and she remembered why. Turning to check the bedside clock she read the display, 02.54.

The only light in the darkened room came from the moon that determinedly slipped through a crack in the curtains, just as Cathy liked it, casting a strip of silvery light onto the bed and towards the door.

Is that a sign? Telling me I need to be with Alfie and Skip, or should I leave them alone and give them this one last night together?

Before she even had chance to answer her own question warm tears filled her eyes as she went over the events of the previous day. They'd called the vet to check on Skip, who hadn't moved for hours, refused to eat and would only take water from a syringe.

After assuring Alfie that Skip wasn't in any pain but it was his time to go, the vet had made a gentle offer to put the old dog to sleep. Alfie flatly refused, and the three of them were left alone to say goodbye.

They'd sat together in front of the fire for hours, watching the rise and fall of Skip's chest and listening to the wheezy puffs of breath and by midnight, Alfie insisted Cathy went to bed. He, however, was staying firmly by Skip's side.

'He's been with me since I was a teenager, my best friend and confidante, he is. One of Sheba's pups. A cracking lass she was. Dad let me pick which pup I wanted, but Skip picked me because while the others suckled, he lifted his head and looked right at me. He was saying, *Pick me.* So just like I were there when he came into the world, I'll be there when he leaves it.'

Cathy knew all this but let him tell her again. Anyway, she couldn't speak. If she opened her mouth, all that would come out was a sob wrapped in heartbreak.

'He's always been by my side, you know. Would walk me to the Land Rover when I was going to school and be waiting by the gate when Dad brought me home. We roamed the fells for hours, just the two of us in rain or shine, snow, whatever. Got me over my first crush did Skip, listening while I wittered on about some lass who went to another school. Didn't even know her name, just used to see her at the bus stop in the village and I were too shy to say hello or owt. He was always there, no matter what, through the good and bad times. Never let me down or made me feel daft and always understood, like he could read my mind. So I owe him this.'

'I'll stay, keep you company. I don't want you to be alone when, you know...' Cathy couldn't say the words or even think about it. The look in Alfie's eyes was bad enough. The raw pain she saw there was unbearable.

'No, love. I'll be fine. Go get some rest. I'll call you if I need you, but I'd like some time alone with Skip, just me and him.' The crack in Alfie's voice splintered Cathy's heart.

Knowing when to take a hint, she was also relieved to turn her back on his pain and her fear of it, like the coward she was starting to feel she was.

And now, alone in the stuffy bedroom, instinct kicked in. Alfie and Skip had had plenty of time to reminisce and say goodbye. She needed to be there as well because she loved that dog, too. And she loved Alfie and wanted to say her goodbyes and be there for both of them.

Pushing back the duvet, she leapt to her feet and after shoving them into her slippers, tentatively made her way downstairs. As she reached the bottom step, her breath caught. She would remember the sight in the kitchen forever.

Alfie lay at Skip's side by the fire, his head resting against his snout, one hand laid on his paw, close as close could be. Seeing Cathy, he smiled.

'I couldn't stay upstairs, Alf. I had to check on you both, but I'll go back up if you prefer. As long as you're okay.'

'No, it's fine, love. He's sleeping and we've had a big chat, haven't we, mate. Talked about all our adventures and scrapes we got into, and he knows how much I'm going to miss him and that I'll never forget him. There'll only be one Skip and that's a fact.' Alfie gently stroked his faithful friend's head, eliciting the merest flicker of an eyelid.

Cathy swallowed and forced herself to be strong and for want of anything else to offer, opted for the practical. 'Shall I make us a brew, or do you think that'll disturb him?'

'A brew would be champion; thanks, love, and don't worry about noise. He's well away in the land of nod.'

Alfie stayed where he was and soon became lost in his own thoughts, so Cathy made her way to the kitchen and flicked on the kettle, forbidding herself to think of the times she'd made Skip a bowl of warm tea, or frothy milk in the winter, his very own doggy-ccino, and always saved him scraps which she'd sneak out of the fridge when they were alone. It was their little secret.

Skip had been such a comfort to her over the years, seeming to know when she was down and needing a nuzzle and a hug. His devotion to Alfie knew no bounds; and he'd been so gentle and patient with Annie's brood as they came along.

The course of the next few hours was inevitable, yet still Cathy wished it wasn't so. They were going to lose their precious friend and he'd take a piece of their hearts with him when he went. It was the worst pain and if it was killing her, she couldn't imagine how Alfie was feeling.

A flicker of latent memories reminded Cathy of the last time they'd said goodbye to someone dear. Jacob, Alfie's dad. But on that occasion it was at the funeral, because by the time they'd found him up on the fells, he was gone. No chance to say how much they loved him one more time and it had been the hardest thing for Alfie to come to terms with. That and not being there for his dad.

Plopping teabags into two mugs, she smiled at the thought of the gentle, rugged man she'd known for a short time because he passed away not quite two years after Alfie brought her to the farm. Jacob had been quite shy, really. Said his piece when he needed to, got on with the business of running the farm as he had since he was a young man, after stepping into his father's boots. Taking care of his family who he loved and the woman he clearly adored was priority. Cricket and the pub came second.

To that day it still amazed Cathy quite how much Jacob adored Bertha, seeing past her brusque ways, perhaps making excuses for her – or maybe he just wanted to keep the peace.

'Owt for a quiet life, lass,' he'd once said to her, as he winked across the kitchen table, both of them eating their tea in silence and staying out of the battle that raged by the stove as Alfred and his mother went head-to-head over something and nothing.

Jacob had been no match for Bertha, not really. He was a kind, honest, moral man while she was the opposite, deceitful and mean and manipulative. He'd been Alfie's hero, so he took it hard when he lost his dad and mentor. Then two years later, as the isolation and instability of Covid was fading into history and the world was getting back on its feet, Albert left, too. Not in a fancy black carriage pulled by four prancing horses, but in an Uber to the airport. And now Alfie was going to lose Skip.

Keep going and be brave, Cathy told herself. *He needs you to be strong more than ever, now. Do not let him down. He was there for you and now you need to be there for him, no matter how much it's hurting inside. Alfie comes first.*

Taking their drinks over to where he and Skip lay, Cathy placed them on the hearth and wished it was colder, because Skip loved the fire, but it was July and far too muggy and might make him uncomfortable. She knew right there and then that whenever she lit one in the future, she would always think of Skip and imagine him lying there warming his belly.

Taking a pillow from the armchair, she settled herself at the side of their beautiful collie, resting her head by his and inhaling the musky scent of his fur. On the other side of sleeping Skip lay Alfie, and as the sun rose between the peaks, they waited. The three of them together.

26

The house seemed too quiet without Alfie. Which was daft because she was used to him being up at the barn, or labouring at a neighbouring farm during the day, only nipping back for his dinner or a brew. Knowing he was only minutes away if she needed him always comforted her and now he was on his way to Amsterdam. Actually, he was in the airport lounge getting hammered, so he'd have the courage to get on the plane.

She could've throttled Dave when he'd suggested going on a three-day bender to Amsterdam but apparently his cousin who lived there had offered to put them up. All they needed was a cheap flight and beer money and seeing as everyone in their man-gang was permanently brassic, it actually worked out cheaper than staying in a hotel in York, or some other well-trod stag weekend destination.

Cathy had been watching Alfie like a hawk for the past couple of weeks because since Skip had left them, there had been another shift in Alfie's mood. As though he had taken a sideways step away from her, turning in on himself.

She was sure it began the day Skip died. She'd woken at

sunrise to find Alfie gone, their beloved dog lying beside her in eternal sleep, covered by his favourite blanket.

Cathy had found Alfie outside by the vegetable patch wall. Hands in pockets, looking ahead at the peaks, just as she had done that first morning at the farm. She'd stood beside him and gently laid her hand on his arm and instantly felt his muscles tense. It hurt but she'd brushed it aside, putting his welfare and feelings before hers.

'Alf, love. I'm so sorry.' She'd expected him to turn to her, so she could hold him and let him cry but instead he brushed away the tears on his sodden face and gave a reply that made her wince.

'I'd best go and dig a hole. Need my big shovel. I'll be back for him soon enough.' And then he turned and walked up towards the barn, his shoulders hunched and his gait slow.

She'd wanted to shout out, *Don't push me away, Alf, not now!* But the words wouldn't come and instead she turned and made her way back to the house to say her own goodbye to Skip.

They buried him under the elm tree in the far corner of the yard, with all the working dogs that had gone before him, plus a long line of cats and Daisy, Annie's rabbit, the one she swore Bertha had murdered.

It was only when they got back to the kitchen and Alf saw the empty spot by the fire that he finally broke down and allowed Cathy to comfort him and for that she was grateful, convincing herself that even though it would take time, Alf would slowly heal. But as the days went by, she noted a gradual change.

Alf was never shy of hard work and long hours and it shouldn't have come as a surprise that he was spending all day up at the barn, taking his mind off things and getting stuck into renovating the camper. The problem was, going by the state of the shell, stripped completely of its interior and sanded down to bare metal, the same as it had been for weeks, Cathy surmised Alfie wasn't actually doing any work.

A couple of times, when she'd nipped up to see if he needed anything, she'd found him sitting on one of the front seats that he'd stored against the wall, staring into space or fast asleep.

Mealtimes were becoming increasingly sombre affairs where she had one-sided conversations with Alfie. When he did deign to join in, she could tell he was forcing it, feigning interest in the latest anecdote about Annie's Eliza, or whatever upbeat story Cathy had heard on the news. She avoided doom and gloom like the plague.

Evenings had fallen into another pattern where after tea, Alfie would slope off to the parlour with a bottle of beer or three and listen to the soundtrack of him and Skip. The playlist he'd started when Skip was only a pup. Or, she wondered, was it him, Skip and Albie. The strains of one track seemed to pop up more than others, a song Cathy knew well. The Waterboys were one of Alfie's favourite bands and the lyrics to 'The Whole of the Moon' became an earworm.

Did they make him think of Albie? The comparison was clear. He was living his dream and had gone off to see the world while Alfie stayed at home, not exactly in his room but it probably felt like it. And the reason for that came down to one person. Bertha.

And then her heart had lurched when the sharp voice inside her head said, *And you.*

It had been an awful moment. A wake-up call really because it was true. The Covid years aside, when much to her delight (if that was even the right word) they'd had no option other than to stay put. But for the past two years they'd remained bound to the farm and the reason for that was simple. Her. Cathy.

She was the one who relished their splendid isolation from

where she micro-managed their lives. As they scrimped a living and plodded, Cathy wore her rose-tinted specs and orbited her own safe-space.

Selfish.

The voice was scathing, and Cathy inwardly shrank from the truth.

So when Dave announced his stag weekend venue, she'd sought to absolve herself of blame by letting Alfie off the leash. Wearing a fake smile and putting all of her niggles to one side, she had encouraged him to go on the trip.

Refusing to watch the imaginary newsreel that conjured up a plane plummeting into the North Sea, or a terrorist attack at the airport, or Alfie being hit by a tram in Amsterdam city. She'd always hated the ones in Manchester, that slid silently along the tracks and scared you half to death with their honking horns.

Those are your fears, so don't saddle Alfie with them. Just let him go and have some fun. He deserves a break from here and from Bertha and from you and your cloying neurosis.

Yes, that had stung, too, but the voice in her head had been on the money, lingering for months, long after the trip was suggested. It was also the reason the second it was booked; she'd transferred the flight money to Dave's bank account. Before she had a wobble and begged Alfie not to go. Instead she repeated a mantra to aid her resolve: *Alfie is going to Amsterdam. I will manage on my own for three days. Nothing bad will happen. The end.*

The kitchen clock told her she had time to kill before Sheena arrived. It also reminded her that mantras don't always work, and she'd failed at the first hurdle because for all her bravado, when the offer came of a sleepover and girlie night in, Cathy grabbed on like her life depended on it.

Sheena was currently in Asda, stuffing all the necessary feast ingredients into the trolley and once she arrived, they were going for a long hike over the tops to work up an appetite. The July weather had been glorious, and now as they nudged into August, the forecast predicted more of the same. It would be good to get some sun on their faces and as Sheena had said, 'We can burn off a shit-load of calories before we ram a million more down our gobs.'

Cathy loved Sheena's 'don't give a damn' outlook and it always buoyed her but then again, being a blonde-bombshell stick-insect who could eat her way through the cake counter and not put on a single ounce, or get one single spot, probably gave Sheena the edge on lovin' life.

Glancing at her notepad, Cathy decided to occupy the minutes by being pro-active and giving the elusive Mr and Mrs Alexander another try. It still baffled her that they relied solely on a landline – even Bertha had a mobile. It had become a bit of a thing for her, calling the number and hoping on the off-chance someone picked up.

Lifting her mobile, Cathy scrolled the list of recent calls and pressed the only one that didn't start with 07.

27

Cathy listened to the familiar ringing and wondered, not for the first time, why they didn't have voice messaging set up. But maybe that was all a bit too fandangle – as Bertha would say – for them. She imagined that miles away, in a hallway decorated in flowery flock wallpaper, an old-fashioned phone rang out. It rested on a dusty mahogany console beneath a gilt-edged mirror beside a wooden coat stand.

She was just about to disconnect when lo and behold, there was a momentary cessation of the rather annoying ringtone, and then, a female voice. Posh and stern. Hyacinth Bucket personified.

'Alexander residence.'

Cathy stifled a giggle, waiting for, 'lady of the house speaking,' but recovering quickly she replied, 'Oh, hello. My name's Cathy and I'm trying to get hold of Guy Alexander. Would that be your husband?'

There was a second or two of silence while the woman at the other end gathered her wits, and then came a question laced with suspicion and a hint of tedium. 'And why would you want to contact my husband? Does he owe you money because if he does then you're barking up the wrong tree. I can assure you of that.'

Buoyed by the confirmation that this was in fact Cressida, Guy's wife, Cathy sought to reassure. 'Oh, no, no. Nothing like that. What it is, we bought his campervan and there were some personal possessions inside that I'd like to return to him, that's if he'd like them back. I've been trying to get in touch for months.'

With this information in hand, Mrs Alexander's attention appeared to have been piqued. 'Well I've been away overseas visiting my sister, and who knows where Guy is from one day to the next. So, tell me. What possessions would they be, exactly?'

'Paintings, really lovely ones, actually. He's ever so talented. Which is why I'd like to return them but thought to check first, rather than put them in the post because if he doesn't want them back, I'd like to keep them.'

When she responded, the boredom and disappointment in Mrs Alexander's voice was impossible to miss. 'Is that all? Blasted paintings. I suppose they're his godawful landscapes. Beastly things.' Next came a loud harrumph before, 'Well in that case, I'll give you his mobile number and you can ask him yourself. Have you got a pen?'

Deciding not to mention that the paintings were of women, very beautiful ones at that, as it might not go down too well, Cathy grabbed her notebook and biro and replied, 'Yes, go ahead.'

It took mere seconds to jot it down and thank Mrs Snippy for the information. 'That's very kind of you. Thanks ever so much. I'll ring him now.'

'Well, best of luck with that. Goodbye.'

Cathy pictured the receiver of the dusty phone being slammed into its cradle and Mrs Alexander storming off down the hall to pour herself a sherry and hate on her husband who was obviously in the doghouse. Poor man.

Mrs Alexander sounded like a right tartar, but then again, going off the evidence, Guy had got them badly into debt so no wonder she was miffed. It also occurred to Cathy that had she said she'd found an antique watch, or some jewellery, Mrs Alexander would have been much more pleasant and probably have come and collected it herself. As it was, she didn't sound much like a fan of Guy's artistry, or even the man himself.

Hearing a car pull up outside, Cathy pushed thoughts of the paintings from her mind and made her way to the door to greet Sheena who was already unloading two huge bags from her younger brother's car.

'Come and grab one of these while I get my things,' called Sheena who deposited the bags on the cobbles, pulled out her wheelie case, slammed the door shut and after reminding revving-Kevin not to drive like Lewis Hamilton on the winding roads down to the village, waved goodbye to the newly passed boy-racer.

Cathy picked up both the bulging bags that clinked and rattled and as they made their way inside. It'd take more than a hike to burn off whatever Sheena had bought for her two-night stay. No matter, at least she had company and that was worth its weight in gold and a hangover from hell by morning.

They were sat at the kitchen table, comfies on, one bottle of wine and two giant pizzas down, when Sheena piped up, 'So are you going to ring this artist bloke and see if he wants his creepy paintings back or what?'

Cathy tutted. 'They are not creepy. I like them. There's an ethereal quality about them, like ghosts from the past that look right into your eyes and soul.'

'What the fuck does *ethereal* mean? And get you, being all arty. You'll be telling me that bowl of fruit is speaking to you, next. Then again you have had two glasses of vino, so I'm not surprised.' Sheena grinned and winked because everyone knew Cathy wasn't a big drinker and got merry on cider fumes.

'Sod off. And it means not of this world, or something like that... but actually, I suppose I could ring him now. It's taken so bloody long to get through to his house maybe I should crack on, in case it takes another three months.'

Sheena patted her hand and stood. 'Good lass. Right, you make the call while I get the cheesecake out of the fridge and some more wine. Then we can chill out and watch a film. That walk knackered me out. Felt like an army drill the way you were marching us up the tops, sergeant major style.'

Cathy ignored Sheena's grumbling and grabbed her phone, typing in the number while more calories were brought from the fridge. Putting it onto speaker so they could both listen but not really expecting an answer, Cathy's wide-eyed reaction matched Sheena's when someone answered. This time, in a less formal manner.

'Hello.'

'Oh hello, Guy. I hope you don't mind me ringing but your wife gave me your number earlier.'

A brief pause preceded a wary response from the well-spoken voice at the other end, 'Oh, she did, did she. What was it you wanted?'

Blimey, thought Cathy, *these two are a right cagey pair.* 'It's nothing to worry about, but we bought your campervan at auction a while back and we found some paintings inside it and wondered if you wanted them back.'

'What, really! You found my ladies? How wonderful. Are they okay?'

Weird way of putting it, *my ladies*, Cathy mused but didn't let on, ignoring the funny look Sheena was giving her as she uncorked the wine

'Yes, they're in great condition. The tube and wrapping they were in seems to have protected them from the elements so don't worry.'

'Oh, that's such a relief and thank you for saving them and yes, I would be most relieved to have them back. They mean a great deal to me.'

Despite harbouring notions of getting them framed, Cathy was glad she'd rang and was doing a good deed. 'Well, I can post them to you next week if you like. Unless you can collect, it's your call.'

'Well I'm away at the moment so I'd prefer to be there when they arrive, and I won't be back for a week or so. I'm in the Lakes at the moment but maybe I could drive to you. Whereabouts are you?'

'Hathersage, just over the Snake Pass. Do you know it? And lucky you, being in the Lakes. It's lovely up there but I've not been for years. Are you on holiday?' Cathy was on a chatty roll now and blamed it on the big gulp of wine she'd just taken from a rather large glass.

'No, I can't say I know your neck of the woods but you're right, this is a marvellous part of the country, and in answer to your question I'm here for the music festival, Kendal Calling. Reliving my misspent youth, I suppose, but don't tell my wife. She doesn't approve of my interests or my paintings unfortunately but that's by the by. I've been staying in a B&B for a few nights before the main event begins tomorrow, now I don't have my camper. Oh I do miss the old girl especially because I'll have to make do with a tent at the festival and these old bones don't take kindly to it.'

Cathy thought he sounded wistful and felt a bit sorry for him because his wife didn't come across as the friendliest person, at which point she was interrupted by Sheena who was making hand signals that appeared to be telling her to press mute.

Cathy said into the phone, 'Could you just hold on one minute, Guy, I just need to speak to someone, won't be a tick.'

Sheena wore an excited expression accompanied by a pre-idea squeal. 'I've had a brilliant thought! Why don't we drive up there tomorrow and hand deliver the paintings. You know, have a girls-on-tour road trip to the Lakes. I bloody love it there and we could make a day of it once we've dropped the paintings off. I'll drive if you don't fancy it. What do you think?'

It could have been the wine or that she was high on the wings of a good deed, but it spurred Cathy into action and for once, she made a snap decision. Unmuting her phone she said, 'Sorry about that, Guy, but me and my friend fancy a drive up to the Lakes tomorrow. We could meet you somewhere and give you the paintings. Our other halves are away on a stag weekend so we're at a loose end–'

Guy jumped in. 'Yes, yes of course. That's wonderful and so very kind of you. I know the perfect place to meet and I'd be happy to reimburse you any expenses.'

'Oh great, and there's no need. So, where shall we meet?' Giving Sheena the thumbs-up, Cathy poised her pen, ready to take down the details. As she listened to Guy's instructions, Cathy was awash with conflicting emotions. She went from excitement at going on a road trip with Sheena, to trepidation at straying so far from home. Then she imagined how proud Alfie would be when he found out. This would prove she was up for their Scotland trip. He'd swallowed his fear of flying for Dave, so she was determined to do the same for Alfie.

It was time to step outside of her very small comfort zone and take a leap of faith, if only in herself.

28

GUY

They're coming home. My beautiful ladies have been saved. This is truly a most wonderful occurrence and my daily manifestations have borne fruit. I always knew it was true: not merely a whim but an actual cosmic gift and my faith in a higher power would eventually be rewarded.

Even when other desires have failed to materialise, slipping through my fingers – I never felt Moroccan sands beneath my feet; my eyes never beheld the Taj Mahal – but maybe the ancient gods and forces beyond our understanding were saving their energy for this most blessed reunion.

Now, I can die happy knowing those I have loved and never forgotten will lie by my side when I take my final journey into the beyond. That's all I wish for. Circumstance and rules and social stigma may have prevented us from being together in life, but in death, we can forever be reunited.

I have spent too many of my years doing the bidding of others. My grandparents, parents and the woman who I didn't choose to be my wife but had foisted on me like a lead weight. I did my duty, and dear lord how it dragged.

That single thought, of the years I've endured with her

reminds me of a time I was out in the back of beyond painting a landscape. I saw a troop of squaddies yomping across the moors. They were on exercise, from Catterick barracks I expect, covered from head to toe in mud and all carrying huge bergens on their backs, fully laden from the looks of them, sodden from wading through rivers, as were their boots and uniforms.

One lad, bringing up the rear, was struggling, his legs buckling under the weight of his load, and as I watched from my vantage point I felt a strange sort of kinship with him. Because that's exactly how I felt. Carrying the burden of marriage, a wife I've never loved, a career I loathed and the rib-crushing pressure of over-bearing parents who dragged me down in their pursuance of pushing me up the societal ladder.

And look at me now. Where did it get them? Here I am. Their only son with nothing more to his name than a home re-mortgaged to the hilt, a clapped-out old car, the spare room and a single bed. Debts I'm about to drown in, a wife who will soon bugger off to live with her sister in southern Spain. She's finally faced up to the fact that the barrel has been well and truly scraped and faces can no longer be saved, and 'we' are nothing more than two names on a marriage certificate.

So actually, now I think of it, another of my manifestations has come to pass and the many hours I channelled speccy Elton, imagining tail-lights taking Cressida off to España on a one-way ticket, actually worked. Fancy that. My powers know no bounds.

And now I must make plans. Should I do as the ball-and-chain asks and sell the cottage, giving her half of whatever pittance remains after the vultures take what's owed? I quite fancy the notion of living on a barge, sedately travelling the waterways of Britain. All I need is a place to rest my head and the simple things in life. Yes, I do like the sound of that.

I can't risk it though. No matter how tempting it is. So I

shall have to stand my ground and fend Cressida off. Adopt stalling tactics. Whatever I thought of my father and his before him, I need to hold on to the last patch of Alexander soil. Yes, that old chestnut should do.

But first things first. Something pleasant to ponder for a change. Not only do I have a whole weekend amongst my kind of people to look forward to, I'll be meeting Cathy tomorrow and then once I have my ladies, we can go home and be together. All of us.

I'm so looking forward to seeing their faces again, which makes me wonder what she looks like, this dear woman, Cathy. She sounded kind, had a softness to her voice and when we arranged to meet, I heard a hint of excitement and nervousness too. I predict she's the cautious type. Quite shy, I expect. I'm good at reading people.

But what of her looks... that's the delicious part. Picturing the face that complements the voice and I see Cathy in her early thirties, a light brunette, almost fair haired. She wears it straight as a die down to her tanned shoulders and... hazel eyes. Petite and dainty. Yes, that's how I see her, but time will tell. I predict she would be the type I'd have sought out, all those years ago.

Oh how I long to be young again and I pray that when I reach the afterlife, I'll be reborn in skin as supple as it was in my twenties. A taut stomach, iron-flat with six rippling sections. Arms toned and muscular and my hair lustrous, not thinning and steel grey with the texture of straw. I won't even deliberate on the rest of my seventy-seven-year-old carcass. Worn out and wrinkled. I find it most debilitating.

They flocked to me then, the beautiful ones, of their own free will but it was holding on to them that was the problem. Exotic birds of paradise I held in my hands for the briefest of time, admiring their colours, silken wings and auras like halos. When we made love under the stars I took them to a place where our souls were as one and then later, it was always so hard to let them go.

And now, like my beauties, Cathy has come to me of her own free will and I wonder if... no, I'm too old to even consider... but what if... What if she's meant to be? The last one. The final bird of paradise to add to my collection. Oh my. Be still, my foolish old heart. Yet is it such a fantasy.

Questions, so many questions shooting like stars inside my head. Is all this – losing my beauties in such a cruel way to have them returned in an act of kindness – a sign?

This stirring inside me tells me it is, and the voice inside my head says I should follow my instincts and be bold. Yes, that's what I shall do. Tomorrow I will take my trusty Nikon with me and ask Cathy if I may take her photo so I can paint her. Immortalise her on canvas, and then... and then... maybe, just maybe, I will take a beauty home with me. One last time.

29

CATHY

The bleep of the alarm on her mobile woke Cathy from a fitful sleep. She had missed Alfie by her side and the tummy-turning anxiety had triumphed over exhaustion and a fair amount of red wine.

It also hadn't helped that Sheena had been in and out of the bathroom all night throwing up, which prompted Cathy to go and check on her.

She found her friend on the bathroom floor hugging the toilet, a bath towel wrapped round her shoulders, the mop bucket and a roll of loo paper by her side.

On seeing Cathy she groaned. 'Maaaaate! I am soooooo rough. Can't work out if it was the pizza or the wine but one of them was deffo dodgy. Are you okay? I've had my head down the loo all night and just now my arse exploded...'

'Jeez, Sheena, that's too much information this time in the morning and yes, I'm fine. Well, I was, but now I feel queasy too, so thanks for that.' Cathy held her breath as she opened the bathroom window.

'And what's the mop bucket for? Did you have splash-back,

or have you missed the target?' Checking the bathroom floor, Cathy hoped it was neither.

'Well I can only use the loo for one thing at a time and seeing as I have a both-ends issue, I had to improvise and now I hate the smell of Dettol. Your mop bucket reeks of the stuff.' Sheena's head flopped back onto her arms, which rested on the toilet seat.

'Yes, you're right, it's Dettol, the green one. I love it. But right now, I need a shower, so do you think you'll be okay on the landing for a few minutes?'

Mindful that it was 10am, Cathy realised they would really need to get their fingers out, as they were supposed to be on the road by eleven. But Sheena wasn't going anywhere fast.

She lifted her head slightly and through half-closed eyes said, 'Mate, can we set off a bit later, or go tomorrow because at this rate I'm going to need rubber knickers and a bucket because I can't stop being– oh God, you'd best go, it's going to be both ends this time...'

Cathy didn't wait for her to finish the sentence and ran for the door which she rammed shut. If she was going to the Lakes, she'd be going alone.

The Defender was ticking over nicely as was Cathy's mind. By her side, next to a bottle of water and her bag, lay the tube of paintings, waiting to be returned to their rightful owner. She never thought she'd say this but if there was a day when she wished Bertha would pull a stunt which meant she had to stay home, today was it.

But even when she'd nipped up the lane with a plate of sandwiches and some leftover cheesecake from the night before, Bertha was engrossed in a re-run of *Heartbeat* and barely acknowledged her. She'd given her all the right cues, but nope, Bertha wasn't going to thwart her trip.

'I'll be gone a while, so if I'm not back by teatime will you be okay popping something in the microwave? I'll nip up as soon as I get home.'

A harrumphing sound was followed by, 'I'm not an invalid yet, so you just get gone. Stop mitherin'.'

'Okay, will do. I've been really looking forward to this trip. Remember I told you I was meeting the man who...' and then Cathy remembered that last time she started to explain about what Alfie had found in the van, Bertha had told her in no uncertain terms she wasn't interested in her rust-bucket-on-wheels or whatever old tat they'd found inside it.

'Best be on your way then. You're interrupting me programme with your goings-on.'

One more try, thought Cathy. 'Sheena can't come with me now because she's poorly so I'm going on my own. It's the first time I've been on a solo road trip for a long time. I feel a bit nervous.' For a bizarre second, Cathy even considered asking Bertha to come along, that's how desperate she was not to make the trip alone.

'It'll do you good 'stead of hanging round here like summat that stuck to me shoe. Flick the kettle on and I'll make a brew to have with me butties. Then you can show yerself out.' Bertha hadn't taken her eyes off the television the whole time she was there, so admitting defeat, Cathy had obeyed.

Sitting in the yard, wiping sweaty palms on her flowery maxi dress, she looked at her phone in its holder, Cathy only needed to press 'Get directions' and then 'Start' and she'd be on her way, yet still her finger hovered over the screen as she listened to the words running through her head.

Bloody Sheena. This was her bright idea and now she's

wimped out. Maybe I should just ring Guy and ask him to come here and pick the paintings up... save me the bother.

No! Stop being soft. You can do this! Just break it down into doable sections. It's a two-hour drive and it'll be nice and peaceful, looking out the window at the gorgeous scenery through the Lakes. It'll be just me and my trusty old Defender. See, even the name means you'll be safe in its care. Just me, the rumble of the engine and the radio.

What if the Defender breaks down?

You have breakdown cover and before you say it, tell them you're a woman on your own: they might even send a lady mechanic.

What about when I get there? There might be swarms of people pushing and shoving.

Then text Guy and ask him to come to the car park or look for somewhere quieter but you won't know till you get there, so go. Go on, push the button and be brave! Do it for Alfie. He'll be so proud.

Sucking in a huge lungful of Derbyshire air, and before she could change her mind, Cathy tapped the phone screen twice, put the Defender into gear and set off down the lane.

The journey had been a piece of cake and as she made her way across the bumpy car park, Cathy swelled with pride at getting that far, emboldened also by the message she'd received from Alfie when he realised she was making the journey to Kendal alone.

You little star. I can't believe you've gone by yourself. Sheena's a melt! I'm so proud of you but please take care and txt me when you get there. Send me a photo. Love you so much xxxx.

Guy had suggested they meet at Abbot Hall, an art gallery and museum close to Kendal town centre. Once she'd parked, Cathy was to head past the children's play area and the lawns, and then wait by the crown bowling green. There were lots of benches to rest on. How simple was that!

After navigating the town with minimum hassle, Cathy parked the Defender and switched off the engine. Stage one of her mission was complete and now she only had to pluck up the courage to meet a total stranger without her sidekick Sheena.

Remembering to text Alfie, she fired off a message. That was the easy bit. All she had to do next was get out.

You have to go, otherwise you've wasted a two-hour drive!

And look, everyone in the town seems friendly. You don't have to stay and chat or have a three-course meal with the man. Just make polite conversation, hand over the tube then go and grab some food and a drink and find a quiet spot to chill out and people watch. Come on. You can do this. Do it for Alfie and Mum and Dad. Imagine how happy they'll be when you send them a photo.

OKAY, okay, I'll do it and I can always come straight back here and drive home if I feel uncomfortable or get spooked... I've got this, again.

Before she could change her mind, Cathy grabbed her phone, bag and the paintings and jumped out of the Defender, then locked the door and set off towards Abbot Hall.

As she walked, clutching the tube to her chest like a shield, Cathy focused on the voices of those around her which muffled the pounding beat of her heart. With every step, each deep intake of breath, Cathy relaxed as the tension in her body ebbed, allowing her to go with the flow.

The gentle rays of the afternoon sun melded with the bonhomie and happy vibes of a beautiful town full of tourists wanting nothing more than to take photos and buy some mint cake. This realisation eased Cathy, relaxing taut muscles, and reminded her of what it was like to be outside, and a little bit free.

She realised she'd made progress on the journey that had started the night she arrived at Blacksheep. All by herself. And that was huge. As a smile crept across her face, another thought, accompanied by the blossoming of hope formed in Cathy's mind and deep inside her chest.

It's going to be okay. Bloody hell. I think it really is!

Outside the grounds of the hall, she checked her watch and thanks to clear roads all the way, she had almost an hour before she met Guy. So rather than head to the meet-up point straight away, Cathy went in search of food.

Her senses were on high alert to the sounds and sights of the town. A cacophony of colours, voices laced with unfamiliar dialects, culinary aromas from the cafés dotting the street, the almost skin-on-skin proximity of strangers.

Keep going, you're doing great.

She bought a baguette and another bottle of water and decided to eat on the green until it was time to meet Guy. It was as she neared the lush expanse of field that her gaze was drawn to a woman sat alone, cross-legged at the foot of a tree.

Dressed in a purple kaftan, the front adorned with silver stars and moons, her flowing grey-white hair almost down to her waist, she was surrounded by candles and an assortment of real and artificial flowers of the kind you see hung around the necks of Hawaiian dancers. In the centre, facing the woman, who appeared to be deep in meditation, giving off an aura of complete calm, tranquil and serene, was a photo frame.

There was just something about her that lured Cathy forward, intrigue guiding her feet, leaving the hubbub behind, and it was only as she neared that she realised what she was looking at. It was a shrine. Not wanting to intrude, yet strangely fascinated, Cathy lingered a few feet away wishing that she too could find such peace.

Taking in everything about the woman, Cathy noticed her tanned arms were lithe and toned, and her bare feet suggested that she was a sun worshipper; red painted toenails and toe rings accompanied a stack of ankle bracelets. Cathy traced the lines on the woman's neck and face that told of wisdom and a life lived, maybe seventy years of travelling and festivals like the one in Kendal, dancing around a campfire in the moonlight under the stars.

Cathy was about to walk away when the woman opened her eyes, deep brown and soulful, and focused immediately on her observer whose first response was to blush and then apologise. 'I'm so sorry for staring but you looked so relaxed and in your own world. I've always wanted to meditate. I just never seem to manage it, not like that anyway.'

At this the woman smiled, as though she'd heard it said before or was grateful for the compliment. 'Believe me it's taken over fifty years of practice. So keep trying, and you'll get there in the end.'

As she finished speaking the woman stood in a fluid motion that Cathy imagined had also taken years of practice, yoga probably. With grace and ease of movement, no sign of creaky joints and a crumbling spine, the woman stepped over the flowers and held out her hand. 'I'm Maddy. It's nice to meet you.'

Taking the offered hand, Cathy responded with her own

name and then a question. 'So are you meditating or praying, or both? And, if you don't mind me asking, who to? I'd love to have deep faith, in something or someone and I'm always envious of those who've made that connection.'

Another kind smile. 'Well, I'm Wiccan, and I was asking for help from the gods and praying for an old friend.'

'Oh, is that who's on the photo?' Cathy gestured to the bed of flowers, trying to see the image inside the frame.

Maddy turned and bent, picked it up and held it out to Cathy. 'It's my friend, Deborah.'

Taking the photo in her hands, Cathy wasn't prepared for what she was about to see, and the connections her brain made between the woman in front of her eyes, and one of the paintings inside the tube wedged under her arm.

Deborah. Surely it can't be her.

Finding her voice, Cathy finally asked, 'Why are you praying for her? Is she poorly?' It was the first thing that sprang into her mind.

Maddy took the frame back as she spoke and looked lovingly at the woman in the photo. 'She was my very best friend, and she went missing in 1979 during the Reading Music Festival.'

Cathy's stomach flipped and heat rose upwards, flushing her neck and cheeks. 'You mean, you haven't seen her since 1979? What happened?'

Maddy sighed. 'That's the big question and it's haunted me for years because I've always believed it was my fault for even suggesting we go in the first place, and for being so high on acid and in love with some guy we'd met on the first day, that I went off and left her alone. The last time I saw her, she was in our tent. When I went back the next day, she was gone, and nobody has seen or heard from her since.'

30

Cathy looked down at the face of the woman and that flicker of recognition returned, accompanied by a sense of dread. She needed to know more before she mentioned the paintings because it was all too mad.

'Oh my God, that's awful. Did the police look for her? Was there a search?'

At this Maddy released a bitter laugh and rolled her eyes. 'They made a half-hearted effort once the festival was over and it was clear she hadn't "shacked up" with someone as they'd put it. It was awful. I searched the whole camp like a mad-woman, asking people if they'd seen her and trying to describe her because at the time I didn't have a photo. That one,' Maddy pointed at the frame, 'was on my camera and hadn't been developed but it's the last snapshot I took of her, the very day before she disappeared.'

Could it be her? My Deborah or is this just a bizarre coincidence?

The photo of a beautiful young woman with cornflower-blue eyes looked straight into Cathy's soul. Her rosebud lips and peach complexion, silky straight brown hair set against the colourful zigzags of a wide bandana were identical to the woman in the painting, rolled up and hidden inside a tube. But before Cathy could verbalise her thoughts, Maddy continued.

'It was sheer torture. Watching as everyone packed up to go and one by one people left on foot or in vehicles, but I waited right until the end. Sat there with my rucksack, determined to stay just in case she showed up and jumped out of some guy's car and said, "Ta-da!" When she didn't, I went to the police because she'd been gone for almost forty-eight hours, and I kicked up an almighty fuss.'

'So the police did look for her?'

Maddy nodded. 'Yes, and there were posters, sniffer dog searches, public appeals but in the end they were convinced she'd met a bloke and would turn up eventually, once the shine of a new romance wore off. But I knew differently. Deborah wasn't like that. She was a dedicated nurse and loved her job. She came from a close family with three younger brothers and a nice mum and dad she adored. She would never do anything to hurt them or me, which is why something bad must have happened to her. Deborah ended up as just another missing person on a register.'

'Is that why you have the shrine and pray?' Cathy indicated the bed of flowers and candles as she passed the photo back.

Maddy clutched it to her chest as she answered. 'This may sound crazy but deep in here, I've never given up hope that one day she might turn up, at a festival, and walk right on up and say, "Ta-da! I'm back".' At this Maddy's voice cracked and a tear escaped which she allowed to roll down her cheek, unashamed of her emotions.

'For the past forty-five years, I've gone back to Reading just in case someone remembers. Perhaps they'd already left when we started searching and they might somehow remember her or have seen something suspicious. And my obsession led to a new way of life and source of income.'

'Really, how? Did you become a policewoman?' It was the first logical thing that pinged into Cathy's mind, so she wasn't expecting the low chuckle it elicited in Maddy.

'Oh goodness, no! I worked in hospitality for many years and then when I retired, I bought a food truck. We, me and my daughter, work around the country at festivals and shows which is why we're here today. My daughter is in charge now, but I still love to come along and so do my grandkids who are around somewhere, on the park wreaking havoc. We'll move to the festival later today and set up. But for now we're having a little break in one of our favourite places.'

'I admire the fact you've never given up on your friend, I really do.' Cathy couldn't imagine the heartache that Maddy had endured.

'That's very kind but this is also about me, absolving myself, freeing my heart and dreams of guilt at leaving Debbie alone.'

Maddy looked into Cathy's eyes and in that moment there was a connection, like an invisible surge of energy and understanding because Cathy also wanted to feel that way. To be free of the dreams and yes, the guilt at being one of those who survived and for making Alfie stay at Blacksheep.

Snapping Cathy into the here and now, Maddy embellished. 'At the start, all those years ago, I was hoping that while someone was buying a wrap or a baked potato, they'd see the poster of Debbie and might be able to help. I still do and I've even got a projection of how she'd look now but so far, it's all led to nothing.'

As Maddy spoke, Cathy could see the sadness in her eyes and years of worry etched in the lines of her suntanned face. She sensed that the toll of guilt still weighed heavy, which was why she hesitated for a second, not wanting to give Maddy false hope by mentioning the painting that looked so much like Deborah. But what if...

Squashing the concerns that were bubbling inside, Cathy had a 'sod it' moment. What was there to lose? So she reached out and gently touched Maddy's arm as she spoke. 'I can see that what happened to Deborah has really affected you and your life and this may sound *really* weird but–'

A phone ringing cut Cathy short as it did Maddy who delved into the deep pockets of her kaftan, apologising as she answered. 'Sorry, it's my daughter. Won't be a tick.'

Cathy waited and listened to a one-sided conversation and quickly picked up that Maddy was being called to some kind of emergency involving one of her grandchildren.

When she hung up, she was in a bit of a tizz. 'I'm so sorry but I'm going to have to shoot off. My grandson's fallen off a swing and hurt his arm. His mum needs me to go. Look, do you want to wait here or meet me later? I sense there's something on your mind and maybe I could do a reading for you, or cast the runes but if you have to go,' – she once again delved into her pocket and pulled out a flyer – 'all my details are on there. So come and find me, or call me, yes?'

Cathy took the leaflet and nodded. 'Yes, yes, you go. I hope he's okay...'

But Maddy was already weaving her way at speed through the passersby, a purple haze of flowing robes, grey hair and panic.

Left alone, Cathy pushed the flyer into her bag and stepped closer to the shrine and knelt, noticing the A4 posters tucked beneath a candle that showed the original missing person photograph from 1983, and by its side, an image of what Deborah, Debbie, might look like now.

Touching the older version, Cathy was overcome by sadness at seeing the face of a life not lived. Or maybe, just maybe, there was a logical explanation for Deborah's disappearance and as Maddy hoped, her friend might one day come home.

Sitting as Maddy had done earlier, amongst the flowers and candles, Cathy soaked it all up and wondered what it must have been like for Maddy and Deborah at that festival in '79 before she was even born.

Taking out her phone, curiosity getting the upper hand, Cathy tapped *Reading, missing woman, Deborah, 1979* and instantly the search led her back in time. Scrolling through the information, it was exactly as Maddy described, and it was as she connected the dots between the face on the screen and the one in the tube by her side, an unsettling thought caused goosebumps to creep up her arms and down the back of her neck.

Without a second's hesitation, Cathy cleared the search bar and typed in a new name and date, and the similar phrase as before, *Krystle, 1970, festival, missing woman.* Her finger hovered for a second over the go button before she pressed, holding her breath as she waited for the blue line to move across the top of the screen.

And there it was. Krystle's face staring right back at Cathy as though she'd travelled through time, her spirit sitting beside her, in communion with Deborah's. With trembling hands, Cathy scanned the sparse details that told of Krystle Moss, age 22, reported missing after the Isle of Wight festival. Her boyfriend had been arrested under suspicion of causing her harm but was later released. Despite searches and public appeals, she was never found and remained a missing person.

Cathy felt heat rush upwards, her pounding heart and the whooshing in her ears drowned out the festival around her and as she swallowed and willed herself to clear the search bar, her eyes pricked with tears. Again her hands trembled, making it hard to type in another name, *Miriam, 1983, festival, missing woman.*

The urge to press the go button was as consuming as the urge not to, and while the conflict raged, her breathing was becoming increasingly shallow. An anxiety attack was setting in, but she had to do it, she had to know. Her thumb hit the button and the blue line did its thing once again.

Miriam Cole, aged 19, reported missing after the Knebworth Festival.

Oh God, oh God... what have you done?

Whoever the paintings belonged to had something to do with the women who'd gone missing and there were two more to check out.

What if ...? What did he do to them? And he's here, you're going to meet him... he'll be waiting by the meet-up point... you have to go, leave right now, hurry up, get away from the danger. Danger is here, it's found you again. DANGER. DANGER. Go, Cathy. GO NOW. You need to get away. RUN!

31

Cathy leapt to her feet and grabbed the tube of paintings. Skewed logic and terror overrode any thoughts of running after Maddy to tell her what she knew, because the need to escape was paramount. At the same time, a wave of anger directed towards herself for going there alone in the first place made her swallow down a scream.

Stupid, stupid, stupid. Danger is everywhere. All around. Waiting for when you least expect it.

Bubbling and boiling into a swell of hysteria, fear coursed through a trembling body that was on the verge of collapse but somehow adrenalin kept her upright and mobile. Cathy began to half-walk, half-run. Impeded by her slip-on sandals and by dawdlers, she pushed past anyone in front, not caring about those she bumped into, ignoring their tuts as she failed to apologise.

It was like before. But this time, instead of the horror being all around, its work was already done, she could sense the hand of evil reaching out. The hairs on her neck stood on end as she imagined the touch of fingers on her skin. Malice trying to grab her from behind and swallow her whole.

Get out, get out, get out.

The whistling in her ears preceded a panic attack. So before it rendered her incapable, sucking in air, she hitched up her dress that kept wrapping round her legs and beat a pathway towards the car park, her feet pounding the ground, out of time with the staccato beat of her heart.

Nearly there, nearly there, just keep going, don't stop, don't stop, Cathy, please don't stop.

The sight of the car park sign registered hope, and then a moment of confusion when she realised that the number of vehicles had swelled since she'd arrived, and she couldn't remember where she'd parked. Which block?

Think, Cathy, think. What letter, what letter? J, no it was L, or was it K? J, it was J definitely J and you were next to the telegraph pole and an old green Jaguar, look for the green Jag.

And then she saw it, the car and the Defender and she may have cried out in relief or maybe it was inside her head, but she'd made it. As she scrambled in her bag for her keys, Cathy fumbled and dropped the tube. For a second she was going to leave it there, so great was the desire to get inside and lock the door against the malevolence about to grab her from behind.

But as she inserted the key, turned the lock then flung open the door, in a fluid movement, she swept the tube from the ground, threw it inside the cab and launched herself straight after it.

Hysteria building, she slammed the door then slapped her hand on the lock button.

Passenger side, PASSENGER SIDE! A voice screeched in her head causing her to lunge across to check the other door was locked, tapping it twice, three times to make sure.

Is the boot locked. IS IT? IS IT? Yes, it's always locked. It's broken, remember, and you have to crawl inside to open it.

Breathe. BREATHE, CATHY!

Safe. I'm safe. I need to go home. I need to ring Alfie. I need to ring the police. NO, you have to go home first. It's safe there. HOME IS SAFE. Start the engine, right now and drive, Cathy, JUST DRIVE.

Cathy couldn't remember a second of the journey home only the map on the screen of her phone, the voice that told her where to go, the thick blue line she followed religiously and the arrow that pointed to safety.

The bleeping of message alerts were ignored, as were the calls. She had to concentrate and there was no way she could explain to Alfie or Sheena what had happened. Not yet. Because she would start to cry and if she did she wouldn't stop, and they'd flap, and Alfie would have a meltdown and make it worse.

And what if it was him? Guy. Wondering where she was. The mere thought made her shudder, so she'd blocked him out.

For the first hour of the journey her hands were glued to the steering wheel, apart from when she changed gear and stopped at traffic lights on the edge of Kendal.

She sent texts to Sheena and Alfie, breaking the law and not caring one bit.

> Leaving now. Will ring when home.

After that her fingers gripped the wheel tight, her mind on nothing but the road ahead. It was around the halfway mark that the tension eased. The food she'd bought remained in the bottom of her bag, but she ignored the weird sounds her stomach was making. No way could she eat anything. It would've come right back up. So instead, she'd sipped from the bottle of water, determined also not to stop for a wee. She'd rather wet her pants than get out. Her focus was solely on the goal of home.

It was when she saw the sign welcoming her to Derbyshire that she allowed herself to think things through, dissemble the whole horrible afternoon and work out what to do next. Being pragmatic was the key now that she'd left evil behind in Kendal.

She would not give in to any more hysteria. Not give any headspace to the man, Guy, who would have by now realised she was a no-show. If he'd texted her, asking where she was, she'd ignore it.

As she drove into the yard at Blacksheep a wave of calm enveloped her and after switching off the engine, Cathy rested back her head and closed her eyes, allowing her body to relax. When she opened them, the sight of home made her smile and within seconds she'd gathered her things, locked the Defender and opened the front door. Stepping inside, she closed it firmly and sighed. This was sanctuary. Here she was safe.

32
GUY

I spotted her in the crowd quite by accident. My tube of paintings she carried under her arm was a giveaway obviously, but she's such a beauty that any red-blooded male couldn't fail to be attracted to her. I felt the stirrings as I watched from a distance, transfixed by that mane of dark hair and her alabaster skin. It was a shame that from where I stood I couldn't see the colour of her eyes, but I assume they are brown. I do love soulful brown eyes.

I didn't approach and instead, enjoyed being the voyeur whilst allowing her time to talk to the woman who had set up some sort of shrine beneath a tree. At this point I'd intended sticking to our arrangement to rendezvous at the official meeting post so there was no hurry. Just more time to gaze and imagine what might have been in another time and place when this old body of mine was that of a toned and horny young man.

After all, that's why I was really at the festival. To reminisce and hunt. Feed the urges that have begun to stir in my groin once again. Fulfil the carnal desire to own something beautiful all for myself. A special prize I could take home from the fair.

It's fate because before, they always came to me willingly. I lured them with ease. They wanted me. All I had to do was wait and choose the perfect one and in some quirk of glorious fate, Cathy, a specimen of pure loveliness had searched me out.

Another twist of fate is that I've never taken anyone from Kendal because when the festival began, around 2006, I'd been behaving myself for a long while, wary of my activities attracting attention and ruining my run of evading the good gentlemen of the law.

I was content with my memories, of heady summer days and the beautiful ladies who, after I absorbed their auras and souls into my own, lived on in my dreams. Their bodies, a temple to our love, lay buried in the woods just beyond my garage with Luna standing guard over them.

But perhaps for my last hurrah, in a change of plan, Cathy can be my swan song. I can't allow her to tell anyone what I fear she knows, and those paintings are the key. My portraits, my beauties, my legend.

I'd watched them as they spoke, the grey-haired one and Cathy and I'm an excellent reader of body language and it was clear that the woman had a tale to tell, and that it had something to do with the photograph they kept looking at. I was intrigued by the interaction especially when Cathy placed her hand on the woman's arm, a gesture of concern, methinks. Then after the woman took a call and left suddenly, Cathy was alone.

I was considering making myself known when she became engrossed in her phone, hand over her mouth in an expression of shock as she read whatever was on the screen and then, quite unexpectedly, she bolted.

I followed but not before rushing over to the shrine to see what had caused such a reaction and it was then, when I saw the photograph of my Deborah, that everything I'd observed slotted into place. Even though I couldn't fathom why the woman was there at Kendal, because I took Deborah from Reading, the cogs whirred in my mind, telling me I was in danger of being exposed.

And worse, Cathy must have recognised her too, from my paintings. That's how good I am. Such a great talent gone to waste. I simply had to get them back and prevent her from telling anyone what she knew. I've come too far, evaded discovery for all these years and kept my ladies safe and close by. That's why I gave chase.

It was easy to spot Cathy up ahead, but she was much faster than me and it was a sobering moment as I puffed and panted trying to keep up while at the same time, plotting my next move.

It was clear she'd been spooked by the shrine and whatever she saw on her phone. In turn, she'd spooked me. I had this sense of everything unravelling and I had to stop it. And the only way to do that was get my paintings back and silence Cathy before she shared whatever it was she knew.

By the time we'd reached the car park I thought my lungs would explode and if not, my heart was about to pack in and while I watched Cathy clamber inside her vehicle, I could only lean on another and gasp for breath. All was not lost though, as I watched her manoeuvre out of the space and drive past me, we were so close I could see her beautiful face in profile, yet she had no idea I was there, taking it all in. The logo on the side of the Land Rover told me all I needed to know, where she was headed. Blacksheep Farm, Hathersage, Derbyshire.

Once I'd recovered from my near-death state I made my way as quickly as I could to my car, which was quite a hike. After chucking my rucksack into the passenger seat, I used the wonderful world wide web to find out exactly where Cathy lived. It took seconds. After a quick visit to the boarding house to collect my meagre belongings and not pay the bill, I did a flit and set off after my prey.

I must have been only an hour or so behind and as I

churned up the miles in pursuit, all I could do was pray that she hadn't spoken to anyone on the way. If she's told them about whatever she saw on that blasted phone of hers, I'm finished. I have to face up to the fact that it could be over for me, already, and these will be my last hours of freedom. Which is why I have absolutely nothing to lose, have I?

One way or another, I want my paintings back. They are my treasure, and she has no right to them. She has no right to even look at them. For my eyes only. And if I manage to get them back, and if I can silence her before she blabs, I'm home and free and I can go back to my ladies. That's all I care about now.

I've parked my car further down the hill, hidden behind some trees along a muddy track. Then I walked the rest of the way using the public footpath that skirts the property, allowing me to scope out the farm and buildings, and ascertain who's home and I think I'm in luck. So far there are no signs of life, and the vehicle is parked out front.

I'm so close, it's quite thrilling. I'm hiding just behind the garden wall in what appears to be a vegetable patch, only feet from the front door. I've not heard voices or even a dog barking, which I'd have expected on a farm. She told me her other half was away for the weekend, which is divine providence if ever I heard it.

There's another door at the rear, to what appears to be a scullery, but it's locked so the only way in is through the front. It's still light. Should I wait until dark to make my move? Something tells me I don't have that much time.

Sound, on the other side of the wall, a latch I think, the creak of wood and then the slam of a door. Please don't let her need anything from the gard– no, I can hear footsteps receding so she must be going towards her car, damn. No, she's still moving so perhaps she's going towards the other dwelling.

Someone must live there. I chance a peep over the wall, and I am, in fact, correct.

Cathy is going up the lane and once she rounds the bend, past the large tree, she'll be out of sight and then I can move.

I'll bet you any money that door is unlocked. And if it is, when she returns, Cathy will have a big surprise waiting for her. Me.

33

CATHY

Bertha was fast asleep in her armchair when Cathy let herself into the cottage, so rather than wake her and get her head bitten off, she'd left a note. It had given Cathy the nervous-giggles, placing it on the table beside the sleeping monster. She half expected Bertha to open one eye and say, 'What the bloody hell d'you think yer doing?'

Cathy's note had invited her to the farm for some supper, 'But if you'd rather not,' it continued, 'you've only to ring and I'll bring it to you later.' Cathy knew it would hinge on whether or not her legs weren't too bad, which basically depended on the weather and which way the wind blew.

Even as she closed the front door carefully so not to wake the beast, Cathy knew she'd be traipsing back later with a tinfoil covered plate, but at least she'd offered. Following the hospital visit, normal belligerent service had resumed.

Still, Cathy imagined it was a long day stuck in the house all alone, watching re-runs of old telly shows. It cost nothing to be civil and maybe – pray for a miracle – 'nice Bertha' would one day return.

Deep down, after the day she'd had, Cathy wasn't looking

forward to spending the evening alone downstairs. Earlier, she'd popped her head in on Sheena who'd been out for the count. So she crept about as she changed out of her sweat-drenched dress, showered and put a wash on. Then she visited Bertha.

Determined to be positive, as she walked back down the track, Cathy decided she was going to make a brew for sleepy-sick-girl and see if she wanted anything to eat. Cathy was desperate for her friend to wake up so she could tell her about Guy and decide what to do.

Annie was still at her mother-in-law's caravan in Rhyl with the kids, so Cathy would have to wait until they were all in bed before they could talk properly. There was no way she could keep it all inside until tomorrow.

It all seemed so... unreal. That was the only way to describe it. Oh, and scary as fuck. Or maybe she was overthinking the whole thing. Or maybe she should ring the police right there and then? Not wait for Sheena to wake up or Annie's kids to nod off.

Would they think she was being dramatic, though? Another over-zealous member of the public who watched too many true crime documentaries, concocting a cold-case mystery on the strength of some watercolours painted over fifty years ago.

They might say she was wasting their time when they had Hathersage hooligans on dirt bikes to chase around the village, or the local shoplifter to apprehend. No, her original plan was the best one. Wait until morning and go to the station in person, with the evidence and Sheena for back-up, and ask to speak to a detective and hope that they'd take her seriously.

Trying to keep a lid on her emotions, Cathy told herself it was natural to be rattled and edgy, but she'd be fine and there was absolutely nothing to worry about. Guy was miles away and he did not know the real reason she'd been a no-show. After ignoring his call while driving home, once she was showered and changed and felt more human, she had finally replied to his brief text, asking where she was. She'd kept it brief.

> So sorry, car trouble, been a nightmare. Will contact to re-arrange.

Cathy also thought, but didn't say, *accompanied by the police.*

Confident that would stall him, and sure he was oblivious to the fact she was on to him; Cathy was reassured and shook off that spooked feeling.

But as she reached the front door, a wave of grief swooshed over her when she thought of Skip. It happened all the time because she couldn't get used to him not being there by the fire and missed the twitch of his ears and the slow thump of his tail on his bed. And acknowledging that she was still bereft made her think of Alfie. *I wish he was home, not in bloody Amsterdam.*

As she flicked the latch and went inside the chilly kitchen, Cathy made up her mind to light a fire, concoct a quick meal for her, Sheena and Bertha and then ring Alfie. His phone had gone to voicemail earlier, so she'd left a message to say she was home. Sheena's was probably still on silent while she slept off her hangover or whatever it was.

Tutting, Cathy took her phone from her jeans pocket and left it on the table next to her bag and the dreaded tube of paintings, then headed over to the fireplace. The fire was already laid, thanks to a habit she'd quickly got into when she'd moved in. She had learned fast how chilly early mornings could be. So once the logs were crackling away and the orangey glow cheered her up and gave the room a cosy vibe, the next task was finding something to eat.

It was as she opened the cupboard door and perused the contents, that she heard the familiar creak of the bottom stair and presumed Sheena was finally awake. The rest happened in the blink of an eye.

Cathy's body reacted swiftly to the panicked message from her brain, telling her something was wrong because Sheena wouldn't creep and stay silent. Her spine stiffened, ears on alert as the hairs on the back of her neck stood to attention, fear rippling through her core. Cathy didn't even have time to turn, grab a knife from the block that – oh God – had one missing, before something sharp prodded her beneath her left shoulder blade.

Next came sour, warm breath on her ear and neck, revulsion was soon followed by a menacing voice, issuing a warning. 'Don't scream, or I'll run this knife right through you, and if you try anything stupid, I'll cut you into tiny pieces and leave them in the fridge. Won't that be a nice surprise for your other half when he gets home from his trip. Now, turn around, very, very slowly.'

Oh God, he knows Alfie's not here. It can't be Guy. How does he know where I live? How can he be here?

Weak with terror, her knees knocking together, Cathy could barely breathe and feared she may faint before completing the instruction but maybe that would be a good thing because then she wouldn't be awake for whatever he was going to do.

Somehow, she remained upright and centimetre by centimetre, turned to come face to face with the man she knew, instinctively and in a flash of panicked intuition, was definitely Guy.

As she took him in, her eyes wide, he smirked as if to say, *yes, it's me.*

His frame was surprisingly stocky, and he stood an inch taller than her. His white-grey hair scraped back into what she presumed was a ponytail. Around his neck, protruding from a dirty, crinkled denim shirt was a black leather necklace holding a silver crucifix. The face showed his age, deep grooves furrowed the forehead, and the track marks of his years were etched into his weather-beaten skin.

His jaw was covered in whiskers which made him look grubby rather than trendy and in one ear he had a silver sleeper. Below the hand that pointed a knife in her face was a wrist stacked with bands. The ancient-hippy look didn't fool or calm Cathy. It only masked what lay beneath: a killer.

The jab of the knife just under her chin made Cathy gasp and squeal. In a voice laced with fear, she said, 'W-what do you want? Please don't hurt me. Is it the paintings? You can take them. I don't want them. They're on the table over there... Look, I'm sorry I left the festival but there was an emergen–'

'Shut up. And don't lie. I know exactly why you left.' Again, the arrogant tone, a verbal sneer to match the one on his face.

'I-I don't know what you mean.' Cathy could barely breathe such was the grip terror had on her insides. It grasped her lungs, restricting the flow of air, and forced her heart to pound so fast she was sure it would burst out of her chest. As her stomach roiled, the most ridiculous thought pinged into her head: that she must not lose control of her churning bowels and bladder. The shame would be as bad as death.

'You saw the photograph of Deborah. I was watching, and then you checked something on your phone and fled. Have you worked it out, pretty Cathy? Who the stars of my paintings are, my beautiful muses?'

As he spoke, Guy slowly traced a line with the tip of the knife, pushing downwards against her throat, skimming her T-shirt, resting finally at the centre of her ribs. There was some tone in his voice that told Cathy he enjoyed doing this, and worse, that he was aroused.

'Did you kill them? Krystle, Deborah, Miriam, all the

227

women in the paintings.' Cathy knew the answer in her heart but there was always the chance…

'Why do you care?'

'Because they're human beings with families and friends who miss them and they've been looking for them for years, praying that one day they'll come home. Will they come home?' Cathy's voice wobbled on the final word.

Guy reacted quite differently to her pointed question, standing straighter, a hint of amusement – or was it pride? He followed up with a question of his own. 'Have you told anyone about this?'

'*No!*' It was the truth and a silly pathetic reaction, saying what she thought he wanted to hear then regretting it immediately, blustering her way through a retraction that she could see wasn't fooling anyone.

'I mean, yes. I left some messages earlier for Alfie and my other friend, a man, who'll be here soon, by the way, so they know what I found, and they already know your name and where you live, from the logbook so…'

'SHUT UP!'

Cathy recoiled and obeyed.

'Do you have my Luna here or have you sold her?'

She was momentarily confused. *Luna, who the hell is Luna? Ah, the van, he must mean that.* And she was shocked, too, by his change of direction. His concern for a rusted lump of metal made her even more convinced that Guy was a full-on psycho. And then out of the blue his unhinged arrogance changed the dynamic.

She was getting a bit pissed off at being shouted at and held hostage in her own home. This was her haven and he'd invaded it. She also figured that if he was going to go stab-crazy, he'd have done it by now, so this time she answered more confidently, adding a touch of sass for good measure.

'It's here. Outside in the barn. Why do you want to know? Have you got another sick little secret hidden inside that you want to perv over? Or do you get a kick out of reminiscing, you know, about the good old days when you murdered innocent women in your shagged-out mobile home?'

A twitch in the corner of his left eye was a tell. It was true. He had killed them. And then a tut and another order. 'Show me! Now, move.'

The terse response again proved to Cathy she'd touched a nerve and emboldened, she stood firm until he reached around the back of her head and grabbed her hair roughly, twisting the ponytail so tightly it pulled on the roots of her scalp, causing her to wince and her eyes to water.

'I said move, NOW!' Guy shoved Cathy roughly and with his arm around her neck and the knife under her chin, they both made for the door.

'And just so you know, all it will take is one slice through your jugular to end you, nice and quick, so don't try anything. Do you understand?'

Gripped once more by terror and pain, her earlier bravado seeping away with every second, Cathy could only make a squeaking sound that he obviously took as a yes. After she flicked the latch and opened the door with trembling hands, they stepped outside into the dimming summer evening.

Ahead, there was just enough time to glimpse the view she'd fallen in love with, that very first morning at Blacksheep, one that had brought her back to life and given her hope. The sight of it caused her to sob out loud and wonder if she'd ever see it again.

34

Turning right, they passed through the herb garden gate and followed the stone path that led along the front of the house. Tears coursed down Cathy's cheeks because she knew she was going to die. He couldn't let her live so was going to kill her, then go back for the sick, evil paintings that were still on the table.

And what about Sheena? Cathy prayed she'd wake up and raise the alarm. But even if Sheena survived, when Alfie got home Cathy would be gone, in every sense of the word. It would kill him, too.

They continued on, around the back, towards the barn which was never locked. When they reached the entrance, Cathy grabbed the edge of the corrugated steel door and yanked it forwards, the metal dragging on the concrete below making the awful screeching sound she knew so well.

Stepping through the gap, Cathy tried to calm herself. Her tear-blurred eyes adjusted to the dim rays of remaining daylight that struggled to illuminate the room via the murky, dust-fogged window on the far wall.

Directly in front of them stood the shell of Luna, another

muse perhaps, and part of his freak-show fantasy life. Something that Guy clung on to like his paintings of those poor dead women.

As they shuffled forward Cathy hoped, prayed, wished and begged to anything and anyone that it would divert his attention enough so she could try to escape. When he released her hair, she found a smidgen of hope, only to have it obliterated by the anger in Guy's voice when he saw his van.

'What the hell have you done to her?'

'We're restoring her. What does it look like.' The spark of rebellion she'd summoned earlier reignited, abetted the stubborn streak that refused to use his pathetic name for the dismantled van. 'We were giving it a new lease of life – but now I wish we'd set fire to it, or the scrap man had crushed it into a cube because it's cursed and vile, like you.'

Guy huffed his derision and it only emboldened Cathy in what she presumed were her last moments. 'That's how you got the women away, isn't it? In that. Are you going to put me in there, too? Once you've had your big hurrah and ruined more people's lives.' Cathy was running on adrenalin now and surprised herself with her erudite thinking and – sod it – telling the psycho exactly what she thought of his death-on-wheels camper.

'Get Agatha Christie here, joining up all the dots. You think you're so smart don't you, and yes, you're right. Luna was the perfect way to spirit my ladies off to a better place once I'd had my fun. And they came to me willingly, just like you did today. Don't you see the symbolism? It's truly beautiful, as are you, and you'll make the perfect final sacrifice.'

'God, you're totally deranged, aren't you! So, I'm your last hurrah, am I? And I take it once you've got rid of me you're going into retirement. Giving up the serial killer day job for your pipe and slippers. What a joke.'

'Oh, it's no joke, dear little Cathy. This has been my life's work, and you'll go down in history as my final masterpiece. I'll paint you once I'm home and put you with the others where you belong.'

'You're sick. You know that, don't you? And I hate to break it to you, but you're not taking me anywhere in that! The engine's in pieces and unless you're blind as well as deranged, it's got no wheels so best of luck sorting that out, mate.'

God she was so angry and although it was risky being arsey, the thought of those beautiful faces meeting their end at the hands of the nutjob holding a knife to her back, ignited such rage she couldn't hold it in any longer.

'You won't get away with it, you know, not these days! It's not the seventies, and someone will have seen you at the festival today. Caught you on their phones or CCTV, and ANPR even as you drove through the village. Christ, they're Ring doorbell mad down there and someone'll have you bang to rights.' Cathy's brain was spinning like an alternator. Ping, ping, ping came the thoughts one by one, counter-arguments, jibes, reasons she might stay alive, firing on all cylinders.

'Loads of people knew I was going to meet you today – my partner for a start – and you'll have a job shutting him up in Amsterdam.'

It then occurred to her that Sheena was in grave danger because she'd been with Cathy when they had first spoken to Guy, unless– *Oh God what if he's already killed her? Did he go upstairs while I was out? Does he know she's here? Bluff it out, try to get him to run.*

'You're the first person the police will come looking for if anything happens to me, so you're well and truly fucked, mate! And then there's Maddy, who will remember seeing me at the festival and she'll tell the police that we were talking about

Deborah, and they'll join the dots and then you're going to prison for the rest of your life–'

The scream that erupted from Guy was sub-human and had he not grabbed her by the hair and flung her to the floor himself, she would have knelt and cowered anyway. As she hit the concrete, her elbow and hips taking the brunt of the fall, the initial pain of grazed skin was obliterated by more, worse, as Guy began a frenzied attack.

Cursing and screaming obscenities. Kicking at any part of her exposed torso, Cathy winced and gasped at each blow inflicted by Guy. Curled into a ball she waited for the end as images of Alfie and Skip and her mum and dad flashed against the black canvas of scrunched-shut eyes that blocked out the crazed man on the other side.

And then there was a thud.

The kicking stopped.

Another thud and a groan, then silence.

Slowly unfurling her hands from around her head, Cathy dared to peep, looking upwards, trying to focus. Seeing first a pair of black wellington boots and then, as her eyes travelled higher, the hem of an unmistakable green mac, and finally, the face of Bertha staring down, holding Alfie's big shovel that was now smeared with blood.

'You all right, lass?'

'Bertha... What...'

Another groan diverted her gaze towards Guy and before Bertha could respond to Cathy, the steel blade of the shovel whacked him again, skull on metal, rendering him silent.

'Bloody basta'd,' muttered Bertha as she kicked the knife across the barn floor, well out of reach, then hobbled back towards Cathy who'd managed to sit, dazed and in agony but awash with relief.

'Bertha, what are you doing... how did you know where to look?'

'Heard that bloody door open, din't I. Right bloody noise it makes. Always got on me nerves did that door. Anyway's, I came to find out what's for me supper, but you'd buggered off, an' I saw fire were lit and yer car out front so thought I'd best have a look round, make sure you weren't up to no good and 'ad remembered to put me chickens to bed.'

Her and her sodding chickens!

Had it not hurt so much Cathy would have laughed.

'Oh, I forgot, you'd best 'ave this.' Bertha reached into her mac pocket and pulled out Cathy's phone and passed it to her.

'Found it on't kitchen table and thought it were a bit odd you'd not tekken it, seein' as you young'uns never go anywhere without one stuck to yer ear. Our Alfred's been ringin, saw 'is name on the screen, not that I were bein' nosy or owt. Oh, and that bloody annoyin' Sheena's prancing around in the kitchen in nowt but her knickers and a vest so I told her to go an' make herself respectable, like.'

Cathy grimaced in pain, but never before had she been so glad to hear Bertha's voice or listen to her grumble on, but then from nowhere her bottom lip wobbled and a bubble of hysteria made its way upwards. It was as though Bertha was oblivious to Cathy's distress or what had just happened. But then again, Bertha was made of strange stuff, probably titanium.

'Thank God you came, Bertha... he was going to... he was... he was going to kill me.'

'Aye, lass. Thought as much when I saw him kicking seven bells out of you. Don't hold wi' blokes hittin' women. Bloody basta'ds. Anyways, less chat and more haste. We need to get you cleaned up an' you'd best ring the coppers so we can have him over there locked up.'

Cathy nodded and sucked in great gulps of air to quell the

urge to cry in front of Bertha, who she knew wouldn't take kindly to a show of weakness.

And as if to prove an unspoken point, Bertha added, 'Or we could get the gun and finish him off, then put him in a sack and bury him on't moor. Shame we never 'ad pigs. Could've chopped him up and fed him to 'em. Job done nice and tidy.'

When Cathy began to laugh, it rapidly turned to the hysteria she'd been holding in ever since she felt the knife at her back and once it was out, she couldn't stop, great big bursts of hiccupping, snorting laughter as she stared at the prone figure of a serial killer.

As Cathy sucked in air and tried desperately to get a grip, Bertha simply tutted and grabbed the phone from Cathy's hand and jabbed the screen, tapping her wellie on the concrete while she waited for someone to pick up. When they did, the person at the other end probably wished they'd called in sick.

'Yes, an' about bloody time too. I want the police and an ambulance up at Blacksheep Farm, quick as you can. We're off the Hathersage Road. What do you want to know me name for? Just bloody listen. There's been an attempted murder. Yes, yes, you 'erd me right. Some lunatic attacked the lass and I whacked 'im wi' the shovel. No he's not dead, don't think he is any road, but that's not my problem, is it! Just send the coppers an' one of them paramedicals and tell 'em to hurry up, I've not 'ad me supper. Right, right, will do.'

'Are they on their way?' Cathy prayed they were.

'Aye, so they said.'

Dread, at the thought of Guy coming round, engulfed Cathy as she stared at the cherry red pool of blood seeping below his head. 'What if he wakes up before they get here?'

Another tut and a roll of the eyes from Bertha who answered, 'Then I'll bash 'is bloody brains in!'

35

August 14th, the day of Dave the Rave's wedding had finally been crossed off the calendar and Cathy welcomed something that would take their minds off the awful events of the previous weeks.

When she teetered downstairs in her very high heels, Alfie was already pacing the floor, his white dress shirt undone at the collar and his bow tie... where was it? Cathy scanned the room and spotted it stretched around the lid of the teapot. Retrieving it quickly, she placed it on the table next to her bag, the wedding card and a box of confetti, and still Alfie hadn't acknowledged her. He continued muttering, squinting his eyes at the words on the A4 sheet, stopping to repeat a sentence then moving on.

He's nervous about his speech. He doesn't mean it. He'll notice you in a minute.

In the end, the need to get going outweighed Cathy's desire for a compliment. Putting her bits and bobs into her handbag, she interrupted Alfie's rehearsal. 'Love, time to go. We can't keep Dave waiting so here, put your tie on and I'll lock up. I'll drive as well. Then you can keep the bridegroom calm on the way to the town hall. Now chop-chop.'

'Bloody hell, Cathy, why didn't you say? I didn't realise... right, right, just pass us it here and I'll put it on in the car. Bloody stupid thing. Why Dave let Sheena talk him into us wearing one of these and that daft bloody top hat I'll never know...' He stuffed the tie in his pocket and headed for the door. 'I'll practice my speech on the way to Dave's mam and dad's.'

Remembering he'd forgot his daft hat, he picked it up from the table and stuffed the speech into his pocket. Then, at last, he looked Cathy up and down. This was followed by a smile. 'You look right nice, love. Proper bonny.'

It was all Cathy had been waiting for and as she blushed, covered up her self-consciousness by checking in the mirror that her coiled hair was still springy. Then she smoothed down the skirt of her new chiffon dress — dusky pink, maxi, dreamily floaty and covered in embroidered flowers. She'd treated herself in the hope that feeling good on the outside would give her confidence on the inside – and so far it was working.

It was going to be a very long day, but she was determined to get through it for herself and also for Alfie whose nerves were getting the better of him already. And of course she wanted to see their friends tie the knot. Dave the Rave and, she chuckled to herself as she closed the front door, the very soon-to-be Sheena the Rave.

Cathy staggered into the kitchen, knees buckling under the weight of her fifteen stone pissed-up partner who she swore was far heavier than he let on. Thankfully, Alfie had managed, with her help, to walk the few feet from the car to the farm door. It had taken three people to get him out of the wedding venue and onto the back seat and in the last few minutes she'd toyed with the idea of getting a blanket and leaving him where he was. But the thought of cleaning the interior if the buffet (two platefuls at that) made a reappearance, left her even more determined to get drunk-boy inside.

After a lot of staggering and colliding with the table, Cathy heaved Alfie onto one of the armchairs by the fire, where she intended leaving him all night, because not a chance would she get him up the stairs. She manhandled him out of his jacket, yanked off his shoes and then covered him with a throw before making herself a much-deserved cup of tea.

Minutes later, her own heels discarded and a brew in hand, she sat opposite and watched Alfie sleep it off. The kitchen bowl was on his knee and a bottle of water tucked down the side of the cushion.

As his chest rose then fell, Cathy pondered what had been a lovely day of sunny weather, Valerie the jolly registrar, a slap-up dinner, Alfie sweating and dabbing his way through what turned out to be an excellent best man speech, and Mr and Mrs Rave taking to the dance floor.

Cathy thought she'd done really well to stay the course but as soon as the disco got into full swing and the noise levels prevented anyone from having a decent conversation, she wanted to bow out and Alfie getting hammered gave her a great excuse.

She'd seen him that way before and it never bothered her because he was a happy drunk, full of bonhomie – yet that evening there was something different. It was as though every drink he threw down his neck acted like rocket fuel, making him talk faster and louder, dead set on being the life and soul until the spark fizzled out and he collapsed in a heap on Sheena's mam's knee.

What was going on in his head? Something wasn't right but that was for another day. She needed to sleep and as she passed Alfie on the way to the stairs, she stopped and kissed his head.

Sleep well, you bloody loon. I love you.

Three days later, the tsunami hit Blacksheep and in hindsight Cathy should have seen it coming. It was as though Alfie had been holding on until he'd got through the wedding, blanking out what had happened up in the barn with Guy, refusing to talk about it, or to look at the photo of Skip on the windowsill.

There'd been moody silences, sleepless nights where he'd kept Cathy awake tossing and turning, then stomping downstairs to watch television till daybreak. He wasn't eating properly and after a post-wedding hangover, was back on the beer again, popping open a bottle, knocking it back like it was saving his life.

It was worse than walking on eggshells, more like landmines, never knowing if one wrong word was going to be the thing that set him off. And in the end it wasn't Cathy asking if he wanted a brew, or the detective who called to give them an update on the investigation into Guy Alexander.

It was a fox.

While DS Lindsay explained where they were up to, Alfie had averted his eyes and picked at a knot of wood on the table, making hmm noises here and there, leaving Cathy to ask questions. She began with what she'd come to refer to in her head as 'death-on-wheels'. The blue camper that they'd fallen in love with, and she'd named Maggie, the thing Alfie had pinned his hopes and summer dreams on, now symbolised the thing she'd been running away from. Evil.

'Will you deal with scrapping the camper van? Me and Alfie don't want to see it ever again and I'm sure nobody will want to buy it, not knowing what happened inside it. We think it's best to get rid of it in case some weirdo ghoul wants to put it in a museum or something. You can give the scrap value to charity if you want. Whatever's best. We'll leave all that to you.' Cathy glanced at Alfie who simply nodded his agreement.

The detective smiled. 'That's fine, just leave it with us and I completely understand where you're coming from.'

Cathy sighed her relief, just wanting an end to the whole hideous event.

'So, to bring you up to date on the investigation, they've wrapped up at the house in York, now all the bodies have been recovered and the rest of the land thoroughly searched. Forensics have what they need, and Alexander has been very forthcoming and compliant, admitting to everything. It makes our life a lot easier and will also save you having to come to court, so long as he doesn't change his plea from guilty.' The DS took a sip of her coffee and waited for the information to sink in.

'And what about his wife? I bet the whole thing was a terrible shock, knowing that those poor women had been there, on their property for years, buried in the woods. It makes me shudder just thinking of it.' Cathy did just that while Alfie seemed unmoved, like he'd switched off to it all.

'She's gone back to her sister's in Spain and, from what I gather, intends to remain there. Looks like she wants to wash her hands of the whole thing, and him, and I suppose you can't blame her.' The DS took another biscuit, the last one of Alfie's favourites and still nothing.

'And Bertha definitely isn't going to get into trouble for hitting him or anything like that?'

A shake of the head confirmed it. 'She acted in defence of you and possible defence of herself when met with violence. It was clear from the injuries you sustained that you'd been attacked, and Alexander admits what he did and the reasons he was at the property. His fingerprints were on the knife he used to–'

When Alfie stood abruptly, knocking the table and causing his full mug of coffee to slop over the sides, Cathy's heart lurched, especially when she saw the look of anger on his deathly pale face.

'I need to be off now, got a job to look at over Stanage way. Back later.' And with that, not even acknowledging Cathy or the DS he almost ran out of the kitchen, jumped into the Defender and leaving a cloud of dust behind, raced away from the farm.

Embarrassed and confused, Cathy stood and busied herself with moving Alfie's cup and clearing the mess on the table. 'I'll come up to Shepherd's with you to update Bertha,' she said. After all, nobody should face the old dragon alone.

And while the DS made small talk with Bertha Walker, Cathy was thinking about Alfie's behaviour and what the hell she was going to do about it.

When she woke the next morning Cathy knew Alfie's side of the bed would be empty. She'd lain awake most of the evening waiting for him to come home, trying to read but failing miserably. As dusk settled, she heard the Defender coming up the lane and her body relaxed. Not her brain and ears, though, because the next few hours were spent wondering why he hadn't come to bed and what he was doing downstairs.

As she listened for noises. Cathy half wanted to go down to see if he was okay, but the other half of her didn't want to get into a row or look at his sullen face. So she'd stayed put, and so did he.

Forcing herself out of bed, she went straight downstairs and found the kitchen empty of humans but scattered with the detritus of what looked like a bacon and egg butty midnight feast, the nauseating stale smell of food lingering in the air. It was as she went to open the kitchen window that she saw the back of Alfie's head below. He was sitting on the bench where he and Skip would spend hours, looking at the view and having a one-sided conversation about rabbits and the weather.

If she closed her eyes she could still imagine Skip sitting by Alfie's side, guarding his best friend and keeping an eye on the yard. It was thinking of Skip that caused her skin to prickle and her insides to tense. So pushing her annoyance at the previous night's performance and the state of the cooker aside, Cathy braved going outside.

Opening the door on a fresh August morning, Cathy was about to inhale the summer breeze when she spotted the shotgun, cocked and resting in the crook of Alfie's arm. Her eyes travelled upwards and met a vacant expression and a face awash with tears, a heaving chest the only movement from a man who appeared to be set in stone.

Approaching slowly, Cathy moved in front of him and crouched on her knees, gravel digging into her skin through her pyjama bottoms.

Gently placing her hands on his arms, she asked softly, 'Alf, sweetheart, what's wrong? Has something happened?'

When he answered immediately it took her by surprise because after the way he'd been of late she expected to have to drag it out of him.

'Bloody bastard fox had some of the chickens and then had a go at Skip's grave. I'm waiting for it then I'm going to kill it.' Still the tears came, like his face was leaking water and there was no tap to turn it off.

'Okay, I get it. Have you sorted Skip out 'cos I don't mind doing it and if there's a mess, I'll deal with the chickens. It's fine. It's going to be okay, love. Don't worry.' Cathy pulled him to her, and he didn't resist, slumping into her body while she held him. 'Alf, please tell me what's going on because I know something's wrong and if you just explain, I can help you sort it out. Is it Skip?'

Cathy didn't think he'd answer because he'd been so closed up of late and anyway, she doubted it was just about losing Skip. He'd lived on a farm forever and understood the circle of life, had told her so many times when they lost lambs and other livestock. So when he spoke into her shoulder, his voice muffled by her pyjama top, it was like whatever he'd been holding in for weeks, months probably, burst forth in a torrent of words and hurt.

'It's everything, Cath. Everything. Me mam being a miserable pain in the arse let-down; our Annie being in the shit with money; and this place going to ruin under our noses; no job, no future; and our Albie being on the other side of the bloody world and Skip... I can't stop thinking about him and I miss him every single minute of the day and then... and then,' he took a breath, 'that fucking bastard psycho came here, to our safe place and was going to kill you and where was I? On a stag-do getting pissed up when I should have been here looking after you and keeping you safe and Jesus, Cath...' – he pulled her to him so tight she thought he might crack a rib – 'I could have lost you and I'm telling you right now if that happens then I'll have nothing, and I can't cope with thinking of life without you. I can't...'

Now Cathy was crying too because she hadn't realised how everything had been building up, locked inside, and she should have known and got him to talk sooner. Her mum had been right, and she'd ignored the signs and been so absorbed in her own issues she'd failed the man she loved. Shame washed over her and then determination stepped in because she was going to put it right. It was her turn to look after Alfie now. She had to be his safe place.

'Alf, let's go inside and I'll make us a drink and then we can have a proper talk and decide what to do, because we can sort this, how you're feeling, I promise.' Cathy's knees were killing, and Alfie was a big bloke to hold up, physically. Mentally was another matter and she swore to take the weight of whatever this was.

Feeling the pressure on her shoulders ease as he raised himself, Cathy carefully picked up the shotgun that had been wedged between them. Once he'd stood, she took his hand and led him inside.

Dr Stevenson had been wonderful. After a brief telephone call with the village surgery where Cathy had insisted that Alfie needed to be seen urgently, they were given a same-day appointment by the huffy receptionist.

Alfie hadn't resisted Cathy's suggestion that he talked it through with a professional. And even though he remained silent during the drive down the hill and sat passively in the waiting room, she felt the tension in his bones when she leaned against him, and his hand gripped hers far too tightly while they sat.

He'd insisted she went in with him. Like she was his security blanket. Earlier, as they talked in the kitchen and he opened up about all the things on his mind, he'd also confessed that when he'd stormed out the day before, he hadn't gone far.

Instead of going to the pub for a bender, he'd had this image of Cathy all alone. So he'd parked up at the bottom of the hill, and once the detective left, blocked the entrance to the lane with the Defender so nobody could get in. And when it got dark he panicked and came back because the fear of something happening to her overwhelmed him. He'd stayed up guarding the house, but the fact he couldn't save the chickens and seeing Skip's grave partially dug up, tipped him over the edge.

And then in the surgery, seated on plastic chairs in front of a fake wooden Formica desk, it hadn't been pleasant, listening to the man she loved falling apart in front of a stranger. Although in a perverse way, Cathy was glad he did because at least the doctor, who listened patiently to it all, witnessed his distress and fragile state of mind for herself.

Kind and understanding, practical and authoritative, after Alfie had confessed to having palpitations, Dr Stevenson listened to his heart and lungs. Next, she booked him in for a same day ECG and a blood MOT with the nurse, just in case he was anaemic or had a thyroid problem. 'Both of those can mimic symptoms of anxiety and depression,' the GP explained.

Alfie bridled slightly when asked about his general mood and if he had any thoughts of harming himself or others, so she assured him it was a precautionary but necessary question as men often downplay their mental health. Then came four short questions to assess his alcohol dependence. 'No, that sounds like normal alcohol use, rather than dependency,' she said reassuringly.

And then came the diagnosis and treatment for what Dr Stevenson considered to be low-level anxiety and depression. 'I'm going to recommend talking therapy, and prescribe some medication,' she said.

'Don't need meds,' said Alfie initially. But after more explanation, he agreed to her writing a prescription. He wouldn't promise to take it immediately so Cathy suggested they could have it at home, just in case, and in the meantime they'd look into therapy and maybe start with an online group.

By the time Dr Stevenson was showing them to the door Cathy was wrung out, but kept her demeanour positive. The GP asked Alfie to return in a fortnight for a review and reminded him that should he take the sertraline and find the side effects unpleasant, he should get in touch.

While Alfie went in for his blood tests, Cathy booked him in for a follow-up appointment and then found a chair at the back of the almost empty waiting room, relishing a few minutes on her own in the quiet. It gave her time to process the last few hours and face something that had been chipping away at her brain during the appointment.

That Alfie was braver than she could ever be because he'd done the thing she couldn't, hadn't. Perhaps if she'd asked for help all those years ago, when she and her life were falling apart, then this might not have happened. One private session, paid for by BUPA, that she walked out of halfway through, didn't cut it.

Yes, there were many factors to Alfie's breakdown, but her reliance on him and the farm to keep her safe had been another burden and she hated that. But this only strengthened her resolve to do whatever it took to get him through, she swore it on her own life. Come hell or high water, Cathy was going to save Alfie right back.

36

ALFIE

It was one of those, 'Uh-oh, what have I done this time' moments when Alfie found Cathy waiting for him at the kitchen table, two mugs of tea and a packet of custard creams laid out, her laptop open, arms folded and, yep, a nervous look on her face.

She'd rang and summoned him minutes earlier, saying that she needed him back at the house, pronto. His first thought as he trudged along the path was that it would be something to do with his mother, which meant he was off the hook, but, as he surveyed the scene in the kitchen, his relief withered like the plants on Bertha's windowsill.

This was followed by a lightning bolt to the heart, forewarning of an email from the bank telling them they were overdrawn again, or maybe it was Albert... yes, that's what it would be. Cathy had planned a Zoom call after filling his brother in on the big meltdown and now he'd have to endure a 'pull yourself together' pep talk. That's all he needed.

As he closed the door behind him, Alfie stifled the irritation that was building inside and warned himself not to fly off the handle before he knew the facts, which prompted him to ask, 'What's going on? Is it Mam?' He could still hope.

'No, love, nothing bad, I promise, now wash your hands and come and have a brew. I've got something I need to tell you, and it's not bad news for a change so don't look so worried.' Cathy added a smile to her statement which relaxed Alfie a lot, and, doing as he was told, he made his way to the sink.

Even if he knew it wasn't going to be the announcement he'd allowed himself to imagine every now and then (the box of Tampax by the loo had made sure of that this month), Cathy's smile allowed the pounding in his chest to abate and that twang of tension to ease a notch.

By the time he was opening the packet of biscuits, he'd convinced himself this was going to be something simple to deal with, like freeing up assets by flogging something they didn't need. Whatever it was, it required the laptop which she was now tapping away at, a smile playing on her lips and a flush creeping up her cheeks. And then as she made eye contact, he caught a definite spark of mischief.

Pushing the laptop to the side before sliding her hands across the table to cover his, which was a bit awkward as he'd got two custard creams wedged in his palms, Cathy spilled the beans.

'Okay... so I don't want any arguments because I've made my mind up and arranged it all. It has been no mean feat, I can tell you, because of your mam mainly, but I'll come to that in a bit...' She came up for air, swallowed, and then squeezed his hands even tighter with no regard for the biscuits whatsoever.

'I've decided what to do with the money Mum and Dad gave me and... we're going on holiday and not just a two-week all-inclusive to Turkey or Greece or somewhere like that.'

At this point Alfie closed his mouth then opened it to protest, no way was she wasting her money. 'Cathy NO, we agreed that it'd be emergency money for if we get in the shit with the bank again and you know, for tests and stuff, important things. Not a fancy holiday.'

But when she raised her hand and gave him the *don't interrupt* stare, he backed down and let Cathy explain, because he was no fool.

'Shush, okay, and don't spoil it, because it's nearly killed me keeping this a secret. So, as I was saying. You and I aren't going on a fancy package holiday. It's a trip of a lifetime, fully sanctioned by Mum and Dad who are over the moon about it. The tickets are booked, and everything is in place here at the farm and this time next week me and thee will be on our way to Thailand, Malaysia and then... wait for it... we're going to stay with Albie who is actually more excited than me if that's even possible. So, what do you think? This is the trip you dreamed of, Alf, the one your dad wanted you to take and something you deserve and need right now. Say something, please, because you're making me nervous.'

It didn't sink in, not really, not at first. They were just words and places and names but slowly the sounds Cathy was making turned into dreams becoming reality, seeing in his mind's eye a face he missed so badly, a brother he could touch. Sand that he'd feel beneath his toes and an ocean he'd swim in. All because of this woman seated opposite who was holding her breath like her life depended on it, waiting for his reaction.

In the seconds before he put his head in his hands, Cathy leapt from her chair and rushed around the table, wrapped her arms around his shoulders, because when it came, there was only one way he could express how he felt.

Thank God for the person who invented kitchen paper, because he and Cathy had gone through at least half a roll as he'd sobbed like a child – he was making a bloody habit of it lately – and she'd followed suit, hopefully knowing his were happy tears and not because he was shit-scared of flying. He'd got into a right lather over a blink-and-you'll-miss-it flight to Amsterdam for Dave's stag. Now he was going halfway round the world!

After pulling themselves together enough to blow their noses, Cathy flicked the kettle on to make a fresh brew and while they waited for it to boil, she explained.

'It was Mum who made me realise that I've been selfish – and before you object, I have, Alf. I'd shut myself off from the outside world as much as possible and while I've been living my best isolated life up here on the hill, you've been struggling, and I became complacent in my care of you. You saved me when I needed it, and just like Julia Roberts said to Richard Gere, because we're obviously dead ringers for the pair of them, it's my turn to save you right back.'

Alfie reached over and twisted his fingers around hers. 'But that money...'

'Alf, stop. We need to do this now. I am not leaving that money in the bank to make zero interest while we plod on here, waiting for your mam to die... and that sounds bloody awful, doesn't it? But that's precisely what we are all doing, marking time and it's not good. Bad karma, negative energy, or whatever you want to call it.

'I just know it's not doing our mental health any good being around someone who is so bitter and twisted that she's poisoning all of us. So we either get away for a while and have some fun and recharge our batteries or we just pack up and leave for good before she sends us to the loony-bin. Or maybe she'll end up there and we spend the rest of our days visiting someone who can't make up her mind if she hates our guts or wants to save our lives!'

Alfie knew that every word was true, and he was glad that

Cathy hadn't sugar-coated it, but he did have one major concern, well, two really.

'But what about you? Will you be able to deal with airports and crowded places? The way I've been lately I'm not exactly what you'd call bodyguard material, bloody crying at the drop of a hat. I got all emosh about that advert where the goats are stuck on the edge of a cliff the other day, proper upset me that did, so if you have a meltdown at check-in, what if I have a panic attack in the departure lounge and need a paper bag to puff into?'

Cathy gripped his fingers tightly. 'Alf, stop. We will be fine I know we will, and you know why.'

'Why?'

'Because I'm pissed off with being scared and I'm not going to let my fear of the outside world hold us back anymore. I will not be a prisoner in my own home and allow the evil people to win. I've done a lot of thinking, and it was seeing you in such a state that brought it all home because what happened to me, the cause and effect, had turned you into a prisoner too. The devastating effect that night had on so many people, the ripples that touched all those lives, is so wrong and for us at least, it has to stop.

'I'd hidden myself away up here. Thinking that the bad people wouldn't find me and look what happened! I finally plucked up the courage to do something that I considered to be brave and ended up bringing evil in the form of a sodding serial killer, right to our door. To my safe haven. How bizarre and messed up is that?

'I tried to do a nice thing for someone, and it went wrong but I know now that I had no control over that series of events. I couldn't have avoided the outcome, the variable timescale that would have affected how it all unfolded, me not bumping into Maddy, taking a different route through the park or even before that, you seeing the camper on the website and buying it at auction. It happened as it happened. The universe had its plan. Simple as that.

'Coming to terms with it made me see that I can't hide forever and the best way to vanquish demons and bad people and blot out the images in my head that give me nightmares, is to face up to them as much as I can. Take new pictures and make new memories to replace the old ones, something to smile about.

'And you know something else? There are other people in all this, who have been worried about us, and gone through our troubles and are aware of more than we give them credit for. By going on an adventure, we can lift them too. Take away some of the anxiety that they feel for us.

'But most of all, Alf, I really do want to save you back and see you live your dreams. Even if, right now, we can't do that here, let's go do it somewhere else while we can.'

Cathy ended on a question. 'So, are we going to do this?'

Alf was stunned and silent. In awe of Cathy who had captured all the horrible, bitter, resentful thoughts that had been swirling inside for so long and made him feel so angry, frustrated, impotent and confused.

Now, letting them go seemed possible. There was a way out. A signpost marked 'freedom this way' and once he'd read the words, a swell of something inside – relief more than anything – began to build and for the first time in ages, Alfie could see another way out. The black clouds were shifting, and the tip of his boots weren't teetering on the highest ledge on the Peaks.

He wasn't looking downwards imagining a swift and lonely descent into oblivion. He was looking up towards a blue sky and white clouds, with the woman he loved more than anything right by his side.

37

CATHY

She knew Alfie was struggling to tap into his emotions. As he avoided eye contact, Cathy watched the rise and fall of his chest and waited for her words to sink in, some she'd rehearsed as she lay by him in bed the night before, some that sprouted from nowhere. She still had more to say, but they would wait.

Cathy watched his face for signs that his fragile soul was going to refuse, put up safety barriers and veto the trip. And she got it, totally. After all, she'd been that person for the last seven years and that was why, she knew with every fibre of her being that he had to say yes. It really was now or never. If they stayed, he'd sink and that meant they both might. And no way was she risking losing the best thing that had ever happened to her.

Giving his hand a wiggle, she caught his attention and when his watery eyes met hers, she noticed the corners begin to crinkle and yes, beneath the beard there was the hint of a smile forming. Then the words she'd waited for.

'Go on then. Let's do it. If you're really sure.'

The whoosh of relief propelled Cathy off her chair and onto Alfie's knee from where she proceeded to strangle-hug the life out of him.

'It's going to be so brilliant, Alf. Honestly, it's nearly done me in keeping everything a secret and arranging it all. But now, we can do the rest together, like plan where we stay in Thailand and all that. I just booked the flights so there was no turning back, but I was pooing myself wondering what I'd do if you refused. Everyone said you'd say yes so I took the chance.

'And we'll need to buy some new clothes, Alf. We've got to look the part of seasoned backpackers so that's on the very big to-do list I've made. Book hotels, buy two huge rucksacks, fill them with our hippy-trail clothes. Ooh, I can't wait. Right.' Cathy clapped her hands as she stood. 'More tea, then we can get cracking.'

Before dazed Alfie could get a word in, she was sprinting across the kitchen towards the kettle, turning once to give him a wink. As she plopped teabags into mugs, Cathy pondered that if she could see auras, there would be a swirling mass of bright colours surrounding Alfie, not a grey or black, or smudgy brown in sight.

The question, when it came, after he'd nipped for a wee and as she poured boiling water onto the teabags, was the one Cathy knew he'd ask first so she'd made damn sure she'd covered every angle of it.

'Cathy, love. What about my mother? She won't be pleased at all and who's going to look after her? She can't manage by herself, and our Annie won't step in. Not that I blame her.'

Bringing the mugs to the table, Cathy resisted the urge to feel smug as she answered, 'Don't fret, my love. I've arranged it all.'

Taking a seat, she explained. 'You know Sheena and Dave are waiting for their house to be finished on the new estate and they absolutely hate living with Dave's mam and dad?'

Alfie nodded.

'Well, they're going to move in here and look after the farm and the chickens, and seeing as it's Sheena's job anyway – you know, being a home help – she's going to keep an eye on your mam and help out if Bertha needs her, just like we do, now.'

'Seriously! She'd do that for us?'

Cathy tutted. 'Of course she will. That's what friends are for, and she'll be getting paid, too. I wouldn't expect anyone to put up with Bertha for free, even though we have to.'

Alfie looked confused. 'But who's going to pay her? We can't afford it and no way are you using your money, I'm adamant about that.'

'Like I said, it's all organised. Your mam can use some of that benefit money, you know, the one the lady from social services arranged, the Attendance Allowance. It'll be going into her account every month and don't forget; she's got plenty stashed in the bank from your dad's insurance. Your mam isn't short of a bob or two so, it's about time she put her hand in her pocket. Instead of expecting everyone to be at her beck and call for free, she can pay someone, like millions of other people have to.'

Alfie had gone from looking confused to stunned. 'And she's agreed to all this, has she?'

'No, not yet. But she will do because our Bertha is going to have three options. Manage by herself in splendid isolation, pay for some care, or go into a home. Simple as that.'

Cathy was aware she sounded very matter-of-fact but as Annie had advised, be firm with Alfie and Mam. Don't let him wimp out or her battle-axe you into submission.

Alfie had now gone very pale. 'Shit, am I going to have to tell her?'

Cathy couldn't help but laugh at the look of abject fear on his face but rather than ruin the mood, she put him out of his

255

misery quickly. 'No, love. I'll tell her myself. Lately I'm the only one who seems to get a word of sense out of her and seeing as all this is my idea, I'll deal with it. But if it makes you feel better, Annie helped me plan it all and is fully supportive. If by some chance there is an emergency, she'll step in but otherwise, is going to leave it to Sheena.

'Annie just wants us to get away, hassle free, okay. But that's why I wanted to tell you first, before Bertha, because I knew if she got wind of it, she'd spoil the surprise out of spite, and then lay a massive guilt trip on you.'

Alfie nodded. 'Bloody Nora. She's not going to be happy, is she? And it's her birthday this week. She'll say we ruined it for her, that's what she's like.'

Cathy smiled. 'No, she isn't, but she's done her fair share of making people unhappy and sometimes karma comes and bites you on the arse. And yes, I know she'll use her birthday to make us feel worse, but we'll deal with it. And I've got her a nice present that might make her smile, so don't fret.'

'Thanks, love. For offering to tell her. She has a way of messing with my head, and I can't be dealing with her right now. I don't think she'll like the idea of Sheena and Dave moving in, either. You know she can't stand Sheena and thinks Dave is a bit simple, always has done since we were kids. The horrible names she called him even when we were at infant school. I remember her telling me and Albert that if he was hers, she'd have sold him to the circus or left him outside an orphanage. How sick is that!?'

Cathy cringed, remembering the very similar vile words that had cut Annie to the quick months before. 'Yes, it is sick but sometimes I wonder if Bertha just likes to shock us and it's all bluster. But anyway, don't dwell on stuff like that, not today.'

At that Alfie just grunted and sipped his brew.

'So, as I was saying, Sheena can dish it out and give as good as she gets, so she's a match for Bertha. Apparently she's used to dealing with worse clients than your mam, if that's even possible. She doesn't stand for any nonsense, but at the same time really loves her job and you can just tell she likes spending time with her clients. So you never know, her and Bertha might become besties. Imagine that.'

Another grunt and a raised eyebrow from Alfie told Cathy he wasn't convinced, and neither was she, to be fair.

'Sheena also gave me a few little gems that might persuade Bertha to see it from our perspective. Basically, that living in the comfort of your own home with someone to come and clean, do your washing and cook your meals is preferable to a poky room at Daisybank Rest Home in the village with set meals, communal dining, and bingo on a Friday followed by chair aerobics. I reckon even your mam will see sense over that!'

'Hmm, well. Rather you than me. But I will come with you, for back-up, if it'll help.' Alfie took another sip of his brew while Cathy chuckled, knowing that it was the last thing he wanted to do, go into battle with Bertha.

'Nope. I'd rather do this myself as long as you promise not to listen to any of her mind games when she starts playing the violin and giving you a guilt trip. Enough is enough and it's not like we're abandoning her. She'll be well cared for, better than some poor old folk in this country, that's for sure.'

'I promise I won't let her get to me and you're right, she'll be fine if Sheena is around and you never know, she might warm to Dave after all these years. Miracles do happen. Look, I found you.'

Cathy rolled her eyes at that but at least he was still on board. No way was Cathy giving Bertha the chance to scupper things which was why she had to keep Alfie away from her as much as possible and, she had one more thing up her sleeve that would hopefully make damn sure he didn't lose his nerve.

'And, I have two more surprises for you.' Cathy's heart beat faster, knowing how much fun the next bit would be.

Raising his eyebrows, Alfie said, 'I don't think I can take much more today. But go on, what else have you been up to?'

'Well, the first one is quite simple really. Albie is FaceTiming us later so we can get all giddy about the trip and make some plans but now, we have to get Annie on the line, she'll be dying to find out what you think. Hold on.'

Cathy slid the laptop across and tapped the messenger app and waited for the screen to show the faces she knew had been waiting at the other end. Within seconds, Annie and Joe appeared, Annie's excitement zapping down the line as she spoke. 'Have you told him? Aw, you have. Just look at his little chufty face and red cheeks. Are you happy, Alf? It's been killing us all waiting to tell you.'

Alfie opened his mouth to answer but before he could, Eliza and Ezra bounded into the room, interrupting the grown-ups. While they piled on to Joe's knee and Annie hoisted Eli onto hers, Eliza whispered something into her dad's ear.

Joe laughed and said, 'Go on then, you tell him.'

Eliza's big bug eyes and smile took up all the screen. 'Uncle Alf, guess what? Just guess, go on you'll not believe it but it's true.' She didn't actually give him time to ask before she exploded with, 'We's coming to Nudezealand to see Uncle Albs and we's meeting you and Aunty Cathy when you get there for a big family holiday and we's going on a huge plane that has an upstairs and a downstairs and it takes more than a day to get there and Dad said we'd better bloody behave ourselves or he'll chuck us out the door and into the ocean, so Ezra started crying and Mam told Dad off for saying stupid things.'

'No, I did not cry, you big fat liar!'

Ezra's protest was ignored by Eliza who was on a roll. 'Yes you did, mardy-bum. Are you happy, Uncle Alf? Cos I am. It's going to be the best most exciting thing ever.'

Chaos. That was the only way Cathy could describe the scene as Ezra and Eliza, oblivious to the fact their uncle was fighting to control his emotions while they fought for screen time and the chance to explain all about where Nudezealand was on the map, and that Uncle Albs was taking them horse riding and camping in the mountains.

What they didn't mention, because it was between the grown-ups at Cathy's insistence, was that once she'd had the idea for the trip, she suggested they all came too, and paid for the flights so that the whole family could be reunited.

Annie had been stubborn at first but knowing Alfie was struggling, and that her beloved dad would have wanted them to be together more than anything, she accepted Cathy's once in a lifetime offer and the flights were booked.

Albie was sorting the accommodation with friends who ran a holiday lodge complex and was giving them mates' rates, so now all they had to do was keep Eliza and Ezra calm for the next six weeks until October half term. Cathy didn't rate Annie and Joe's chances and was glad she'd be miles away, preferably on a nice quiet beach in Thailand.

All that was left now was to face the beast up the hill, but she was going to tackle that tomorrow. Today was for making plans and hitting the online shops or heading to Go Outdoors and going crazy in the rucksack department.

No matter what, Cathy was determined to ride the happy wave because the scene in their kitchen was just the start. Taking her phone from her back pocket, she captured the moment for posterity with a photo and made a mental note to do the same later, when Albie called.

The two photographs would go on the first page of the

album she was going to buy the next day. Something she could touch and feel and remember and hold against her heart. To remind herself that no matter what life threw at them, loss, sadness, bad people, psycho artists and possibly the worst mother in the whole of Derbyshire, they'd get through the darkest of times. Together, as a family.

38

BERTHA

Bertha flicked off the television and huffed loudly. Looking at her phone on the arm of the chair she pondered on whether to ring Cathy and think of an excuse to get her to come up. Stubborn pride got in the way as always and instead of admitting she'd like a bit of company; she flicked open the magazine that rested on the other arm and seethed silently.

Well they can all sod off. Ungrateful lot. There's me putting a roof over Alfred's head and he can't even be bothered to call in and say hello.

And that Ann keeps the kiddies away out of spite and as for Albert, well, if he thinks snubbing me will make me lose sleep, he's wrong.

It's a bloody good job for them that me and Jacob made a joint will, otherwise I'd have rang that there solicitor in town and changed it. Left the lot to some charity or other, one that'd right piss them all off.

And then, with punishing her kids one last time in mind, she thought of the perfect beneficiary. Bertha imagined them all sitting around the solicitor's desk, dressed in black, sombre faces masking their anticipation as the last will and testament of

Bertha Walker was read and finding out she'd left her entire estate to The Conservative Party. She was just having a chuckle to herself when the sounds of the front door opening and Cathy's voice snapped her out of her happy place.

'It's only me.'

Bertha rolled her eyes. *Yes, it's only you. S'pose you'll have to do, seein' as no bugger else can be bothered.*

Straightening in her armchair, she feigned great interest in her magazine and waited for her visitor to appear.

'Sorry I'm late popping up.' Cathy placed her load on the kitchen table as she explained. 'We had a lie-in for a change and I treated Alfie to a cooked breakfast. I see you've had your porridge, good. It's much better for you than a fry-up. But I got you a nice cream cake assortment and some pasties from Greggs. Naughty but nice.'

Bertha forced a smile as Cathy winked and made her way over to the sofa opposite and began plumping cushions and stacking magazines.

'I'll just have a quick tickle round the kitchen then I'll make us a nice brew. Tea or coffee?'

'Tea, in the pot, if you're stopping. And I might as well have a cake, seein' as you made the effort.'

'Of course I did, anything to make the almost-birthday girl crack a smile.' Cathy finished faffing and went back into the kitchen, humming the birthday song which was bloody annoying.

'It's not me birthday till Friday an' anyways, I don't hold with making a fuss. Nowt special about bein' as old as I am. I'll be gone soon an' then you can all 'ave a proper celebration.' Bertha folded her arms and huffed, knowing deep down her erudite words were true, even if she did wonder now and then if anyone would actually miss her when she popped her clogs.

'Yes, I know it's on Friday, and if you behave yourself maybe

Annie will let the kids come up and give you a card and of course me and Alfie will pop in, unless you fancy coming down for tea. I'll make you something nice, whatever you want.'

Bertha tutted. 'I'll have a think on it and see how me legs are. I'm not going in that wheelchair contraption or pushing that stupid frame thing, either. And that's before you suggest it. I'm not a cripple yet.'

It was Cathy's turn to huff as she put her hand on her hip and attempted a stern look at Bertha, not that it did any good because everyone knew Cathy didn't have it in her to be tough, not with anyone.

'Whatever you say, grumpy guts. Just have a think if there's anything special you'd like, as long as it's not offal I'll cook it, okay! No tripe or liver: it makes me feel sick. Right, kettle on, cake, natter. Won't be a tick.'

Cathy got on with faffing under Bertha's watchful gaze and it was as she observed the laying out of cakes and warming of the teapot, she realised there was something else.

Bertha couldn't put her finger on it. Like the lass was nervous. A bit too bright and chirpy, as though she had something to say or on her mind. Far too jolly. Bertha couldn't remember her being like this before. Cathy always seemed relaxed, especially after the daft lass convinced herself they'd formed a bond.

A secret p'raps. Bertha twisted further in her chair to get a better look at Cathy as she pottered about, clattering dishes in the sink, squirting Fairy Liquid, opening cupboards and storing the shopping she'd brought, and humming again. That was getting right on her nerves.

Bertha considered herself good at reading people. She'd always known when one of her three had something to hide and never failed to get it out of them in them end. Shifty little bastards they were. Like when Ann and Albert hid the rabbit in the barn. Bertha soon put a stop to that. Yes, Cathy was definitely on edge.

Might be she'd heard something about that bloody nutter. Bertha wondered if they'd let him out, but that was impossible because he'd pleaded guilty and once the court doo-das were over he'd be stuck in jail for the rest of his life, or so the coppers said. Well, if that low-life ever showed up there again Bertha would take the gun to him this time, no messing about. Never had time for trespassers, especially mental ones.

Perhaps Alfred had had one of his funny turns. He was a soft lad at times and just remembering the state he was in when he got back from Amsterdam made her shake her head in dismay, and disgust that he'd even been there in the first place. Full of prostitutes and diseases and he'd be riddled with the clap, now. She blamed that stupid Dave for suggesting it in the first place. She'd never liked him and told Cathy to make sure Alfred got a shot of penicillin just to be on the safe side.

No wonder Alfred went all daft in the head, probably from too much beer and sex... oh, and that whacky baccy that you could buy in the corner shop. Bertha didn't know what the world was coming to and the sooner she was with Jacob, away from head cases and sex-mad drug addicts, the better.

Bertha reckoned Alfred might have been hallucinating or still under the influence, that's why he took it all so badly, thinking that Cathy might have been murdered and Bertha was going to get locked up for whacking the mad bloke with the shovel. It had taken the coppers to put him straight and assure him it were self-defence; any daft beggar knew that.

Bertha tutted, irritated by the memory of Alfred's meltdown. She shoved it from her mind and instead, focused on Cathy who gave her a bright smile.

'Almost done. I'll bring it over on the tray then you can choose your cake.'

'If there's an éclair, I'll have that. Don't suppose you'll want one, seein' as you've had a big breakfast.' No way was she sharing her cakes.

Even that, a Bertha special, a cracking curmudgeonly comment hadn't wiped the smile off Cathy's face. Maybe she was losing her touch or maybe, the reason Cathy wasn't taking the bait was she was happy.

Uh-oh. That was it. She was up the tub, at last. Served herself right if she was, especially after Bertha had told her and Ann what she thought about bairns tying you down and ruining your life. But then again, nobody took any notice of what she said.

Like when she'd seen the photos in the paper. The one she kept hidden under the cushion of her armchair, that she'd take out and have a look at now and then. It also gave her immense pleasure having it there because when she broke wind, his face was directly under her bottom. Simple pleasures were always the best.

Front page news it was. All about the loony artist who'd tried to kill Cathy and had gone around in his campervan murdering all those other lasses. Poor buggers.

Bertha was as gobsmacked as everyone else though, when the coppers came and told them they'd found all them bodies buried in his garden. He'd started his killing spree in the seventies apparently, and even then she'd not put two and two together, not until Cathy came with the newspaper.

Nothing could have prepared Bertha for that shock. She'd recognised him straight away from the old photo, from back in the seventies, in his hippy days. No mistaking him. Took her breath right out of her lungs and gave her bad dreams for days after. If she'd known who he was when she'd hit him with the big shovel, she'd have given him a few more whacks for good measure! And chopped his wotsit off, too!

They'd even shown a photo of the van from back then. It looked nothing like the heap of scrap that Alfie had been planning to do up. She'd watched the police put it on a low-loader and take it away for forensic examination. Not that they'd found much: Alfred had stripped it down to the metal, ripped the insides and the engine out and destroyed any evidence. Bloody idiot!

That's why Bertha hadn't recognised it, or him, not after fifty-odd years and to be fair she only saw the back of his head when she walloped him, then he was covered in dust and blood while they waited for the coppers and the ambulance to arrive. Took bloody ages it did. Bertha had been miffed about not getting her tea, but that Sheena made herself useful for once and went to the chippy. After she'd put some clothes on, the floozy.

Bertha still wasn't going to say owt. There was no point for a start. It wouldn't change anything. It wouldn't save those poor lasses and it wouldn't surprise her if they thought she was making it up or going doo-lally. But she knew what she knew, no matter how bloody mad it all was.

No, it was nobody's business but her own and the secret she'd guarded for all of them years was going with her to the grave. Anyroad, no good would come of thinking about it at the moment. Best to focus on the present and Cathy who was on her way over with the tray.

Bertha locked Cathy in her sights and yes, she was definitely being shifty, nervous in fact. She rubbed her hands together in glee, not necessarily at the assortment of cakes, more in anticipation at the challenge ahead.

An éclair and a vanilla slice and a mug of tea down, Bertha was relieved Cathy hadn't eaten one of the cakes. There was a jam and cream doughnut and a custard tart left. They'd talked about everything under the sun, like how mild it was for

September and that Alfred was busy working over at Bedford's Farm, and in the meantime Bertha was losing the will to live.

In the end, she couldn't take the nervous yakking and asked, 'Is summat up, lass? You don't seem right. Been proper twitchy since you got here, you have. You can tell me, you know. I don't always bite and thanks to them cakes, I've been fed.'

Bertha thought a bit of levity might encourage the loosening of lips so when Cathy's eyes widened, and she sucked in a breath, Bertha knew she was on the money and a big announcement, or even better, a confession, was on the cards. After shuffling in her chair to get comfy, she waited impatiently for Cathy to spill the beans.

39
CATHY

Their afternoon tea and cakes session had gone so well that Cathy was contemplating saving the big announcement for the next day, or even the one after that. However, being well and truly caught in Bertha's headlights made wimping out a non-option. She had to get it over with and today was the day.

Sucking in a deep breath before responding to Bertha's question, Cathy began with a compliment. 'You don't miss a trick, do you? Actually, there is something I need to talk to you about while Alfie isn't around.'

'Oh aye, what's he done now? Been a lazy beggar I expect, just like his brother.'

'No, no, nothing like that but as you know he's not been right for a while and after he got...' Cathy was wary of saying anything that would encourage Bertha to put Alfie down. '...a bit overwrought the other week, well, I've been trying to think of a way to cheer him up.'

Bertha rolled her eyes, huffed and folded her arms under her ample bosom but thankfully kept her pursed lips firmly closed.

Cathy prayed for strength then ploughed on. 'Anyway... and

please don't get annoyed or worried because I've thought of everything and there's a solid plan in place.' She paused to gauge Bertha's pre-announcement reaction and steel herself for the big moment. On seeing the set-in-stone expression, Cathy just went for it.

'I've booked me and Alfie a holiday. Well, it's more of a once-in-a-lifetime trip because we'll be gone for a few months, seeing as we're going to the Far East and also...' Cathy knew this bit wouldn't go down well, '...to see Albie in New Zealand. I think it's just what Alfie needs to perk him up and it's been his lifelong dream, to go backpacking. So that's what we're doing.'

Silence. Absolute and utter silence, accompanied by a cold hard glare, followed Cathy's big reveal and as she waited for Bertha to react, her heart pounded so badly.

Eventually, the mothership spoke. 'And how long is "a few months", exactly? Is that some poncy way of dressing up the fact that you're leaving for good? Like that lazy-arse Albert. Abandoning a crippled pensioner in the back of beyond while you two go off finding yourselves on the other side of the world.'

Jesus Christ, talk about dramatic. Cathy thought it but didn't say it. This was more or less the self-centred reaction she'd imagined when rehearsing this speech.

Cathy's 'NO!' came out a bit louder and more emphatic than intended and made Bertha start. 'It's not forever but the joy of backpacking is going where the mood takes you and I don't want to limit our time with Albie because Alf has missed him a lot, and so have I.'

'Aye, just like Albert was s'posed to be going for six months and look what happened there! Them New Zealanders must be a bit stuck for decent workers if they're letting him extend his visa every five bloody minutes, that's all I can say. Or 'as he finally found a lass that'll put up with him? Is that it? He's all loved up. About time too, was starting to think he might be one of them gays but then again, over my dead body would one o' my sons turn out like that. Proper Walkers they are. Men through an' through.'

Cathy sighed, not wanting to discuss Albie's love life because there'd be murders. And she didn't want to go back around the houses with the 'you're the sodding reason why he left in the first place,' argument. So she changed tack. 'I have no intention of settling overseas as I'd miss my parents,' – she swallowed first and crossed her fingers – 'and you too much. But Alfie is my top priority right now and as I said earlier, I've put things in place to make sure you and the farm are well cared for while we're away. So there's absolutely no reason to be worried or get your knickers in a twist, okay?'

'What the bloody hell do you mean by that? *Put things in place*. I'm not a bleedin' invalid or going gaga, so if you think you're going to shove me in one of them homes for oldies, you'd better think again.'

Cathy tutted. 'Well that's funny because two minutes ago you were accusing us of abandoning a crippled pensioner in the back of beyond, so make your mind up, Bertha!'

It was Bertha's turn to tut, and when she'd unfolded her arms, Cathy noticed her fingers tapping the arm of the chair and her right foot kept the beat. A sure sign an explosion was on the cards. But first, came a question.

'So, I take it you're going to enlighten me, and explain how you're going to run my life while you're off enjoying yours oh, and while you're at it, how've you managed to afford a fancy holiday? I thought you two were skint, which, I'd like to remind you, is why I'm kind enough not to charge you rent for your lodgings in my house.'

Cathy wasn't expecting that little gem, hence why her mouth was making an O-shape. She was momentarily stumped for a comeback. Her gobsmacked brain was on pause, perhaps knowing that right now wasn't the time to lose her shit. Nor was it the time to point out that due to the two-faced injured party seated opposite, Alfie had lost his livelihood. And not just that, remind Bertha that it was his home, too. And that dear, sweet Jacob, had always insisted that his sons, and Cathy, were to regard it as such. Not just that, they paid all the bills, council tax, water rates, everything and maintained the property. Cathy was livid.

When her brain kicked into gear, the voice of reason inside her head advised caution because the next part was even more pivotal than the opening gambit. If Bertha rebelled in any way, Cathy knew there was a chance Alfie would cave and call off the trip, so she had to get this right. Staring Bertha the beast in the eye, Cathy straightened her spine, and got on with it.

The tiny cottage lounge-cum-kitchen had never felt so small, and Cathy was sure the walls were closing in. Or was that because her ribcage was doing the same thing, crushing her heart and making her feel a bit panicky. She was desperate to flee into the safety zone of the kitchen, away from the death-ray glare that was burning holes into her head.

Get a grip, you've said it now. Ride the storm for Alfie's sake.

When finally she spoke, Bertha's voice dripped a lethal concoction of sarcasm, anger, obstinance and yes, Cathy heard a hint of jealousy.

'So let me get this right. Your mam and dad gave you a big fat cheque and now, instead of doing something sensible with it, you're treating yerself to a fancy holiday. Buggering off, while I sit here on my own. And not even the offer of a day at the seaside.'

Bertha paused to warn Cathy off interrupting – a raised finger was all it took. 'And to add insult to injury, you've arranged for that slapper Sheena to look after me, and I'll have to pay her for the privilege while her and that daft, lanky streak of piss husband live in the farmhouse – my farmhouse – free of charge. Well, young lady, you can think again.'

Another twitch of the finger silenced Cathy in an instant. 'And who knows what them two will get up to while you're away. And as for me, she'll leave me up here to rot, I'm telling you that for nowt. I'll be dead in a fortnight so I will, and it'll be you and Alfred to blame. I never 'eard owt like it in me life. Shocking. Absolutely shocking behaviour. Selfish to the core and cruel with it.'

Arms once again folded across her heaving chest, Bertha's lips were pursed tighter than a cat's bum, as Alfie would say, and while Cathy had experienced a moment of relief at getting it all off her chest, the realisation that the battle of wills was about to commence hit her hard.

As did the knowledge that she'd done the right thing not bringing Alfie with her. This was going to be the presentation of her life. A conference hall packed with thousands of delegates was nothing compared to bargaining with the devil's big sister.

'Right.' It was Cathy's turn to raise her hand. 'That's enough. I think you're getting this all out of proportion, so I'm going to make us another cup of tea and when you've calmed down, we can discuss this sensibly and then hopefully you'll realise that nothing much is going to change and me and Alfie aren't cruel or selfish, or whatever else is going on in your head. The only difference will be the face of the person doing a bit of cleaning and shopping for you, and making your tea and who knows, you might even be grateful of some fresh company. And as I said, it's not forever.'

Not giving Bertha time to come back with a barbed retort, Cathy gathered the cups and plates from earlier and shot off into the kitchen.

Not a word was spoken in the time it took to boil the kettle and wash the dishes and when she returned to the sofa, Cathy noticed that Bertha was relaxed back in her armchair, no foot-tapping, fingers of one hand still, the other hand mithering a thread on her cardy, eyes averted.

'Okay, so, can we please start again? The last thing I want is to upset you, Bertha, but Alfie really needs this holiday and I swear, if I didn't think you'd be well looked after I wouldn't go and neither would Alf. That's a given. Which is why I really want you to try and see this from our point of view and, I suppose, give us your blessing and let us go. The time will fly and winter's coming up and you don't like going out in the bad weather, so you'll be safe and toasty, well fed and cared for right here.'

Nothing.

'And we'll ring you all the time if you want. And I can send Sheena photos so she can show you, or if you want I'll get you a new phone that can receive picture messages, then you can look at them yourself. Anything to make you happy. All you have to do is ask.'

Bertha's head jerked up. 'Well in that case, I'm askin' you not to go.'

Touché, was the first word that pinged into Cathy's head. 'I'm sorry, Bertha, but I can't do that. I've already told Alf and Albie and they're both looking forward to seeing each other so I won't let them down and I hope you won't, either.' She wasn't up to mentioning that Annie was going, too. That was too much information and best left for another day.

'I don't care. I won't have that Sheena coming up 'ere or staying at the farmhouse. It's an invasion of privacy, that's what it is.' Bertha had adopted the 'petulant child' attitude, not quite teenage tantrum, but there was always time.

Cathy sighed, exhausted by the sheer effort of appeasement.

'The thing is, Bertha, we need to put some safeguarding measures in place, just as a precaution. You remember what it was like when you came out of hospital, and they wouldn't let you home until they knew you'd have care in place. If you don't let Sheena help, then I can't promise that the care team won't make you go into Daisybank Rest Home down in the village.' Cathy was aware she sounded like she'd swallowed a social services pamphlet, but needs must and planting the care home seed was one of them.

'And seeing as Sheena does this for a living you'll be in really good hands. She's such a kind person and funny, too, if you give her a chance and she'll take your lead on everything. If you're managing on your own then fine, but at least you'll have the comfort of knowing there's someone close by if you want help. Not a lot of elderly people have that luxury, you know. You're really lucky, having your independence here at the cottage but still within minutes of assistance and company.'

At that, Bertha squinted, as if trying to work out if Cathy was being patronising or talking sense. Cathy admitted to herself it was a bit of both.

'Well,' Bertha muttered, 'at least you're not trying to put me in a home. That's summat, I s'pose.'

Seizing a golden opportunity, Cathy jumped in, 'Oh, Bertha, that's the last thing I'd want for you, I swear. But at the same time, the last thing any of us wants is you taking a tumble or a turn for the worse. Which is why Sheena is the best bet.

'And I know you don't have the best opinion of him, but Dave's been Alfie's best friend since nursery and won't let him down. He's promised to look after the farm and the chickens and do any odd jobs that come up and as for not paying rent, it'll help them out while they save up for new furniture for their house, never mind get them from under Dave's mum's feet. In return you get a housekeeper and caretaker, all rolled into one. Sheena only wants half of what she gets paid at work, which is a really good deal because home helps aren't cheap.'

Tension and mental exhaustion were taking their toll on Cathy who after picking up her mug, slumped into the battered sofa and waited for the next round to begin.

'Well, I don't blame Dave for wanting to be away from that mother of his. Nasty old bat she is. Never 'ad a good word to say about anyone and a face like the back end of a bus most days, miserable cow. Always thought she were better than the rest of the mams at the gate she did. Fur coat and no knickers in my opinion and far too fond of the gin, an' that's a fact.'

The irony of Bertha's analysis wasn't lost on Cathy, and she averted her eye from the half bottle on the side, oh, and the brimming ashtray by Bertha's chair. So much for looking after her health. Knowing when it was best to keep schtum, she did just that while Bertha made her other feelings felt.

'And as for them social worker do-gooder types, they can bugger off. Don't want them nosing about up 'ere. It's bad enough 'em making out I need that there wheelchair and that walking contraption, like I'm some kind of limpy invalid. Cheeky beggars.' A loud huff thankfully ended that little speech.

At last, the tension inside Cathy receded, like a gentle tide of anxiety washing out to sea, and then...

'So what 'as that one down in the village said about you buggering off? Or 'aven't you told her yet? Don't blame you either. Bet our Ann won't be pleased when she finds out you're off on a fancy holiday to see her precious big brother. Never did like bein' left out, that one. She'll kick up a right fuss, you mark my words. Selfish as they come, that one is.'

Just when Cathy thought she was on safe ground, rough water appeared on the horizon. Placing her mug on the table, she prepared for a tsunami of epic proportions. Bracing herself, she took a very deep breath and said in a voice laced with trepidation, 'Well, it's funny you should mention that...'

40

BERTHA

*Well, what a bloody fine birthday this is turning out to be. No
bugger has been to see me. No cards or owt. Not even a kiss me
arse or nothing. Bet they've forgot. That'll be it. Can't blame 'em,
I s'pose. Not like I ever made a fuss over their birthdays, but
you'd think Cathy might've called up seein' as we're the only
ones on proper speaking terms. She knows it's me birthday as
well.*

The bitter thoughts hadn't even had time to settle when
Bertha heard the front door opening and footsteps along the
hall. Then Cathy appeared and behind her, looking sheepish,
was Alfred.

'Happy birthday, Bertha. Thought we'd pop up and give
you your pressie and have a birthday brew with you. Did you
sleep well? Alfie can't stay long as he's got a job on, but I
brought an apple pie with me and you can share, if you like.'

Completely ignoring her son, who hovered at the hall door,
and Cathy's nervous witterings, Bertha experienced a moment
of unexpected pleasure when she noticed Cathy was carrying a
box tied with a ribbon and topped with one of them fancy bows,

and a card. And a carrier bag. The day was looking up, especially if there was a bottle of gin inside.

Cathy flicked the kettle on and then bustled into the lounge and plonked herself down on the sofa while Alfred shuffled to the door and leant against the frame.

'Happy birthday, Mam. Hope you like your present.'

Bertha gave him one of her special looks, up and down without making eye contact and then finished with a harrumph. That seemed to do the trick.

'Right, I'll be off then and leave you two to your pie. Have a good one, Mam.'

And before she could ignore him further he'd turned away and his work boots could be heard stomping down the hallway.

When she focused on Cathy, the lass was giving her a look. Was it disappointment? Probably supposed to make Bertha feel guilty, which she certainly did not. She wasn't the one buggering off and leaving someone behind. Alfred was!

'Here, open your card.' Cathy passed it over.

Deciding to play along, Bertha graciously opened it and feigned interest as she read the words. Nothing special, just the usual platitudes more than likely written with as much sincerity as the ones she'd printed in cards for her children when they were young. And once Jacob was dead she'd given up the charade altogether.

'See there's nowt from Albert and Ann, or the kiddies.' Bertha watched Cathy squirm as she tried to think of an excuse, but in the end she chose to ignore the question. So Bertha hit her with another. 'All packed for your trip, then?'

Cathy nodded. 'Getting there. Now, here's your pressie. I hope you like it. I found it online specially.'

'What, so it's second-hand? I don't want nobody's cast-offs.' Bertha grimaced at the box that Cathy had placed on her knee.

'No, it's not a cast-off. Go on, open it.'

When she looked up, Bertha saw a child's expectation in Cathy's eyes, which were bright with excitement and what looked like joy at seeing someone open a present. And it pissed Bertha right off. And she also saw the perfect opportunity to punish Cathy for taking Alfred away and leaving her with that tarty Sheena.

'I think I'll open it later on. I'm feeling tired and need a nap, so you get off. I'm sure you've plenty to do. You can show yerself out.' Bertha watched and enjoyed every detail of the crestfallen look that swept across Cathy's face.

And then, the soft lass surprised her. 'Right, fine. If that's how you want it, I'll get off. I'll leave the apple pie on the side, and you can have it when you wake up. Have a good nap and I'll try and pop up later.' With that she stood and in a huff, marched to the door then turned, as if she'd remembered something.

Bertha waited, amused by Cathy's sudden show of attitude.

'You know what, Bertha? You can play your mind games all you want but it's not going to change the fact we are going to go on holiday and when it boils down to it, the reason why you've not been invited, and why you will be home alone for the foreseeable, is totally down to the way you treat people. And it's why nobody apart from me and Alf have bothered with your birthday. So think on that. Just open your present, okay. You never know, you might actually like it and crack a smile. Have a nice day, on your own!' And with that she was gone.

Bertha tutted, then rested her hands on the top of the gift and fiddled with the fancy bow and contemplated opening the box, curious as to what it contained. But then if she did, and she liked it, that would make Cathy right. And worse, she'd have to say thank you.

Decision made, regardless of her curiosity, Bertha put the

gift on the side and went into the kitchen. She tutted, realising Cathy never made her a brew.

On the other hand, now she'd buggered off, it meant she wouldn't have to share the pie. See, it was turning out to be a good birthday, after all.

41

ALFIE AND CATHY

Their matching his 'n' hers rucksacks were leaning against the kitchen wall, stuffed to the brim with all the things Cathy insisted they'd need for an open-ended trip to paradise and beyond. Paradise was Phuket and the beyond bit meant seeing Albie, and Alfie could not wait to be reunited with his brother. He didn't care that he was scared to death of flying and would be on a plane for twelve hours and sixteen minutes precisely. He was going and that was that.

He'd got some tablets from the health food shop that the assistant assured him should take the edge off his anxiety because getting plastered in the bar wasn't on the cards, not this time. He wanted to remember every minute of this trip with Cathy. From the ride to the airport, the posh lounge her mum had booked them as a treat, the whole experience of going on the adventure of a lifetime but most importantly, he *had* to be in the moment for her.

This was going to be a big deal for Cathy, and she needed him to be strong no matter what it took; he wasn't going to let her down. In return, as was her way, she'd been doing everything to reassure him she was totally prepared for what lay ahead. That they'd get through each leg of the journey and any wobbles along the way, together.

And Alfie believed her because while she'd always seen him as her crutch, her safety net and protector, it was actually the other way round because since she came into his life, he'd had a purpose. With her by his side, Alfie could do anything and face anyone. Like his mother who'd taken the huff of all huffs since she'd heard they were going on the trip.

He'd eventually plucked up the courage to go and see her on her birthday, with Cathy as his shield, but it had been excruciatingly awkward so after wishing her the best, he'd made his excuses and left them to it. It seemed that Cathy was the only person who could get through to Bertha these days or get a word out of her at least. His mother had burnt that many bridges she was running out of options.

Annie still refused to speak to her, saying they were done for good and had forbidden Joe to take the kids within a foot of her if he called at the farm. When his sister was on one, *nobody* with any sense disobeyed. But Alfie understood why she didn't want Eliza and Ezra being infected or affected by their grandmother's special brand of poison. Little Eli was lucky, too small to be bothered by the worst gran ever.

What a state of affairs. His mam had the ability to piss people off even when they were on the other side of the globe. Albie had been incensed when he heard all about what Bertha had said to Annie, which had only made him more resolute that he'd never speak to their mother again or return to the farm while she was alive.

Alfie didn't like to hear the bitterness in the voices of his brother and sister. He found aggression and negativity hard to cope with, so he'd stepped away from those conversations, just like the online support forum had advised. Joining the men-only group had been a revelation, and a lifeline. Alfie was convinced it had helped him more than the still unopened packet of anti-depressants could have done. Just talking to other men who were having similar thoughts and feelings made him feel less vulnerable and alone. He'd felt a kinship with a distant brotherhood of blokes from all walks of life who understood.

Alfie had listened and learned, shared when he was ready. Following some simple advice, like cutting down on the booze, had really helped.

He'd been empowered and now he was about to put all that advice into practice. He was also determined to check into the group during their trip to update them on his progress like they'd asked. Perhaps his physical journey to the other side of the world might help some of them take small steps of their own.

His moment of reflection was disturbed by the sound of Cathy bounding down the stairs after her third and final check of the house. She'd been fussing around for days, making up one of the larger bedrooms for Dave and Sheena, dusting, polishing, hoovering like her life depended on it, and bleaching the bathroom like she and Alfie had the plague.

'Right. All done. Did you have a wee like I told you to? I've just put bleach down the loo, so you better have!' Cathy stood with her hands on her hips, scrutinising Alfie.

'Yep. Safety wee all done, boss.' Alfie saluted but kept to himself the fact he'd not followed orders. NO WAY was he risking the wrath of the bleach monster. He'd just cross his legs till they got to the airport.

Cathy scanned the kitchen once more and Alfie could almost hear her mind ticking from where he stood by the door, listening for Dave the Rave who was their taxi ride to the airport. She was nervous too, he could tell, and keeping busy was her way of coping.

'Good, well. I think that's everything done.' She puffed out her cheeks and exhaled. 'It's all sparkling and ready for when they move in later. I've left them a bottle of wine in the fridge to say welcome and told them to use up whatever is in the freezer.' Cathy turned, speaking to herself more than Alfie.

'The checklist is in the drawer with numbers for the doctor and the community nurse in case Sheena needs to ring them for Bertha, and the vet in case the chickens get poorly... and the home insurance in case there's a leak or something... I think that's everything. Do you think that's everything, love?'

When she turned and saw Alfie's amused expression, she smiled too. He opened his arms wide and she scooted across the kitchen to let him fold her in a hug as he whispered, 'I think that's everything. Mr and Mrs Rave are going to be okay, and the house will be too. We've got this, so try to relax. Just remember that together we can do anything and that I love you, and we are going to have the best time on this adventure. Just thought I'd tell you again before Dave gets here and ruins the moment.'

Alfie kissed the top of her head and when she looked up Cathy simply replied, 'Ditto.'

An enthusiastic honking horn forced them apart and within seconds, after one more glance around the kitchen, Alfie and Cathy had gathered their things, closed the door behind them and assembled on the cobbles.

He had no idea when they'd be back, but common sense told him it wasn't something he should dwell on. While he'd been desperate to cut the cord for so long, right then he felt the tug of the farm, an invisible force pulling him back, asking him not to go. Or was that his own voice, his insecurities and lack of confidence masquerading as a friend called familiarity?

Which was why, shaking loose the ties that bound him, Alfie sprang forward, severing the hold Blacksheep had on him and grabbing both the rucksacks, strode purposefully towards the boot of Dave's car.

It was done. All they had to do now was drive out of the gate and Alfie Walker would be free.

Cathy

Cathy's heart swelled with a mixture of pride and love as she watched Alfie spring into action and hoist the laden rucksacks from the cobbles.

'Right, let's get a move on. Don't want to get stuck in traffic and we've got that fancy lounge to make the most of once we've checked in. Cathy, you get in, love, I'll sort this.' Alfie was already at the boot and loading their things as Dave watched on.

Looking forward to the lounge her wise mum had booked for them, saying it would be a calmer environment to wait in before boarding their flight, Cathy reminded herself to take a photo of them lording it up. It'd make her parents smile and after all, without them, none of this would have been possible.

She was about to do as Alfie said and had opened the car door when something caught her eye further up the track. Her heart lurched when she homed in on Bertha.

NO! Not now, not today. Please don't spoil this moment for us.

They'd said their strained goodbyes earlier that morning. She and Alfie had gone to say farewell and on the walk towards the cottage, Cathy had repeatedly prayed that Bertha wouldn't unleash one of her bitter diatribes and upset Alfie. She needn't have worried because where he was concerned, Bertha continued to snub him as she'd done ever since the trip was mentioned. With tuts, shoulder shrugs and silence.

The meeting had lasted minutes with Alfie mumbling,

'Take care of yourself, Mam, and let Sheena know if there's owt you want, and we'll ring you every week for a catch-up.'

That received a huff.

'Right, I'll be off then. Got some bits to do up the yard so I'll leave Cathy to check you've everything you need.'

That was met with a tut and a surly look to which Alfie responded by turning and walking out of the room.

Swallowing her annoyance but reminding herself she'd not been expecting much anyway, Cathy had gone over everything one more time. 'Right. This is a list of important phone numbers, but they're all programmed into your new phone anyway.' Cathy had bought Bertha a simple to use smartphone so they could video call her, that's if she deigned to answer.

'And remember you can send voice and video messages too, if you don't want to text. I've even wrote down a step-by-step guide in case you've forgotten but you can always ask Sheena to help you if you get stuck.'

This at least elicited a response. 'I'm not simple, you know. I understood the first time you showed me. Anyways, hadn't you best be getting off? Don't want to hold you up and me programme's starting soon and yer in me way. Show yerself out.'

Bertha was avoiding eye contact even though Cathy was standing directly in front of her but knowing when she was beat, decided it was time to give up and go. As she turned, on the sideboard she noticed the birthday present she'd given Bertha, still wrapped with the bow intact.

'I wish you'd open your present, Bertha. I know you'll like it and... and it'll show you how much I care about you.' Cathy waited for a response, but Bertha was busy rummaging around the pile of all sorts on the table by her chair. She eventually picked up the remote control and her telly magazine.

Cathy gave it one last shot. 'You know, the thing with gifts is that when you take the fancy wrapping off, you often find something very special inside. And it's the same with family. Underneath all those tough layers they might just be hiding their true feelings, and you never know, if you're willing to take a chance you might be surprised that despite everything, deep down, they do love you.'

At this, Bertha had raised an eyebrow, reached out her arm and clicked the remote. With the opening bars to *This Morning* ringing in her ears Cathy had sighed, then turned and left the room.

And now, as Cathy's stomach swirled with nerves, she watched Bertha make her way slowly down the lane, avoiding potholes as she pushed her wheely-walking frame, the one she refused to use, towards the car.

If Cathy knew Bertha at all, she was about to play her final hand and do or say something to spoil everything for everyone. And apart from knock her out, or drag Alfie into the car, there was nothing she could do to stop her. Not a single damn thing.

As if sensing she was behind him and following Cathy's wide-eyed stare, Alfie turned to greet his mother. 'All right, Mam. What you doing out and about?' If he was surprised Alfie hid it well and after he slammed the boot shut and Dave stepped slowly away from the beast and slipped into the driving seat, Cathy gripped the passenger door of the car and watched on.

Bertha had paused and made a point of taking a loud, deep breath, clearly fatigued from the exertion of her stroll downhill. 'So, you're going then?'

Cathy wasn't sure if that was a statement or a question but either way the tone was laced with accusation. Alfie was deserting and guilty as charged in Bertha's eyes.

'Yes, all ready for the off so can't hang about. Don't want to miss the flight.' His voice was too jolly, forced and an octave higher than normal.

Go away, Bertha. Please, just this once let him be.

'Right, well. Don't let me stop you. Just wanted to say bye.' She held Alfie in her sights, gripping the arms of the walking frame as if daring him to go.

'Oh, right. Well, like I said before, you take care, and we'll see you soon.'

No, you shouldn't have said that, Alf.

But it was too late.

'Aye let's hope so. Can't be promisin' I'll be here when you get back, though, can I?'

You cow.

At that, Alfie was rendered speechless unlike Bertha.

'An' if you will, say hello to Albert from me, seein' as I 'aven't heard a word from him since he left. Give him me best. An' I hope you all have a nice time together when Ann and the kiddies join you. Be nice will that, all of you together. I'll be thinkin' of you when I'm sat up there on me tod.'

Jesus Christ. She knows how to twist the knife.

So before Bertha could wind Alfie up any further with her pitiful hypocrisy, Cathy called time on the heart-warming scene. 'Yes, of course we will, Bertha. Now we really do have to go. Come on, Alfie, chop-chop, otherwise we'll hit rush hour on the motorway. Best get in.'

While Cathy felt sick, her words seemed to have broken the spell Bertha had cast over Alfie. He turned and made his way to the front of the car. But before he got inside he looked back at his mother. 'You'd best get back inside now. Looks like rain.' The second's pause seemed interminable until he said, 'Love you, Mam.'

Those three simple words floated in the air, suspended on a shred of hope as Alfie waited, just a heartbeat and when Bertha didn't respond, he quickly got inside, slammed the door and fastened his seat belt.

Holding in her utter despair and the temptation to scream in temper, Cathy dropped Dave the hint. 'Let's get this show on the road, then. Start her up, Dave.'

The sound of the engine soothed Cathy somewhat, but she was still tempted to ask Dave to lock all the doors and put his bloody foot down. As the car finally began to move towards the gate and then bank gently to the left and down the hill, Cathy focused on the scene ahead, the one she'd fallen in love with on that first morning at Blacksheep. The dark and craggy twin peaks on either side of the valley, the silver lake below and in between, endless pale blue sky.

Forcing herself not to cry, telling herself she'd be home soon, and her beloved farm would be waiting for her, Cathy also forbade herself to turn and say *à bientôt* as she'd planned. No way would she give Bertha what she wanted. The satisfaction of being the star of the scene she'd set so well. Where a lone elderly woman, leant heavily on her walking frame, in a desolate abandoned farmyard before an empty home.

Instead Cathy committed the view through the windscreen to memory, just like she had the first time she saw it. The late September sun was dropping behind the peaks to the west, casting a gentle golden glow across the moors, mirroring the warmth in her heart that swelled with love for Alfie.

Reaching forward Cathy rested a hand on his shoulder and after giving it a squeeze, sat back in her seat, took a deep breath and focused on the journey ahead. Leaving Bertha and Blacksheep Farm behind.

42

CATHY

The captain had just given them their ETA and local weather report. The temperature outside was ten degrees: quite normal for a grey Manchester afternoon in November.

Cathy pondered on the next day or two when the skies would be filled with fireworks and smoke once bonfire night got underway. As always, the booms and bangs would remind her of one thing in particular, but she would focus only on the good and that New Year's Eve when Alfie came to her rescue and drove her to Blacksheep and safety.

Until then, there were other issues to deal with and plans to make which wouldn't be easy. Thinking of what lay ahead, she looked to her left and passed a smile to Alfie who, dragging himself from his soundtrack, passed one back. This lifted her because he'd spent most of the twenty-three-hour flight in deep contemplation, only joining in conversation when prompted or when they changed flights at Singapore.

Nudging Alfie to attract his attention again, she watched as he removed his earphones and his tired eyes focused on her face. They were both travel weary but soon they'd be home, in their own bed and that was always something to look forward to. A very simple pleasure in a very complicated life.

'Not long now and we'll be landing. It looks grim out there, and I *really* hope Annie's put the heating on for when we get back.'

Alfie took her hand. 'I'm sure she will have, and if we're lucky the chippy will still be open, then we can pick something up on the way through the village. I fancy pie and chips, and peas. And gravy... and a sausage.'

The thought of food always cheered Alfie up and Cathy couldn't help laughing at the memory of all the delicious and exotic meals they'd eaten over the last couple of months, yet here he was looking forward to a chippy tea.

Deciding to pack everything away for landing, Cathy left Alfie to plan his tea, and folded away her iPad case. During the flight she'd occupied herself with the usual long-haul entertainment, but found it hard to concentrate so instead had cheered herself up by looking through the albums on her phone: Thailand, Malaysia, New Zealand but her favourite was simply titled Family.

It had been the best time with Annie and her brood and seeing her reunion at the airport with Albie, well, it still brought tears to her eyes, just like the moment Alfie saw his brother waiting in the arrivals hall in Auckland.

Sucking in air brought some self-control which was followed by blinking back happy tears. She was over emotional and sad things aside, even thinking back to the happiest of times could set her off.

It was those memories, of them all being together again, and how hard it was when they had to say goodbye to Annie and her lot that had given Albie food for thought.

In the days after Annie's departure, they'd talked it round the houses, the three of them, and as much as Cathy had wanted to beg him to come back, she and Alfie had agreed that it had to be his decision and they couldn't put any pressure on him one way or another.

What had irritated them all, Annie especially, was the fact there were two huge obstacles stopping Albie from coming home to the family, the niece and nephews, the farm, his friends in the village he'd grown up in. He'd admitted to missing them all like a limb. The stumbling blocks were pride, and Bertha. But now those obstacles had been removed and Albie was free to return to Blacksheep.

Turning her head to the right, Cathy observed Albie who had pushed his face closer to the window, watching the Cheshire plains below. He was hoping to spot the Jodrell Bank Observatory, with its Lovell Telescope, and as he'd pointed out landmarks during the flight, she likened him to a kid on a school trip, wanting to be the one who spotted Blackpool Tower first and got 1 op off the teacher.

Throughout the trip from Auckland it had been Albie who'd buoyed them, been their unofficial guide and leader, assuming the role that had always come naturally to him. Keeping their spirits up, remaining practical, kind and tactful when Alfie needed him to be.

When Annie rang to give them the news about Bertha, five days before they were due to fly home, it had come as an immense shock followed by waves of so many different emotions. A squall of jumbled feelings that they'd all expressed openly, and none of them surprised Cathy at all. Albie was stoical and pragmatic, booking himself onto the same flight as Cathy and Alfie while liaising with Annie who was organising things at home. Alfie went to pieces.

It was Sheena who'd found her, poor thing. But she'd assured Annie, who then related the scene to the others, that it looked like she'd just fallen asleep in her chair in front of the telly. It was sometime before bedtime as she was dressed in her pyjamas and dressing gown, slippers on her feet. There was a cold mug of tea by her side and half a piece of toast which she religiously had every night for supper. It had a bite mark, and Sheena said it had made her feel glad that she'd had something to eat before she went. Cathy had smiled at that because it was a nice thought.

There was another thing that when she heard it, rocked Cathy in a way she'd still not come to terms with. It had made her cry private tears and hurt her heart at the same time as giving her great comfort. Somewhere in between the two, remained a ball of confusion but that was Bertha all over.

It seemed that on the table by her comfy chair, was a pile of wrapping paper and an opened box. On Bertha's knee was an old vinyl album, by someone called Donny Osmond and on the top a tag that said:

To Bertha, I didn't forget. Happy birthday, with love from Cathy x

Sheena had wondered why after refusing to open it for so long, Bertha had asked her to fetch it over and leave it on the table. Apparently every time Sheena dusted it she'd suggested Bertha 'just bloody open it' to which she received the usual tut and 'mind yer own business.'

For some reason, the night she passed, after Sheena helped her get ready for bed and made her supper, as she said goodbye, Bertha asked for the gift, saying, 'Me legs are bad, and I feel a bit jiggered.'

And for the first time ever, she'd thanked Sheena. 'Ta, for me supper, lass, an' you know, doin' me bits an' bobs. Show yerself out.'

Sheena was beside herself when she found Bertha the next

morning, saying she should have known something wasn't right and that in her own odd way Bertha was saying goodbye.

Annie had assured her that de-coding Bertha Walker would test the most beautiful minds of MI5 and Bletchley Park and the main thing was that she'd gone peacefully, after tea and toast and finally opening a very strange pressie from Cathy.

Once again holding in her tears, determined to get through the next few hours without blubbing be it for Bertha or the man who sat to her left. Alfie was convinced his mother knew she was going to die and would never see him again. And like Sheena, he thought he would have realised. If only he'd listened properly on the day they said goodbye.

Then what? That's what Cathy had asked him. Would he have stayed at Blacksheep and missed out on the happiest time of their lives? Missed out on filling pages and pages of their photo album when they got home. Not played cricket on the sand with Eliza and Ezra and Eli. Missed out on horse riding through the bush with Annie, camping under the stars beneath Mount Cook with the whole family, seeing the kids squeal with delight when they visited Hanmer Springs thermal pools.

Both she and Albie had told him, Annie too, that Bertha was messing with his head that day at the farm and was still doing it even though she was gone. He had to stop allowing her access, for his own good. He got it, but a lifetime of game playing and mental abuse at the hands of what Cathy could only describe as a master narcissist, wasn't easy to shake off and it might take years before Bertha's influence, and the scars she'd inflicted, faded away.

Seeing the air crew swinging into action, guided Cathy's mind away from Bertha and as the rest of the passengers prepared for landing, alerted by Cathy's fussing with her bag, Albie dragged himself away from the window and leant forward to speak to Alfie.

'I want the same as you, bro. And a fish. I've dreamt about a chippy tea from Po Fongs for ages. They'd better be open now you've mentioned it, otherwise I'm going to be devastated. What you having, Cathy? Chips and gravy as usual for our veggie warrior, or you could go mad and have curry sauce for a change.' Albie rubbed his stomach and gave her a wink.

Resting her head against her seat, Cathy smiled. This was what she'd longed for but didn't dare believe in. The three of them back together again, brotherly banter, two sets of muddy work boots by the kitchen door, and a chippy tea round the big pine table.

43

The funeral dust had settled and after doing right by their mother, the Walker family were about to gather around the kitchen table to discuss what happened next. There was a pot of tea at the ready, wearing one of Cathy's knitted cosies, and home-made pies were warming in the oven giving the room a comforting ambience.

Temperatures had dropped overnight, and the tops of the Peaks were covered in a glistening sheen of white. Cathy thrived on making Blacksheep a comforting place to be and since the passing of Bertha creating an aura of calm had seemed so much easier.

Albie was shuffling papers while Annie brought mugs and milk. Joe was stacking cardboard boxes outside the door in preparation for the next task – clearing out Shepherd's Cottage. Nobody had been up there since Bertha died, apart from Sheena who'd done the basics and emptied the fridge and perishables before she and Dave moved out of Blacksheep and into their own new home.

It had occurred to Cathy, even though it was a bit of an 'out there' thought, that Bertha had checked out when she did, on purpose. Knowing that it would always bother Alfie that he didn't get to see her again and knowing it would put the mockers on Christmas for everyone. Annie for one, agreed.

They'd given Bertha the send-off their father would have wanted her to have – a surprisingly well-attended church service made up of the old guard of neighbouring farmers and a handful of villagers. During the proceedings, immersed in silent contemplation and a bizarre blurring of bittersweet sadness and guilty relief, Cathy had pondered that the mourners were most likely there out of respect to Jacob, rather than to his widow.

After Bertha's service, they all trooped off to the pub for the wake and once they'd thanked those attending and stayed for as long as was deemed appropriate, the Walker clan beat a hasty retreat.

In the Land Rover, Annie, Joe and Cathy huddled in the back with Albie and Alfie up front. As they pulled out of the car park, they allowed themselves a unified sigh of relief, which in turn morphed into semi-horrified laughter at their inappropriate response.

It was Albie that had broken the hex and said it like it was. 'Right, that's that done with and we did Mam and Dad proud. So I reckon we should spring Eliza from school, get Ezra from nursery, pick Eli up from Joe's mam's and all camp out at Blacksheep tonight. Have a Walker family sleepover. We'll order pizzas on me and get some beers in. Does that sound like a plan?'

The unanimous response was 'plan'.

Now, two days later, it was time to make more. They were seated around the table – Annie and Joe on one side with Cathy and Alfie opposite and Albie at the top, in Jacob's old place. Since he'd arrived at the farm, he'd taken control and steered the ship and jollied them along, showing them the way.

Whether his choice of seat was symbolic or a sign, it gave

Cathy immense comfort to see him there and after a swift glance at Annie, the hope in her heart was reflected in her sister-in-law's eyes. Would Albie take this opportunity to announce his plans and say he was leaving after Christmas or would he stay, like they all silently hoped?

Nobody had put any pressure on him to make his decision, but at the same time the question was on all of their lips and minds.

Taking a swig of tea, Albie place his mug on the table and after a quick look at whatever was written on his notepad, addressed them all. 'Right, let's get this show on the road and before we sort out the practicalities, there's something that needs saying because I want you to know where my head's at.'

Uh-oh. That sounded a bit formal. Please let it be good news.

Cathy saw Alfie stiffen and a flash of worry skitter across Annie's face as they waited.

'I know Dad always wanted me to take over the farm with Alfie by my side and Annie doing her thing in her dairy.'

It was as though the whole room was holding its breath. Waiting for the axe to fall.

'But just because I'm the oldest, I don't think that I should be in charge and if we're going to make a go of Blacksheep then it has to be a joint venture where we all have an equal say, and nobody rules the roost. There's been enough of all that.'

Annie's eyes were wide, and she was sitting bolt upright, 'So does that mean what I think it means, that you're staying? We didn't want to pressure you, but it's all we've thought about since you got back.'

Albie reached over and took her hand in his. 'Yes, sis, I'm staying. I wasn't sure about anything when I got on the plane, so I wanted to see how I felt when I got here, but as soon as I drove through the gate, I knew I was home. We had stuff to sort out first and I needed time to think the future through so thank you for giving me space, that goes for all of you.'

Of course, at this point Annie burst into tears which set Cathy off while to her right, she saw Alfie lean across the table and fist-pump Joe. Once everyone had settled down and dried their eyes, it was Alfie's turn to speak.

'Well, as you can tell we're all chuffed to bits you're staying on, Albs, but, and I might be speaking for myself here, I want you to know that I have no problem at all with you taking Dad's role and being in charge. Not one bit. It's how I always saw it and it's your rightful place as eldest son, just like Dad and his dad before him. It's how Walkers have always run the farm and I'd like it to continue. What do you say, Annie?'

Annie nodded like her head was going to fall off and then, 'I agree. Someone has to take the lead. It's kind of comforting and not just that, we can always blame you if things go tits-up!'

The laughter around the table was much needed as it had all been intense so far. But Albie appeared to be pleased and smiled when he received a wink from Cathy that told him it was all going to be okay.

'Right, well, if that's what you want, let's see how we go. But this is a family farm and we're going to run it as such, once we get the funds in place. Which brings me to my discussion with the solicitor earlier.'

Albie briefly consulted his notes then continued. 'According to Mr Hammond, Mam and Dad's joint will is straightforward and everything now passes to the three of us in equal shares. Once probate is complete he'll arrange for the bank to release the funds into the relevant accounts and also notify the land registry, et cetera. Until then, I suppose all we can do is mark time and prepare for the future. But for now, I think we have to address Annie and Joe's situation first, because time's running out.'

Since Bertha had put the mockers on Annie's plans, she and Joe had decided to extend their lease for six months and see if they could make ends meet by tightening their belts so hard that it might cut off circulation. Annie would be doing weekday twilight shifts at Asda, still working at the pub at weekends. It was going to be tough, but they didn't fancy the alternative, a smaller house and a move nearer to Sheffield or down the valley into Tameside.

At this juncture, Cathy dived in. 'Well the offer is still there, for you all to move in here like we'd planned.' She omitted to mention that Annie's nemesis was no longer around to make things difficult. 'And even with Albie back home, there's still plenty of bedroom space if Ezra and Eli share and Eliza has the smaller box room. Can you get out of the new lease, though?'

Joe looked at Annie who smiled a yes, then replied, 'We were due to sign it next week, on the 1st of December but the landlord did mention about a hundred times that he had a queue of other tenants wanting it, so I reckon he won't kick up a fuss. Shall I give him a ring and ask?'

Joe found himself being ordered into the parlour immediately to make the call while Annie thanked Cathy and Alfie profusely.

Alfie replied, 'It's your home too, Annie. You need to get that into your head, okay.'

'I know, but it's really been yours and Cathy's for ages and I respect that you've had the place to yourselves and now it's going to be overrun by three very noisy kids, so I hope you know what you're letting yourself in for!'

Cathy was the one to answer. 'We love the kids and it'll be fun having a house full and anyway, two of them will be at school most of the day and if Eli gets too much his uncles can take a shift looking after him.' She winked at Annie. 'We can spread the childcare and the love between us.'

She nudged Alfie who grimaced, no doubt remembering what a handful Eli could be now he was walking.

When Joe returned, they could tell by the look on his face that it was good news. 'He says it's fine, seeing as we've given him enough notice to get someone else in. We'll have to be out by the end of December but that's doable. So, folks. It looks like we're moving in!'

Albie drummed the table. 'Excellent news. And it looks like a big family get-together is on the cards at Blacksheep this year. I really missed being home for Christmas and this one is going to be special. We'll let the New Year in under one roof, not on Zoom like last time.'

And as the kitchen descended into voices making plans involving Christmas trees and telling the kids the news, Cathy stood and made her way to the oven to check the food. As she did, the skin on her arms prickled and instinctively she looked towards the window half forgetting that the shadow she expected to see passing by, wasn't there.

Maybe it was her imagination, but she swore she could sense Bertha hovering somewhere on the periphery, ever watchful. Shaking the thought away, Cathy grabbed her oven gloves and opened the door, resigning herself to the fact that even though Bertha was gone, her memory and dubious legacy might linger for a while yet.

And even though none of the others would share that sentiment, Cathy was glad to have her around, even in her imagination.

44

Cathy and Annie had insisted that they be the ones to sort through Bertha's things up at Shepherd's Cottage. It was a woman's job, they'd said. Both had expected it to take no more than a few hours as there wasn't much, so after emptying the kitchen cupboards of crockery and food stuffs, they'd moved onto the lounge area.

The plan was that once all the personal items were sorted, the menfolk would remove Bertha's old-fashioned furniture, re-paint the whole cottage and re-fit it with more contemporary, functional items that would suit a holiday let. Then they could get it on Airbnb as soon as possible and create some much-needed revenue.

Perhaps it was because the cottage was freezing and they were loath to put the heating on for a couple of hours, and no amount of woolly jumpers and thick clothing would take off the chill or gloom that hung in the air, but there was just something unsettling about being in Bertha's home. More than once Cathy had to tell herself not to be so stupid, yet she still sensed the presence of an angry spirit.

Cathy wondered if Annie felt the same so had been keeping

an eye on her, watching for signs that it was all too much. Wary also, that whatever feelings she harboured towards her mum would bubble to the surface as they navigated what is always an awful job for any relative.

Dismantling a life, deciding what to keep for posterity, discarding unwanted remnants that symbolise years and years of them being them, and being alive, leaving fingerprints on cups, the odd stray hair on the back of the sofa, indents in their slippers by the gas fire. And on top of that, battling the overwhelming guilt that such a simple act brings. Of putting those things in a bin bag and throwing it over the wall at the tip. Gone forever, like them.

It was easy with the kitchen stuff because Bertha had left all of her crockery and utensils behind at the farm and bought new, basic items enough for one person. But now, they were onto the more personal belongings and Cathy sensed the atmosphere had changed. Like the tension of being in Bertha's lair had cranked up a notch. Attempting to make things easier, Cathy decided to take charge.

Flinging open the door of the cupboard underneath the television where Bertha kept all sorts, she sucked in air and said, 'Right, I'll empty this and then we can take it all down to the farm and let Alb's look through any paperwork. There's not much so it'll only take a few minutes.'

Resting a cardboard box on her hip, Cathy glanced around the sparse room which silently nodded its agreement. Apart from Bertha's armchair and the two-seater sofa that used to be in the parlour down at the farm, all that remained was a dated mahogany coffee table scattered with magazines, and a matching occasional table which, to Cathy's despair, still held the Donny Osmond album.

Underneath lay the scrunched up wrapping paper that had concealed the surprise gift Bertha had waited decades to receive, along with Cathy's subliminal message that she hoped Bertha had understood.

In the doorway, Annie stood with her hands on her hips and a frown that betrayed what she was thinking before she spoke. 'Hmm, well it's not like she kept a shrine to her family, is it? The only photos are of her and Dad. I'll do the bedroom and empty that hideous wardrobe and chest of drawers. The bedding can go to the tip with the rest of the unwanted stuff, like that manky armchair.'

Annie pointed to where Sheena had found Bertha, and as Cathy's eyes followed Annie's finger, she noticed something popping out from under the seat cushion. It was a folded newspaper. On closer inspection, Cathy noticed it was left open, face up and on the full page spread about Guy and his poor victims.

'Look at this. I wonder why she kept it? And that's odd, she's drawn a square around the photo of that nutter when he was young. So weird.'

Cathy glanced over to the pen on the side table that Bertha always used to underline the programmes she wanted to watch, so she never missed any of her favourite shows.

When she looked up, she was met by Annie's raised eyebrow and an unsurprising comment. 'Who knows why she did anything. I gave up trying to work her out years ago. Right, I'll go and do the bedroom and leave you to it. Won't be long.'

Cathy nodded and went back to the newspaper, unable to shake off her curiosity.

Maybe Bertha was in a bad mood, so drew a frame around the photo. She'd pressed hard with the biro, Cathy could tell, and wondered if Bertha was imagining bashing the young Guy's brains in because if she had, he wouldn't have carried out such awful acts. And it wasn't like she wasn't capable. After all, she'd given old-man Guy a damn good walloping that day in the barn.

Content with her resolution because Annie was right, second-guessing Bertha was a fool's errand, Cathy got stuck into the task in hand. After stuffing a pile of old magazines into a bin liner, she focused on the telly cabinet where she found two small photo albums crammed with, as Annie had said, photos of Bertha and Jacob. Not a child in sight.

Next, she found a battered red biscuit tin, ironically branded 'Family Favourites' and after lifting the lid and finding what looked like bills and bank statements, all opened but still in their envelopes, and some velvet jewellery boxes which she suspected might have belonged to Jacob, so she decided to give them to Albie to sort through, then moved on to the side table.

The *Take A Break* and *Woman's Friend* magazines also went in the bin liner but smiling Donny Osmond was going in the box, along with the tag. Even if none of Bertha's kids wanted to listen to it, Cathy was going to. She was intrigued to hear the voice and lyrics that had obviously meant so much to a young, miserable girl living on a remote farm full of cold-hearted men. Flipping the album over Cathy saw one of the tracks was called 'Puppy Love' and she wondered if when Bertha met Jacob, that's how she felt about him.

Placing the album on the top of the tin, Cathy dithered over the newspaper because there was just something... and then she thought better of it, stuffing the face of a monster deep inside the bin liner.

Next was Bertha's phone that was still plugged into the charger and flashed into life when she unplugged it from the wall. Remembering how she'd sat with Bertha and patiently explained how to use it, even writing a step-by-step guide in the notebook in case she got muddled, made Cathy smile. The screen didn't have any personalisation, just the factory setting icons that Cathy had narrowed down to Call, WhatsApp, Camera and Photos. It had been a waste of time really.

She'd sent lots of photos of their trip and umpteen messages giving Bertha an update on where they were and what they were doing and asking after her. While they knew Bertha had read them all, the two blue ticks giving her nosy nature away, she'd stubbornly refused to reply or answer their calls.

If it hadn't been for reassurances from Sheena that Bertha was alive and still being a pain in the arse, the lack of response would have had them panicking.

Out of curiosity, and knowing she wasn't invading a dead woman's privacy because the only texts and photos she'd see would be from herself, Cathy tapped the photo album. Feeling nostalgic, she wanted to remind herself of the last photo she'd sent, and what Bertha had seen.

However, rather than there being one of them all waving Annie, Joe and the kids off at the airport, to Cathy's surprise the last icon in the album was a video. It appeared to be a black screen and in the bottom right-hand corner, it showed the length of the recording. Nearly twenty-five minutes. Knowing it definitely wasn't something she'd sent, intrigued, Cathy's finger hovered over the video, about to tap.

Then the screaming began.

Ramming the phone into her back pocket, heart racing, Cathy leapt over the cardboard box and sprinted out of the lounge, through the kitchen and down the corridor towards the bedroom on the left. Bursting through the doorway, terrified at what she'd find, her eyes landed on Annie who was pressed up against the wall to Cathy's right, opposite the open wardrobe, her hands over her face, shoulders heaving as she sucked in deep breaths.

Crouching, Cathy gently rested her hands on Annie's arm, 'Annie, love, what's happened? It's okay, just take deep breaths, I'm here now...'

Looking around the room, expecting to see... What? An

intruder, a giant spider, a ghost? Cathy couldn't identify anything that would cause Annie to scream in such a blood-curdling way, until her eyes landed on something on the floor, just in front of the open wardrobe doors. A small brown suitcase with the lid up, and inside what looked like a carrier bag. Nothing scary there.

Turning back to Annie, Cathy tentatively prised her hands from her face which, when revealed, was ashen.

'Annie, whatever is the matter? You look like you've seen a ghost. Don't tell me Bertha came back for one last hurrah when she found you rummaging round her knicker drawer.' Cathy forced a laugh, hoping it might do the trick, release the skin-pricking tension and get a smile, or an answer out of Annie.

Swallowing, keeping her eyes firmly fixed on Cathy's face, as though she was too scared to look elsewhere, Annie gripped Cathy's arm and whispered, 'Oh God. Cathy... it's too awful... don't look whatever you do. Just ring the lads, get them to come right now. PLEASE.' Her voice bordered on hysteria. 'Get them right now.'

Heeding the warning and now too terrified to move her head in case she saw the awful thing, Cathy stared into Annie's wide, frightened eyes and had to ask, 'What is it? What have you found? You're scaring me, Annie, so just tell me...'

A heartbeat passed, and then as her lip wobbled and tears leaked from her eyes, Annie whispered, 'A skeleton, in that brown suitcase. It's wrapped in some material, inside a carrier bag.' Annie inclined her head, still not looking.

Cathy, thinking she'd misheard, asked, 'What do you mean, a skeleton? A human one?'

When Annie nodded, Cathy thought her heart might stop but there was more and through her sobs, Annie managed another piece of truly horrific information.

'And... and... oh God. Cathy. It's a baby. The bones of a tiny baby... I saw it, the skull, all of it... in that suitcase.'

When her crouched legs gave way, Cathy slumped next to Annie who she pulled towards her, wrapping one arm tightly around Annie's shoulder to give comfort to both their trembling bodies. Realising her own phone was in the kitchen and not wanting to leave Annie who was now distraught, Cathy pulled Bertha's phone from her pocket and tapped Alfie's number.

It occurred to her, in that moment of blind panic and horror that it would freak him out, seeing his mother's number flash up on his screen. But that would pale into insignificance when he and Albie arrived at the cottage. Resting her head against Annie's as she listened to her sobs and Alfie's ringtone, Cathy's eyes were drawn to the brown suitcase that held much more than the skeleton of a baby. It held a secret, and it was one that only Bertha could tell.

45

They were all huddled around the fire in the parlour. Outside the wind and rain lashed at the windows while the slate grey clouds shrouded the farm in gloom, as if they needed any more of that. Even though it was only just past midday it felt like early evening.

The glow from the logs did nothing more than focus their eyes on something warm and bright and deepened the shadows that lurked in the corner of the normally cosy room. Creeped out, Cathy stood and went over to the sideboard and flicked on the lamp, and then another by the door and instantly the ghouls in her mind vanished.

Taking her seat on the sofa opposite Joe and Annie, Cathy wrapped her hand around Alfie's. He responded with a firm squeeze. To her left, in the armchair facing the fire sat Albie, his face sombre and lost in thought. They all were.

Cathy was just about warming up and had stopped shaking while poor Annie looked dreadful, wrapped in a blanket and scrunched into Joe who was as shell-shocked as everyone else. His mum was minding Eli for the morning but had now been enlisted to collect Ezra from nursery and Eliza from school and would keep them at hers for as long as necessary. Not that she knew the real reason she'd had to step into the breach, and instead, they'd invented a family crisis, the nature of which was yet to be decided.

One thing that was for sure, they weren't going to tell her what Annie, and then her brothers, had seen inside the suitcase. It was the first thing Albie had said when they got back to the farm and placed it reverently on the kitchen table.

'This stays between us, okay. Until we decide what to do.'

Up at the cottage Cathy hadn't dared look inside, knowing she'd have nightmares about it forever but just listening to the exclamations of 'Jesus Christ' and 'what the fuck' had been enough to sear an image onto her brain. One of a tiny baby skeleton, wrapped in a cotton dress, and hidden inside a Woolworth's carrier bag, locked in the brown suitcase for many years.

Cathy was trying to erase the picture from her mind when to all their surprise from underneath her blanket and the crook of Joe's arm, Annie spoke in a dreamlike voice, as though she'd woken in the night and wasn't quite awake yet desperate to get a nightmare out of her system.

'I didn't notice it at first because it was right at the back and hidden by a blanket and underneath piles of old jumpers. I realised straight away it was the one Dad always used to refer to when he told us how he and Mam eloped that day at the market. He said that all she had was a tatty brown case and a carrier bag of belongings, hidden inside one of those wheelie trolleys. When I found it, it was zipped shut and buckled tight and I thought that when I opened it I'd find some old love letters – which would have been a shock as I don't think Dad was the writing type – or old photos, something like that. I couldn't believe it... when I looked inside the bag and unwrapped the fabric...'

'Shush, love. Don't go over it. It'll upset you again.' Joe rubbed Annie's arm and his words seemed to sink in and she fell back into her silent state.

Alfie spoke next. 'What I want to know is whether the baby was in the case when she brought it here, or if... if she had it when she was with Dad which means it's our brother or sister, which is just sick.'

Cathy answered, 'She was only just seventeen when she met your dad and, from what she told me in the hospital that night, had led a really sheltered life on the farm. Sounded like her dad more or less kept her there as an unpaid housekeeper, so I doubt she'd had a boyfriend before Jacob.'

'Which means the baby was Dad's and for whatever reason, she hid it and kept it a secret and the only reason anyone would do that is if...' Albie faltered, then dragged his hand across his face, unable to say the words.

Annie did it for him. 'If she'd killed it on purpose. That's what you're thinking, isn't it? I am, I bet we all are. Cathy, what do you think?'

She hated being under scrutiny, but this wasn't the time for shying away from the truth, not when it was something as serious as this, and as the memory of a late-night conversation floated into her consciousness, a chill trickled slowly down Cathy's spine.

'Well for a start, I don't like speaking ill of the dead and we have to remember that your mam isn't here to defend herself or explain the circumstances...' Cathy paused, the voice of a sleepy woman high on painkillers drifted on the woodsmoke and she wished the words would float up the chimney and over the Peaks so she wouldn't have to say them out loud.

I've never told anyone the truth about it, not even my Jacob. Especially my Jacob.

And then... *I did it for Jacob because I loved him and 'avin*

310

bairns is a wife's duty they reckon, and I didn't want to disappoint 'im. Then, when they came along I hated sharing him with them... and I hated them because he loved 'em more than me.

'But?' Annie prodded, expecting an answer from the person who'd been closest to Bertha.

Taking a breath, Cathy ignored the notion she was betraying Bertha and instead remained loyal to the living who desperately needed answers. 'I can't help thinking about that conversation we had when she was poorly in hospital, and at the time I assumed it was the strong painkillers they'd given her because she was hallucinating and thought her mum had been to see her.'

Cathy swallowed, nervous now because she'd never divulged the more hurtful elements of the conversation with Bertha and instead, had focused on the things she'd said about her dad and brothers. Damage limitation and family relations had guided her decision, especially knowing how fractured Annie's relationship with her mam was at the time. But now, Cathy had to tell them everything, and relate the whole conversation as she remembered it.

Looking Annie in the eye, Cathy told them the truth.

A hush had once again fallen on the room as three siblings and a silent husband contemplated Bertha's words.

Albie eventually broke the dark spell. 'So that proves it. At some point, she managed to conceal her pregnancy from Dad and when the baby was born, she got rid of it.'

Alfie threw his head back against the sofa and closed his eyes as if to block out the reality of his brother's words. 'Christ, she was a monster, wasn't she?'

Cathy's stomach churned with nerves because despite the evidence saying otherwise, she still needed to defend Bertha and no matter how dreadfully she'd behaved in life, surely she deserved the benefit of the doubt so, risking the wrath of Annie, she spoke for the one person who couldn't do so herself.

'But we don't know that she... you know... killed her baby. We weren't there, and what if she was depressed or scared?'

Albie shook his head and asked, 'Scared of who? Not Dad, that's for sure because he was a gentle giant and adored Mam, everyone knew that. And don't forget what she said to Annie's face, about never wanting her, especially a girl.'

He looked around the room and was met by nods and murmurs of agreement. 'And like Cathy told us, she didn't want kids in the first place and preferred it to be just her and Dad. The only reason she gave in was probably to please him, so it makes sense that possibly after Annie, she had another baby that she got rid of. But why the hell she kept it hidden all these years is another mystery and weird as fuck. Just like her and this whole thing.'

Alfie interrupted, sounding weary of it all. 'Well that's something we'll never know so maybe we should focus on the practicalities like what the hell are we going to do now? Do we have to report it to the police? And then what? Have a burial or something because we can't just leave the poor thing like that, can we?'

'What good will telling the police do?' Albie's voice sounded sharper now. Maybe it was strain, but it was clear that the legal route wasn't on his agenda. 'They can't bring him or her back to life, or lock Mam up for infanticide because that's probably what we're dealing with here, and I don't know about everyone else, but the last thing I want is this getting out and the Walker name and the farm being dragged through the mud. No matter what we thought about Mam, her and Dad were well respected around here and I can't bear the thought of people gossiping about them.'

Alfie agreed. 'Albs is right. A police investigation won't

change what's happened and we'll be the ones to suffer in the long run and I for one have had just about as much as I can take of Mam's behaviour and how it affected us all our lives, so I say it stops here. Today.'

Annie spoke next, directing her question towards Albie. 'So what do you suggest we do? With the suitcase. And come to think of it, Mam's ashes when we get them back. We've not even talked about that.'

When he answered, Albie's voice was laced with anger. 'Well right now, I feel like putting them in the wheelie bin. But let's focus on the innocent for now. We can sort out what to do with Mam later.'

Alfie spoke next. 'Agreed. I think we should give that baby a respectful burial somewhere on the farm. They never had the chance to grow up as one of us but the least we can do is keep them here, close by us, as part of the family they never had. What do you all say? Will it bother you, being reminded of whatever our mother did and knowing what's buried there? Or do you think we should put them together?' Alfie searched everyone's faces and waited for an answer.

'I don't know about Mam. The way I see it she didn't want the baby anyway, and only kept the body close to protect her secret. As for the baby, we could put it... them – I hate saying "it" – up with the pets, under the tree. We loved all our dogs and cats–' Albie's suggestion was received by unanimous nods of approval.

'And my rabbit that she killed, too!' Annie was getting angry again.

Just the mention of the rabbit made Cathy squirm, so she attempted to alleviate the growing tension in the room. 'I think a burial up by the elm tree, with all the pets you've loved, is perfect and we can mark it with something special. None of us are religious and plenty of people have humanist ceremonies so we can have one of our own. I could look online, to find the right words to say, and maybe, Albie, you could read them, as head of the family. What's most important is that we do right by that little baby and somehow show them love and respect and try to put all the other stuff behind us.'

Cathy felt Alfie's hand on her back, a gentle touch that meant he agreed and whilst it was reassuring, the gesture threatened to break her resolve.

Needing to compose herself, she stood. 'I'll go and make us all another drink while you talk it over because it's a lot to take in and I don't think we should make any snap decisions, about what to do with Bertha, either.' With that she gathered the empty mugs and the clanking of pottery against the backdrop of hush made her want to escape even more.

Leaving them alone, Cathy made her way to the kitchen and after depositing the mugs in the sink and filling the kettle, she turned and faced the thing her eyes had avoided on entering the room. Walking slowly over to where the suitcase lay on the tabletop, she placed the palm of her hand on the lid and spoke to the tiny thing that lay inside.

'I'm so sorry for whatever happened to you, little one. But I promise that we will say goodbye to you properly and I will come up and see you lots to say hello. I won't forget about you, I swear. I hope you're happy wherever you are and know that your brothers and sister would have loved you very much. And so would I.'

Wiping away a tear, Cathy was about to return to the sink when Bertha's phone caught her eye, and she remembered the out of place video from earlier. Picking up the phone she opened the photo album and without overthinking it, tapped on the blackened image and pressed play.

Seconds later she was racing back down the hall towards the parlour and after she burst through the door, causing everyone to jump, she held up Bertha's phone and to four sets of startled eyes said, 'You need to listen to this. It's a message, from your mum.'

Walking into the centre of the room, she placed the phone on the coffee table, took a seat next to Alfie and then pressed play. After some rustling noises, loud tuts and a sigh, the room was filled with one very recognisable voice. Bertha Walker was about to speak to her family for one last time.

46

BERTHA

I've been buggerin' about wi' this bloody fandangle contraption for ages, on account of losing that bit of paper what Cathy left instructions on but anyroad, I reckon it's working now. I'm not doing a proper video wi' me face showing because all I could see were me double chin and up me nose, so you'll have to make do wi' listening instead. I'm not the best at reading and letters so din't want to make a fool of meself writing all this down, so I fancy this'll be the best way of sayin' goodbye.

Right then. I expects by now you'll have found me suitcase and if you 'aven't you need to go and look in me wardrobe. It's at the bottom, at the back covered wi' a blanket.

See, I know I've not been the easiest to live with an' no doubt you all hate me guts, but I can't go without sayin' I'm sorry for what you'll find in that case and explaining why it's there. I expect yer thinkin' all sorts about me an' I wouldn't blame yer.

Best I start at the beginning I s'pose, an' by that I mean before I came to live at Blacksheep wi' yer dad. I've always split my life into two parts, you see. Before I met him and after.

Before were crap. Living wi' a nasty bunch of men in the

middle of bloody nowhere. Me da was too handy wi' is fists and me brothers not much better and had vicious tongues on 'em, too. When me mam was alive things were different an' I was loved. I was happy. I even went to school but once she were gone I was good for nowt but cooking and cleaning and bein' used as a punch bag when me da had too much to drink.

He blamed me, you see, for Mam dying because I were what they called 'a time of life baby', and by all accounts she were never right after she had me. So when she passed, he punished me every day, one way or another, for takin' a breath and losing him his housekeeper and punch bag. I was his replacement for both.

Anyroad, after Mam, I rarely went to school and spent most of the day alone keeping house. I didn't have any friends because nobody would come up to the farm. It were a shithole no matter how hard I tried to keep it clean and tidy, and once I left school they all forgot about me. Then one afternoon, everything changed with a knock at the door. Me life and me future. I were a naïve fifteen-year-old at the time. Nowt but a little lass.

It was the middle of a boiling hot summer, 1973, and I was so fed up, being on my own on a dingy farm so when I heard tapping on the door my heart lifted. I knew straight away it would be a stranger wanting milk, one of the campers from the site down the lane. Da had a sign on our gatepost saying we sold fresh milk daily and it was my job to fill up the bottles and take the money. Maybe I was hoping for it to be some kids, sent up by their parents, who I could make friends with.

When I opened the door I got the shock of my life because there on the step was the spitting image of Jim Morrison, all bare chested and tanned, his long curly hair flowing down his shoulders. I thought he was the most beautiful thing I ever saw in my whole life.

I remember his voice to this day, like treacle or hot chocolate, smooth. He was posh, like the man who read the news on the BBC but instead of being stern and formal, Jim Morrison was polite and friendly, and he smiled like he meant it when he asked if he could buy a pint of milk.

I asked him to wait while I fetched it and took my time because I didn't want to let him go. When I got back, he passed me the money but didn't leave like I expected him to and instead, he started to chat, asking me about the farm and who worked there, and what I did.

I think he knew I was shy so did most of the talking but I was so desperate to keep him there that I forced myself to answer and soon, I'd told him everything about me. It was like I couldn't shut up and when he asked how old I was I said sixteen and he believed me.

I also noticed how he kept looking at my legs which were bare and tanned from working outside in the yard. I was wearing some cut-off shorts and a used-to-be-white T-shirt and as we talked, he seemed to be admiring the whole of me which was something new and exciting.

He told me he was from the other side of York, a student, studying law, and was on his way south to a music festival. Cheltenham. A place I'd never heard of let alone visited. I tried to act all clever, like I knew what he was talking about, and didn't dare admit that my musical knowledge was based on *Top of the Pops* and my first and only love was Donny Osmond.

I bravely asked him how long he was staying, and he explained that his van had broken down and one of his travelling friends was fixing it. Once they'd found the part he needed, then he'd be on his way. Even though I'd only just set eyes on him the thought of him leaving made me sad so when it was time for him to go, I made up an excuse to walk with him. Said I was going to see a friend and the campsite was on the way and I could show him a shortcut, through our woods.

I've no need to explain to you what happened after we stopped awhile in a shady spot under the trees. You all know about the birds and the bees but for the next two days, just after my da and brothers went off to the fields, he came up to the farm to buy milk and after he'd put the money in the jar, we went upstairs to my room.

I was besotted, not just with him but the tales of his travels, university and music festivals where everyone slept under the stars, and it seemed like heaven. He told me he really wanted to be an artist and go to somewhere called St Martin's in London, but his parents had other plans so in the summer, during the long holiday, he escaped them and was free to be himself.

On the third day he told me his van was fixed and even though it would break his heart, the next morning he'd be on his way. I thought I would die when he said it and in a moment of sheer panic I asked him if he would take me too. He said yes.

And just like that, I almost died from pure happiness at the thought of escaping the farm and my da. I swore to meself that once I left I'd never go back, and I'd spend the rest of my life travelling the world with Jim Morrison. I was only a child really and I believed it.

It was the longest night because after I stuffed clothes into a small brown suitcase I'd found in the boxroom, I lay on my bed for hours, counting down the minutes until I'd escape. I left the minute my dad and brothers set off for work, sneaking across the yard before running all the way to the stile on the B-road where he was going to pick me up.

I waited for over an hour, scanning the traffic, watching for the blue van that was his pride and joy. He'd told me all about it and I couldn't wait to ride away with him but when he didn't show up, I realised what had happened. He'd broken down again. With hope lodged in my heart I raced to the campsite, carrying my suitcase that banged against my legs as I ran. I didn't care that I'd have bruises, that I was getting too hot and I was thirsty and hungry after being too excited to eat breakfast.

All I wanted was to see his face but when I got to the field, the sight in front of me was worse than a punch to the stomach from Da. I searched from corner to corner but saw only tents, no blue campervans and as hope withered, I realised that Jim Morrison had gone. And with it, he'd taken my heart and chance to escape.

As I made my way back to the farm, I had never felt so worthless, alone and empty. Little did I know that Jim Morrison hadn't entirely abandoned me because he'd left something behind. His seed. The pit of hurt deep inside of me soon began to fill and as my stomach grew, I likened meself to one of the heifers in the field, swelling with every month.

I found some of Mam's old dresses and I worried that Da would notice and tell me to take them off. I needn't have fretted because none of them really saw me, or the bump. They just laughed at me and said I was getting fat. And no matter how I tried to will it away, growing up on a farm I knew that what was inside me had to come out, just like I'd seen the heifers deliver their calves. I was terrified.

The night it came out, almost nine months later, was the most horrible, torturous thing that had ever happened to me, and I thought I was going to be ripped apart. As I clutched a pillow to my face to muffle my cries, I prayed to die and whimpered for my mam.

At 3.23am it was finally over. I lay on my bedroom floor, grateful that the pain had stopped, and the fact the baby made no noise and didn't wake the others.

I woke at 5.54am to a silent May morning and was so exhausted I hadn't even heard the cock crow. In the quiet of the room, I did the only thing I could and cleared up the mess on the wooden floor. I pulled a dress from my wardrobe and wrapped the still and silent baby inside. I put her in a carrier bag and then after dragging the defunct suitcase from under my bed, put her inside, zipped it up and fastened the buckles tightly. Then I hid it in the bottom of my wardrobe and closed the doors, shutting out the past nine months and Jim Morrison. I swore never to think of him again.

That was the easy part. The hard bit was coping with what was going on in my head because for the longest time I was numb to everything and everyone one minute, in floods of tears the next, consumed by anger then devoured by shame. I hated the world and meself and I thought I was going mad.

I had to keep my bedroom windows open through the hottest summer for years and during the longest nights crying meself to sleep, begging my mam to somehow help me. I went over and over it in my head. What to do with the suitcase. I was just too scared to take it out of its hiding place and get rid of it. For a start I didn't have a clue where to put it.

I thought about digging a big hole in the woods and burying it but imagined animals sniffing it out and clawing it up and I didn't want that. The same with hiding it somewhere on the farm. There was always a chance that one day it would be discovered and the shame of my family finding out what I'd done terrified me.

So I left it where it was. Eventually, and thankfully before winter came, I could close the windows in my room and put the few items of clothing I had back in the wardrobe.

For the next year or so, I somehow managed to breathe, walk, eat, cook, clean, function. Being a robot got me through the days. And then just after my seventeenth birthday, Da rang

321

and asked me to bring his wallet to the auction and the rest is history, mine and your dad's, and yours. You know our story well enough.

And yes, I brought the suitcase with me because I couldn't leave it behind for my family to find and when I got to Blacksheep, I hid it in my wardrobe because while it was close to me, my secret was safe.

After we were wed, I managed to stall Jacob for six years one way or another, faking visits to the doctor who had supposedly reassured me that it would happen when the time was right. Thank heaven for contraceptives but in the end I gave in. I put Jacob above myself because I lived to make him happy and thought that if I didn't, he wouldn't love me anymore.

I gave Jacob the sons he wanted. The doctor could tell Albert wasn't going to be my first baby but in those days, dads weren't soft and didn't come to every single appointment like they do now, so Jacob was none the wiser. I told the doctor I'd lost one, before I moved to Blacksheep and reminded him that it was my business, and it was to stay that way. And it did.

Of all the bad things I've done and said, this is the one that has weighed heavy on me, ever since the day I gave birth in my old bedroom.

That's why before I go, I had to make sure that when you found the suitcase, you didn't carry my burden onwards. I hope now, you understand why it's there.

47

CATHY

It was impossible to listen to more because Alfie was distraught, and not one of them had dry eyes. Annie looked like she was set in stone. Her alabaster face streaked with tears as she stared at the phone and gripped a scrunched soggy tissue in one hand, the other clutching on to Joe.

It was Albie who pressed the pause button. Knowing that there was more to come because the video hadn't ended, Cathy was relieved. They needed a few moments to process what Bertha had told them about a secret part of her life – but at least now they understood some of what had made Bertha tick.

Albie held a knuckle to his mouth, biting down as if to give him strength or help him hold it together.

Wiping her own eyes and face with the sleeve of her jumper, Cathy sniffed and took deep breaths while beside her, Alfie sobbed. Placing her hand on his back, she let him get it all out while she tried to take it all in.

As she'd listened to Bertha's story, Cathy's skin had prickled at the mention of her Jim Morrison lookalike, and then his yearning to be an artist, but it was the mention of a blue camper that drove home the possibility that fifty years after they first met, fates had collided. Was it really Guy who'd called at Bertha's home, all those years before? Could he have been on his way to another summer killing spree? Did Bertha swerve being murdered like the other women?

Perhaps that was the key word. Women. All the others were older, and Bertha was just a child. A shiver rippled through Cathy's body with her next unbidden thought because something inside told her that Guy always knew Bertha wasn't really sixteen and had used an innocent and vulnerable young girl. God, how she hoped he'd get his brains bashed in while he rotted in prison because that's what he deserved.

They would never know for sure if it was him because Bertha never said his name in the video, although one thing she was sure of, it definitely wasn't Jim Morrison that came calling.

No, the evidence pointed right at Guy, because why else would Bertha have marked his photo in the newspaper? And when Alfie bought the campervan, it had the original blue paintwork, and the logbook confirmed it. It was covered up when it arrived, and Alfie had sanded it all down straight away so even if she had seen it on one of her early-morning skulks around the farm, she wouldn't have known it used to be blue and had no reason to suspect who once owned it.

And then another thought. How must Bertha have felt when she realised who the man she'd whacked with shovel was? It was so like her to keep it all to herself. The same way she'd locked the painful parts of her past away, hidden deep inside, for her entire adult life.

It was then, in a blinding moment of clarity that Cathy realised what Bertha's message really meant. It was her way of setting them free. From the secret she'd hidden at Blacksheep Farm and the tainted memories they had of her.

And there was something else that made Cathy's heart ache with love and such bittersweet realisation. That Jacob had taken

Bertha away from a terrible life, and those bad memories, of things a young woman had wanted to forget, was their connection. Cathy's and Bertha's. Blacksheep Farm, Jacob and his son, had given them the most precious of things. Sanctuary.

Looking around the room at her shell-shocked family, Cathy wondered what was going on in their heads but didn't dare ask because she wasn't sure what they'd say. She hoped they'd find it in their hearts to forgive Bertha for some of it, or at least try to understand the complex person that gave life to them, despite everything she'd been through and everything she got wrong afterwards.

When Albie coughed, all eyes turned his way as they waited for him to break the silence. 'Well, that were a bloody shock and it's going to take a while for it all to sink in, that's for sure... Are you okay, Annie? You look like you've seen a ghost.'

Eyes then shifted to the other side of the room from where Annie managed a response as Alfie composed himself and lifted his head to listen.

'No, I mean yes, I'm okay but... oh, Mam, why didn't you tell Dad or someone, and then you could have got help? I'm sure he'd have understood and then you wouldn't have had to keep it to yourself and let it ruin everyone's lives, never mind your own. It's just all too bloody sad.' Annie was talking softly to the phone screen as though Bertha was listening.

Cathy spoke next; she was compelled to whether it was the right time or not. She owed it to Bertha, for the moments they'd shared at the hospital when she'd attempted to tell Cathy her deepest secret, and also, to the memory of an innocent little baby.

'Well now we know the truth, about what happened to your mam when she was no more than a child, and that the baby was a little girl – your sister. I think she needs to be recognised properly. Which means we will have to tell someone in

authority, no matter how awkward it is. She deserves a name –
you could pick one you all like – and we can bury her properly
on the farm and mark her grave. We can't just put her in a
cardboard box with the pets. Your poor mam didn't know what
to do for the best all those years ago. She was probably in shock
and in a state of grief. It must have been horrendous so at least
we can put that right, for her and the baby... Sorry if I'm
speaking out of turn but I feel really strongly about it.' Cathy
swallowed down a sob and braved meeting the eyes of the
others.

Annie replied instantly. 'Cathy, you're not speaking out of
turn at all, and I agree. We have to do the right thing now we
know the real circumstances and I feel terrible about thinking
that Mam could have... you know...'

Alfie agreed. 'Me too, so we should do what Cathy says.
Make things right. Albie?'

Everyone's eyes turned to the eldest. 'It's true. She would
have been our sister and that makes her family, so we'll register
her properly, her birth and death, and give her a name, our
name, Walker, and sod what anyone thinks.'

Annie wiped her eyes, her lips wobbling as she spoke but
managing to keep a grip on her emotions as she nodded towards
the phone and asked Albie, 'Was that it? Does she say any
more?'

Albie tapped the phone screen. 'It says there's a few more
minutes.'

Annie sat forward, staring at the phone in Albie's hand. 'I
want to hear the rest, I need to know what else she said, doesn't
everyone else?'

Cathy nodded and turned to Alfie. 'Love, do you want to
listen or is it a bit too much? We get it if it is, don't we?' She
looked up to see everyone nodding but hoped he'd say yes.

'It's fine, let's listen. I'll be okay.' Alfie sat up straight as though he was preparing for bad news or a judge to send him to jail.

Cathy grabbed his hand and prayed it was neither. That the last words they'd hear from their mother wouldn't break her children's hearts all over again. As Albie nodded and went to press play, Cathy spoke silently to a woman who held the future in the palm of her hand.

You've got one last chance, Bertha, so please don't let them down.

48

BERTHA

So there you 'ave it. The next part is simple really. When I moved up here, to Shepherd's Cottage, the suitcase came with me so I could keep my secret safe.

Then we 'ad all that palaver with the lunatic and it got me thinking about the past and people I wanted to forget. Not just that, either. See, lately, I've not been feeling too good, 'specially at nights and as much as I tried to ignore them, I know the signs.

Thing is, I don't reckon I've got long left on this earth which is a bit of a bugger because I'm not at the end of *Bridgerton* yet, and I really want that chubby lass to get with the snooty fella even though he gets right on me nerves.

Anyroad, I've realised it's impossible to protect my secret forever and it's too late to get rid of it, being bad on my legs and all that. Which is why I've told you about it now. Stupid really, that I left it so late, but I thought I had plenty of time, but don't we all? At least you know the truth, in case I peg it in me sleep. Better safe than sorry, eh?

So now we've got all that bother out of the way there's a couple of things I need to say afore I bugger off to meet yer dad. I'm right looking forwards to seein' him again and me Mam, that's a fact, and these past few days I've felt them both close, like they're waiting for me, so I'd best get a shuffle on.

Which reminds me. I know I made a fuss about yer dad's ashes, and even though I dint want him sprinkled up on the moor with the sheep shit, after thinking on it, and if you can be bothered, I'd like you to do the same wi' me. Otherwise, feed me to the chickens, they'll eat owt.

Now... what else is there? Oh yes. The biscuit tin. I know you all resent me for being a tight-fisted bugger these past years, but I knew you'd get it all in the end, but to make up for some of it, if you look in the tin there's some things of your dad's that I'd like the lads to have. Nowt special as he weren't one for fancy stuff, but his grandad's pocket watch is in there, and his medals from the Great War which yer dad were right proud of, as you know. Then there's his old watch, a Timex, and it still ticks cos I wind it up regular, an' his wedding ring. It's up to you who gets what, but I know you'll treasure them.

I din't 'ave nowt of me mam's, just her photo, but I do 'ave me wedding ring and I'd like our Ann to have that. It's my pride and joy is that ring. My marriage is my greatest treasure so I'd like Ann to look after it. I'll understand if she doesn't want to, but maybe Joe will make an honest woman of her one day. It's about bloody time an' that's a bloody fact.

There's some bits of jewellery in the box what my Jacob gave me an' I'd like Cathy to 'ave something, too, because she's been a kind lass to me, an' even though I never said it, we're a bit the same, her an' me. I was thinking on it the other night, goin' over stuff in me head.

You see, my Jacob came and got me that day, saved me from me da and being a skivvy. He brought me here to Blacksheep and gave me a proper home and respect and most of all, he made me feel safe. Our Alfie did the same for Cathy. He went and got her that night when she were proper fed up and brought her home, to a safe place. We both found sanctuary at Blacksheep even though it were for different reasons.

Anyroad, I'm getting soppy in me old age and we can't 'ave that, can we. Right, best get on afore I forget what I wanted to say.

Whatever you do, don't throw me woolly socks out because that's where I keep me money. In the bottom drawer in me bedroom, rolled up inside, is mine and yer dad's pension money and whatever we didn't tell that greedy bloody taxman about. Didn't have owt to spend it on really, apart from ciggies and gin and that bloody lottery which is a waste of time, so I kept it there, in me socks.

There's a tidy sum and it should tide you all over till you get your inheritance. Maybe you can take the kiddies out somewhere nice, and Cathy can get her bits an' bobs looked at proper. Bloody NHS is crap so don't be waiting on them.

Oh, that reminds me. Cathy, thank you very much for me present which you'll be surprised to hear made me smile. Seeing Donny's face again was a proper treat and the fact you remembered I wanted it all of them years ago meant a lot. It also got me thinkin' about what you said at the time, about family and if you look underneath the wrapping, you'll be surprised what's waiting for you.

Well I've finally taken my wrapping paper off and showed you all what's inside, and I hope it goes some way to makin' amends.

You're a good lass, Cathy, an' I'm glad Alfred has you by his side, even though you can be a bit soft and need to get some meat pies down you now an' then. Won't do you no harm, you know.

Our Joe's a good lad too, a worker and he'll look after Ann and the kiddies so I can rest in peace knowing that.

Albert, I think it's about time you found yerself a nice lass and settled down. I'm sure there's someone out there who'd have you.

This bit's just for Albert, Alfred and Ann, because there's something I need to get off me chest with you three more than anyone.

Now, as I'm sure you can imagine, I don't find it easy sayin' this, but I'm sorry. I really am.

And if I had me time again I'd try to be a better mam to you than I was an' that's a fact, but hand on heart, there were just summat inside me that wouldn't let me. Like there were a brick wall stopping me showing affection. I'm not even going to make excuses and blame it on the past because it were down to me.

Maybe I am a bad bugger like me da were, but I did me best by you and made sure you were fed, and had clean clothes and a warm bed to sleep in. The rest yer dad made up for and I'm thankful for that.

I s'pose what I'm trying to say is that I wish I could have loved you like you deserved, and I am sorry that I couldn't.

I hope you'll all be happy at Blacksheep and make a go of the farm like you planned. Look to the future, forget about the past if you can because it'll do none of you any good.

Right, I think that's everything, so I'll be going now. That's if I can turn this bloody phone off proper.

Take care of each other and do yer dad proud.

I'll show meself out.

Mam.

THE END

ALSO BY PATRICIA DIXON

WOMEN'S FICTION / FAMILY SAGAS

A Family Affair

They Don't Know

Resistance

The Destiny Series:

Rosie and Ruby

Anna

Tilly

Grace

Destiny

PSYCHOLOGICAL THRILLERS / SUSPENSE / DRAMAS

Over My Shoulder

The Secrets of Tenley House

#MeToo

Liars (co-authored with Anita Waller)

Blame

The Other Woman

Coming Home

Venus Was Her Name

A Good Mother

ACKNOWLEDGEMENTS

Dear reader,

Thank you so much for reading my story.

The idea for Sanctuary came from conversations I've had over the years with female friends who'd confided in me that whilst they love my stories, they have struggled to connect with the 'good mother' characters in some of them. After telling me of their experiences and explaining why it was hard for them to read about a relationship they never had, I decided to write a character and a story for them.

One friend kindly and bravely took the time to send me notes sharing some of her sad and damaging memories, the essence of which, with her permission, I've fictionalised and embellished within *Sanctuary*.

And whilst her story is ongoing and I have no idea how it will end, in mine, I hope I have found a way to tell Bertha's tale in its inglorious honesty but perhaps, I've also given you, the reader, the means to forgive her or at least understand. If nothing else, there's plenty to think about.

The fear of the outside world and the evils within it is something many of us struggle with and have to face on a daily basis as we watch the news, or travel about, or whilst doing simple things like visiting a shopping centre. And it's a fact of life that bad things can happen when we least expect it, at any time, to good people going about their everyday lives.

Cathy and Alfie's tale touches on this and combines their separate struggles with mental health issues. Woven into their fictitious story is the tragic, real-life event that occurred in Manchester in 2017, the Arena bombing. I remember afterwards, my daughter was terrified of going into the city centre and I'm sure many people for their own reasons had similar experiences. I have striven to write about this catastrophic night with sensitivity and respect because even now it hurts my heart to think of it, those innocents who lost their lives or were injured and everyone who was affected by it in a myriad of ways.

I love my city and the people in it which is why I dedicated the book to Manchester.

I have enjoyed writing every single word of *Sanctuary* for you. It's a story that encompasses family, love, heartache, loyalty, compassion, separation, and the battles many of us face in our everyday lives and minds. I hope you enjoyed it and thank you for reading about the Walker family.

More thank-yous now, and I have to start with the magnificent team at Bloodhound Books who work so hard behind the scenes to get my manuscript up to scratch and out there into the world.

To Clare, my wonderful editor. From the second my manuscript lands on your desk I wait nervously for your verdict because your opinion means so much to me, as does your guidance and input throughout the editorial journey. Over the years you've worked out what makes me tick, where my characters are coming from and what I want to convey in between the lines, even if I might sometimes need reining in. That connection is priceless. Your quirky notes in the margin always make me smile, especially when you say I've done good. Thank you, Clare, for every minute you spent making *Sanctuary* shine.

To Abbie, thank you a million times for your meticulous eye for detail and dedication. For understanding my northernisms, ethos and sense of humour because being on the same page really makes a difference to the end product. Your critique is always much awaited because your professional opinion means a great deal to me, as does your friendship so thank you again, for both.

Thanks to Maria who gives everything the final beady-eye check. You are the first person to read the finished article, so I really hope you enjoyed it.

To Tara, the Queen Of The Spreadsheet and deliverer of schedules, who steers us through the whole process from the day our books are signed, right up until they're ready to go out into the world. You made *Sanctuary* look beautiful on the inside and as you know, I also get a bit emotional when I see it in all its formatted glory but this time, with the bee emblem and dedication, it was perfect. So thank you, for all that you do but most of all, for being a wonderful friend, too.

To Hannah and Lexi, who work their socks off behind the scenes, creating the best images, videos and content for my book and then spreading the word far and wide. I love working with you both and want to thank you from the bottom of my heart for all that you do, for *Sanctuary* and all of my books. You are superstars.

And finally to Betsy and Fred. Without your vision and dedication to Bloodhound Books, none of this would be possible. You make my dreams and those of so many writers come true. But most of all, thank you for always believing in me. You're the best.

Whilst writing Sanctuary, in order to make sure the nitty-gritty aspects were covered, I drew on the support and experience of fellow authors and friends who very generously gave me their time.

First of all, thanks to Nicki Murphy who over the years has become a trusted friend and supporter. She also shared some very private memories with me and this insight into her past helped form the basis of Bertha's character and her relationship with her children. Nicki, I will always be immensely grateful for your help but most of all, for having you in my life. Eat chocolate, be happy, you deserve it.

Sue Baker (or SuperSue) who I called on for her veterinary knowledge because I wanted to make sure saying goodbye to dear Skip was handled correctly. Thank you Sue for answering my questions and also, for being a fabulous friend and supporter over the years.

Doctor Charlotte Stevenson, who also happens to be a brilliant author (*The Serial Killer's Son* and *The Guests* just in case you're curious) for her immense patience and advice with regards to Alfie. He's one of my favourite characters and I had to make sure I looked after him properly. So thank you Charlotte, for our virtual doctors' appointments with a made-up person. I wish all doctors were like you and that's a fact!

Big thank you to another fellow Bloodhound writer, the fabulous James Woolf (*Indefensible* and *The Company She Keeps*) who put me in touch with forensic scientist David Tadd. It was imperative that the sad discovery in the suitcase was portrayed accurately, for example the condition of the contents after so many years. So thank you, David, for taking the time to answer my questions and for sending such a detailed explanation. Greatly appreciated.

And now to my very special group of super-readers who very kindly read early copies of my books, feeding back their thoughts and writing reviews. Thank you a thousand times. I hope you know how much I value not only the hours you spend reading the ARC, but the support and friendship you give me in our group and along the way. I feel that just like Alfie, I have a bunch of great mates around me, and I'm also wondering if I should give you all special names, like Dave the Rave and Chippy Van Tony, have! Watch this space.

Anyone who has read my other books will know that I always save the last words for my precious family. They are the reason I get up in the morning, are at the centre of my life and the heart of everything I do. Soon, we will be welcoming two new members to our tribe, and I cannot wait for them to arrive because then I'll be able to write their names in black and white in a book. For now, to Brian, Amy, Mark, Harry, Owen, Jess and the dachshund's Albie and Elvis, I love you more than all the words in all of my books could ever say.

And on that note, I shall show myself out.

x

A NOTE FROM THE PUBLISHER

Thank you for reading this book. If you enjoyed it please do consider leaving a review on Amazon to help others find it too.

We hate typos. All of our books have been rigorously edited and proofread, but sometimes mistakes do slip through. If you have spotted a typo, please do let us know and we can get it amended within hours.

info@bloodhoundbooks.com

Printed in Great Britain
by Amazon

50688620R00195